Deferred Interest

By Ryan Pollyea

Deferred Interest by Ryan Pollyea

First printing, 2016

ISBN 978-0-9968461-1-0

www.ryanpollyea.com

Published by: Ryan J Pollyea Publications, Chicago, IL
Edited by: Daniel Solera
Cover Art by: Jonathan Kreyer
Book Jacket Design by: Jennifer Gadus
Interior Layout by: Jennifer Gadus and Ryan Pollyea

This book is set in Crimson Text, © 2010 by Sebastian Kosch

This is a work of fiction. All characters are fictional, as are the places and events described herein.

Introduction

EACH YEAR, at an idyllic location far from each of their campuses, presidents from several of the finest universities in the United States meet for a distinguished summit. Recently, at one of these gatherings, the presidents sat for a session focused on dangerous antics insidiously enveloping their schools.

Research data suggested that this on-campus chicanery was directly linked to parodies of college life made famous by popular culture. Overly fictionalized movies, television shows, and tall tales were throwing askew students' expectations of collegiate life. In these over-the-top stories, a student performed an idiotic task, fought against learning from their mistakes, and eventually saved their skin by conveniently recalling a lesson from a single lecture they attended long ago. What's more, these yarns almost always came with a perilous omission: the consequences.

This pop culture attack was so unnerving that the committee resolved to find a widely available and powerful way to combat it. Dissatisfied with the methods they were already using to guide students away from delinquency, the university heads concluded it was time to disseminate a story about real life disobedience and the crime's very real punishment.

Their goal was not to create propaganda, but merely to highlight what is typically hiding silently in illusory depictions of college life. As opposed to picking apart popular movies one cliché at a time, the delegation's tale would provide young minds with a healthy alternate benchmark for understanding the college experience.

Ultimately they decided a book would be the best way to reach the public at large, including prospective students anxious to read about college life and the parents who were eager to read about what their children were omitting from their phone calls home.

To find the tale that would scare America's youth into a path paved with learning and devoid of damnable intentions, the delegation's research staff consulted administrators from universities across the nation. To their surprise, they found their cautionary tale from an institution in their own ranks, my employer, the upstanding Pemberton University. The story belonged to Charles "Chip" Lockwood, who attended Pemberton in the early 2000s.

Once the topic was chosen, I was asked to compile the facts into an unbendingly honest depiction. This job fell to me, the entirety of the University Archives, as I was present when the tale took place (I have been here since the first brick was laid in Pemberton's foundation, in fact) and I intimately know each of the characters involved.

The board desired a stern message that would disillusion students who felt they could slug their way through college between disciplinary mishaps and sagging grades and come out four years later unscathed.

The problem with Charles Lockwood's story, however, as I tried tirelessly to explain to the cabal, is that it could not be farther from what they wanted. Despite my efforts, the committee pushed forward with the commission of this tale. Although I attributed their decision to the fact that these leaders are not always in lockstep with the needs of the general public, select moments of this story do lend themselves to the morality fable genre.[1]

---

[1] Some in the committee wanted this book to be released as a textbook co-published by all of the participating universities, a move which would have increased the consumer price threefold.

To create a truthful retelling, I have compiled this story using my extensive knowledge of the events, as well as information gleaned from emails, text messages, and interviews. Some names have been changed for various reasons, and I should note I have accepted only a fraction of the vetoes sent forth by the university's censors. Additionally, to ensure focus remains affixed on Pemberton's story and not on other institutions, I am consciously omitting the names of most of the other universities in this text.

Regardless of my reservations, I promise to tell this story as accurately as I can and you may make your own conclusions around what the delegation wanted you to see in these pages.

Chapter 1: Charles "Chip" Lockwood

THE BEST place in Lockwood's less than esteemed academic career to pinpoint this tale's beginning is around two a.m. on October the eighteenth of 2005. It was a Tuesday and Charles Lockwood was relaxing underneath a lilac ceiling, between bed sheets belonging to a girl who believed his name was Jia Xiong.

Earlier that night, Lockwood found himself not where the university wanted him, which was at a discussion section to receive the results of his latest midterm, but at an off-campus bar called Home Reading. As he'd chosen to fill out the exam with little regard for the correct answers, he felt no need to retrieve it.

The bar was a hot spot for PMU students, especially those who found humor in saying they spent a night "at Home Reading" as it sounded more like they were studying, not drinking pitchers of beer through garden hoses.

In an example of Lockwood's extremely good fortune, the junior learned while at the bar that an attractive coed he had been eyeing was mutually interested. The young lady was a freshman who was convinced the very Caucasian Lockwood was the PhD student from China who was serving as her Teaching Assistant in Seventeenth Century European Conflict (EURP-180, offered FALL and WTR). As she believed she was failing this class, her goal was to find her TA at his favorite bar, woo him into bed, and coerce him into boosting her grade.

Even after the three rounds of a game called "quarters" he played (according to those who were present and later questioned by my staff), the young man was able to piece together the girl's scheme without letting on that he knew something was awry. Upon realizing that she was coherent and perhaps just hard of sight, he proceeded to let the intriguing opportunity take him where it might.

*   *   *

In his first two years at Pemberton, Charles Lockwood did little academically or civically notable with the exception of being barred from ever again entering the state of Ohio.

When this story began, he was a man of twenty-one who lived by an untamable appetite for recreation and a carefree attitude that flirted with unflinchingly indifferent. In all, he would have been difficult to love if society didn't encourage others to emulate his boldest qualities.

He stood about six foot three inches when not slouched over a coffee table piled high with beer cans. Accompanying his face's strong features were pale blue eyes he inherited from his mother and surfer blonde hair that highlighted his southern California roots. His classic mid-20th Century good looks even landed him on the cover of an admissions packet his sophomore year, amid students joyously watching a PMU football game. In the picture, Lockwood was smiling at the camera with his perfect teeth, welcoming eyes, and strong chest visible under a PMU shirt emblazoned with an aggressive-looking butcher knife. (Incidentally, the Admissions Office later found out that off camera he was, in fact, not wearing pants.)

Either through courtesy of his upbringing, the freedom afforded by his wealth, or a combination therein, his cushioned existence's protective coating preemptively brushed away life's harsher circumstances at all times. Winds changed in his favor when at sea and consequences of any severity voluntarily altered themselves in his wake. It was almost as if fate herself not only existed, but she interacted with mortals solely to protect Lockwood.

From his first days at Pemberton, he did not use his powers to strengthen his business acumen, benefit charity, or help classmates realize their potential. Rather, Charles Lockwood was often busy using his abilities to be Charles Lockwood. He was not being asked to live in simple terms, so he naturally did not respect certain societal norms.

During his freshman year he grew famous for having convinced a yacht owner in South Beach to allow forty students onto the ship on a whim. (The party was halted before he managed to steer the boat to Havana.) His past also featured a visit to Chicago during which he became the only Pemberton student in history to spontaneously place a bid on and drunkenly attempt to sign a lease for the purchase of one of the city's grand museums. He also gave the school an international first on a flight from Los Angeles to Sydney at the age of twenty when he became its first student to organize an in-flight beer pong tournament on a major airline.

His antics were the kernel of fraternity legend. His ability to avoid penalties was hurtful to anyone with a conscience. And to administrators who dealt with the costs he ignored and the students who felt they could sculpt their reputations in his image, Lockwood's presence was, at times, simply destructive.

So it is no coincidence that his most storied misadventure at Pemberton begins here.

*   *   *

After thirty minutes of talking, during which the intoxicated Lockwood noted the freshman never once asked him his name or major, twenty of walking, and fifteen of what students in the mid-2000s considered courting, the couple made it into her dorm room. Not terribly long after that, two a.m. arrived.

Looking up at the lilac ceiling, Lockwood smiled and the girl giggled. Lockwood recognized it as a cue that a conversation might start. His eyes remained on the ceiling.

"So I had a great time," she began, rolling onto her side and away from Lockwood, "and I hate to bring this up now, but about the midterm…"

Lockwood recalled who he was supposed to be. "Should I have seen this coming?"

"I don't want you think this was only about that," she replied insistently. "I just really need to know that grade before class."

Had he been listening, Lockwood might have brainstormed a way to dull the agony of the pending moment when the girl discovered he was not Jia Xiong. He opted for a higher risk response. "It'll all work out, baby."

The girl laughed, signaling what sounded like a temporary truce.

"So, what's with the ceiling?" he asked. "I thought you couldn't paint dorms."

The girl turned on her back. "I heard that whoever had this room two years ago was some rebel who was sick of not being able to change anything here. She got fed up one night and painted it out of some sort of protest."

"What kind of rebel thinks light purple makes a big statement?"

"I don't know," the girl said with a shrug. "But the school got upset and told her she had to paint it over or pay some huge fine."

"What'd she do?"

"My RA said she refused and the school charged her a thousand dollars to clean it."

Lockwood tried to make sense of the story but couldn't. "But it's still purple."

"I know. Weird, huh? It's like the school got the money and just forgot. Speaking of something totally different," she continued enthusiastically, "can we talk about the midterm now?"

"Wow, really? Why?"

"Because I'm worried about it, Jia!"

Despite being called a name that was not his own while nude in bed, Lockwood managed to simultaneously dodge the issue and offer support. "Listen, it'll sort itself out, believe me."

Although the topic of academic excellence was brought up under questionable circumstances, her concern was justified. For decades, Pemberton has been one of the most respected, prestigiously ranked, and selective universities in the nation.

Since its founding in 1857 as Pemberton Methodist University and Culinary Institute, PMU has enjoyed a reputation of the highest caliber. Cradled by the shoreline of one of the country's greatest lakes, Pemberton has been a peaceful source of mental rapture and emotional growth for hundreds of thousands of students. By the time the culinary school closed in 1872 and "Methodist" was dropped from its name, Pemberton had grown from a notable yet quaint institution into a nationally renowned powerhouse of education, research, and civic significance.

In Lockwood's case, worrying about classes was not an affliction he was capable of developing. It was not for a lack of intelligence, as results from the standardized test scores attached to his application showed, rather it was due to his mindset about academia as a whole. He decided as a child that learning class material strictly for a test or a grade wasn't beneficial. The problem morphed when he learned he could find a way around anything he felt was superfluous to the learning process, namely lectures, course work, and often common decency.

What helped drive his reprehensible attitude was a theory he tested regularly: no teacher he would meet was really going to fail a student. Whether it was thanks to his privileged life or by accident, his theory typically worked for him. Even instructors who didn't know his family's history seemed to be hesitant to let him fail their class.

At PMU Lockwood regularly attended three sessions of any given course: the first day (to sign the university's only official attendance form), the day of the midterm (to get through the questions as rapidly as he could), and the day of the final (to pass the exam using notes he pilfered from students he met while handing in his midterm).

During most classes he had been able to correctly deduce enough exam answers to pass. This led to a rarely spectacular GPA, but a passing one nonetheless. At one point the previous year his theory appeared to waver when he narrowly avoided a spot on the

Provost's Procedures Committee's Watch List. An abnormally high score in American History 1914–Present Day (AMER 212-2, offered WTR) bumped his GPA enough to keep off the list by summer.

His lax attitude bled heavily into his early morning talk that Tuesday in October.

The girl offered: "I'm sorry for making you talk class in bed."

"Wouldn't being sorry stop you from bringing it up?"

"I only want to know if I need to drop the class. You don't have to change anything for me. You looked in class like you really wanted to help your students."

"I've been told I'm a different person outside of class." He smiled at the thought of the next interaction between the girl and the real Jia Xiong. *Now that's a class I would show up to*, he thought. His mind then drifted to the girl's plan and its aura of oddity. "Why are you pushing for this now? The drop date isn't for three weeks. You have time."

"Sure, if I want a D slapped on my midterm grade report. Law schools will see that. My parents will see that. I'd rather drop it now to make it disappear and make it up next semester."

The statement confused Lockwood. The suddenly observant girl noticed and continued. "My RA told me if I wait for my midterm report to see I'm failing, the school will have an official record of it. If I drop it before the report comes out, then it disappears. The school doesn't bother putting dropped classes on midterm reports. That's why I need to know now."

Thanks to a somewhat outdated policy, the girl was correct. Early in the 1980s, a major student loan provider told administrators that PMU had some of their bank's highest stability ratings in every category but one: the number of dropped classes seen on official documents. When PMU overseers set out to lower the statistic, an analyst offered two solutions. They could either invest heavily in instructors and support staff who could help struggling students early on or simply remove incompletes from documents wherever possible. The administrators went with the free alternative, and though the loan landscape changed greatly by 2005, the policy remained.

Her honesty impressed him. "I like your style. If it were up to me, you'd get that C."

The girl's head snapped in Lockwood's direction. "I thought the grade is your decision."

Opting to pretend he was drunk and rude instead of caring and attentive (which wasn't hard), Lockwood replied, "I can't believe all that freaking beer I had, man."

"What?" the girl asked with a rapid headshake.

Lockwood let the back of his head put on an effective show to convince the girl it was bedtime. Eventually her eyelids and her questions begrudgingly agreed.

Around three a.m., long after his temporary roommate fell asleep, Lockwood crept out of bed and slid over to her desk, where he shook the mouse until the computer screen popped to life. As that semester had been particularly unruly, he decided to check on his grades.

He'd known for semesters he could check his grades online, and in following with tradition, he only did so to confirm he wasn't in danger of failing.

With five pre-midterm scores revealing themselves on the monitor, the young man whose disposition rarely called for worry began feeling a quickening heart rate.

You see, as someone brought up amid infinite routes of opportunity, Lockwood also grew up with only one steadfast rule: he was not under any circumstances to fail out of Pemberton.

Despite the late hour, the five markings launched him into persuasive letter writing mode.

It had been a difficult term due to his work with the End Gun Violence blood drive, one section of the note explained. Donating blood twice that semester to keep the drive going forced an enormous strain onto his body. This extra stress prompted flashbacks to injuries he sustained as a semi-professional school athlete the year before, exacerbating his ability to focus on schoolwork.

His words conveyed that he would hoist his grades after the midterms if the letter's recipient could kindly tweak the score in the meantime. An "uncharacteristically low mark" (his best fictional prose of college) might prevent him from leading the upcoming spring break volunteering trip he had been planning for months, and so on.

After editing the letter to ensure it looked nothing like previous versions he'd composed, he sent out five nearly identical copies to five professors. Then, out of admiration for the only careful work he'd submitted all semester, he sent an edited copy to the real Jia Xiong from the young lady's email account. He then set an early eight a.m. alarm and got back into bed.

Though confidence helped him assume his situation would not worsen, he still treated it with care. He was not yet in danger, but at that moment, Charles Lockwood could still see the ominous truth shining back at him: he was on pace to fail all five of his classes.

Chapter 2: Alistair Lockwood III

THE UNION between the university and the Lockwoods began in 1873 when Connecticut shipping magnate Alistair Lockwood III decided his eldest son Calvin would attend the still young Pemberton Methodist University. It didn't take long for the tradition of sending Lockwoods to Pemberton to grow and evolve. As the Lockwood flock widened, their impact on campus became more noticeable. For instance, there was the era during World War I when three brothers led PMU to Debate, Fencing, and Chemistry Association national prizes in a single year. During Prohibition, four Lockwoods led the university's football team to back-to-back perfect seasons.

The family's most prominent time came between 1958 and 1967 when they helped boost the school's academic reputation and also broaden its civic outreach by founding two sororities and one fraternity. Charles Lockwood's own father attended during this era, as did his father's younger brother Arthur, who was the family's sole attendee during the tail end of the acme.[2]

---

[2] In addition, I have been told the first few years of the 20th Century hosted several notable Lockwood Pemberton Pact anecdotes, but as my official records from that time are regrettably spotty, stories from that span will not be included here.

By the 1960s, the family's name was so embedded in the campus that when the dormitory August P. Lockwood Hall was erected it had to be referred to as "August Hall" or "AP Hall" to reduce confusion with PMU's central Science building, Lockwood Family Hall.

The family's prominence at Pemberton did not always sit well with Charles Lockwood. At times while growing up he felt as if he existed only to be assailed by facts about PMU. It was not just the tradition, relatives explained, but the ability to contribute to the school in a greater way than anyone else.

When he arrived in 2003, though, it seemed there was nothing new to bring to life at PMU thanks to a longstanding, sturdy saturation of overachievers. Even worse, the only other Lockwoods on campus graduated at the end of his sophomore year, leaving him as the lone torchbearer in the autumn of 2005. Somehow, of the eight branches of the Lockwood line, only Charles "Chip" Lockwood was available to continue the ritual as an undergraduate during his (scheduled) junior and senior years.

Given his penchant for extracurricular activities, it was odd that he was left alone at Pemberton even for a single day. But by 2005, the only relatives who could take up graduate studies were too focused on bond trading and financial analysis to consider a provisional career halt for the benefit of keeping their cousin company. This itself was a sign that the bond was not as strong as it once had been. But the Lockwoods knew the union would inevitably return to a spot of glory at some point, namely after Charles Lockwood left campus and took with him his contributions of pranks and poor marks. No national academic records would be broken by the boy who once glued quarters to the change bins of every vending machine in the student union and who once handed in an essay-based midterm having only written: "Is this shit going to be on the final?"

Another one of his infamous practical jokes came his sophomore year when his girlfriend of two months left him over questionable reasons. Shortly after her departure, late one night he went to her sorority house, which decades earlier had been dubbed the Monterey House by its founder (a Lockwood, incidentally), and he silently pumped three feet of water into its uninhabited basement dining hall. No one in the sorority was laughing after waking up to find dozens of bits of sugary cereal floating atop feet of standing water.

As he did elsewhere, he lived free from worry at Pemberton, save the one problem he was forced to recall regularly: the Lockwood line had never been sullied by failure or expulsion.

Lockwoods had transferred or had willingly chosen other universities for study, but as long as there was another present at the time, such actions were acceptable. But there was to be no failing at Pemberton. Underage drinking, promiscuous sex, or disheartening the proletariat were markedly lower on the list of sins.

At this point some readers may conclude that his family must have been willing to tolerate failure.

Charles Lockwood's lax view of academia was not due to a lack of trying on his parents' part. Though not the strictest of disciplinarians, they did consistently remind their son of his duties. With help from his entire family, refreshers were offered at each stage of his childhood.

Since these lectures came from his least favorite relatives, like the mother of his pompous cousin Craig, as well as from the ones he adored the most, like Uncle Arthur and Great Aunt Adelaide, young Charles Lockwood didn't know how to handle the negative reinforcement, so he shifted his attention to alternate solutions. This led to his first great discovery, which was mentioned in part earlier: most instructors had little desire to fail him.

The idea worked well through grade school and some of high school. During this time, his parents assumed that silence from Lockwood's teachers signified progress. This would later haunt them as their son continued for years to lean on his well-built crutch.

In high school, he encountered some instructors who required more coaxing to align with his mantra's goals. The issue intensified at the end of his sophomore year when his parents had to wring a barely passing grade out of a macroeconomics instructor who also had close ties to Pemberton.

The grade and the battle that led to it startled his parents' resolve. The lectures the boy hated so much returned, and he grew angered that only one slip up turned him back into a pariah. He later translated this example's message into another misaligned lesson: only register for courses with instructors he knew he could influence.

The family sermons, which he ritualistically ignored, continued through his junior year, ultimately leading to what he should have seen as a denunciation of his flawed life view: his failing of Advanced American Literature. He'd known this outcome was possible, but instead of tending to altering the grade, he affixed his attention on an upcoming eight day trip to Valencia, Spain with his best friend. What's more, as he knew the resoundingly excellent grade he would receive in French History would boost his GPA, he opted to not worry.

When his grades arrived in his parents' mailbox the day he flew to Europe, the pair was intolerably livid. This behavior would not be abided. What they needed, they decided, was a lesson so severe that their son would never again deviate.

Their rebuttal began while Lockwood was on his way to Spain. First his mother cancelled all of his credit cards. Then his father called his travel partner's parents to explain that Lockwood hadn't followed through with booking his trip and he failed to inform his friend. The friend, at Lockwood's father's insistence, should fly elsewhere instead.

By the end of his first night in Spain, the only night he pre-paid for a hotel room, Lockwood realized something catastrophic had happened. He called his parents to hear a less than endearing reply. After letting the phone ring a few extra times, his mother answered and read aloud his full grade report. She then informed her son that he was cut off until he returned. His parents would accept only one collect phone call from Valencia that week, and if their son wanted assistance, during that call he would have to offer a detailed outline of the steps he would take to ensure he would never fail another class. If he didn't like feeling stranded, they added, he should think hard before any repeat performances.

The marooning left Lockwood shattered, if only for a moment.

Although only seventeen years old (or nineteen based on his fake ID designed to get him into Valencia's bars), he empathized with his parents' desire to educate him. As opposed to the lesson they wanted to teach him, though, he felt it would be more valuable to demonstrate to them that he was growing smarter thanks to skills that were more valuable than homework. With this in mind, he opted to showcase his ingenuity to his parents instead of cowering with halfhearted repentance.

He first asked his hotel's concierge which beaches American students used. He then found the beach and located a group of students who had a guitar. With his charm and his fake ID as collateral, he would ask to borrow the guitar to earn some beer money (a portion of which would go to the guitar's owner). Then, he would busk to entertain passersby until his hat was full of euros. Once this happened, he would return the guitar, enjoy drinks with his new friends, and find a hostel for the night before repeating the steps the next day.

The plan, though inventive, did not sit well with his parents. This wasn't just because he'd avoided heeding their message again, but because he didn't contact them at all until the seventh day of his trip. (Also, he arrived back in Los Angeles intoxicated.)

After Valencia, his parents spent the summer before Lockwood's senior year bluntly stating that he was too unintelligent for college. As they did in his younger years, Lockwood's favorite relatives weighed in on the matter. Arthur played the role of peacekeeper all summer and Adelaide unexpectedly excoriated the teenager. Whether she'd grown weary of his indiscretions or was standing up for the whole family, she delivered to him one final, acerbic speech before refusing to see or talk to him ever again.

It was Adelaide, then, who helped at least temporarily push Lockwood in the right direction. His senior year's report cards saw straight A's due to a combination of a less intensive course load and a minimal amount of added effort.

College then began and with it came extra temptations, looser schedules, and a set of what looked to Lockwood like entirely malleable rules. Ruefully for his clan, the reward of playing the role of

Charles Lockwood remained too grand to focus on anything else.

His relatives' lectures did not come to mind while he was ditching classes by the dozen, spending nights gift-wrapping animals scheduled for dissection in pre-med classes, or covering red hand rails with ketchup. The talks, however, did stick out vividly while he was checking his preliminary grades that night in October.

His mother's stern words were the first thing on his mind when he awoke minutes before his alarm, careful to not stir the person who would be distressed to discover he wasn't Chinese.

The morning began like many of Lockwood's mornings in freshman dorms, with an examination of the resident's medicine cabinet for signs of prescriptions linked to sexually transmitted diseases. After feeling confident with the lack of findings, he flicked the computer's mouse and opened his email account to see five new emails.

All five notes began with "I regret to inform you" (a phrase he'd never seen before). He glared through a dumbfounded haze as he sifted through his professors' undeniable rejections.

Lockwood, who was almost never rebuffed, was having difficulty with the five refusals staring back at him.

For comparison's sake, he signed out of his email and opened the girl's account that was winking at him from a row of minimized windows. He found a reply from the real Jia Xiong, who altered her score thanks to coercion provided by the man pretending to be him.

As his grades painted a darker portrait, the boy who often lived without care finally realized the weight of being the only Lockwood on campus after one hundred and thirty-two years.

Chapter 3: Madame "E.D." Grafe

DESPITE THE opinion held by many with whom she had dealt, PMU junior Edie Grafe did not rise each morning desiring to make someone's day miserable. Truthfully, though, she was always innately happy to know it was bound to happen at some point in the day.

Edie Grafe, whose last name was pronounced like graph paper and whose first name was not really Edie, awoke early to pangs of discomfort behind her eyes courtesy of the vodka diet sodas she consumed the night before. Rolling over in her bed, she looked around for clues about why she set an alarm more than three hours before her first class.

On her dresser, atop a small mirror sat a delicately cut yellow wristband, reminding her that Charles Lockwood, her best friend running on two years, chose their Monday night plans. The sight reminded her that her alarm was set early so she could rush to the Freshman Quad and mock Lockwood face to face as opposed to the convenient electronic options at her disposal.

She did not know where he would be simply because he was conventional. Rather, Edie knew he slept at a freshman's dorm because she helped facilitate his rendezvous.

"I can't tell if that's him or not!" Edie recalled hearing over the thumping music at Home Reading the night before. The speaker was a pleasant looking brunette who was leaning up to a lankier female companion. Both were clearly freshmen, despite their yellow wristbands. "It better be him. I have to get that grade up!" The brunette stood on her toes and bit her lip for a better look across the room.

Her interest instantly aflame, Edie scanned the room until her gaze landed on the owner of the room's only white and blue shirt: Lockwood. She then turned to the girls with a stunning smile. "The cutie by the pool table? Good choice," she purred in a polite tone.

The girls somehow decided she was trustworthy. "You don't know him do you? He kind of looks like my European History TA. And I kind of need to…talk with him."

Edie pursed her lips sympathetically, denoting she understood without judgment.

The girl gave a timid look. "Does this make me a bad person?"

"Of course not!" Edie insisted warmly. "Tons of students every day ask for better grades. Why should you get punished for being direct?" She nudged a laugh out of the girl.

"Yeah," the girl replied, squinting out of uncertainty. "But he looks a different in class."

"He's friends with my roomie but I'm really bad with names. What's your TA's name?"

"Jia Xiong," the brunette noted.

The comment forced a fraction of a giggle out of Edie, who pretended to sip her cocktail. Not wanting anyone to realize the absurdity of the statement, she declared, "That *is* his name!"

Staring at her gratified face in the mirror that morning, Edie was again happy to have a friend like Lockwood who not only shared her love of mischief but whose actions seemed to brew it. He kept her entertained even when she wasn't toying with the campus herself. [3]

---

[3] Her favorite prank in her arsenal was executed whenever she could find any female's unguarded cellular phone. She would pick up the phone as if it were her own, locate a male's phone number among her contacts, type in the message "A little friend is 3 weeks late" and send the message before leaving the phone where she found it.

Her personality wasn't much more endearing than her shenanigans, as those acquainted with the 21-year-old Business major from a suburb of Philadelphia knew quite well. She was undeniably pleasant around a select few but in the presence of most she was nearly unbearable. In fact, she could be so antagonizing at times that she was the only member of her sorority (which her family forced her to join for posterity) who was allowed to skip any chapter meeting she wished. Once she learned of her influence over her house's meetings, though, she attended every session without fail.

While her visage was often inhospitable, her beauty was so palatable it was even noted in the campus archives thanks to various emails. In September of 2005, for example, PMU's board of governor's black tie gala was approaching and the Fundraising Department received four emails from the wives of professors stating their refusal to sit near Edie at the upcoming event. It was not for her snide remarks, rather they feared their husbands would look lecherous if they were seen near or photographed with the fetching Edie, a regular attendee of such events. (In her defense, though she enjoyed the chance to don her formal attire, Edie found the events boring, and only attended when forced by her absent relatives.)

Those involved in the letter campaign were elated that their requests had been granted when they saw Edie gracefully entered the campus' grand hall donning a backless green gown that highlighted her enviable figure and brilliantly emerald eyes. Her midnight black hair, gleaming white teeth, and iridescent red smile all spent the night at a table of octogenarian professors and their wives who continued to ask if she was related to "the gal who played Ava Gardner in that Howard Hughes Martin somebody movie."

It was her beauty paired with her intense personality that inspired Lockwood to give her the nickname Edie. Her frightening wit and magnificent allure came across as so startling, Lockwood joked, that Edie at her most direct could give young men who approached her "a serious and long lasting case of erectile dysfunction."

While others may have complained, Edie was entertained. Soon after altering the gender confusing acronym of "E.D." to Edie, she became known at Pemberton strictly by this moniker.

Prior to bestowing the nickname, Lockwood met Edie their freshman year at a new student week event in the Grafe Arts Building. She was uncontrollably lethargic and he was circling the event donning a nametag that read "Lamont" and swapping out the building's dry erase markers with permanent ones. Their first exchange came as she helped Lockwood convince an egotistical looking student that legendary status was bestowed each year upon the first freshman to urinate on the Waterman Building (home to PMU's University Police Department).

The latest in Lockwood's seemingly unlimited cache of non-standard moments came that Tuesday morning when Edie found him already at her sorority house's doorstep waiting for her. After recovering from the initial surprise, she could see something was awry in his face but couldn't identify what it was.

While the seated Lockwood analyzed papers, Edie pivoted towards the heart of campus, suggesting he should follow or be left behind. "What could that girl have possibly done to get you out of her bed this early?"

He folded the sheets and stood as the wind sent his hair fluttering. "We gotta talk."

"Ooh! So serious. What'd she do? Plan a nice trip to Montreal for you?" Edie suggested coyly.

"Sadly, no, last night was different."

"Different like she changed your world?" she playfully teased. "She woke you up early because she knows the *real* you?" Edie knew her line of questioning was too far from the truth to be taken seriously, especially since one of Lockwood's mottos was "the only true form of unprotected sex is when the girl knows your full name."

"No, she was great."

"So what's the problem then? Did you...find out she's a congressman's daughter? Or she's actually a reporter posing as a student to expose your evil immature tricks to the world?"

"No, I," Lockwood stammered in an almost embarrassed tone. "I think I'm flunking out."

"Oh, ha, ha," Edie said with strained sarcasm.

"I'm serious. This could be a real problem."

Edie shook her head. "I didn't wake up early to hear about problems. I woke up to hear about the valedictorian you carried out of Home Reading last night."

Lockwood, who was glad to forget his situation for a few moments, gleefully noted, "It was pretty funny actually. This freakishly hot freshman walked up to me and said she wanted to nail me. And get this: she thought I was a Chinese guy!" The comment's accompanying chuckle was soon joined by a confused-looking brow. "That's kinda weird now that I think about it."

"Maybe she saw you across the room and could tell that you had a tiny dick," Edie nonchalantly sung. "Or...maybe she had a gentle shove from a friend."

Lockwood shook his head. "You? Damn! Nice job." His smile faded as the urgency returned and he placed a piece of paper in Edie's hands.

Edie looked over the data in admiration at how much effort he must have exerted to get such low scores. "Busy semester?" Edie tossed the paper back.

"I'm serious. I think I'm going to fail."

"Don't insult me," she replied with her eyes affixed anywhere but the pleading boy. "There's nothing on that page you can't change without quick emails to your profs and slow repetition of your last name."

"Already did that," Lockwood said. "Come on, why aren't you listening to me?"

"Because even if you're 'failing' you're not really failing!"

Although she was usually more supportive, it was not Edie's fault for being distant. Grades as a subject never arose organically in their conversations, despite the fact that they were both students. Edie knew Lockwood exercised his standard operating procedure for floating through classes more often than his calculation for how many push-ups one had to do in private before walking into a dorm hallway shirtless (which was a formula he used often). While some planned their semesters around their core curriculum or a finals schedule that could give them a few extra days of winter break, Lockwood avoided anything with midterm essays, lengthy handwritten finals, or classes that carried more than a small risk of failure.

As they continued, Edie for a second wondered if he truly felt he was in peril but she promptly dashed the thought. Stories of misbehaving rich kids in college were too cliché for her attention. And if she hated anything, it was predictability and patterns.

This trend started in high school when she learned that most people utilized a blueprint for pointless chit chat in nearly every conversation. She went on to observe that these needless talks filled identical days. Even milestones like birthdays and graduations were treated with such rote behavior that no event was too strong to break the predetermined pattern.

The college visits she took during high school only sharpened her dislike of the configurations she continued spotting. As a Grafe, another well-established PMU family, her mind was set on Pemberton from the start of her process, but she visited fourteen colleges nonetheless. She did so in part to get away from her monotonous classmates and also to see if a place existed that offered a four-year plan that was not a duplicate of every roadmap available.

During her travels she found patterns were even more prevalent in college than high school. Each clique had a nice girl destined for law or medicine, a funny guy who would end up as a nameless company's class clown, an overly excitable attractive girl with large breasts, and so on. From that point on, instantly ignoring or casting away friends at the first sign of tedium was common in Edie's life.

Her hatred of banality helped draw her to Lockwood initially since he was rarely predictable. Just as importantly, their relationship was not romantic. Only once for roughly five minutes did their amity approach anything near adoring before she rapidly dissolved the sentiment. In that short period, her mind jumped ahead to their wild courtship, loud dating, and exuberant engagement. The thoughts stretched farther, seeing their premiere apartment, the birth of their first child, and all the way through the realization their dreams had been swapped out for the more important desires of their little one. She was frightened; this much foresight was extreme even for her. The scorn with which she greeted Lockwood after their brief flirtation conditioned him to never again do anything that would threaten their platonic friendship.

Although his sudden interest in academia was atypical, the idea of Lockwood failing still seemed too farfetched to her. "Let's get back to how Little Miss Brilliant reacted when she found out you weren't the one who could solve her problems."

"Oh I did solve her problems. Both of them."

"Let's be clear: she needed a better grade, she wasn't just cruising for your dick."

"You know the email I sent my professors?" he asked, holding up document as proof. "I sent it to her TA and he fell for it."

"So sleeping with you actually helped this girl's grade? Amazing even for you."

"Good, I got your attention. Now, when are we going to talk about this for real?"

"Why bother? You're never failing out of Pemberton. Period."

The reply stunned Lockwood as it used the same exact words as his mother's favorite saying. "If that's true, there's no reason you can't look at the scores. Right?"

"Should I assume 'scores' is your new way to covertly bring up unplanned pregnancy?"

"No one's knocked up," he stated casually. "I just can't flunk. No Lockwood has flunked out of Pemberton ever. This is as serious as herpes in an orgy."

Edie pondered and draped a sarcastic expression over her eyes. Begrudgingly she took the documents and used them to signal towards a nearby on-campus coffee shop.

The two trotted on, Lockwood grinning over his fleeting victory.

"I'm still waiting for some gratitude for the lay," she noted.

"It makes up for the last time. Remember that girl you found in the VD clinic?"

"I won't apologize for thinking a girl buying penicillin looked like your type."

"I have more than one type. The chick last night was girl next door cute. Are you saying she looks like a girl with VD?"

"If she didn't before sleeping with you, she certainly does now."

After enjoying two coffees served by someone who Edie felt looked too old to be working at a college cafeteria and ten minutes of calculations, breakfast was nearing an ill-fated end.[4]

Upon reviewing the syllabi and scores provided by Lockwood, she couldn't help but feel her body language grow tense. "You've outdone yourself this time," she stated.

"Shit, that's not possible. I cannot fail."

"It looks like you're doing a pretty great job of it to me."

"You don't get it. I am not allowed to fail out of PMU. How bad is it really?"

"According to these numbers, there's statistically no way you can pass."

---

[4] Edie was noticing the results of a joint project led by the Alumni Relations Department and the university's catering provider. Starting in 2001, to combat the school's shrinking job placement numbers, PMU started offering on-campus food service positions to recent graduates who were seeking employment. Their contracts lasted twelve months and helped boost the percentage of "full time" jobs Alumni Relations helped its graduates find.

Chapter 4: Great Uncle Alvin, Ian, and Adelaide Lockwood

AFTER MAKING sure no one in the shop was eavesdropping, Edie proceeded.

In one class, Lockwood amassed what Edie and Pemberton alike considered a pitiful forty-four percent. The outlook grew bleaker as she analyzed how the grade was distributed. The assignments to date were three quizzes comprising twenty percent of the overall grade, an essay (which he didn't submit) worth ten percent, and a midterm worth thirty-five percent. The remaining thirty-five percent was linked to the final exam, and with a miraculous and unlikely perfect score, his overall grade would come out around sixty-three percent.

Under normal circumstances, if a student raised their grade that much in the semester's second half, a reasonable professor might bump the final grade up. But as professors would rarely feel an urge to boost a student to a higher grade *before* any effort was exerted, Edie knew Lockwood could not hope for a generously rounded score by Friday.

As a tangent, she wondered if calculations were even necessary since the king of persuasion received five rejections stating creative grading adjustments were out of the question. Was something pre-meditated to blame for this situation?

Conspiracy theory aside, the remainder of Lockwood's classes looked worse than the first. One class, led by a professor who evidently did not care much for final exams, was already eighty-five percent in the books. Another showed that with an unlikely spike in performance, Lockwood could squeak by with a sixty-one percent: another shining D in his impeccably awful semester.

"So realistically," she concluded, "you're fucked."

To the displeasure of Lockwood's social calendar, her numbers were correct.

Without so much as a confused look as to how he could be failing five of the easiest classes in which a junior could enroll, Lockwood comatosely stated, "This might end up being a pretty shitty time to be the only Lockwood here."

"You're really the only one? Wow. That's amazingly bad family planning. I wouldn't ask you to save a seat in a movie theater, much less save a hundred plus year tradition."

"Even if my shitty cousin Craig who's doing a PhD overseas could transfer, that ain't gonna happen until next semester at the earliest. Either way: if I fail, I'm done as a Lockwood."

The comment and his body language forced Edie to pause. Typically at his worst he appeared slightly disjointed but nowhere near panicked, and that morning she could tell there was a little fear behind his dehydrated eyes. She also knew about his past academic dalliances. The issues that led to Valencia, the accusations he cheated his way through high school French, and other episodes where his parents came to his rescue. Though unsure of why he was so certain this time was different, she was confident she wouldn't find anything nearly as entertaining that week as watching this story unfold.

Lockwood expeditiously gathered the papers and stood. "Time to pull out," he noted with a quick chuckle.

The pair departed to test Lockwood's next attempt to evade the consequences of his intentional and consistent actions. If coercion would not help and the grades were etched not in stone but in digital ink, he felt all he needed was someone who could alter those pixels.

"Well then, Charles," she prodded, with a rare use of his Christian name. "Want to share your grand plan?"

"We," he began with a matter-of-fact grin, "are going to see Alf."

"Alf?" Edie asked, perplexed as she expected to hear a name of someone whose morals were almost as despicable as her own or Lockwood's.

Though savvy with popular consumer technology, Lockwood knew little about PMU's digital infrastructure. That's where Alf, the most mild-mannered of Lockwood's close circle, would come in. (It was odd that Alf was introduced to Lockwood's plot in the context of cyber terrorism as his expertise was often used for altruistic purposes, like building the network which Lockwood planned to ask him to hack.)

As Lockwood wasn't terribly fond of asking Alf to do anything illegal, his trek to the Northeast Quad began by convincing himself the task surely fell in a gray area. By the letter of the law, of course, the act was definitely illegal. But in Lockwood's mind, since he had no other way to obtain passing grades, online espionage was in a moral middle ground.

Less concerned about the deed's scruples, Edie was more than willing to express her lack of faith in the idea. "Did you get this entire plan from an 80s movie?"

"Until I beg my ass off, which I'd love to avoid, it makes sense to try something simple first," he stated coolly. "All we have to do is hack into the system and get me some C's."

"We?" Edie asked with a stretched out inflection on the vowel.

"We as in Alf. And C's as in B minuses. Come on, I'm in serious trouble."

"If you were in trouble you'd use that fancy grade changing device called your parents."

Lockwood vehemently shook off the idea. "No chance. Definitely can't call them."

"Why not? They bailed your dumb ass out after homecoming last year."

"Entirely different story."

"How is it any different? Both stories center on you being a total shit-iot."

"No, this is as serious as it gets. I cannot fail."

"Did you consider sharing that with your grades?"

"If they find out I got this close to fucking this up," he pleaded while clinging to at least a hint of his bravado, "they'll help me now and then bury me. I'll make it through the semester then someone else will transfer in for an MBA and I'll be dead to them."

"That seems pretty extreme."

"They won't give me another chance to mess this up. My family is not an easy crowd. I once almost got my Aunt Adelaide to talk to me again but then I failed that dumbass theater class. That was one class. Try five."

"How does failing a theater class make you underqualified to be a Lockwood? I thought it just made you overqualified to work at a doughnut shop."

The subsequent silence suggested to Edie that either he didn't like her joke or he was too deep in thought to catch it. She pushed to keep the session a collaborative one. "I don't see why you can't bullshit an excuse that makes you the victim. Then your family will be happy to help keep the streak alive. I mean, how often have Lockwoods come close to flunking?"

"There's been a few who had *way* better reasons than anything I could think up."

Lockwood went on to describe a set of near failures that ultimately ended up as the cherished stuff of family lore.

First he told of his Great Uncle Alvin, who decades earlier had to deal with a faction of professors who privately rallied to break the streak after Alvin's father received a prestigious judgeship over the Dean of Pemberton's law school, Orrington Kieft. These professors graded Alvin's papers and examinations with far too strict of a hand during the first semester of his final year. Once he noticed the discrepancy, he fought back with everything he had. The administrators, convinced its professors weren't capable of such petty acts, refused to re-examine any of Alvin's work.[5] With help from his father, the university was forced to allow a board of professors from other universities to grade his final exams. Alvin scored perfectly on all four exams and passed three of his four classes, making it through the semester.

Also in line with the boldest of beleaguered Lockwoods was Ian Lockwood, a great figure who amiably juggled classes and kept his father's business afloat while also tending to his duties as a husband, father, and brother. In one semester, he helped his wife raise their newborn twins while simultaneously caring for his parents who fell sick with rubella. During another semester, he tutored his brother who'd lost a leg in fighting in The Great War only weeks before enrolling at Pemberton with a full course load.

He then explained the story of Adelaide Lockwood's younger, intrepid college years when she was one of the first women to gain entry into the school's Business Department. After the untimely death of her brother Richard at the Battle of Guadalcanal, Adelaide took to the war effort by starting her own scrap metal recovery company. This activity took more time as the venture boomed during her junior year. In classes she was ignored by members of the faculty whose views about women were less than progressive. One professor in particular who despised her pioneering attitude seized his chance to teach her a lesson during her senior year when she enrolled in three of his classes at once. During each class's last session, which she'd missed to tend to her work duties, he abruptly changed the dates and locations of the final exams, knowing she would never hear the updated locations and miss each test.

Luckily for Adelaide, her evenings were spent at the county's most popular destinations where she was joined by many of her

---

[5] In Alvin Lockwood's defense, the campus leaders at the time were among the worst in PMU's history. They spent little time focusing on the students yet the institution flourished around them nonetheless. This isn't terribly relevant, but as I wasn't fond of them at the time and I don't have many chances to speak ill of them, there you have it.

classmates. These men gladly told her the exams' correct dates and rooms. She went onto ace each class despite her professor's efforts.

"There have been rough times," he explained, "but not disease, teachers, or Pemberton itself could ever stop a Lockwood from doing what they were here to do."

"Too bad all you're here to do is drink, party, and splooge in girls' bath towels."

"Damn right." He felt a wave of relief while thoughts of recent weeks returned. "Man, it's been a good semester."

Edie nodded. "It really has."

Lockwood sped up as if they were running behind. "But it's all over if I fail. I'll have to change my name and move to a country where people tape gloves to their feet for shoes."

They walked in silence a moment, prompting Edie's suspicions to latch onto the intrigue featured in two of his tales.

"You know, your situation is sort of like Alvin's. After years of being fine with grade inflation now none of your professors are willing to change your grades? Something's up."

"Even if that's true I don't have enough time to root out the cause of some conspiracy. What I need is a trump card. And that card," Lockwood said, as he raised an arm towards the building they were approaching, "is in beautiful Auggie Hall."

"What do you mean you don't have enough time? You have all semester to fix this fuck up."

"I gotta strike before Friday at noon. Can't have any official proof that I'm about to fail."

"Seriously?"

"Yeah. Last year I dropped Science of City Planning in October to avoid the 'failure is folly' lecture at Thanksgiving. I planned on telling my parents the grade was a typo up but when the midterm grades showed up, the class wasn't on it."

"Got it. And you can't do that for all five at once because then you're a dropout."

"That's right. That's why we need our Alf."

"Good thing we didn't have anything else to do this week."

Chapter 5: Alf

PEMBERTON UNIVERSITY'S square-shaped August P. Lockwood Hall is four levels tall, one level deep, and its floors of connected hallways form a center-less box. With two hundred eighty two student dorm rooms spread across its three upper levels, it sits as one of the more formidable housing buildings at Pemberton.

The dorm is one of six residence halls in the area of campus known as the Northeast Quad, which also contains a gym, six fraternity houses, and a delicately bricked common area at the center. One dorm, Colonial Hall, and the lengthy gymnasium make up the Quad's northern border, which is only one hundred yards from the campus' shoreline along its Great Lake.

August Hall boldly forms much of the Quad's eastern wall, with Glazier Hall to its left. The building, which was named after Charles Lockwood's great grandfather, was one of four dormitories built in the early 1960s in response to the Baby Boom.

The hollowed out area at August Hall's center was originally going to host a robust courtyard that would connect out to the Quad through flowered pathways. The building's designs were changed due to the wishes of then Dean of Students Sheridan, as part of his movement to keep delinquent students from being able to sneak in and out of dorms as they saw fit. Under the new blueprints, students on the second floor were perched at least fifteen feet above the ground, farther, he felt, than anyone would be willing to jump to surreptitiously sneak out.

Redesigns sealed off the inner courtyard and introduced a new basement and first level to the building. The new design chopped up the first floor into two halves. Those entering from the main entrance were greeted by a central Recreation Room that took up the western half of the level. Behind the Rec Room, on the eastern half, the planners drew a small café. The spacious restyled basement, which could no longer host dorm rooms as the redesigns stripped the rooms of their windows, was populated by dozens of storage spaces. Amid these units, designers added their crown jewel: a high-ceilinged multipurpose space that could serve as a concert stage, theater venue, or event hall. The site was wildly popular during its first thirty years, often boasting a weeks-long waiting list filled with student groups yearning to use it. The room was still getting use by the turn of the 21st Century, but mainly by theater groups, who had also taken over a number of the basement's storage units.

Since first opening its doors to undergraduate students in 1961, August Hall experienced its fair share of notable moments. For instance, while studying in a lounge in the spring of 1966, Walt Morrison, a man who would later become a United States Congressman, proposed to the love of his life, Amanda Miller. Their first meeting took place in that same spot during an impromptu party one warm September night in 1964 as a love song was playing on a nearby turntable.

In 1969 a similar study lounge in the building played host to the first meeting of the group that would one day infamously be known as the Pemberton Eight.

Elsewhere in the building, Betsy Wagner, a graduate of the class of 1978, grew distracted one evening while watching the 1976 Winter Games in Austria instead of studying for an Anthropology of South America (ANTHRO 214-1, offered WTR) exam. After failing the test in the class that was vital for her major, she opted to focus on her secondary concentration in medicine. She went on to become one of the foremost pancreatic cancer specialists in the nation.

While the building's forty plus year history spurred countless memoirs, its most significant would be set in motion that Tuesday morning when Charles Lockwood casually strolled into the lobby with the intention of visiting Alf for counsel.

*   *   *

To show his family cared about the state of the dorm named after one of its most beloved patriarchs, Lockwood was obligated to live in August Hall every day of his college career. During his junior year, while his official residence was in August, his main residence was an off-campus apartment he shared with a fraternity brother. His dorm room, meanwhile, was often empty outside of his somewhat regular visits.

Lockwood and Alf met at the tail end of the latter's New Student Week in 2004 as Alf was settling into his new home in August 4017, which happened to be the same dorm Lockwood occupied the previous year.

Thanks to wild partying and a reckless reliance on muscle memory while intoxicated, Lockwood first encountered Alf after mistaking August 4017 for his own bedroom late one night. Had this happened only once they might not have become friends. The alcohol-fueled event, however, took place five nights in that week alone.

Lockwood enjoyed his new acquaintance but had difficulty determining why Alf was always occupying what he thought was his dorm room. The well-mannered Alf watched Lockwood with the smallest bit of shock initially, and in trying to be the gracious host he'd been taught to be, he sat for a drink with his guest the first two nights. He greeted his later arrivals with snacks and movie screenings based on conversations from earlier in the week. During one of these visits, Lockwood also drunkenly conjured up Alf's nickname in a conversation whose finer details were remembered by neither one of them the next morning.

That Tuesday in 2005 Lockwood and Edie found the sophomore as he was preparing for a full day out: first a shift working at the Registrar's Office as a part-time programmer, then two classes, one discussion section, and two or three hours at the library.

Once he was facing the open doorway of Alf's room, Lockwood explained his newest quandary while advising Alf to ignore possible ethical dilemmas when debating his answer.

An unfazed Alf answered with the sincerity of a companion and the emotional distance of a scientist. Digitally altering grades, he explained, was not feasible.

"Beyond the monumental task of hacking in, the system has checks that protect against malicious or opportunistic grade changes." Alf paused and saw both visitors were firmly focused on his explanation. It was odd. "First, the program looks at the IP address that submitted the grades initially and checks to see if the one making the edits is different. If the IPs don't match and the computer making the edits is outside of PMU's network, the system goes into lockdown. At that point, changing any grade in that class requires sign off from two sources. One source has to come from the Registrar, the other one from a university office or PMU-owned laptop."

"Why would you build it so air tight?"

"I didn't think while helping design it that you would need me to break it."

Edie piped up, noting, "That was shortsighted of you."

Ready to move onto another option that could be more beneficial, Lockwood asked, "What else are we going to do if hacking in won't work?"

"I don't know." Alf grabbed two packs of fruit snacks and a sports drink, tossed them into his backpack, and zipped it up. "But I'd be happy to brainstorm as long as the suggestions don't get me expelled, and if we can talk while walking because I'm almost late for work."

"This is no time to be thinking about work," Edie joked. "You know, if I weren't so busy not taking this seriously, I would be inclined to say you're not either."

The three exited the room as Alf chuckled and closed the door. They then made their way towards a staircase while Lockwood's brain went into a type of crisis management mode.

As they departed the building, Edie surveyed the area determined to find the route that was farthest from other ears as possible. There were no students along the Northeast Quad's lakefront path save one loner on a park bench who was toting a pompously bright yoga mat.

"Here's what we do," Lockwood began as Edie led them towards the walkway, "we find a way to stop professors from submitting their grades electronically. Maybe disable their emails with spam. That will give us time to find a way to get other grades in."

Alf shook his head. "Professors can phone in grades, too."

"Then we disable their phones."

"Man, they can walk in grades. If this is the best you have—"

"Next idea," Lockwood said. "We study the people who work at the Registrar, how they get in, how they punch in the grades, and Thursday night we bust in and change them ourselves."

Alf politely searched for words that could say this was the worst idea yet. For help, he looked at Edie, who seemed more interested in the lake than Lockwood's mental state. "Edie, anything to say? Don't you want to tell him this idea is idiotic?"

"If I tell him this one idea is stupid," she replied, her gaze switching from the waves to the lone student in their midst, "it would be unfair to all his other totally stupid ideas today."

"Fine!" Lockwood stated. "Just tell me what makes the idea awful."

"Beyond the problem of getting in there, you'll need class-specific override codes that only the Registrar has and a department code that only professors get."

"Shit, man!" Lockwood declared before repeating: "Why would you build it like that?"

"I didn't build that part." Alf could see Lockwood was still straining for any idea he could. "It wouldn't be worth it anyway. There are definitely security cameras in there."

Lockwood considered showing up masked to get his updated scores in and then abandoned the idea upon realizing the security footage would encourage officials to search their records to see which grades had been changed. For safety he would have to update dozens, maybe hundreds of students' grades to cover his tracks.

Alas, he found a silver lining. Altering grades wouldn't work. Delaying the grades from getting published could, though. He just had to stop the grades from being printed.

Through a quickly forming smile, Lockwood asked, "Then we don't need to change the grades; we just need to party our asses off in the Registrar's Office."

Edie remained far from impressed. "Do you want to elaborate?"

"If it's too risky to bust in there and change my grades, let's destroy the computer that holds the grades. If we go in there attacking the computer, it's suspicious as hell. But…"

"But if it looks like an accident," Edie said, "They're looking for partiers, not jihadists."

Lockwood nodded, as the trio absentmindedly approached the one occupied bench along the lakefront and its neon yoga mat that could likely be seen by boats off at sea. "So, Thursday night we get maybe two hundred random people, as many beers as we can carry, and party in the Registrar's Office until something breaks off." Lockwood tried to let the idea sink in before allowing his smile to spread too broadly. It was difficult, since he felt he finally found the key.

At that, the lakefront's only other guest joined in the conversation. "There's no breaking into that place," the female student offered without bothering to look up at the loud passersby.

Edie similarly didn't get a look at the speaker's face, only the back of her head and her lilac jacket. "Excuse me? I couldn't hear you over our warm invitation into our conversation."

The young lady, believing facts would quiet the three more than a witty retort, stated: "A big protest happened there in the 60s. Now the Registrar is the most protected building on campus. So if you're going to protest you have to do it somewhere else."

"Oh, we're not here to protest, baby," Lockwood replied, hoping his condescending tone would get the stranger forget their talk more rapidly. "We're here to party."

The student dug her face even further into her textbook thanks to the comment. "You enjoy that, then," she coldly hissed, wondering what went wrong with students since the 1960s.

Edie motioned towards a more private path. Once alone, Alf declared, "So that's out."

The interaction left Lockwood confused. "Protest? I'm not trying to protest."

Edie rolled her eyes. "Alf has work, I've got a class I'm not willing to miss for this mess, and you may have crabs after last night. So you should get that checked out."

Feeling no farther along and with time still ticking down, Lockwood knew he had to flirt with an option he did not care for. "Thankfully you won't have to see this next part. Alf, thanks for your help. Edie, I'll see you after Econ?"

"I'll count the moments."

Chapter 6: William Allton

TWO HOURS later, Lockwood found himself sitting on the concrete steps leading up to Rosemond Hall in a dejected mood and waiting for Edie's class to end.

He stared at a single sheet of paper, which a professor printed for him during a hasty visit. The terse note stated the university was cracking down on the "senseless practice" of grade inflation.[6] All grading patterns that semester would be studied by an inquiry board, the letter continued, and if evidence suggested that grades were unfairly changed, the professor would be held accountable. The letter was unsigned aside from the indecipherable acronym "PAGIP."

The notification was a torpedo fired directly at Lockwood's primary survival mechanism.

After the strong flow of departing students calmed down to a trickle, Edie exited and instantly knew from Lockwood's posture that his morning did not go well. She casually assumed the seat next to him and he handed her the paper.

---

[6] Grade inflation involves a professor raising results of the lowest performing students (or every student) to keep the class's pass rate statistically high. Some instructors find it detrimental while others feel it is a key component of their curriculum.

Her eyes darted quickly over the report. "Did all five get this?"

"I think. The first and third mentioned it and it's the only thing the fourth gave to me."

"Someone's screwing with you. You're telling me every professor got these and no one told our parents? Or the school paper?"

Lockwood hoisted himself up and Edie followed. "That's not the problem."

They walked almost aimlessly until, for reasons unknown, he began ambling towards a building whose interior he had only glimpsed in two years: the library. They scanned their student IDs and stepped through a turnstile, moving past many erudite PMU Blades who were studying, a habit thankfully many felt necessary, unlike Lockwood.

"If they're going to throw some bullshit," he said, "there has to be a way to fight back."

"That would be true if the university considered accurate grading to be bullshit."

As this was not the reply Lockwood wanted to hear, they continued deeper into the library. The eclectic mix of strangers both disgusted Edie and depressed Lockwood a little, in that his opportunities to ever meet them would soon be eliminated.

"I could say I cheated," he suggested prematurely. "Then there'd be an inquiry, right?"

"Who's going to believe you cheated for those shitty grades?"

He nodded solemnly while looking at the cover of a book that appeared at a distance to have a dirty sounding title. As he got closer he realized it did not and lost interest. "Then we need another way to Uncle Alvin this."

"I did the numbers twice. Best case scenario you still fail." For a nudge in the right direction, she urged, "Come on, Chip Lockwood. Give us your real idea."

Lockwood brandished the email with fervor. "We need someone who can decipher this," he stated, halting their stroll. "I'm stuck because I don't know how this place works. We need someone who does everything to stay in the lines. They'll know how to fight this."

Edie happily nodded at the rebound. "So is that why we're at the library?"

"Nope, it's why *they're* at the library," he triumphantly exhaled as an epiphany occurred to him. He then pivoted to a librarian. "Excuse me, where are the library's quietest study areas?"

*　　　*　　　*

Sophomore William Allton was sitting unobtrusively in the library's second floor quiet study area, a favorite location he very carefully chose. He regarded the spot as the second quietest place in the library. (The most noiseless locale was always filled with the terminally stressed, so he often chose the silver medalist instead.)

His preferred study area that Tuesday morning wasn't nearly as serene as he'd hoped. For over an hour, two students had been chattering away about various non-academic topics. In an email he planned to send to the library staff, William described this egregious breaking of the quiet rule. Before sending it, he pondered what would happen if the librarian dispatched to clean up the issue called out the email's author by name and a messy confrontation ensued. He then promptly deleted the email.

Had he been paying more attention to his surroundings, he certainly would have noticed two students approaching with their eyes set specifically on him. After guiding the email to its death, he turned his head and was devastated to see Lockwood and his "relentlessly psychotic counterpart" (his words) lurching towards him with ghoulish grins stitched to their faces.

The ensuing moments went in flashes for William. Arms flailed, books flew, he clutched his backpack for life, and then he sprinted for a small staircase in a foolish act.

Before William knew it, Lockwood foiled his escape attempt by leaping on top of him and pinning him down on the stairs that would have brought him freedom.

"Come on, Little Willy," Edie called out. "Give us a kiss."

*　　　*　　　*

William Allton liked the library. It was safe. It was calming. Most importantly, it was the one place on campus he believed he would never encounter anyone on his ever-expanding list of people he could not stand at Pemberton.

A bookish young man who could be described as one of PMU's countless overachievers, on most days William directly interacted with very few people. This had not always been the case. His high school transcript detailed many forays into activities and sports. A well-liked, intelligent, outgoing fellow, his peers expected him to make a big splash at Pemberton.

While some incoming freshmen find themselves lost at the start of college only to regain their amiability after testing out the new environment, the exact opposite happened with William. The social skills garnered from his years high school in suburban Cleveland all but disappeared within his first week at PMU after an accident swiftly placed him on bad terms with the school.

During his move in day he and his roommate hosted their first visitor, a vivaciously attractive girl who was encouraging freshmen to sign up for campus activities. Without reading what they were signing, both volunteered for whatever groups they could find in her clipboard, and William became the only member of the misprinted Anti-Anti-Racism Society. After three strenuous disciplinary meetings, the incident was declared as an inopportune mishap.

Over the course of his freshman year, he lost nearly all the muscle mass he'd built up in high school athletics, as well as other fine traits which initially made Pemberton interested in him. This process began around the time he shaved his regrettable post-high school goatee. The transformation, with help from his features (pale skin, brown hair, brown eyes), made the retired athlete fairly cookie cutter in his new surroundings.

"Dude, calm down," Lockwood said while still perched atop William. "We just need your help for a quick five minutes."

"A polite email might have worked!" William yelped.

Lockwood shifted his weight slightly. "What I'm about to tell you is a secret, so this is between you, me, and the floor."

"No, *I'm* between you and the floor. And if you've got a secret this is not the best spot since I'm guessing people are staring."

Lockwood and Edie turned to see approximately fifty students studying them. Lockwood relaxed his grip and stood with an extended hand for William. The sophomore debated darting away cowardly before deciding it was best to listen and accept it.

Edie, who was triggered by a smell and deliberately ignorant of how the scene looked, asked: "Did you shower yet? You smell like a strawberry daiquiri's walk of shame."

The trio located a private study room and closed the door. "I'm having a problem with one of my professors," Lockwood solemnly stated. "He wants to fail me."

"That can happen when you refuse to show up to class," William replied frankly.

"This is not a usual class. He gave me something and I need you to take a look." Lockwood procured the note as William flinched.

The sophomore looked at the unentertained Edie and then the surprisingly worried Lockwood before turning his attention to the paper. Hesitantly picking it up, William recalled the first time Lockwood needed his help.

It was earlier that calendar year, while William debated if Pemberton really was for him. Two sets of midterms, one of final exams, and two rounds of finding seats in new semesters' classes had passed already, signaling sadly that he and Pemberton appeared stuck together. In an optimistic moment, he decided it was time to try to start fresh again.

The first stretch of college made him a loner, and secretly he wanted to be the person he once was, friendly, talkative, and not afraid to go into any room and introduce himself. He wanted to make friends but he needed a structured, safe way to show one person at a time the real William.

Upon searching, he found a study aide program. The service existed for injured student athletes who were provisionally unable to attend classes, take notes, or discuss course material with instructors or other students.

Around that same time, PMU's intramural ice hockey team played a tough away match against one of the larger schools in Ohio.

During the game several members of the home team forcefully took down one of PMU's second-string wings. The encounter involved Pemberton's wing starting a bench-clearing brawl all while the referee was re-setting the puck. Shortly thereafter, Charles Lockwood returned to campus with a dislocated elbow, a black eye, six stitches along his knuckles, and thanks to other events I am not allowed to discuss in full here, an invitation to permanently stay out of Ohio. It was then determined he would be unable to take notes for American History 1914–Present Day (AMER 212-2, offered WTR).

So Lockwood and William were paired up as study partners. The term partners wore off rapidly, as William realized Lockwood was relying on his help to pass the class while putting forth no effort. But William needed at least one friend, so he soldiered on, providing Lockwood with exact duplicates of class notes, and eventually, against his better judgment, a "preview" copy of his final essay. William bought Lockwood's excuse that writing the essay himself would slow his recovery so he had to use the freshman's work. William hated the decision, but he resigned himself to writing two term papers, one for Lockwood, one for himself.

The attempt at making a colleague failed pitifully, and the delicate studier returned to his hole, hoping to never again see the man who convinced him to abed academic dishonesty. (Details as to why Allton wanted to avoid Edie, meanwhile, were shady at best. I can only assume his distaste for her arose during the one night the pair took William carousing far from campus. That night probably also prompted the birth of William's nickname "Creamer" which he despised and I refuse to use herein for a number of reasons.)

Only minutes after being embarrassed in front of dozens, William was simultaneously reviewing Lockwood's paper and hoping he could find a replacement study fortress before finals. Returning to the second quietest spot was no longer an option.

William tried poorly to hide his disappointment. "I've never heard of anything like this. But it looks pretty legitimate except the lack of a signature."

"Does that mean I can challenge it?" Lockwood queried with a slice of hope.

William hoped his answer didn't prolong his captivity. "If grade inflation was the only way you were going to pass, there's nothing you can fight."

William's remark muzzled the room. Lockwood pensively stared into a corner and Edie monitored William with hope he was bluffing. Truthfully, lying was not on his mind. He was merely trying to escape before anything worse happened. Allton, whose parents attended small liberal arts colleges far from PMU, had no connection to the school. He was very aware that special rules existed for Edie and Lockwood but not for him.

"Man, this place kind of sucks," Lockwood remarked.

William nodded. "Welcome to our world. I think your best bet is the F."

Lockwood exhaled slowly and noisily, almost to prevent his upcoming sentence from happening. "It's not that simple," he wheezed.

William apprehensively swallowed. "You're failing more than one class, aren't you?"

Lockwood held up five fingers. William's first reaction was to run and never look back. Instead, he meekly demanded, "You have to let me go."

Lockwood shook his head. "We need you, man."

Although not expecting to be let out after calmly stating his case, the denial hurt. In a dual nervous twitch and scream he let out a louder, "You have to let me go!"

Lockwood slammed his hands on the table. "Dude, focus up. I cannot fail."

"It sounds like you already are failing!" moaned William.

Edie chuckled. "Ha. That's what I said to him, too."

"Give me a second here," Lockwood said while lifting his hands to a more neutral position. "My family has had someone here for every year for over a century. No one has ever been flunked, expelled, or anything. Don't you want the chance to do something amazing here?"

"Helping keep you here will only be amazing for the skyrocketing chlamydia rates."

"This is part of Pemberton, man! This tradition survived decades of change. Shit, there were only 38 states when this started. All of PMU shouldn't suffer just because I messed up."

Against his best judgment, William pondered the consequences of an unceremonious end to the Lockwood Pemberton Pact. He could see alumni donations dropping, average class test scores decreasing, and most annoyingly, older PMU graduates asking him for the rest of his life why his generation was the dumbest in Pemberton's history. Despite his questionable logic, he began hating the parts of his mind that were agreeing with the far from helpless soul.

He looked up at the junior. "Even if I wanted to help, you're out of options. This entire school is set up to prevent this from ever happening to you, but somehow it happened. That's it."

The last comment hit Lockwood somewhat hard, considering he had been riding a wave of good luck since first spotting William.

"Now can I leave?" William asked.

"Not until you tell us our options. There must be something we're missing."

"Nothing but the chance to get a quality education. The only good ways out of here are getting a degree or transferring."

"Neither one's going to work right now. What else you got?"

"You could always fail or get expelled."

"Really not the options I was looking for."

"You're asking me the impossible! You can't magically get your grades changed, you can't get a degree in October, and you can't get some sort of free pass like the Pemberton Eight did!"

Edie's and Lockwood's heads turned towards William in such perfect synch that their spry interest startled any fragment of his mind was not already mortified.

"The Pemberton Eight?" Lockwood eagerly asked.

"Who are they?" Edie chimed in.

William considered his position for a moment. "I'll tell you...but you'll have to promise to leave me alone once I do."

Chapter 7: The Pemberton Eight

WATCHING WARILY for exits should one become necessary, William led Lockwood and Edie into the library's Hall of University History. The eighty foot long corridor connected the newer, larger section of the library, which was built in the early 1970s, with the older, pre-Depression library building. Instead of adding books into the cramped hallway, the library's staff turned the hall into a showcase with photographs and captions playing out vignettes along each wall.

Lockwood's eyes signaled he was befuddled that his attempt to get through college brought him to a place as odd as a library. An annoyed Edie wondered how the hall showed anything notable aside from an old picture of her grandmother in her days as a PMU student.

"What is this place?" Lockwood asked, looking over one of four lithograph reprints of the beaver-filled, uninhabited land that would one day become PMU.

"This hall covers every major event in the school's history. And we..." William trailed off as his attention switched from talking to searching, "are heading to the 1960s." It took him a moment to find the section of interest as he'd rarely re-examined it after his first of many visits.

William pointed to a photograph of a small protest in a bare area of South Campus. "It was the spring of 1969 and students were getting vocal about their disagreement with the Vietnam War."

Edie asked, "Even though the school had nothing to do with it?"

"Many felt a disproportionate number of professors were teaching pro-war lessons."

(I should note that although I have very personal views about this story, in order to keep the re-telling accurate, I will silently defer to the explanation William Allton offered at the time.)

"The protests started heating up around midterms," William continued. "One night, eight campus leaders banded together to do something about all the anger."

As William went on, Lockwood inspected a photograph of an impassioned student shouting into a microphone. The well-worn caption, which amassed a large number of scratches over the student's name, read: *Student Council Vice President and Debate Team Captain* [words unrecognizable] *addresses students outside of Liberty Hall.*

"These students were huge deals. Each one ran student groups that were so big that combined they were in direct contact with half of the student body." William moved their attention to a photograph of the Registrar's Office as it looked in 1969. "One Monday morning, they filled backpacks with food, water, candles, and matches and they stormed the Registrar's Office, forcing employees out and locking themselves in. They then sent telegraphs to every major university office demanding that the university president, provost, and board of trustees denounce the school's pro-Vietnam War stance that its students considered repellent."

Suddenly interested, Lockwood asked, "What happened then?"

"The school ignored them, obviously. The dean figured they would get bored and wander out looking for weed after a few hours. By the end of the day, he realized he was wrong."

The three looked over a picture showing crowds forming around the Registrar's Office.

"People started to show up, but the school still ignored their demands. After twenty four hours, the school cut the power and the water. Then the crowds kept getting bigger."

Lockwood's eyes wandered to a photo whose caption read: *six of the Pemberton Eight wait in the Registrar's Office during the second night of occupation. This is one of only three photos from inside the building that remain. Photo courtesy of PMU Students Against War.*

"They sat by candlelight for the second and third nights, lived off granola and apples, and took shifts to watch for people trying to sneak in." William pointed to the next photo, a shot of a large gathering of angered students holding banners. "By Thursday morning, an estimated thirty percent of campus was watching. Then the Eight started playing hardball: they announced that if they didn't hear back from the school in an hour, they would start burning every document in the university's archives. Every thirty minutes another entire semester's records would go."

Lockwood started to laugh. "So you're telling me I have to start burning shit?"

"No, no, of course not."

"Well it worked for them, didn't it?" Lockwood asked.

Edie suggested, "Should we hear the rest before we light anything on fire?"

Lockwood shifted his attention to a candid picture of the chief of university police looking distraught as he received a lecture from the infuriated Dean Sheridan.

"The school called the their bluff and sure enough, at ten, the Eight found the 1899 Fall Semester records, took them to an isolated bathroom, and burned them."

The next image showed an aerial view of the Registrar engulfed by a crowd of hundreds.

"Every half hour for six hours, they threw another batch of ashes out a window, hearing cheers every time. Finally, the dean gave police the order to bust down the doors."

Lockwood's mood saddened as he saw the Student Council Vice President defiantly grinning while being handcuffed by a police officer. The photo's caption had entirely worn off.

"What the hell?" Edie asked. "I thought you said they got special treatment."

"They did. The school learned the Eight were not only top students, they were loved by the whole school. Pemberton couldn't risk upsetting the entire campus by kicking out their leaders, so they were forced to find a middle ground."

Lockwood suggested, "So they lit shit on fire and they didn't get kicked out?"

"They were expelled but the school altered the terms. Since, with the exception of the fire, the students were expressing their First Amendment rights, they were expelled with what the school called a high level of honors."

"So they still got kicked out? That doesn't help me!" Lockwood blurted, the color in his face moving from a gentle tan to a pinkish fury.

As Lockwood puffed and William cowered, Edie, who knew Lockwood wasn't really upset, turned back to photographs.

Lockwood asked: "You know how screwed I am and you bring me here for this crap?"

Edie, still focused on the wall, declared, "Oh my God..."

"'Oh my God' what?" William asked, turning with Lockwood to the picture. Upon seeing what made Edie cry out, William moved instantly from praising the distraction to staring in awe.

It was an arrest photo that took their attention. In it, deputies lead the Eight through the crowd. Seven of them looked like non-descript, unwashed students. The eighth student had a bright smile, fashionable clothing, and with the exception of his longer hair and sideburns, he looked startlingly similar to one of their own.

Under the photograph, the caption read: *The Pemberton Eight being led off. Pictured: Lois Conner,* [name unrecognizable due to scratches], *Patrick Byrne, Rebecca Stevens, Amanda Dorn, Kurt Blackwelder, Vanessa Hines, and Arthur Lockwood.*

Edie slyly smiled. "It looks like the magnificent chain's already been broken."

*   *   *

Lockwood bolted down the hallway feverishly searching for a number in his cellular phone. Upon finding it, he pressed a key to dial it, taking no notice of the NO CELL PHONES signs featured throughout the library.

Had he been paying more attention, he may have noticed the girl who had been watching his every move from the moment he ambled into the library until his disappearance with William. She was stationed at the far end of the lounge, attempting to be inconspicuous. She was a mousy looking thing, donning a bright red autumn overcoat not suitable for surveillance. The coat was paired with a logo-less black baseball cap that hid her wavy brown hair. Ducking further behind a computer in case Edie returned, the girl patiently watched Lockwood's gallop from afar. Alas, we will get to her story shortly.

Lockwood stepped outside just as his call was placed through to his uncle.

"Chip, my boy!" Arthur cheerfully asked upon picking up the phone in his Wilmington law office. "What's happening in the exciting world of Pemberton?"

"Tell me about the Pemberton Eight," he replied, silencing the jovial tone and ending the portion of the call from which I may directly quote.

Arthur skipped all formalities. Without knowing why his nephew required assistance, he explained the incident was real it was true he had been expelled. It was also true no other Lockwood was attending Pemberton at the time. But, he explained, he did not break the streak.

Arthur clarified that although his expulsion remained an important part of the Lockwood legacy at Pemberton, decades later it still wasn't a story in which most Lockwoods took pride. As Charles Lockwood's own father argued at the time, since Arthur was helping the voiceless express their rights, Arthur's sacrifice marked a luminous moment for every Lockwood. On top of that, he did come home with a degree, albeit not a desirable one.

As Arthur began detailing the penalties of his actions, his nephew's focus wavered. He felt this selective listening was necessary as it blocked key facts from slowing him down, notably that Arthur's act took weeks of preparation with eight plotters. Lockwood had only days, and at best a less devoted team that was only half the size. He also felt it was imperative to ignore his uncle's blunt references to the doom one could face if they tried to mimic the Eight.

Arthur noted PMU wanted them out at any cost to avoid an insurrection. As they could not expel the Eight outright, each student was granted what was called an Undergraduate Pemberton Associate's Certificate, or UPAC for short. The UPAC was "about as legitimate as half a BA in Film Studies," Arthur explained. It could stand as a launching point for a degree elsewhere, but it was far from a full or admirable college degree.

Within a week of the raid's end, Charles Lockwood's grandfather agreed that Arthur's action was in line with the ideals for which the Pemberton Lockwood Pact stood. Therefore, the degree would suffice and his act had not broken the chain. Arthur promptly started applying to colleges and his younger sister Laura filed papers to transfer in from another university that next semester.

Still having failed to hear any downside, Lockwood pressed for more UPAC details. The degree, he learned, had a caveat stating it could not carry an official grade point average. This was expertly included by the dean, who desired to make the UPAC as undesirable as possible to dissuade other protestors. As the campus continued approaching anarchy each moment the Eight appeared to have lost their rights, Dean Sheridan explained at the time that all grades, not just those from that semester, would be altered to Pass/Fail transfer style grades to expedite the printing of the degrees. For Arthur, accepting the paper wiped clear his cumulative GPA of three point seven out of four.

Despite the fearsome account, Lockwood was so jubilant he nearly dropped his phone.

"There wasn't a single part of this that wasn't gravely serious," Arthur began earnestly. "You won't learn this there but the heart of it all was Abraham Rayburn, a born leader and great friend. He was also the only one of us who refused to accept the UPAC. When he got drafted a few weeks after we got kicked out, we couldn't believe it. But he was too much of a patriot to run from his duty. When he got killed in action halfway into his tour, it took years for the stinging to go away." Arthur paused. "We helped pave the way for major change that week but we paid an enormous price. The only consolation for a while was that we believed in what we were standing up for."

*   *   *

Years after the Pemberton Eight's ado, it could be confidently stated the UPAC was imperfect in every way except its ability to prevent copycats. The post-Pemberton Eight waves of social change of which Arthur Lockwood spoke did occur eventually. But no Vietnam War-related demonstration came close in size or impact as the Eight's Raid. Between 1969 and 2005, only one other person, a student in 1974, received a UPAC. By 2005, few even remembered its existence, and it should go without saying (or it would in any other tale) that no one ever had actively tried to obtain a UPAC to obliterate their own horrendous GPA.

A beaming Lockwood located Edie, who let William scurry away earlier. Through a far too easygoing smile he said: "We got three days to get my ass kicked out before I flunk out."

Chapter 8: Kathie Kieft

THE SIGNIFICANCE of Lockwood's family's permanent residence at Pemberton was one that frequently cursed the mind of the young woman spying on Lockwood that day.

As Kathie grew up in a family whose history at Pemberton (and other storied East Coast universities) was almost as heralded as the company Charles Lockwood kept, she learned early on to despise the rival clan. Her odium grew throughout her life, especially while at PMU. She often pivoted around campus in lengthy detours to avoid even the tiniest glimpse of either August or Lockwood Hall.

By the time she spotted her nemesis jauntily chasing an anonymous male, her morning was already a mess. Amid suffering the agony of having lost her prized smartphone for the sixteenth or so time that semester, seeing Lockwood brought forth a stiffly rooted cache of anger. This thrust her into a search to unveil the dubious impetus behind his actions.

Paradoxically, Kathie's revulsion was so achingly deep it stifled her ability to accept her place as the only person who truly knew what was happening to the young man.

*   *   *

Kathie Kieft was never the most emotionally generous student at Pemberton. In fact, from the moment she filled out her application, she was quite the opposite. From the January afternoon when she was admitted, she instinctively assumed most of her classmates would be "assholes" (her words). Most people were assholes, in her opinion, and she didn't mind blindly classifying them as such. This was her belief, her mantra, and the essence of the senior will listed in her high school yearbook. She firmly believed that most people upon meeting her gave her the benefit of the doubt for at most thirty seconds before deciding to move on. Thus, while only a teenager, she started treating strangers with as little respect as she could muster.

She had a shrewd countenance that was permanently one motion away from displaying unremitting animosity. That face possessed nosy chestnut eyes and a tiny mouth powered by viciously powerful vocal chords. Her pallid skin, petite frame, and etched away fingernails each interpreted without context could suggest she was a nervous or frail soul. In truth, they were side effects of her ruthlessness. Inaction led her to agitation, thus the nails, at which she picked while sitting in lectures she felt weren't living up to their potential. Eating left no great taste in her mouth. You couldn't "win" at eating. Studying, attending administrative meetings, and bettering herself while alone helped keep her skin clear and pale. She had no desire to encourage acne through eating pizza at group "study sessions" that often became grope fests.

As much as she disliked Pemberton prior to arriving, she sprinted into activities quickly by obtaining a part time job even before starting classes. Coincidentally, the position was less of a way to convince classmates she wasn't painfully grating and more of an excuse to let others despise her before stepping foot into a classroom.

Her duties centered on performing Internet searches on each incoming freshman to ensure no admitted students had taken any legal liberties after graduating high school. To stave off invasion of privacy lawsuits should her job become public, she was to do nothing more intrusive than a search engine query.

Kathie spent six weeks performing checks on each student, all of whom were still strangers to this vividly smart and impressionable young lady. (Before you start to feel sympathy, I should note this job was created for Kathie specifically on her request.) No name was too long, no recommendations came from too reliable of a source, and no detail was tiny enough to escape scrutiny. Who cared if the Admissions Board and my own office accepted each person on the list? Kathie had to make her own decision.

Since most accepted students do little that is illegal until after they enter college, the task mainly turned out to be an exercise for improving Kathie's already well-honed Internet research skills. Her pace of seventy students per day lasted until midway through the "L's" when just the most recent forty five articles about a student named Charles Lockwood took six hours to get through. Suddenly she had new justification for her feelings towards the family.

When she finished with the deed, school authorities analyzed her findings. While a small fraction of the work was considered useful, the bulk of it was deemed potentially dangerous for the university— and Kathie— to have at their disposal. The school initially reacted by doing nothing. Ultimately, after hearing from a trustee/golf friend of her grandfather's that they hadn't treated her brilliant work appropriately, administrators scrambled for a solution. One resolved the issue by appointing Kathie as the first student in over thirty years to have a permanent seat on the Provost's Procedures Committee. The move seemed appropriate as the administrative group's banal discussions rarely raised pulses. Nevertheless, having assumed this new position before other incoming freshmen even moved into their dorms, Kathie entered Pemberton with a heightened feeling of entitlement, which was a trait that already appeared fuller than necessary.

When classes started, Kathie's impression of the school's stringent social structure promptly exasperated her. Battling with genius level international students in class, attractive sorority sisters roaming the campus, and "body spray-tastic, starchy pink shirted, upper crust fraternity boys" virtually everywhere showed her PMU was sadly all she expected it to be.

But it is not Kathie's lack of social skills that brings her into this story, rather it is her connection to Charles Lockwood. Their association, which began with online stalking that left her without a single picture of the boy's face, was forged thanks to a lovely young woman named Sarah Warren and the easily irresistible Lynette Darcy.

*   *   *

In September of his freshman year, Lockwood met fellow newcomer Sarah Warren, with whom he was instantly enamored. Sadly, at the time he was dating Lynette Darcy.

Lynette was a film and theater double major whose behavior was so uncouth that it made unhinged garage bands look civilized. She met Lockwood at a fraternity party during a part of the term where freshmen were not allowed on fraternity grounds. Their sparse talks served only to pass time between absurdly noisy arguments in public and intentionally loud sex in private. Soon after meeting Sarah Warren, Lockwood knew it was time to end things with Lynette.

When he mentioned the idea that they might not be compatible, Lynette grew combative. Suspecting a third party was involved, she warned him that the last time her heart was broken over another girl, she "pounded out the pretty" of her old boyfriend's new femme.

The idea of Lynette coming between he and Sarah was bad enough, but to think Sarah might become Lynette's next target was too much for Lockwood to bear.

Never the worrier, with relative ease Lockwood thought up a way out. And so he did something that was terribly out of character: he went to class.

The class was English Fiction Survey (ENLT 211, offered FALL), which was mainly comprised of freshmen girls he didn't know. After searching the crowd he found a girl who he could instantly tell was a "pain in the ass" in the nearly empty second row. He picked a seat one space away from her and his brief but important courting of Kathie Kieft began.

Kathie, while exuding her cold exterior she had perfected over many lectures, was astonished that a young man would not only sit next to her but also ask her out after class. He seemed familiar somehow, but when he introduced himself as Arthur, the mystery ended. She knew no Arthurs.

They had their first date that day and two more that week. Even the cynical Kathie was swept away. Lockwood was quite charming despite his constant habit of looking over his shoulder. She didn't mind his fussiness; she was happy he always let her choose talking points, which tended to focus on how nearly everyone at PMU was an asshole.

For their fifth date he took her to the Film Department's feminist cinema double feature event. Minutes into the first film, Lynette noticed the pair. While brewing the harshest of thoughts, Lynette waited until Kathie stood to use the rest room, followed her in, and mercilessly pounced. She landed four fierce while shouting "Chip is *mine!*" A janitor stepped in to swiftly end the quarrel before Lynette could do any serious harm.

The next day, Lynette was shocked to hear she was being expelled without the ability to appeal. As it turned out, she had been on academic probation since the start of the term and the assault came too early in the year for her to keep her seat.

Hearing she was already on probation stunned Lynette. The three film and two theater classes in which she was enrolled had at that point only assigned two papers, one of which pressed the author to write about their favorite cinematic color.

She went on to learn that someone that summer found a plethora of information she never submitted to the Admissions Department, including problems she'd had with her local police department and actions strong enough to expel her from her school's senior honors association.

So, Lynette was sent home, Kathie's physical wounds healed, and Lockwood was free to date Sarah Warren. The pair dated for a fruitful three weeks before both losing interest. Shortly before their last date in the city center, Kathie stumbled upon them, and amid the ire she finally fully understood her attacker's war cry.

From then on, in addition to graduating at the top of her class, Kathie's new life goal was making Lockwood pay. Thanks to her relatives' stories of the Lockwood Pemberton Pact, she knew exactly where she would one day strike.

*   *   *

Kathie's monthly to do list always had one coded entry to which she would attend if able: RCL (decoded as: Ruin Chip Lockwood). For the sake of her mental health, he was not always on her mind. She knew his wiliness and his family's influence made RCL a difficult task, so for the most part she kept the quest as a footnote beneath her primary goals.

As Fall Semester of 2005 had been a difficult one for Kathie, when she nearly ran into Lockwood, she almost decided to avoid him for another month. She had more pressing issues, notably locating her missing electronic comfort blanket yet again.

She received the magical tool as a gift that summer and had grown frighteningly reliant upon it. She loved the device. Not only did it set her apart from nearly all other students (not even Edie owned one), it reminded professors and others that she was as refined and mature as they were. Of course losing the device regularly didn't help prove that point.

Had she not spent most of that Tuesday morning focused on recovering her phone, their library encounter would have likely gone differently. Under better circumstances, there was a chance Kathie would have remembered the five unsigned letters she sent to specific professors at the start of the semester detailing a very fictionalized grade monitoring initiative.

To Kathie's credit, it was a great RCL plan, especially as Lockwood seemed almost determined to flunk out that semester without any outside help.

In recent semesters she had grown irritated over traps she'd set that Lockwood was able to escape with ease. His charm, intuitiveness, and well-connected parents protected him from vulnerability. That semester Kathie sought to destroy him by toppling one of those pillars.

She surmised that she had to show Lockwood's parents how truly awful their son was by revealing that he was recklessly relying solely on luck to keep their beloved tradition going. This led Kathie to the best place to start: grade inflation.

With just one letter, the "randomly selected" professors imagined firings, slicing of retirement benefits, and freezing of research funds. (None of them knew the university would not even allow auditors to examine student loan distribution or food contracts much less grade inflation).

Ruefully for Kathie, she did not connect these letters to Lockwood's odd movements. She was only focused on learning what Lockwood and his cronies were up to. Knowing she couldn't ask Lockwood or the loathsome Edie, she set her sights on the weaker one.

She positioned herself by the library entrance from which he attempted to flee earlier and strategized. Should she pretend to console the stranger to get him talking? No. She would not suffer the humiliation of approaching him as an ally and having him laugh in her face. Should she befriend him? No. The boy clearly wasn't that great at making friends.

The boy emerged, briskly speeding away. She followed and attacked.

"Excuse me, young man!" she formally demanded (she felt mature language would convince him that she had stature). But he did not turn. "Young man!" *This might be tough*, Kathie thought, *he's not even blinking.* "You must answer for your actions."

William had his fill of both conflict and human interaction for the day, so to block yet another emotional pummeling, he employed a rarely used defense mechanism: pretend your confronter is talking to someone else.

Kathie steeled herself for a fight as the pair continued walking. There was something odd about his defiance. It was not the polished refusal that Lockwood's privileged pals would use. "I'm shocked that you think you're allowed to waltz away."

William kept moving.

"If you think the library is your play place, you're sorely mistaken," she stated, hoping to strike a nerve. "I'm going to have to write you up. What is your name?"

The agitated sophomore almost entirely forgot his surroundings and his inquisitor. *I knew it. Of course I'm the one who gets in trouble, not him.*

Still walking at a hurried pace, William decided on a new solution. He would walk to the nearby Seward Hall, weave past the lecture halls to their sandwich shop, buy enough food to last for two days, and hide in his dorm until the campus once again forgot about him.

As William pressed forward he procured from his pocket his student ID, which also doubled as his campus credit card. Kathie, assuming he was taking the card out for her, reached in to grab it. William swiftly pulled his hand back away from the person he'd nearly forgotten. He examined the girl who had been barking at him and noticed she looked even younger than she sounded. "Wait. You're a student? What are you doing drilling me?"

"I'm...I'm trying to help you," Kathie snapped. "You don't know what you're—"

"Who the hell do you think you are?" William spat, with a sliver of his old self emerging.

Kathie stood brazenly. "I'm Kathie Kieft. Who the hell do you think you are?"

"Kieft?" he asked amid shock. "As in Kieft like the dorm? Did I hit a hive of you people today?"

"What's that supposed to mean?" she asked, disgusted. *It's just one more of his loathsome friends.*

By this point, William was only partially listening as he saw his destination ahead.

Kathie pressed on nonetheless. "You think you can just run this place. One day you're going to learn you can't float through college doing whatever you want to do."

The comment's insipid tone and its callous insinuation hit William harder than any other comment that morning. "If you only knew," he muttered, before jogging to Seward Hall.

What does that mean? Kathie wondered. Feeling the need to try once more to procure answers, she shouted: "A polite person would have just given me their name!"

From the steps of Seward Hall, William opted to reply as his brash, more confident seventeen year old self. "You don't care about my name. It's not on any of the buildings."

With that, he disappeared into Seward Hall. Despite his efforts to retain his anonymity, Kathie garnered valuable clues from their talk. From his accent he was Midwestern, he didn't look like one who ditched classes so he was either a regular at Sandy's Sandwiches or he had a Tuesday/Thursday afternoon class in Seward, and most importantly: he did confirm Lockwood was up to no good. Kathie was confident that with a bit more digging it would be impossible to not find out who he was.

While questions played a heated round of jai alai in her head, she focused on two in particular: *who is CL's mystery man* and *why was CL in the library without a visible beer?*

Had Kathie been more observant she may have added a third, much more interesting question: Why am I not the only person spying on CL right now?

Chapter 9: Squanto

IT FIRST happened at August Hall, where Lockwood asked for Alf's help without a single thought to stop by the room six doors down. Then there were professors and a library visit to loop in a stranger who seemed to selfishly refuse to help. Clearly Lockwood was not taking his situation (whatever it was) seriously if he failed to ask the one person so willing to assist him that he would spy on him all morning. This logic was typical of the student known as Squanto.

He had been on the hunt longer than Kathie, yet unlike Kieft, who could have understood the scenario if she wanted, the tragically nicknamed junior was almost entirely in the dark.

After hours of observations Squanto was prepared to insert himself into Lockwood's day. He watched from behind a bookshelf as Lockwood first took three books on the Vietnam War, then moved to two on the Berkeley riots and finally one about anti-nuclear protests.

Having just accessed a library search tool to check for common references, Squanto stealthily pulled off a nearby shelf any book he could find that referenced at least three of Lockwood's titles. He then remained in the aisle, sitting atop his claimed books like a protective mother hen.

Squanto was a Biology student from Tampa who was seen typically as a cross between a social sponge covered in abrasive thorns and an abject creep. The emotionally bullish boy had the appearance of most slight, brown haired men at the school. What set him apart were two non-physical traits: his inability to be polite and his raging hatred of foreigners.

Far from his dislikes were Lockwood and his friends, whom he adored. He'd petitioned Resident Services five times to let him move in as Alf's or Lockwood's roommate, unremittingly demanding a place among them by free will or force. At one point he attempted to run off Alf's roommate by trying to convince him their room was haunted. Squanto's tactics, which included leaving a burning cross in a pot outside Alf's door, ended up being more racist than ghostly.

His run-ins with Lockwood and Edie always started thanks to his own efforts and usually ended promptly thanks to Edie, who thought their exchanges would end after nicknaming him in a far from politically correct way (it was based on his lack of hygiene, savagery around women, and voice which belonged to "a person no one wants to listen to"). He proudly wore his nickname both because Edie bestowed it and it insulted "reds" whenever anyone uttered it.

*   *   *

Lockwood's research about student assembly in the second half of the 20th Century was enlightening yet depressing, and potentially detrimental to the continuation of his plan.

The battles interested him, as were the times in which historians were able to show a clear path from an issue's origin through its escalation, boiling point, and resolution. Similarly he was astonished by the passion with which students banded together, often facing jail sentences or risking injury. These furious arguments and the students championed them, however, were far different than what Lockwood had ever seen.

The only debates he'd encountered in the few Pemberton classes he'd attended were typically led by students who rattled off points until ending up off topic. Regardless of class size, rarely did more than six students ever enter the fray. Concurrently, arguments in the bleachers over sports and bickering in bars over women did not come close to the fervor seen in the books.

He realized that his desperately needed focal point had to be controversial enough to stir the imaginations and rile the passions of a populace that seemed to lack both qualities.

After all of his reading and his relatively current knowledge of topical issues, his mind latched onto nothing. Reactions to the two ongoing wars, flare-ups around *Roe v Wade*, and outbursts over taxes were the only protests he could recall. None would get him anywhere near a UPAC. Was there a way to interest students *that* much to cause a campus-enraging protest?

If such a magic bullet protest existed for his generation, he felt, someone would have found it already. He was going to need an unconventional course of action.

While pondering, a set of six books loudly dropped onto the texts in front of him. As the set fanned out he noticed two of them were books he was about to locate. Unnerved, he looked up to see the handiwork was Squanto's, who let his impatience get the best of his intentions.

Squanto's presence usually unsettled anyone. Once Lockwood pieced together why Squanto had these books, his feelings turned to spiteful suspicion. *How much does this little shit know?* he wondered.

"Thanks for the invite, buddy," Squanto began as he hovered over the table.

"I'm a bit busy here. Thanks for heading out."

"Busy like when you and Edie were walking around with that shit ass looking gay kid who was about to cry?"

Not wanting to be caught with a suspicious look on his face, Lockwood shifted his attention to his phone. "I'm sure you were dying to say hi then."

"No way! Edie never wants to talk for some reason," he pleaded miserably.

"You sure it's not because you tried to date rape her old roommate?"

"That was a misunderstanding!" Squanto squealed. "And it was just alleged date drugging. There's no proof I tried to do anything else."

"'Date drugging' still sounds pretty shitty."

"Date vitamin-ing, okay? All I did was put a diet pill in her drink when we were out at dinner. People like four tables away flipped out and she yelled and ran and shit wasn't my fault!"

"Did she ask you to put a diet pill in her drink?"

"Of course she did!" Squanto bellowed, as if the answer should have been clear before the question was posed. "Well...she was about to."

"How the hell did you know that? And don't say because she was fat."

Squanto's neck and cheeks bulged as if he were about to spit out an unpleasant mouthful of food but restraint prevented it. "I didn't know it had more uses until after!"

If Squanto had a super power it was his ability to weasel out of situations in which he rightly deserved punishment. Unlike when Lockwood used his similar ability, Squanto's transgressions often put others in real danger. Often he evaded repercussions because even the disciplinarians charged with putting him in line didn't want to interact with him. He didn't always escape punishment, but often enough he slithered away without it. In the case of Edie's sorority sister, University Police had no evidence as Squanto promptly drank the girl's beverage himself and later claimed he had been drugged by an anonymous fraternity prior to dinner, leaving him allegedly with no recollection of the date at all.

As was usually the case with Squanto, the talk in the library hit a sore subject quickly. As he sat down across from Lockwood, the latter asked: "What are you doing?"

Squanto leaned back in his chair and grinned. "The real question is what are *you* doing? You never ever study, dude. Bro. Lock-migo. Lock-fraire."

"I'm studying, Squan-tool. Now get lost."

"Shit no, you're not! I'm sick you guys leaving me out of your fun shit."

"No. You can leave."

"No way, man. I've been watching you with your books and

shit. You've got something going on, don't you?"

In an attempt to prevent a scene, Lockwood then dropped his imaginary reluctance and outlined his latest ruse to evade Squanto. It was something his fictional cousin at USC called "Dicks-n-every book" (modeled lovingly after the word "dictionary"). It involved a group of male students photocopying pictures of their genitals and taping the images into hundreds of books. The prank required a sparse paper trail, so to dole out assignments, Lockwood would direct students to a library shelf whose book titles were in alphabetical order. *LBJ's Tremendous White House Era*, *Mass Military at Berkeley*, and *A Nuclear Future World* weren't study materials, they were vessels containing work orders for helpers with last names starting with L, M, and N.

The idea, which Lockwood deliberately made absurd, sucked Squanto in straight away. He demanded to participate and Lockwood instructed him to start in the European History section. Squanto objected, stating European History books were on the ninth floor and it was his favorite in the building since "it's the only place I can go without the chinks and Japs following me."[7] Lockwood guided him elsewhere and gladly watched him leave.

With Squanto gone, Lockwood shifted to writings on modern protests, which when viewed did not give him much with which to work. Eventually he saw the corporatization of American universities emerge as a pattern but it didn't seem strong enough to be helpful.

The groups and their goal would have never shined in Lockwood's thoughts amid the more accessible anti-war protests that harkened back to the days of the Pemberton Eight. There was good reason for this. By the fall of 2005 their cause had only grown slightly in reputation from its humble roots. The school of thought consisted of separate pods of activists protesting issues like the rapidly expanding importance of corporate sponsorships of colleges, extreme escala-

---

[7] Squanto based his thinking off of the fact that the number nine is unlucky in some Asian countries, a fact he was overly happy to learn in high school while on his school's golf team.

tion of tuition fees, and questionable tactics of the student loan industry. Between those protests and other related issues, the voices were backed by data but possessed little weight.

At first glance this idea fit much of what he was trying to accomplish. But it was impossible to ignore the fact that it appeared hard to promote in a tight timeline to an apathetic audience. Above all, Lockwood felt the issues didn't seem to have any connection to Pemberton.

I suppose we should not be surprised that a boy failing Corporate Environmental Awareness was quite wrong about the effects commercial powers had on his school. Examples existed all over campus. Even his great grandfather's namesake was not immune to outside forces beating down the quality of life at PMU. Over the decades August Hall remained a lively place despite a number of incidents that all affected the resident experience in some way.

For one, in the 1970s, local fire officials decided that an underground passageway that connected the Great Hall to neighboring Colonial Hall was not up to local fire codes. Instead of filling in the tunnel to dismantle it permanently, as was recommended, administrators found it more economical to paint over the entrances and remove the hallway from all campus maps. The decision saved money but data hidden in the archives showed the move led to a higher than average number of bronchial infections in students living near the hallway in either building. Also, it certainly would have posed a security risk if anyone remembered the hall's existence years later. Along the same lines, by 1983 the university began charging outside vendors and student groups alike to utilize the Great Room, and these fees were more than most student groups could afford. Additionally, in the early 1990s the university boarded up August's dining hall, along with three others, when it was decided the real money was generated by having food service providers pay to utilize the building's cold storage units which they helped build.

August's residents sometimes posed questions about oddities in their dorm, like where the café went or why loud trucks noisily and regularly drove by during pre-dawn hours. For the most part, the tiny shifts in service were spread out enough to go mostly unnoticed, and the dorm adapted along with others on campus, each time emerging as a slightly weaker version of a home it once was. But information describing practices like these at Pemberton would not help Lockwood as this data was confidential at the time and far from Lockwood's eyes.

Regardless of what he did not know about his university, he knew he was still far from an answer that would propel him to his expulsion, and he began to sense that the real answer was not in books. He required something darker, something far from straightforward.

As his research continued, his focus drifted back to Squanto and rested upon two thoughts. The first was his hope that Squanto's pending arrest due to exposure would encourage him to care less about Lockwood's activities. More disturbingly than the thought of Squanto rubbing himself on library books, Lockwood realized Squanto was unfortunately the typical PMU student in that he embodied how students would react to any type of spontaneous, politically-steeped protest: with bland disregard.

With this thought came his breakthrough: to dismantle his classmates' stubbornness he didn't need a cause; all he needed was a spectacle big enough to grab and keep their attention. The desire to not be left out would then fan the fire throughout campus. He would merely have to find the loudest voice in the crowd and carry their cause farther than anyone would dare. As stepping over boundaries was his specialty, he was confident he would do well at that stage.

The remaining problem, of course, was he had to first find that spectacle of an argument that could neither be shot down and nor embraced by the university. Was such a task possible? Being Charles Lockwood, he arrogantly answered with a strong affirmative. But even more enticing to Lockwood was the other question: since it was possible, could it be made easier?

Was an Abraham Rayburn of his generation out there already looking for a way to get their classmates to rise up? If so, might they be willing to do Lockwood's work for him?

Chapter 10: Eva Yesterday

FOR AS long as she could remember, Eva Yesterday, an effervescent twenty-one year old native of Portland, Oregon, had sought the truest of all opportunities: to flex her Constitutional rights to assemble for a just cause. But she was never once directly involved in a battle that was worthy of the epic stories on which she was raised, even though she knew that she was destined to one day deliver a speech capable of burning a hole through a megaphone.

After four years of fighting whatever battles she could find in high school, her college years gradually taught her that her generation was little like the students of the sixties and seventies whom she greatly admired. Those predecessors impressed her so much while growing up that her appreciation for their era's culture evolved into an obsession. Even her nickname, Eva Yesterday, which she chose at fourteen after mishearing a lyric in David Bowie's "Young Americans," was an attempt to pay homage to that great generation of civil fortitude.

Early on at Pemberton she found a battle or two and fought as hard as she could for them. Her most notable accomplishment was shifting the publication of the student newspaper six hours earlier. *The Nightly Pembertonian* (formerly *The Daily Pembertonian*) was a campus staple since its formation in 1914.

During the winter of Eva's freshman year, students began grousing (in hindsight, perhaps sarcastically) that it was useless for PMU to distribute the paper early in the morning as it was primarily used for its crossword puzzle. As many of its "readers" frequented bars on weeknights, the unimaginably tedious task of stopping for a paper on the way to class was a nuisance, if not a danger. As there were no other grand tasks to undertake, Eva honed in on altering the *Pembertonian* to suit the needs of these students. At first the university laughed at her, but she held strong and led a tough battle. Regardless of how silly administrators made her arguments seem, in each round of sparring she found ways to keep her cause alive. This continued for weeks until a scandal erupted elsewhere on campus grounds.[8] To divert attention from the issue, administrators opted to shift the printing time. As the paper's staff was not thrilled they had to alter every aspect of every schedule, they changed the paper's name to *The Nightly Pembertonian* to highlight the crusade's ridiculousness. The change also prompted the paper's new motto "Literally printing yesterday's news." Thus Eva had her first victory.

This win helped secure what the Provost's Procedures Committee considered to be a coveted role in student government: the university's student liaison, whom they would call upon to determine the legitimacy of each student protest. This practice of gauging demonstrations was born out of a desire to keep risk and liability at bay.

Every so often the university would call on Eva to look in on a new student-based protest group. If their cause seemed legitimate, the PPC would classify it as a sanctioned organization, provide the group with spaces for events, as well as a stipend from a university-run student fund. (What Eva didn't know at first was that once groups accepted the non-negotiable funds, their days as an effective module for change were numbered.) Alternatively, if Eva declared

---

[8] In the aftermath of the flooding of Monterey House, fire officials accused Resident Services of neglect when the water damage revealed a spate of wiring and building code violations that apparently had long gone unnoticed.

that the group was not acting as a legitimate vehicle for self-expression, it was treated as hostile and their protests were guided by university officials to end as soon as possible.

Eva was not entirely fond of taking part in the charade but she told herself it did at least some good, and she knew without taking part she would lose a role in maintaining her post as a campus VIP. She would need a role like that, her high school guidance counselor once warned, as her looks did not set her out tremendously.[9] At five feet nine inches tall, the brunette with inquisitive hazel eyes was slightly taller than most females at Pemberton and louder than nearly all others when she chose to be. She had a healthy, trim frame thanks to a sensible diet, yoga (her bright, rainbow-infused yoga mat was a mainstay on campus), and favorable genetics.

On that October afternoon it wasn't the fear of going unnoticed or a lack of a real battle that dominated her thoughts. It was a terrible idea that made her question whether her efforts were for nothing: the greatest protest idea she'd ever heard wasn't really for a protest, but for the biggest keg party in PMU history.

She'd heard the idea earlier that day from "some ungodly annoying, cookie cutter frat boy." Hours later, sitting in the student union overlooking ships distantly strolling across the lake, she couldn't strip the boy's carelessness from her mind. She couldn't tell what upset her more: the student's offended reply when she mistook his idea for a demonstration or the fact that she couldn't come up with better ideas for self-expression.

Eva allotted only five more minutes to focus on the anonymous party animal. Before switching topics, she unintentionally crinkled her face into a scowl and wondered how far he got in his party plans instead of taking time to study the world around him.

---

[9] Like with nearly all of her other charges, Eva's guidance counselor talked less of Eva's competencies and more of her looks and religious background. The counselor was promptly fired upon Eva's acceptance into five national powerhouse universities, including Pemberton.

*   *   *

Oddly, at that exact moment Lockwood was entering his seventh hour of studying.

At this point, kind reader, I know what you may be thinking: this is the part in which the hero, a devoted opponent of all aspects of academia, starts his life anew by taking his nascent excitement for research to forge a respectable path in life. This was not the case.

It was true that Lockwood was studying like he never had before, but what he was really doing was working just hard enough to attain the lowest measurable mark of success. (This is a commonality at many universities, I understand.) This, frankly, isn't studying; it's cheating oneself from living up to their potential. In Lockwood's case it was a last resort after years of ignoring other options. I only mention this in the hopes that reading of Lockwood's challenges encourages at least one student to avoid this often used tactic.

His intentions aside, Lockwood did cover a reputable amount, and as much as it pains me to admit it, what he'd come up with was surprisingly insightful. What he still lacked, however, was the big spectacle behind which he could rally the troops.

For forty minutes he searched his notes for anything that could point him to a protest whose roots were so solid that it could not be stopped by anything short of the university stuffing a UPAC in his hands. He knew the idea had to be enraging, and each side of the argument could possess no chance of being declared wholly wrong. After finding his notes didn't hold the key, he logged into a computer and executed whatever Internet searches came to mind.

After running a web search for "school protests" he stumbled on a wave of articles detailing the same issue arising in middle schools, high schools, and colleges nationwide. Many articles' pictures featured angry white men hurling statements at stoic opponents. Despite the fact that all the recipients of these enraged remarks wanted to do was change school mascots from Native American caricatures to something less insensitive, the opposition refused to budge.

With this discovery, Lockwood's posture straightened, his excitement rose far beyond his normal library levels, and he could practically taste the victory beer he would soon serve himself.

After unwillingly embracing with disappointment, he'd finally returned to an emotion with which he was more at ease: a combination of victory and smug satisfaction.

He loved this Native American idea. The argument was emotional, it was not so narrow that he couldn't later connect it into other student-centric themes if needed, and although the plaintiffs had valid points, their opponents could not be considered wrong because that would invalidate the origins of their nation's history as it was widely taught.

Giddily eager to proceed, he reached for his phone and sent three text messages. The first, to Edie, said: *Auggie Hall, 9pm, bring dinner for 4, will pay u back*. The second and third went to Alf and William. Each message read *My room, 9pm, be there*.

*   *   *

The campus' central clock tower and four others tolled their eight p.m. tones. As the alma mater chimed from the bells above Liberty Hall, the players regrouped.

Eva Yesterday left the student union for home, finally having plucked her nameless enemy from her mind. Squanto exited the university's police station and retreated towards August Hall, having avoided disciplinary action by reminding the arresting officers he never fully brandished any of his anatomy before being apprehended.

Alf finished his long day by skipping his customary burrito shop stop on his way home. William, meanwhile, ignored Lockwood's request to meet him at his off-campus apartment while wondering about the life he could have had if college had started a little differently.

While waiting at the student union's Italian food counter for the team's meals, Edie re-read printed copies of two *Nightly Pembertonian* articles that mentioned the student body's lead "protest liaison" yet did not fully explain why such a title existed. She studied the girl's picture, and while wondering when their paths might meet, she grew annoyed by the capricious Asian student nearby who was beaming at his laptop. Edie was unaware that this European History PhD student (who hadn't been to Home Reading in three weeks) was joyously re-reading an email from one of his very attractive first year students whom he hoped could provide some non-academic rewards in exchange for boosting her grade. At the same time, the imposter who already reaped those benefits was washing off his long day in the shower.

Kathie, meanwhile, was sitting in the basement of the student union in front of a laptop connected to a bulky machine, which stored every student, faculty, and staff ID photo taken between 1988 and 2005. After wasting hours poring over photos, she could not turn up anything on Lockwood's mystery man. The closest she came to finding a match was a year-old photo of a bearded student with a heftier build who may have been a white supremacist. The near match suggested to her that her search would never come to fruition without additional help.

Tearing through the halls of the staffed section of the union, she sought out anyone who might be able to help at that hour. Upon realizing no one would still be around that late, she returned to the ID machine, located the emergency contact list that was taped to its side, and began dialing numbers from the office phone line.

After being unable to connect with any of the university employees listed, she went in for a closer look at the bottom line of the list. Much to her ire, this last name belonged to a student. The explanation offered under the student's name irked her even more: "contact if student rights questions arise due to inappropriate or potentially offensive photos."

Although she didn't feel she should have to contact a fellow student about the issue, the name was obviously there for a reason, and by Kathie's thinking, it was another person she could yell at. She dialed Eva Yesterday's phone number post haste.

Eva answered the call after three rings. "Hello?"

"Yes, I'm calling with the Provost's Procedures Committee. I'm researching an incident in the library today. I'm looking through the ID card archive and it looks—"

"Who is this?" Eva asked, suspicious of a voice that sounded so young.

"This is Kathie Kieft."

"Kathie Kieft the undergrad?"

"Yes but I'm—"

"The undergrad, who like all others, is not authorized to look into photo archives?"

"I have been supervising the work of a staff member, thank you very much," Kathie snidely remarked. "We are looking for someone who was causing trouble in the library today and he isn't in the system. Have you had any glitches in your software lately?"

"None at all," Eva replied dryly, "because that's not my software, I don't work there, and neither do you." (As it were, Eva's name was on the machine's call list as a result of one of her mini crusades the previous year which had led to a mostly meaningless victory.)

"Well your name is on the machine's emergency call list," Kathie spat. "So someone thinks you're important enough to answer questions about the software."

Eva let out an exhausted breath. She disliked dealing with Kathie even on a good day. As this day started with a reminder that her labors as a steward of student rights may have been a pointless endeavor, interacting with Kathie, who seemed to also want to point out the idiocy of Eva's dream, was more draining.

Pushing past the hopefully temporary angst, Eva asked bluntly: "Is the staff member you're helping engaged in an investigation that could at some point suppress a student's rights to assemble, to express themselves, or to study in a safe environment?"

Ignoring the remark, Kathie aggressively moved forward with her attempt to either guilt or bully information out of Eva. "The incident in the library started as a distraction and is now a security issue since the culprit doesn't appear to be in the directory of every undergrad, grad student, PhD candidate, and part-time student."

"Have you considered the possibility that he wasn't a Pemberton student?"

"I saw a student ID in his hands. How could he not be in the system?"

"According to an email I got a few weeks ago saying a bunch of fake university IDs have turned up this semester. Bars and bouncers at frat parties have been turning in a bunch."

At this, Kathie promptly (perhaps a little too promptly) concluded that this rash of fake IDs certainly fit into Lockwood's plans somehow. *Also,* she wondered, *how's this bitch getting private school emails that I'm not getting?* "How would you have gotten an email like that if I didn't? I'm supposed to believe this coming from someone like you?"

Eva laughed briefly and silently thanked Kathie. Tearing through the negativity pressed upon her that day, this snide reply reminded Eva that her struggles were not for nothing. She was there at Pemberton, she resolved, to stop people like Kathie from thinking and serving as the only authority students needed. "Don't call again, Kathie."

Kathie hung up, ceasing the call which discomposed both participants. She focused again on Lockwood, wondering how his prank would weave in this network of teens posing as real students. As Kathie then wondered how to ensure that this would be Lockwood's last stunt at PMU, Eva steadfastly vowed to punish the next person who attempted to paint her work as pointless.

Chapter 11: The War Room

EDIE'S GENEROUS offerings were well received upon her arrival at Alf's dorm room. As she dabbed at her sushi, Alf ate fried rice (his favorite on-campus food), and Lockwood tore at two slices of greasy pizza while explaining his findings. The fourth dish, a dull bowl of buttered noodles purchased for a mystery guest, sat uneaten.

After clueing Alf into the reason they were gathered, Lockwood was immensely thankful that Alf still wanted to help with his perilous quest. He wondered what inspired the computer whiz to help but shied away from the query quickly. The question was an apt one which likely later puzzled some administrators, but not me.

Alf's principal motive was that Lockwood reminded him of Professor Russell, his favorite instructor and the primary reason he chose to study at Pemberton. To Alf, both Lockwood and Russell fit the mold of the type of person who could change the world. The comparison was far from academic, as Russell possessed a doctorate and other degrees from elite universities in California and England, and Lockwood spent most of his time at PMU drinking, partying, and vomiting. Alf believed that those who were charismatic, unabashedly dauntless, and who also had access to wealth, like Lockwood and Russell (who was one of the first backers of three technology titans of the 1990s) would mold humankind time and time again.

Earlier that semester, Russell presented his students with a challenge to impress him. The cavalier suggestion stemmed from a push to provide students with both in-class instruction and extemporaneous challenges. It also didn't hurt that with his experience, prestige, and independent wealth, posing such a test could not possibly later haunt his career.

Skip ahead to October eighteenth. As Alf believed helping Lockwood was both a good deed and a way to rise to the challenge set forth by his instructor, the choice was simple. If Lockwood made a big enough spectacle, Alf could exhibit his mastery on a grand scale and use Russell to evade potential trouble. If Lockwood failed, Alf would fall back on his previous attempt to impress Russell (the new security features of the Registrar's grading system).

During the feast Lockwood covered everything from the evolution of campus protests to the protracted timeline needed to create a real demonstration. He also outlined that he would gain Pemberton's attention with some grand, yet undetermined gesture and not let go until receiving a glorious expulsion. To start, he said, they would drum up attention by protesting PMU's treatment of Native Americans, a ploy which would lead them to a more gripping topic.

"Native American mascots?" Alf asked with more than a hint of confusion. "You do remember our mascot is a knife set, right?"[10]

Edie's nod gradually gained speed, denoting approval. "The world's first totally crowd sourced expulsion. I think I like it."

"You're damn right for liking it," Lockwood replied.

"Two problems though," Edie noted. "One: it has to look like you're coming up with the big ideas yourself. If you don't, people will think you're mocking them for attention."

"I know. That's why we need William help us cover our tracks. Has anyone seen him?"

---

[10] Alf was correct. Many of the advertisements from PMU's early years touted its culinary school, so for decades a set of anthropomorphic (and at times racially insensitive) knives served as the school's unofficial mascot. In the 1930s the mascot became official.

Edie's head tilted at the remark. "Seen him since you stepped on his face in front of the only twenty people on campus he wasn't scared around? Um...no, I have not."

"Maybe he'll show soon."

"Second problem: you're down to sixty-three hours and still don't have a *how*. As in: how will you use to your advantage something no one's ever cared about in history?"

"Not gonna lie: no clue. That's why we're here in the war room."

Alf glanced at the walls, which were adorned by his favorite movie posters: *Lawrence of Arabia, Platoon, Zulu*, and *Full Metal Jacket*. "Is that because of the war movie posters or because this is supposed to be your headquarters? Again, I do still live here."

"It's the war room because we're here to think! So let's throw out ideas. Even bad ones."

Edie offered: "If we're listing bad ideas let's start with how your 'place to think' is a building where you've studied zero times in two years."

"I don't need logic, baby, I need emotion."

"Self-immolation is emotional," Edie said, kicking up her feet and leaning back on the couch. "But it might be a bit extreme."

Lockwood, launching into a more active mode, announced, "All right, let's do this! Let's uh, spray buildings with Indian war paint."

"Lame," Edie replied, her head in a magazine. "Sounds like an art project."

"If you had more time," Alf suggested, "You could do something big at the football game Saturday. Like storm the field and do an Indian rain dance."

"Something like that would end too fast," Lockwood replied. "There would be no time to generate more momentum. And don't forget we can't do anything that seems like a prank."

"So you need actual protest ideas."

"No, we need something that people actually respond to. We're thinking small. Sit-ins, tiny rallies, letter writing campaigns..." Lockwood slowed after hearing the options out loud. "Wow. Nonviolent protest sounds useless, huh?"

At that moment, the door flew open. "Como te llamas, pussies?" Squanto bellowed.

His scan of the room showed Alf staring into his computer, Edie trained on a magazine, and Lockwood pacing. Squanto's face illuminated. "What's up? Twice in one day! Crazy."

Lockwood waved him off, hoping he would take the cue. "We're a little busy."

Squanto feigned shock with a halfhearted gasp. "Oh, you're busy *again*? Should I assume this asshole is in on your big project, too?"

"I'm only here because they think this is their room," Alf noted.

"And what are they busy with?" Squanto piped up.

"Ideas for getting kicked out—" Alf absentmindedly stated before stopping his gaffe.

Lockwood's neck muscles tense up at the words. *Squanto can't know about this,* he avowed. *That shit eater ruins everything.*

"Kicked out?" Squanto screeched. "Of what? School?"

"No, his roommate, uh," Alf stumbled momentarily.

Edie, simulating disinterest at the potentially deadly faux pas, swept in. "Chip's roommate kicked him out last night over something gross he did. Now Chip has to convince their landlord his roommate did something worse to get his roommate kicked out instead."

"I'll be your fucking roommate, jack ass!"

"I may be in a bad spot," Lockwood threw back, "but no one's ever been that desperate."

Squanto waltzed through the room, eyeing Lockwood. "That's bullshit. You're really planning your next prank, right?"

Lockwood released some uneasy laughter and Alf mimicked it.

"Damnit!" Squanto whined. "You guys never let me in on this stuff!"

Edie cooed, "There's a reason for that, Squnt. We can't stand you."

"I let you in on the library prank," Lockwood replied. "How did that go?"

"Almost got me arrested, dick," Squanto said as he deliberately fell backwards onto the couch next to Edie. She sneered at him before looking back at her reading. "Now let's hear your ideas or I won't leave your precious private party."

In unison, Lockwood, Edie, and Alf all went silent, with Lockwood adding in extra effort to blankly stare down Squanto until he got the point. It took a few uncomfortably long minutes (far more than it would have taken for anyone who could read normal social cues).

"You guys," Squanto began as he slowly stretched his legs to stand, "are being real fucking slits about this shit. Pretty damn soon, you're gonna need help from this guy. And where am I going to be? Hitting up the late night sub shop scopin' freshman girls in short ass shorts and getting my twelve inch ham on!" After one last wink at Edie, he reached for the door. "So much for sticking around until you had a good idea, Cockwood. Ha!" Squanto laughed. "If you shits had to stay until you got a half decent idea for a prank you'd be here for weeks. Total lockdown with the cock down."

At that, Lockwood's eyes sparked and Edie perked up behind the magazine. His stare shifted slowly towards Alf, who had ceased typing.

Squanto exited yet no one spoke for thirty, sixty, ninety seconds. Immediately following the sojourn, the trio could barely contain itself.

Lockwood didn't love the idea's origin but he felt he had in his hands the golden suggestion to get the campus's attention. What better way to involve all of campus, he thought, than roping in four hundred students without even asking them to leave their rooms?

"Alf," he started, "we're gonna skip over you almost blowing this like a horny chick at a date party. Second, this could work right?"

Edie smiled. "It would be a big enough gesture."

Alf added, "I could wire up the security system to take care of the automated locks."

After another suggestion was posited that someone should also manually secure the doors and windows near the ground (I have been asked to not attribute that quote to any particular individual), the plan seemed more robust.

"It's bold," Lockwood stated, "and I've got a pretty good feeling it's never been done before." He glanced at Edie and then Alf. "People, let's move some asses."

*   *   *

Thanks to two warring opinions, this next passage is an incredibly delicate one. On one side, I have been asked to accurately recite all events connected to Lockwood's siege with all of the data at my disposal. However, certain administrators have decried disseminating detailed descriptions of students willingly breaking university policy as well as several laws.

I may broadly explain the plan, though.

The initial focus was the locking of the building both physically and digitally. Secondary tasks came next, like spreading news of the protest and impressing upon the students that they were patriotic assistants and not captives. To accomplish this, Lockwood utilized an energy that was rarely seen from him when not prepping for a bar crawl or a keg race.

Lockwood effortlessly rounded up aides almost immediately. The additions were a friendly PMU linebacker nicknamed Dipshit and a dozen freshman girls. The young females helped primarily because they were enamored with Lockwood. The committed student athlete, meanwhile, was eager to help the man who had been the first (and for a period only) fan to support him after a he made a controversial decision in a big football match the previous October. One half of the volunteer squad followed Edie and Dipshit for security assignments and the other descended to the basement to procure supplies from the rented storage spaces.

Dipshit focused on draping chains and locks on doors, and other volunteers, where appropriate, covered up select windows to intrigue outsiders. Some recruits, still unclear as to the end goals of their actions, created murals out of large sheets of butcher paper and blanketed the first floor windows with the signs as a diversion. Surprisingly, the crew did not encounter any students coming or going during their preparations.

Alf, after having recoded August Hall's digital door lock program, made quick work of its pair of security cameras. After minutes of tinkering, the two cameras were pumping out looped footage of an empty Rec Room and a bare basement.

If I may pause again to discuss some issues which were being neglected in this highly illegal act: they had no plan for food, water, or what to do if the electricity was turned off. They didn't know how exactly they were going to engage in polite discourse with the university, nor did they possess more than a weak understanding of what they were doing.

But they had passion, and Lockwood specifically was moving as if little could stop him.

The dorm's clocks approached 10:30 by the time Lockwood re-entered the Rec Room to see nearly all of the windows decked with slogan-covered placards, and for some reason, a few outward facing murals of an eagle attacking a horse. The possibly jingoistic paintings hardly compared to the outsized bravado with which Lockwood rejoined his team thanks to his headgear, an overtly disrespectful faux-Native American headdress found in storage.

The building was almost entirely locked down. All windows near ground level had been nailed or clamped shut, windows peering into the side exits had been blocked, and all but the two sets of double doors at the main entrance were locked and chained. Next to those main doors stood an anonymous helper holding a set of chains and a lock. Dipshit stood nearby, leaning on a set of large metal desks, which were to be jammed up against the front doors as soon as the order was given. Garbage cans throughout August, though bulky enough to help, could not be used. Enough mischievous acts in the past forced the university to chain each one to nearby walls.

Lockwood approached the main doors, the feathers of his headdress grazing walls and spectators as he passed. In his hands he held a piece of paper primed at the corners with tape. The document, printed in a fine hand in red ink, proclaimed, "We the students, who serve as the proper deed owners are seizing this land from the university that never legally or spiritually owned it. We shall hold this as our own until PMU addresses concerns facing the university's residents."

Lockwood approached the outer set of double doors and taped to them the notice with the print facing out. He then retreated into the Rec Room and gave the order to chain both sets of doors and barricade the entrance. The anonymous student and Dipshit worked in tandem, first by chaining the doors and second by placing the obstacles around them. Lockwood, who was skipping over his scheme's lack of morality for the sixty-fifth minute in a row, approached Edie and Alf, whose computer was hooked into an electrical panel.

"What do we got?" Lockwood asked with a feverish zeal.

"Almost ready," Alf replied. "I just need a minute for QA."

"Which icon does it? This one with my picture on it?"

Alf nodded. "Yes, but we shouldn't do anything until—"

A whimsical Lockwood reached over Alf, seized the laptop's mouse, and clicked the button to execute Alf's program.

An instant later, the entire building's power went out.

Chapter 12: The Very Empty Northeast Quad

WHEN THE lights went out over William's head, his first thought was not of Lockwood. As he rifled through his backpack for a flashlight, the troublemaker was the last thing on his mind. That had not been the case earlier.

After locking himself in his dorm room built for one that afternoon, he swore off ever again seeing Lockwood, Edie, and the strange Kathie who accosted him.

The emotion was soon replaced with an antagonizing notion: he did not really despise Lockwood, rather he sought his acceptance. Regardless of how furiously he studied, the feelings of wanting more would not subside. His books could only afford his secondary attention after the desire to create his own entertaining stories, and if possible, once again be who he used to be.

At six p.m., after hours of torment and more than a full year in captivity, William decided it was time to embrace the life he always wanted to lead in college. His first act was emailing the object of his purest desires, a nimble and gregarious southern belle known as Carolina (nicknamed for an approximate assessment of her origin) asking for a study date that evening. Fortuitously she responded with an affirmative and suggested her own room in August Hall as the locale. He quickly packed a bag with books and departed, ignoring Lockwood's text, which he thought was directing him to meet at Lockwood's off-campus apartment.

As he walked through the building later guided by his flashlight, his mind ran through his most recent conversation, the one he'd been waiting months to have with Carolina.

"Before it gets too late," Carolina endearingly began minutes earlier, "I have to say I was really, really happy when you emailed."

William hoped earnestly to match her sincerity without overdoing it. "I was happy you were up for it."

"I have to ask: why'd you choose today? I mean, we don't have any classes together this semester and you didn't take me up on my invites when we had Econ last year."

"I'm still sorry about that..." he started slowly, sputtering out words that struggled to express for the first time something he'd wistfully told himself over and over. "I haven't been a lot of fun in college and that's all my fault. I didn't realize that until some total ass told me that one day I was going to learn this wasn't just a place to do whatever I want."

Carolina seemed a bit confused. "Why would someone so rude mean anything to you?"

"Because it made me realize I haven't done *anything* I wanted. I learned college wasn't made for goofing off on my third day here. I want to have fun and know good people like you."

The response elicited a warm, pleased reaction, although William wondered if he was seeing in her face a touch of worry that he was projecting too much on her. "I like that attitude," she stated resolutely. "And I know precisely who you need to meet to enjoy college more. He actually kind of lives here and he gives everyone these funny nicknames—"

The power cutting out at that precise moment prevented William from being asked if he'd ever had a nickname, so he was grateful for the incident. Then, as he wanted to appear as a helpful alpha male, he instantly volunteered to find the source of the problem.

Once he arrived in the Rec Room, his flashlight beam landed on a boy at a computer connected to what appeared to be a fuse box. The flashlight panned up at a hulking behemoth, three attractive girls dressed in Native American-like garb, and finally on Lockwood, who was wearing a gigantically objectionable headdress.

"Oh shit," William ruefully uttered.

Lockwood's headgear and eyes pivoted to William and his grin grew. "You made it for the protest! Also: do you know anything about fuses?"

Thinking the annoying encounter would be brief, the disgruntled William pressed ahead instead of backing off. "What are you protesting? High electric bills or the Union cavalry?"

"Native American displacement."

William tried to determine if it was a joke. "That's the dumbest idea I've ever heard."

"No, it's an idea that will upset people for no good reason," Lockwood suggested as he stepped closer. "Whenever Native Americans ask for anything people don't just ignore them, they flip out because they think they're going to lose something if the Indians win."

"Okay it's not the dumbest thing ever," William replied, "it's the most horrible."

"Thank you," Edie coyly remarked with a smile. The tiny remark was enough to make William flinch and regret his evening's choices even more. "That's sweet of you to say."

"How is turning off the power going to get students involved?"

"It won't. Locking their asses inside will!" Lockwood replied gleefully. With that, Alf's hard work paid off and the power kicked back on.

With the lights working, William seized a closer look at the lobby. Couches were overturned, chains and locks were wrapped around the front doors, and large desks were piled like firewood near them. Skipping over what he could see of the window-covering avant-garde artwork that signified warfare or bestiality, he concluded promptly that there was no escape.

Ignoring William's jaw figuratively hitting the floor, Lockwood and Edie approached the entrance to see no one had taken notice of the building yet. The front doors were flanked by wide floor to ceiling steel-reinforced windows, and through both the windows and the doors, the same barren scene was visible. In a manner more closely matching a person commenting on a dreary autumn afternoon than a criminal act, Lockwood declared, "I thought they'd be here faster."

"Please tell me this is for a student film or a play." William stammered.

"Fuck no. We're locking up the building with everyone inside until I get kicked out."

William, feeling nothing but sheer panic, sprinted to find any window that would open.

After enjoying William's humorously terrified display for two minutes or so, Lockwood signaled to Dipshit to intervene. The obliging athlete wrapped William in a bear hug and the meek sophomore was stuck yet again.

Edie advanced and took William's jaw in her hands. "Whether you like it or not, you're here until this is done. So calm down so you can come up with other ways to get people here."

"I refuse to take part in this! Nothing good happened to the Pemberton Eight and they weren't stupid enough to imprison hundreds of people!"

"You're not doing the trapping," Lockwood stated. "You're helping get me attention."

William let out a hysterical chuckle. "Attention for what? Your fictional protest or the fact you blocked anyone's chance of escaping if there's an emergency or a fire?"

Alf stood up and nodded to the room. "That'll work. A fire alarm will get officials here."

"Wait a second—" William said in vain.

"It's gotta happen," Lockwood replied. "Spark it up, Alf."

"Gladly," Alf said, hitting a key to set an alarm blaring all over the building.

The noise caused Lockwood to adopt the appearance of an overjoyed child on Christmas who was unsure where exactly to look for his presents. Swiping his head back and forth between the view of the NEQ and August's stairwells, he didn't seem to hear the screeching.

The alarm continued and he soon found himself checking his phone once, twice, three times. His smile faded when he confirmed time wasn't stuck; rather no one was going to show.

"What the hell is wrong with these people?" he asked.

"I don't know," Alf shouted. "I always leave my room when I hear an alarm."

"What happened," Edie yelled, "is you took over campus' deafest, least hostile dorm."

With that, a stairwell door opened and all eyes darted towards the movement. Would they see hundreds of students? An entire hallway intrigued by what Lockwood was about to present?

Instead, a single student bumbled in. His Rastafarian hat and floppy smile made it evident he did not notice the disturbing nature of the lobby or the half-naked warrior clutching a pale sophomore. Without pause he walked directly for the vending machines.

Lockwood sized up the student. Slowly a coin was raised to one of the machines. It disappeared into the metal and clinked. At a dawdling rate, another was produced for the same dance. "What are you doing?" Lockwood asked.

"Dude," the guest replied through squinted eyes. "Munchies. Sub shop's too far."

In an ironic move, Lockwood became the scene's authority figure. "Don't you hear that? That sound that's telling you to escape a fire?"

"I thought the fire protection guy was a big bear, not an Indian Chief."

Lockwood inched closer to the student and Dipshit lowered the subdued William to show he was willing to enter the discussion, as well.

"Woah kemosabe, just kidding," the hungry student replied. "When the alarm goes off I always check out the window for people running. Empty quad equals false alarm, so I lock my door and if anyone knocks I pretend I'm not home." The student took his snacks and walked back towards his room. "Everybody does it. It's just a stupid drill."

Before Lockwood could react, Alf instructed everyone to get down and hide.

Lockwood ducked as a Fire Marshall made his way up the front steps. "Hell yes!" he said to Edie. "Finally!"

The crew watched with heavy anticipation as the man climbed each step as if there was no rush to get into the potentially burning building. Without a look at the decorations or acknowledging the lack of students waiting to reenter the building, the man tried to open the door. His first tug did nothing.

The second tug provided the same response.

With that, he stepped to the side and approached a wall-mounted metallic box. He took out a set of keys, opened the box, and flipped switches until the alarm ceased. He then closed the box and departed.

The bewildered Lockwood remained motionless. *This was supposed to work,* he thought. To highlight the command of the English language which he'd honed through years of the finest educational facilities in the land, he summarized his grief with a single word: "Shit."

With the shrieking fire alarm gone, the truth sunk in that no troops would follow to fill in the Marshall's investigatory gaps.

"Would somebody tell me what the hell just happened?" Lockwood asked.

Edie was the first to speak up. "Nothing just happened."

Lockwood pulled William (who hoped he had been forgotten) to his feet and brought him to the front door. "How am I supposed to stand up for anything if I'm just going to get ignored?"

William was taken aback by Lockwood's honest to goodness, legitimate question. Lockwood took the reaction as an insult.

"What's wrong?" he asked.

"It's a valid question. It just threw me off," William responded, wondering if Lockwood suddenly cared about carrying out a real protest after seeing his rally disintegrate.

Lockwood continued with: "What kind of jihad is it if we can't get anyone's attention?" and swiftly ended William's suspicion that he was dealing with a new man.

"Where did you come up with jihad?"

"Wrong part of the world, friend," Edie offered.

Instead of replying, Lockwood bolted towards a stairwell. Edie grabbed William and followed him.

Lockwood, from a half flight above, called, "Maybe there's people gathering in the Quad and we can't see them yet!"

Edie replied in pursuit. "It's only been a few minutes!"

"It should've worked already though!" whined Lockwood. "It's how jihads work!"

"It's not a jihad, damn it!" William shouted.

Lockwood pushed his way into Alf's room and left the door open behind him. "I must have at least done something."

They looked out at the Quad, where nothing resembling a crowd had formed. In fact, only one individual could be spotted: Squanto. He stood wearing a disappointed expression before taking note of the three (spending much more time on William). The resentful resident moved his sub sandwich to his soda hand and used his free hand to extend a middle finger towards them.

Lockwood dismissed Squanto at once. "Why isn't anyone pissed off?"

"Because you haven't disrupted anyone yet," Edie replied.

"Of course I have! They can't go out to bars! What else is there to do?"

"Follow me."

Edie led Lockwood into a study lounge. The scene, which was replicated in fifteen other study rooms in August Hall, was terribly foreign to Lockwood. Students were nestled comfortably in couches and upholstered chairs and reading from large textbooks. Edie put her hand on his shoulder and reminded him: "It's that thing from the brochure: studying."

Lockwood dourly examined the study room. *Is this going to end up being actually tough?*

Edie continued. "You might not realize it but once people wake up tomorrow and see what you've done, you'll be the most wanted person at this school."

Lockwood glumly considered her words long enough for a few students to turn to see who was examining them like babies in a maternity ward.

"Okay," Lockwood said, putting his arm around William. "Let's get back to my place."

"About that," William replied, "I was hoping to hang out with Carolina...."

"Hell, my room is practically exactly the same as hers. You won't regret coming by."

"I can almost guarantee you're wrong," replied an immediately grumpy William.

*   *   *

Lockwood's dorm room contained not one "beer fridge" but four. Anchoring one side of the room was a couch, which according to the blurred official records provided by some faculty members, Lockwood either purchased or pilfered from the Anthropology Department faculty lounge the previous year. Two standard issue dorm chairs and a swiveling leather chair all sat near his desk. The remainder of the room was filled in with one bed instead of the standard two, and two dressers, each filled partially with clothes, snacks, and prophylactics. The walls were decorated with sports pennants and an odd set of photographs.

He had traveled all over the world, but whenever possible he avoided taking pictures of only himself. Rather, as was visible on each wall, whenever he found the opportunity at a tourist destination, he would ask a helpful guide to take a photograph, join up unannounced with other tourists, and have a photo snapped. Typically these photos showed off at least part of a famous monument, a beaming Lockwood, and sincerely perplexed strangers who would never again see Lockwood or learn their faces made it up onto his wall.

After leading Edie and William in, Lockwood strolled towards one of his refrigerators with the purpose of "getting shit faced drunk." Although he didn't need permission from anyone, he first looked at Edie, who nodded, and then William, who surprisingly shrugged in agreement. This was likely due to the fact that en route to Lockwood's room William spied Carolina's door was closed. He assumed the room would remain off limits for the whole night.

At a dazzling pace they could not explain later, the three got intoxicated rapidly. As they consumed thirty-three beers over three hours, their talk covered a variety of gossipy and college age topics. One of the more peculiar themes came while Lockwood brought up his unwritten thesis "Breakfast, Weed, and Surfboards: A Study in West Coast Nutrition."

The talks continued until two a.m. when William, for some unannounced reason, stumbled out of the room. Lockwood grabbed two beers and wandered out, as well. Edie opted to find a pillow, climb into bed, and retire with the hope that Wednesday would bring greater riches than Tuesday.

Chapter 13: The Quickest Route to Advanced Russian Literature (RUS-305)

WEDNESDAY MORNING in August Hall started peacefully enough.[11]

Sophomore Terry Orton awoke at 6:15 for a thirty-minute shower, or rather, five minutes of showering and twenty-five minutes of hoping the water pounding on him would tear the remaining alcohol from his bloodstream. This was his usual Wednesday morning routine after a night of rough drinking at Sporty's, a local bar known for serving ten-cent pitchers of beer on Tuesdays between four and six p.m. As the previous night he had been "obliterated" (per his friends) by seven p.m., he slept through the night's shrieking fire alarm.

When his shower was complete, he donned his most comfortable shirt and climbed back into the beer-splattered jeans he wore the

---

[11] Incidentally, only four students attempted to re-enter the building in the hours between the power outage and sunrise. Each opted to sleep elsewhere after departing the NEQ without enough concern to phone in what they thought was a prank the school would cease by morning.

night before. He then made his way to the dorm's Southeast door. As he was still intoxicated, the door's reluctance to open did not initially startle him. The crudely reinforced dead bolts, the chain weaved around the push bar, and the bake sale-style poster reading "act out, protest your right now!" covering the door's window meant nothing to him. He determined that the obstacle was a sign to return to bed. Interpersonal Communication One (COMM 180-1, offered FALL) would have to wait.

Minutes later, sophomore Beth Dane was engaged in a battle with the Southwest corner door. Her synapses fired at a heated pace while analyzing the door and wondering why the chain lock adorning it had not been secured. (The answer was that Dipshit lost interest on this, his second to last door. Despite his laziness, it was still locked.) Dane examined the poster that read "Remember the Maine" which was the handiwork of freshman Dana White, a kindhearted Spanish Literature major whose American history knowledge centered solely on the 1890s.

Dane conjectured correctly that some sort of statement was being made. She then guessed the signs must have been in honor of VE Day (actually May eighth, not October nineteenth) and decided this meant classes for the day were cancelled.

Had he been awake, Lockwood could have seen that by 7:20 a.m., all his plan did was convince two students skip class and force Squanto to sleep in the Mathematics Library.

As fate would have it, predictable lady luck was stumping for Lockwood when sophomore Becky Kernel exited her room at 7:27 hoping to leave the building by 7:31.

Kernel did not often have such precise timing; she only took up this pace on Wednesdays when her boyfriend deserved stern words for doing something less than honorable the night before. Her alarm allowed her enough time to get out of bed, shower, dress, and use the lakefront path's quickest route to her boyfriend's only compulsory class of the week by 7:50.

However that morning, when she got to the door to find it was locked, she felt fretted over the crushing of her plans. After she raced around to the Northwest door to find the same response, she sprinted to the front entrance. Once there she found two possible clues: a set of desks blocking the doors and a scrawny boy who had fallen asleep on top of them.

The boy was William, who had stumbled out of Lockwood's room earlier that morning in a final attempt to escape. After very slowly descending four steps of the SW stairwell, he opted to slide shoulder first down the remaining stairs. Once on the first floor he staggered to the Rec Room. After a futile attempt to bypass the obstacles blocking egress, he fell asleep on a desk with one hand raised in the air, clutching the immovable push bar.

Becky, being a young woman who never shied away from a challenge, took William's presence as a call to action. It was time to wake the entire building.

She fled the lobby quietly and ran back to her room, where she shared the news to her roommate and two neighboring friends. The quartet then employed a rarely used announcement tactic of pounding on each door while yelling a location or directive. This usually took place late at night to "out" residents attempting to covertly use the dorm's showers for unclean activities.

It only took a few minutes to gather the second and fourth floors and eight minutes to rally the third floor residents minus a few freshman girls who, as hall rumors had it, stayed up late playing some form of dress up game.

Generally the door-pounding tactic stirred around eighty percent of the students. At eight a.m., Kernel's efforts only summoned one third of residents to the main lobby.

Unfortunately for William, who stirred amid unmistakable nearby noises of students complaining, the tactic was effective.

He awoke to see the same lobby in which Lockwood clamored for an audience hours before, packed with residents. Some were visibly annoyed, others were still half asleep. Nearly all wondered who had destroyed the lobby.

Becky stepped forward. "Does anyone know what's going on?"

By this point, William concluded he was not dreaming. In his defense, it had been a long time since that many people were focused on him. Having grown accustomed to staging a plate and a half empty glass of soda at the seat across from him in the dining hall to throw off suspicion that he was alone, William was no longer used to crowds.

"Well?" Becky demanded once more.

Mistakenly thinking the girl was talking to him, William's lips let an unimaginative "uh…" escape. Students turned to him as surprise and panic sabotaged his eloquence. "The thing is…" His head, neck, and left shoulder were pounding so ferociously he was having trouble remembering anything from the night before. As answers seeped into his brain, like how he got to his bed facsimile and why the doors were locked, his struggle grew.

Then, in front of more than one hundred classmates, William sprung up to kneel on all fours on a desk, slid open a drawer, and vomited into it.

Amid groans and giggles, one boy exclaimed, "All right! Ten cent pitchers win again!"

*   *   *

The intense rapping on Lockwood's dorm room minutes earlier had been enough to wake Edie. Rising rapidly, she recalled what brought her to that particular spot. After thanking the heavens for not waking to a weeping William in bed next to her, she moved on, knowing she had to find Lockwood without delay.

She put on her shoes, rose to her feet, and swept a hand through her very presentable hair before exiting the room. Immediately grabbing the arm of an unsuspecting male resident, she demanded: "Who's the dumbest, hottest girl in this hallway?"

The boy looked puzzled. "Is this a trick question?"

Edie shook her head. "Answer."

The boy nodded, undeterred. "Michelle. Four doors down on the right."

Characteristically omitting pleasantries, Edie walked down the hall and stopped at a door marked *Michelle and Candy!* After finding a sliver of the door's surface that was not covered in glitter or puff paint, Edie pounded until she could hear movement.

A female voice from inside said, "Come in."

Edie opened the door to see a girl under covers watching Lockwood put his pants on.

"Move faster," Edie instructed. "Somebody's gathering people downstairs."

Lockwood threw on a shoe, advanced on what looked like a makeshift pill cabinet atop a dresser, and grabbed a bottle of generic pain relief pills. "Great. Where's William? And did you punch him in the face last night?"

"Haven't seen him. And possibly yes to the punch."

Lockwood nodded, tossed two pills into his mouth, and drank them down with the remnants of a nearby beer. "What's the crowd like? We need them pissed and on our side—" Lockwood cut himself off to turn to Michelle. "You didn't have anything besides ibuprofen in here, right?"

The pause from Michelle, which was longer than Lockwood hoped, was followed by a peppy nod. Grabbing the door, Lockwood exclaimed, "Let's rock."

Taking meticulous steps to hide his enthusiasm, Lockwood glided down the stairs thinking more about how he looked instead of what he would say. With that remarkable attention to detail occupying his thoughts, he pushed open a door to the lobby and sized up the scene. A healthy number of agitated students were crammed into the Rec Room. Joining the crowd were a fully blocked main entryway and William hunched over a desk being used as a trash can as the building's other receptacles were chained to walls far, far away.

Lockwood and Edie circumnavigated the crowd and took their place between the students and their lowly cohort. In a deep voice, Lockwood announced, "Good morning everyone. Thank you for coming to hear about our quest."

"What's going on?" replied one girl.

A few shouts of agreement followed from the befuddled yet mostly docile crowd. "We're all in here to make a better Pemberton," Lockwood noted in a calming tone.

"What does that even mean?" another person queried.

They're not getting it, he thought. *Maybe I'm too vague?* "I'm taking a stand against Pemberton because none of us can let it continue doing what it's been doing lately," Lockwood declared as Alf emerged from the crowd to hand William a water bottle. "For decades the university ignored the plight of so many, spent decadently, and silenced the truth behind its history. The school forced me to lock those doors until the truth comes out."

He scanned the crowd to see that his speech did little besides raise confusion and give students a chance to become entranced by the hall's bizarre murals.

Lockwood leaned back to his counsel and whispered, "Why don't they get it?"

Alf stated as politely as he could, "Because you sound f-ing crazy!"

"Oh, that makes sense," Lockwood replied. He turned back to the students and studied the faces. As his dehydrated mind dug around its archives for hints of a direction in which to go, onlookers grew more suspect. And then as the glares began to grow more tiresome, a recollection popped into his mind. "Just like what happened to tens of thousands of natives in the past, the day we got here, those running PMU took something from every one of us and they never ever plan on giving it back." He and two of his lieutenants watched as more faces adopted inquisitive expressions to figure out what had been taken from them personally. (His third lieutenant saw only his provisional toilet.) "Today you need to think hard to remember what's been taken."

The silent crowd, while not entirely cognizant of what was being said, knew something important was happening. Lockwood pointed dramatically to the lobby's papered windows.

"Examine it well," he commanded, not realizing he was pointing towards one of the racier images. "It just might help you remember what they took. I'll be on Four West if you need to talk with me."

The crowd remained nonresponsive as the information was processed. As Lockwood continued to stare, one student queried, "So we can't go to class today?"

"Correct," Lockwood replied. "This is our sacrifice."

"So wait," the student continued. "This means we're *allowed* to miss class?"

"Um…" he replied as he wondered what was heard versus what he said. "Yes?"

At that, the majority of the students filtered back to their rooms, even a speechless Becky, who was trying to discern what she was missing. Meanwhile, outside of Advanced Russian Literature (RUS-305), Becky's boyfriend stood indignantly holding a photograph of the lower-maintenance girl for whom he was going to dump her. He waited for fifteen minutes while rehearsing his speech. When she didn't show, his emotions flowed from anger to regret and longing, and he determined he was overreacting.

Following his address, Lockwood brought his advisors back to Alf's room. The leader tried rubbing the headache out of his forehead as Edie typed away at her phone, asking friends if any news about August had gotten to them. Alf examined whether anyone tried to remotely override the security system, and William reeled over Alf's small trash bin.

Edie threw William a playful elbow at his head.

William moaned. "Where is death's sweet embrace?"

"Well," Lockwood stated, skipping the question, "That didn't go as planned."

Edie glared. "Not to plan? Chip, there was no plan."

Alf offered, "At least your speech didn't make them any *less* enthusiastic."

Scornfully Edie proceeded: "An enema crammed with downers couldn't make them less enthusiastic. I thought you guys said we just needed to get to morning and we'd be golden."

"It's still too early," Alf noted. "No one in IT has noticed the new security code yet and I don't think any admins have even gotten to their offices yet."

"We better see shit soon, because right now we're looking pretty bad," Lockwood remarked, still unable to process why his plan had failed thus far. "People are off watching DVD box sets, no protestors are outside, and no one from the school has asked for my scalp yet."

Edie pursed her lips. "Too soon for scalping jokes."

William, despite his limited physical and mental mobility, opted to join the session. "It's not like trustees swing by dorms daily to make sure everything works. But soon someone will realize four hundred students aren't in the library or the gym or in classes and they're going to look for them." William leaned back on Alf's couch. "In some building out there, in some big board room, a committee is gonna meet...and your only shot is pissing them off beyond belief. So you better hope you're on their agenda."

Chapter 14: Some Big Board Room in Some Building Out There

AS FAR as the students, staff, or community leaders who needed PMU's blessings were concerned, the Provost's Procedures Committee was the university's ultimate point of authority.

The team met each Wednesday at one p.m. to discuss both new and old business. Luckily for Lockwood, his stunt landed on the right day of the week. Unluckily, his cannonball outburst had hardly made a ripple by the time the week's meeting agenda was drawn up.

The PPC was comprised of twenty-two faculty members and one student. Each of the six undergraduate schools provided a representative, as did the five graduate and professional schools. Employees from the Registrar's and Bursar's offices, as well as Finance and External Consultancy had seats at the table, along with the board's leader, Provost Harold Asbury.

The university provost was a humorless, grave man who was secretly enamored with academia. His nearly four decades in the international relations departments of three prestigious universities focused on U.S. foreign policy. The educator's repertoire contained lectures that were so fascinatingly detailed that colleagues were convinced his death would bring about an irreparable loss of data to his field. Despite what some students felt about his disposition, when in a classroom he was a truly great educator.

After spending a few years in the 1960s as an Associate Professor at Pemberton he shifted to an opportunity out west for the ensuing decade. Later, during his time at a revered university in Manhattan, he took on the title of Department Chair. He returned to teach at Pemberton in the early 1990s and in 1999 he became the university's twenty-sixth Provost at sixty-three years of age.

He was a stern man who often reiterated that his position did not exist solely to deal with rich students who felt they had free reign at Pemberton. In his mind, this task belonged to the university president. This brash perspective, too, had an invitation to attend all PPC meetings.

Asbury's pushiness did not make him the PPC's most hated member. This role was filled by Kathie Kieft, who insisted each week on being combative and ritualistically unpleasant. To Kathie, those surrounding her were punctuation marks highlighting years of selfless service outlined on her resume. She cared little for their decades of experience in education and was unimpressed with their histories.

As for her demeanor on October nineteenth, she was even more of herself than normal. She'd been in a vile mood since overhearing numerous students mention her least favorite word: Lockwood. It was not unusual to hear his name, but four times in one day was uncommon, not to mention annoying, especially as she hadn't yet unraveled his latest scheme.

Unlike Kathie's morning, which was full of Lockwood, the PPC meeting was not. By halfway through, his actions had not been a topic of conversation.

The closest the group came to discussing Lockwood was when an open letter from the fire department was read aloud. The letter explained the department's displeasure with the lack of student response at fire drills at August Hall. The recital of the letter was cut short thanks to Kathie, whose boredom grew with each sentence.

"Fine, on to old business," Provost Asbury announced.

A mention of Lockwood in this final agenda item was not likely.

The same four topics reflecting short term and upcoming needs were discussed each week. They were: undergraduate applications, alumni donations, library usage, and class attendance. The first three figures were procured using standard methods and the forth was calculated thanks to paid student volunteers who took unofficial attendance records in each class, as professors were not obligated to do so.

A noble member of the Registrar's team presented the data. Undergraduate applications were up three percent from the year before. Alumni donations remained steady, and all libraries saw an expected post-midterm decrease in usage with the exception of the law library.

The final topic, the concerned analyst noted, presented most unusual results. She received the concerning data before the weekly session and she hoped a mid-meeting refresh would shift the trend. It did not. "I'm afraid we have a rather disturbing attendance report for this week."

At that, every member of the board save Kathie and Asbury turned to the analyst, eager to learn what could possibly be described as "disturbing" attendance data.

"Attendance records were normal through the week, but on top of the typical Wednesday absenteeism, we saw a drop of more than four percent today." She looked up from her computer to see a table bordered by blank looks and one childish snicker.

Asbury, the last person the analyst hoped would respond, asked, "What does that mean?"

"Students take a day off from time to time," one representative noted with a wretched condescending tone. "This is college. Haven't you seen that what's his name's semester abroad movie?"

Most of the room laughed at the misplaced reference. The analyst did not desist. "This means beyond the number of students who normally miss Wednesday classes, an additional four hundred students skipped this morning."

"Four hundred?" Asbury cried, slapping the table, rattling anything nearby. "Why didn't you say that in the first place? How often does this happen?"

"With the exception of national days of mourning, we have never seen this big of a drop on a Wednesday. Fridays before away foot-ball games can see a five percent drop, and the Friday before Spring Break has seen a nine percent drop, but those are special cases."

The instructor with faulty knowledge of film titles would not be swayed. "Couldn't this be due to a simple explanation? The flu? Late midterm cramming?"

"It's far from likely."

"Maybe a wild party? Perhaps our student friend here could help us with details. Miss Kieft, did you see any more party invita-tions than normal this week?"

Both the inquisitor and responder knew Kathie was in no posi-tion to answer. The junior, who gained notoriety as a freshman for forwarding party invitations to campus police, hadn't received a sin-gle invitation in over a year and a half.

Kathie shrugged. "I didn't see any more than usual," she replied, hiding her contempt by focusing her attention on deleting emails from the inbox displayed on her phone's screen. "Maybe it's time to move on or end the meeting," she added impatiently.

Asbury slammed his fist on the table again. "I want to know who thinks they can miss this much class. Is it the football team dick-ing around again?"

The Registrar's number cruncher examined her laptop. "It does look like a lot of these new absences came from students in the Northeast Quad. Many athletes do live there."

Asbury grinned at the thought of handing an administrator a high-octane thrashing. "Get A.D. Emerson on my office line in fifteen minutes," he said to no one in particular.

Kathie, having heard all the attendance data she could stand, carefully held onto ten percent of her charm to try to steer the meet-ing (a personal goal of hers for each week). "Respectfully, Sir, I think this conversation may be better offline. I'm not sure if we should—"

"I don't mean to stop you," the analyst called, breaking the board's meager standard operating procedure of never interrupting Kathie, "but it appears the absences are even more centralized than I thought." This garnered the attention of everyone but the girl whose words were silenced for the intrusion. "Only two students from August Hall attended class today."

This drew Kathie's interest.

Amid grumblings around the table, Kathie recalled words from conversations she passed by earlier. The students were saying something about protesting and "Auggie Lockwood" which she had taken to be a reference to Lockwood himself. In her email account, she sped to the Junk Mail section and saw she had four emails on the subject. The notes were clear enough to show Lockwood may have finally purchased a one-way ticket out of Pemberton. *Oh that sweet stupid bastard*, she thought. "We have to move on this now," Kathie stated authoritatively.

The comment ceased every side conversation as all eyes turned towards Kathie.

"Excuse me?" Asbury asked.

"I feel..." she began, her words lazily catching up with her eager desire to draw attention to Lockwood without broadcasting how much she knew, "strongly that residents skipping classes is something the school should investigate. Unless, of course, you want students telling their parents that the school doesn't really care if they show up or not."

A number of representatives sunk back into their chairs. Asbury, though, lost interest as soon as Kathie gained it. He dryly replied: "I see your decades in academia have given you quite the understanding of parent/student/teacher relationships."

Kathie heard how absurd her argument sounded but she did not want to be the first to give Lockwood's name and present a personal bias. So in response she nodded curtly.

"Actually," another voice added, "this reminds me of some strange emails I received today." Kathie could hardly contain her delight as the man continued. "I didn't think much of it earlier, but a History professor forwarded me a message he received that reads: 'Dear Prof: a guy who locked up my dorm says we can't leave because of some India protest.' I have three more emails and if I'm reading them correctly..." he trailed off to squint at his laptop. "Two list the student responsible for locking them in."

A suddenly interested Asbury pried, "A student is behind this?"

The professor nodded. "A boy named Chip Lockwood."

Kathie faked a shocked look as others rolled their eyes. Asbury groaned. "Lockwood? He may be cocky but he's not a moron."

Kathie bit her tongue at the audacious error.

Asbury continued, producing more heartbreak for Kathie. "If it's Lockwood we don't have a problem, just buffoonery." Reaching out with weathered fingers, he picked up the conference table's phone and stabbed an extension into the dial pad. "This is Provost Asbury. Get a car out to August P. Hall for a walkthrough and have them tell me exactly what they see." After a pause, which shifted his tone from general to targeted disdain, he stated: "Yes, I'll hold. Is someone on their way? Good! Put them through." His left index finger stamped the phone's speaker phone button and he placed the receiver on the table.

As the room waited, Kathie mapped out her plan with ferocious speed. She knew she had to convince the university that Lockwood was dangerous. Surmising if the university dragged out Lockwood immediately, they would only achieve ACLP: annoy Charles Lockwood's parents. That wasn't on her to do list. RCL was.

Jumping over the fact that no rumors had been confirmed, Kathie decided the best way to keep Lockwood's farce going was to convince the PPC he was leading a legitimate protest. The PPC would predictably reach out to the flighty Eva Yesterday for counsel, who would do whatever she could to get the idiot Lockwood out of her way. *As long as he acted as stupid as normal,* she thought, *the plan would be foolproof.*

Through the speakerphone, rustling noises grew louder and mumbled voices blurred into coherency. One voice shouted an unabashed, "Oh holy shit, Marty."

"Shhh," another voice replied. "We're on with Asbury."

Asbury cleared his throat. "You're on with the entire PPC. Skip the radio babble and tell us what you see."

"Well, Sir, it appears the doors have been locked from the inside and our keys aren't working." Representatives exchanged apprehensive glances with their watches and some jotted notes that would become condolence cards for their evening plans. "Windows are covered with posters depicting—" the man stopped. "Hey Teddy, does this look like a horse doing a grizzly?"

"Marty, you gotta take a look at this!" Teddy howled.

A period of silence followed before Marty said, "Sir, there's like a declaration taped to the front door."

Kathie gripped her chair with vehement anticipation.

The man read Lockwood's proclamation, prompting board members to cringe at what lay ahead and launching Kathie's copious appreciation for Lockwood's fatuousness.

"Should we call in for back-up to diffuse this, Sir?"

"No, don't bother," Asbury replied gruffly. "It's just another prank. Have the Fire Department break down the doors and charge Lockwood's parents for new ones."

Kathie reacted immediately to the unsatisfactory response. Broken doors meant no protest, no protest meant Lockwood couldn't dig deeper, normal depth hole meant only standard punishment, which meant more Lockwood. "We cannot do that if this is a protest!"

Asbury grimaced.

"This is a prank, end of story," Asbury declared.

"But what if it's not?" Kathie asked, setting aside the stupidity of her statement. "I know he is fond of adolescent pranks. But if he's serious *or* working with brighter students who are serious and you go in wielding axes this could look like PMU is smashing students' rights."

Asbury's mannerisms mutated from annoyed to incensed. "No one in academia loses face for squashing pranks."

"We need to make sure! Do we even have rules on how to proceed if this is a protest?" Kathie asked despite knowing the answer already.

The Registrar's representative piped up. "I'm looking through the school charter now."

Into the phone Asbury ordered, "Stand down, we'll call back

with orders," and hung up. He shifted his stare to the many who had already bowed out of the fight. It was arduously irritating that in a room of colleagues few could stand up to an unremittingly correct pre-adult.

"It says here," the analyst began, "first we must contact the student assembly liaison to see if this is a sanctioned student protest."

With that, the PPC called for an investigation into the validity of the rumors despite Asbury's belief none present would ever hear about the event again after that evening.

Kathie, while displaying a front of concern, couldn't be happier. Thanks to her, the PPC was going to take his latest scheme seriously and "bounce that douche burger out of Pemberton so hard it will bust his tailbone" (her words). What Kathie didn't realize, of course, was she helped turn a largely Lockwood-less PPC meeting into one that could actually help his cause.

Chapter 15: Sacred Indian Ground

THE HOURS without contact from the university were tedious for Lockwood. During this lull, he mulled over his ever-deepening predicament while staring at the ceiling of his room and blasting what he called his "Hangover Mix" CD. He even remained fairly motionless after hearing he would have a guest from the university in less than an hour.

His friends were less inactive. Alf, to learn more about the campus' reactions, set up alerts that would notify him every time the word "August" or "Lockwood" appeared on the website of the school newspaper or on any pages indexed by either of campus' two most used search engines. Edie enlisted Dipshit to stockpile water by cleaning and filling up plastic storage bins most students owned. William walked the halls with Carolina, who insisted on distributing cookies to students to keep morale up.

Lockwood continued to ponder a single question: what if he really did fail? The cost of this "pansy ass spirit quest" (Edie's words) would soon become irrevocable.

Forty minutes after hearing about his pending visitor, Lockwood had done no planning at all. He did find a toy telescope, though, which he used to search for his incoming foe. Little did he know a second and equally important visitor was en route, one who thankfully didn't recall meeting him the day before.

*   *   *

Eva Yesterday stepped out of her off-campus apartment at around five after two and began her fifteen-minute trek to the Northeast Quad, a favorite pastime of hers in the gorgeous autumn months. When the call came in asking her to walk to August Hall to help with a situation that might develop into a larger issue, she was willing to oblige.

Although she disliked the practice of "sanctioning" protests for a number of reasons (primarily that she rarely found a worthy cause that could gain traction), feelings of excited anticipation always stoked her senses when approaching a potential stronghold of assembly.

Questions sped through her thoughts as her feet brought her closer and closer to the NEQ. The intrigue, not to mention the optimism she always felt on the approach, nearly drowned out the pessimistic thoughts that occupied her mind the day before when others question her goals.

The instant she arrived on the scene, her positivity faded. The first two sights she encountered at the scene were the image of a Caucasian boy dancing inside his dorm room in the captive August Hall wearing only a Rastafarian hat and the dorm's front lawn, which did not have a single student showing any interest in the so-called protest.

The third sight was of a young man throwing a foam football into one of August's windows. This handily suggested her report might not end up being terribly serious.

*   *   *

The bouncy ball landed three feet away from a freshman who was studying in her room. She picked up the ball and read its inscription: "bring me to Chip Lockwood, bitch and or dick."

Minutes later she came upon an open door in her hall to find two people looking out the window through gaps in the curtains, one with binoculars, the other with a cheap toy telescope. "Do either of you know Chip Lockwood?" she asked.

The pair turned and Lockwood kept the apparatus pressed to his eye. Assuming he was staring at her breasts, the student lifted the football to block his view. "I think this is for you."

Edie lowered her counterpart's telescope and the girl handed over the ball.

"Thanks," Lockwood said with half of his attention on the ball and half on the girl as she made her exit. "Do you think it's from the school?"

Suddenly, Lockwood dropped the football as it began trembling and emitting a muffled noise. After a few seconds, Edie picked up the ball, found a knife mark in the material, reached in, and pulled out a cellular phone. The two exchanged confused looks before Lockwood opened the phone to answer the call. "Hello?"

"Thank God it's finally you!" the unnecessarily shrill voice on the other end of the line replied. "Does your asshole face know how hard it is to get you on the phone?"

Lockwood groaned and Edie poked him for information. "What do you want, Squanto?"

"I want you to freaking let me back in, man!" Squanto whined. "Last night it was a funny joke, I totally got it. But let me back in before I lose my chance!"

"Your chance for what?"

"My chance for serious poon-age! If you wait too long, they'll tear up your fiesta and I'll miss the whole thing!"

Lockwood's attention for the call sagged when he spotted an impatient looking middle-aged man lumbering towards August Hall with a clipboard, a megaphone, and a disdainful visage.

"You have to let me back in, jack ass! I've got info you're seriously going to need!"

This piqued Lockwood's awareness. "What information?"

"Information that says," Squanto began with a whisper, "if you let me back in I'm definitely gonna get my dick sucked!"

Lockwood disconnected the call and dropped the phone to better focus on the university's foot soldier who was already making notes about the area.

"That's our guy," Lockwood declared with excitement.

"Good. Do you remember what you're doing?"

"I'm going to demand to be heard and make ridiculous statements he can't argue with." Upon realizing he might be moving too fast for someone who hadn't really prepared himself, he decided he needed his helper who "spoke school" nearby. "Find William...he might know a trick or two for dealing with this guy."

Edie threw a thumbs up at the clearly half-baked plan. "If he's not shitting himself in fear I'm sure he'll shit with joy when he learns that you need him."

"Awesome, meet me in Alf's room in five."

Outside, the dutiful representative examined the property and documented his findings. He confirmed by hand that each door was locked. Additionally, in the six or seven rooms he was able to cursorily observe, it looked like all of the students were doing homework or studying.

He positioned himself fifteen yards from the main entrance and swung the megaphone to his mouth. "Residents of August Hall. My name is [REDACTED]. I'm here to speak with whomever posted the note on your front door." The announcement caught the attention of a few students and a group of a dozen or so formed near the speaker.

Then, a window on the fourth floor swung open and Lockwood leaned out, displaying more gusto than was fitting. PMU's man noted Lockwood's change in expression upon seeing only a handful of students outside.

Before proceeding, I must note there is a simple reason why Lockwood performed terribly that afternoon: he never actually studied. Do you recall when I urged you to not confuse studying with cramming? You may have been tempted to think his rapid research would save our protagonist, especially considering the examples set by various cinematic characters you've seen who pass exams thanks to last minute scrambling or boldfaced cheating. You will read the message here again: cramming doesn't pay, but real studying does.

It is true that Lockwood did a lot in a short amount of time that week. But he was nowhere as well versed in revolutionary rhetoric as the Pemberton Eight had been. He was a twenty-one year old trying to bluff his way through an impossible situation.

"Are you the student responsible here?"

Lockwood nodded. "I am Chip Lockwood," he shouted, his voice roaring through the nearly empty quad. As the echo returned, he noticed a sorority had set up a tiny bake sale stand at the far end of the NEQ, seemingly unaware of his quest. "I am here to speak for those whom this university has chosen to silence!"

The representative plainly replied, "Whom have we silenced?"

The direct question caught Lockwood off guard. It was so confusing that he turned his head into Alf's room for help but he learned he was still alone. Turning back towards the square, he replied: "If I shouted the names of every voice that PMU has silenced, I would lose my own."

Eva, from her position far behind the sickly small audience, took note of Lockwood's possibly profound statement and wondered if he said it on accident.

Lockwood then remembered his initial plan and stomped to pieces any doubt in Eva's mind. "But mainly I am here to speak up for the Indians!"

The representative asked: "The Indians?"

The repetition jostled Lockwood, who was still trying to process the lack of an audience. All clarity returned once he spotted Squanto watching the proceedings with an infuriated glare.

"The eviction of good, honest Americans is what I am fighting!" Lockwood cried. "Too many Indians have been pushed out of their homes and this university needs to explain why it did that and other actions!"

Confused students standing around the representative struggled to make sense of Lockwood's words. Squanto just shook his head.

Inside, the door to Alf's room opened and Edie and William entered. Most didn't notice Lockwood turn and flap his arms, but the negotiator did deduce that Lockwood was not alone.

"How's it going?" Edie asked as she and William hit the floor and slid to the window.

"Not so hot, but I'm picking it up!" Lockwood lied.

"Let me get this straight, son," his opponent stated into the megaphone. "You are upset that the university has kicked out...whom?"

"The Indians!" Lockwood replied.

William shook his head vigorously. "They're Native Americans!"

"Huh?" He couldn't clearly hear William but he had little time to reply, so he latched onto a word he thought he heard that also often came up in his French classes. "I am here to protect the Native Algerians!"

Edie's kick to Lockwood's shin forced him to buckle, causing more commotion in his spectators' minds. With force, William whispered, "Native-Fucking-Americans!"

"I'm taking a stand for the," Lockwood paused to make sure he got William's exact tone right, "Native-Fucking-Americans!"

William dropped his head into his hands and Edie deliberated the response, eventually giving the point to Lockwood.

The representative was not fazed. "For which tribe are you speaking out?"

Lockwood, who clearly wasn't expecting such a simple question, replied with his first thought: "You mean there's more than one?" A second kick from Edie suggested he come up with another answer. His mind sprinted for anything that would help him answer. He looked around the War Room for any clues that could help. *Alf's computer, the pile of laundry, the movie posters?* He impulsively shouted, "Zulu! I fight for the Zulu!"

Lockwood grinned until he saw Edie and William both shaking their heads.

"So you're telling me your protest is about Pemberton expelling from university land a tribe of people that lives thousands of miles away in southern Africa?"

"The answer you seek is in your own heart, faithless stranger."

Unsure how to follow the absurd answer, the representative

commanded: "Son, I need you to unlock these doors and stop endangering the lives of those students inside."

"That will absolutely not happen before I am heard!" he replied defiantly.

"Stand down," the man repeated. "There are forums for this—"

"Enough! We will not be silenced!" Lockwood shouted with enough determination it startled even Eva. "The university selfishly wasted their time to discuss this appropriately!"

Edie rejoiced at Lockwood's response. He needed to end on a high note. (William, meanwhile, was just thankful that Lockwood hadn't repeated "jihad" in front of the group).

The representative, realizing real progress would be limited at that point, switched to logistical queries. "I will report that. For now I need from you a head count for safety reasons."

A confused Lockwood shrugged. "Three, maybe four times this week." A menacing blow to his shinbone that nearly doubled him over followed. "Ah, jihad!" Before any questions could be asked, he avowed, "This session is over! You know my demands!" before closing the blinds.

The representative made a few more notes as the bemused few students watching dispersed. After one last look at the building, he departed. Eva then retreated and surmised a report would not be necessary. The incident was a farce; an unfunny practical joke at best. What's worse: it did not live up to the high standards she had set for herself, especially the ideals she set in her mind for Charles Lockwood and his crew.

*   *   *

By this hour, Asbury was so convinced that Lockwood's siege was a "non-issue" that thoughts of the boy and his family's dorm hadn't slowed down his afternoon workload at all. He was so unfocused on the matter that he didn't even read the official recap of the negotiation session until it had been on his desk for fifteen minutes.

The short missive reassured Asbury that the situation was far from dire. There was little chance the exercise would last the evening, but still he was prepared to call the Fire Department. He would have made the call more promptly if he hadn't been distracted by thoughts of another disconcerting matter: the PPC's beleaguering ineptitude at debating whether this had been a protest or a party.

As he recalled real instances of hardship on school campuses, his vexation expanded. Students assembling in California and being thrown down hard stone steps was a protest. He knew this well. Students like Lockwood drinking too much and falling down Glazier Hall's steps stone drunk was a party. Teachers, staff, and students having to walk along rows of armed soldiers to get to class saw real hardship. Students playing with butcher paper and making murals in AP Hall was not. *What happened at the Registrar in sixty nine—* he thought before stopping cold, unwilling to remember more.

He knew what he had to do. The university president, the dean, Alumni Relations, and others would surely be annoyed at him for a fortnight or two. It was time to end the charade.

Before he could pick up the telephone, the door to his office forcefully opened, revealing an exasperated Athletic Director who looked a touch out of breath.

"Stop!" the visitor called. "You can't break down the doors of a building in the NEQ!"

*   *   *

Backing up a bit, this scene would have gone differently if not for Kathie.

As soon as the negotiator returned to Liberty Hall ready to write up his lackluster report, Kathie intercepted him and his summary. It didn't take long for both to annoy her.

Something was amiss, clearly.

In the tiny window she had before Asbury would make a rash (but correct) decision about August Hall, she proceeded with fire, first by racing to the NEQ.

En route, she fired off a text message to Eva which read: *where's your summary of AP Hall protest? Did not see it yet.* While still on the war path, Eva's reply came: *i didn't write it, it wasn't worth it thanks to lockwood.*

The entire text concerned Kathie, not just Eva's aggravatingly poor use of capital letters. Before wasting too much time thinking about Eva's statement, Kathie arrived at the NEQ to confirm neither report was inaccurate. *How can this be? There's no way he performed that abysmally. Not when he's this far in.*

She was determined to not let Lockwood's grandest attempt to embarrass himself out of a college degree slip away, even these summaries suggested he wasn't as committed. But what could she use to prolong the sham? What could be so important to a school, she wondered, that it would take precedence over the safety of its students?

As she let her eyes roam from one featureless scene to the next in a search for that answer, they drifted surely towards the NEQ's enormous gym and a pack of student athletes practicing outdoors. Kathie had the answer she craved: a school like PMU would do most anything to quell the threat of a damaged or unprofitable athletic brand.

Intrigued by the idea, she took a quick look at August Hall to ensure she wasn't being watched and strolled to the gym to figure out the best way into the vaulted Athletic Department.

Fate seemed to be on her side that day as an option present itself promptly. In front of the hulking structure, she happened upon a sign embedded into a garden which stated "Welcome to the [REDACTED COMPANY NAME] Northeast Quad" as opposed to listing it as simply the Northeast Quad, which was how most visitors knew it. [12]

She walked into the gym and headed straight for the membership office near its entrance. After showing herself in, she politely smiled at the office's plump sales events associate.

"May I help you, young lady?" the staffer asked warmly.

"Yes please," she sweetly replied. "I was wondering if you could answer sort of a weird question: why does the sign out front say the [REDACTED] NEQ?"

"Sure thing! They are one of our gracious sponsors. The Quad

---

[12] As the Public Relations representatives of this successful company will not have the opportunity to review this manuscript until after its publication, they will be left anonymous.

and the gym's parking lot always tend to attract our best fans on big game days, so they contribute each year to make sure our facilities look sharp and our athletes practice with the best equipment."

"Wow! I've walked by that sign for two years and I always wondered," Kathie replied through enthusiasm that sounded far from forced. "They don't ask for anything in return?"

"It's very symbiotic. They help keep it looking nice outside and we mention their name when we have big events. Anytime the events provide great photos they pay a pretty penny, too."

Ten minutes later the scheming Kathie was hunkered down in one of the unoccupied back rooms of the Math Library with her ear was pressed up against the office's phone. As soon as the Athletic Director greeted her, the ballet began.

"I'm calling from the Provost's advisory board," Kathie stated expeditiously in a professional tone. "I've been asked to call to double check that no athletic department is hosting a pep rally or event in August Hall or the [REDACTED] NEQ today."

"My secretary told me you said this was urgent. Why didn't you just ask her?"

"I was told to speak directly with you as the Provost plans to end this unsanctioned event by ramming through a set of barricaded doors in AP Hall and setting up triage in the NEQ."

"What?" the AD screamed. "Why? Does Asbury have any idea how bad that could be for us if— what's going on there anyway?"

"There is an unsanctioned protest taking place in the dorm. It appears a student named Charles Lockwood is at the center of it."

"That frat kid from that homecoming prank last year? This has to be another prank. Does Asbury have any idea how much we could lose if it looks like he's seen strong-arming students in that Quad?"

"I'm sure he has taken that into consideration," a calculating Kathie replied.

"I can tell I've known the man longer than you have and I guarantee he hasn't considered any of this. How can I stop him?"

With just a little more goading and a veiled suggestion that the AD should rally a major administrative department against Asbury,

Kathie's mission was complete. Before long, the provost had a very unwelcome visitor who shared with him more than an earful about how the Athletic Department and the President alike would handle the August situation differently.

Asbury was unwilling to take such a battle to heart, namely because he knew the Athletic Department would soon realize they wanted nothing to do with the mess. Once that happened, he could end it the way he wanted *and* he would get to rip apart the AD when all was settled.

He sent to the PPC a brief message noting the Athletic Director was going to organize his own inquiry and if no action was taken before midnight, "the PPC will take care of the situation ourselves and Lockwood will face stiff, very serious consequences."[13]

As she skimmed the email, Kathie relished her latest discovery: Asbury's hands were more tied than she'd imagined. If she did her homework, she could certainly buy Lockwood enough time to make him look like the fool he really was.

---

[13] It is perhaps needless to mention that the Athletic Department did not assign anyone to investigate the matter.

Chapter 16: Sub Two Cold Storage

IMMEDIATELY FOLLOWING his poor showing, an unfamiliar feeling of desperation forced Lockwood into a near catatonic state as he sat in his room. His unpreparedness, combined with the lack of student response, formed a potent cocktail of despair for the often boundlessly optimistic boy.

If I had been watching this as a casual observer, I honestly would not have known if Lockwood gained his second wind by chance, determination, or because he thought he was merely whittling down the hours until his doom became official. In truth, it was his hatred of despair that pushed him to vow that if these were his last hours on campus they would not be quiet ones. What he needed to do, he decided, was face this like he did every other challenging situation: play like he was already winning (his words and motto, not mine).

To wrest the trio from inaction, Lockwood unglued himself from his mentally frozen perch and swiftly produced six shot glasses from a drawer. "It's time to Drain Storm."

Edie pulled a pillow off of the couch, placed it on the ground, and sat on it, grabbing her shot glasses to signify she would join the game.

William, feeling a pinch of heartache at being separated from his books as well as his attempt to woo Carolina, asked, "Does Drain Storm mean 'let William go back to studying?'"

"It's brainstorming with booze. Take a seat." With delight he produced three forty ounce bottles of malt liquor. He placed one in front of Edie, gave William one, and sat with his.

"I'm guessing I'm allowed to opt out, right?" William asked to no avail.

Lockwood popped the top of his bottle and filled both glasses in front of him. "So it's just like a normal brainstorming but when you say an idea, you take a shot."

"But if you don't want to drink there's no incentive to come up with ideas."

Lockwood took a swig directly from his bottle. "When someone comes up with an idea before you do, you have to take two shots."

William ruefully opened his first ever bottle of malt liquor.

"Clear on the rules?" Edie prodded. "All you have to do is get Chip a solution. Like bribe a school official or demand a new negotiator or throw furniture out the windows for attention."

"Got it."

Edie glared at William. "That was three ideas. Should we wait for you all night?"

"But I thought—" he stopped upon seeing Lockwood gulp shot after shot. He knew arguing would not help him so he rapidly filled and emptied his glasses.

"I liked the throwing the furniture out the windows idea," Lockwood said as he refilled. "But maybe we just throw all the books out instead?"

Edie slammed a shot and reached for her second. "The school won't care." She took her second shot and nudged William's hesitant hand closer to his mouth. "They would just sell everyone the same books back afterwards."

William tried to think but all coherent thoughts were pushed out by the question of how Lockwood or Edie could talk while drinking as fast as they were.

"Let's get a real Native American here!" Lockwood declared.

"To do what?" Edie asked. "Tell the school you're definitely full of shit?"

"Let's light school papers on fire," Lockwood suggested between sips, borrowing a classic of which I was not terribly fond.

The others drank and shook their heads, Edie in regards to the idea, William in regards to the game.

"We don't have any school papers," William said.

"Do we have anything in the building they would want?" Lockwood asked.

Edie downed a shot and poured one for William to be a hassle. "Just the students."

"We could give up now," William suggested. "Don't look at me like that. I'm going to keep saying it until you're drunk enough to agree."

"New rule," Edie replied. "You drink three shots every time you repeat an idea."

"Why? That's not fair!" William complained.

"That's for coming up with a stupid idea," she replied.

William cradled a glass near his chest and grumbled, "Lots of these are stupid."

Edie chortled. "You're right. They're just like all of Chip's other stupid ideas that get attention around here."

Lockwood's slightly bleary eyes flashed at Edie's statement. "That's it! I just need to treat this like it's really a prank! I've gotten the school's attention tons of times but with stupid shit I knew would piss them off, not serious stuff!"

Edie held back a question while trying to hold onto sobriety with a glass in hand. William, trying to not move for fear the liquor would start pouring back out, remained motionless until Lockwood slapped his back excitedly.

Lockwood clutched the bottle triumphantly. "It's time for a fucking party, guys!"

William didn't know how the game was handled once a winning idea was suggested, so he continued to drink at a tremendous pace while the others spoke.

Edie replied with: "I like it. But one problem: what are we going to drink?"

William gestured towards the room's refrigerators.

Lockwood laughed coldly. "This wouldn't last ten minutes."

"I got it," Edie declared before elbowing William. "This is going to be five shots for you at least. The RAs must shut down a dozen parties a night here. There's no chance they throw the drinks out after. They have to have a sweet stash somewhere."

Lockwood smiled. "Do you even know how much I love you right now?"

"No but considering your head count lately I'm glad it goes unsaid." Edie braced herself and stood. Lockwood followed, bouncing onto his feet.

"Now," he began while typing a text message to Dipshit, "about finding the RAs..."

*   *   *

This portion of the tale is, at least to some at the university, a tad embarrassing. By midafternoon, not one of August Hall's Residential Assistants, who were technically the only students with authority in the building, had reported the incidents. Similarly, despite their status, Lockwood gave them no special attention when locking up the building as he didn't think they posed much of a threat to his plans. To the chagrin of the Residential Affairs Department, his assumption was correct.

With Lockwood leading the way, Edie behind measuring her actions to hide the malt liquor's impact, and William half stumbling at the rear, the three located the pre-determined rendezvous spot, where they found Dipshit guarding a door. At Lockwood's request, the athlete managed to round up half of the building's RAs. Lockwood, Edie, and William entered the room to find eight anxious looking hall monitors.

"I need information," Lockwood demanded. Some exchanged looks as they awaited instructions. "I need to know where you keep all the confiscated booze."

Two RAs tensed up. A third shook his head and stated, "It's our job to pour the alcohol down the drain right after busting parties."

"Bullshit," Lockwood replied, making his way to the pair who flinched. "You wouldn't look so nervous if it all went down the drain, huh? Where is it?"

"Are you from the school?" a solemn RA asked. "Are you here to bust us for the stash?"

"I am definitely not from the school. But the only way Asbury's not going to find out about your booze cans is if it all disappears tonight." He watched the thought sink into the RAs' heads like confiscated beer into a shower drain.

"We keep a list," an RA stated amid some quiet opposition. "Then we store it all in a room on Four that's been empty since the second week of school. My copy of the list is in the bottom drawer over there."

Taking a cue from the RA's directions, Lockwood rifled through the desk until he found the envelope. He tore it open and made sense of the encoded data. "Twenty two bottles of liquor, thirty bottles of wine, and about seven cases of beer. That's still not enough."

A new voice, that of a senior named Kyle, joined in. "Uh, Chip is it? I think I know what you're trying to do…and I have an idea but I need some guarantees."

"You have got five minutes," an unusually stern Lockwood replied.

"Wow, I didn't really think of you as a workhorse."

"It's not that. We may be on the verge of blacking out so if you don't talk fast I might forget ever meeting you."

"Gotchya. I can get you what you need but a: we want in on the party and b: you can't tell anyone ever that we helped you."

Lockwood's gut told him Kyle was trustworthy but he wasn't certain. He looked at Edie, who was calculating the risks, as well. Sadly for PMU, suspicion was not necessary as Kyle had no intention of abandoning his brewing scheme in favor of fulfilling his obligations to the school.

"Deal. Let's hear the idea," Lockwood said.

Kyle sat up straight for his tale. "Everyone who's lived here has heard those annoying trucks that come every morning. People have been complaining for years but nobody's ever been able to stop it and no one has ever explained why they're here. So I decided to stake it out and I learned it's the campus caterer's delivery truck."

Lockwood was unmoved. "Probably for the vending machines. Doesn't help me."

"They're not stocking the vending machines and there ain't no dining hall here. But we do have a gigantic refrigeration unit that the caterers use for big events like alumni gatherings."

The prospect of what could be hidden beneath their feet was almost too enticing for Lockwood to bear. "Show me. Now."

*   *   *

Kyle, Lockwood, Edie, and William descended the stairs to the basement and proceeded towards a corner of the building that was rarely used publicly.

"So you've never been in this storage room?" Lockwood asked.

"I saw it from the outside once," Kyle replied as he pulled open a door connecting the Great Hall to the hallway of storage units running along its southern wall.

"So how do you know anything's in there?"

"I watched them every morning for two weeks. Each day they wheeled in a ton of stuff." The group approached a second door and Kyle sifted through his key ring to gain access.

He unlocked a door and pushed it open to expose a chilly anteroom. To the left was a door marked "Cleaning Supplies" and to the right was a door without a label. Directly ahead was a wall of steel, twenty feet wide, and accessible by a padlocked door.

Lockwood examined both of the door's unremarkable locks and took a photograph of them with his cell phone. He then looked around for a blunt object. Seeing only a fire extinguisher nearby, he unhooked it and with careless judgment, bashed the locks until each fell off, broken and covered in red slashes. Setting the tool down, Lockwood tugged the door open.

A gust of cool air stung Lockwood's face and blew back Edie's hair. The sight of the treasure trove instantaneously shocked them all.

Cases upon cases of wine and champagne were stacked along one wall. Beside this dazzling site were at least five crates each of gin, vodka, and whiskey. Assorted boxes of crackers, cheese, and appetizers caught their attention, but they were far from claiming the title of the room's gleaming centerpiece: approximately three dozen presumably full kegs of beer.

Lockwood didn't know whether to laugh or cry. Edie opted for the former. Kyle fell to his knees and chose the latter. William, with the help of the malt liquor and shock, fainted body first onto the cold ground and face second into a large bag of coffee beans. Recalling the boy's rarely used nickname, Edie chuckled to herself at the pairing of coffee and creamer.

Lockwood inhaled a deep breath and relished in the room's glory. "Know what this is, Edie?" he asked rhetorically. "This is playing like you've already won."

*   *   *

The party began promptly at four thirty p.m. with grandeur.

Two kegs were hauled up to opposing corners of the second floor by RAs. Quickly thereafter each vessel was paired with a set of computer speakers. One set announced the party's presence by blasting early 2000s pop and hip hop songs.

Residents filed out of their rooms, at first armed with curiosity and shortly thereafter with plastic cups that seemed to materialize out of thin air. They pieced the scene together quickly: music, free beer, RAs present with drinks in hand, a bold supply of buttery crackers, and of course, no campus police to shut the party down.

As the second floor filled up and music tastes diverged, students realized they could organize their own smaller parties and the gathering grew larger. Techno Rooms sprung up on Three East and Four South, and an "R&B Groove Shack" took over a third floor study hall. Elsewhere, sets of speakers in twelve adjacent rooms kept music going in the fourth floor's "Strictly Dance Party Hallway."

More kegs were placed around the building and a shocking

number of assorted "self-catered" cans and bottles flowed strongly out of dorm rooms. This should come as a complete surprise since more than eighty percent of August Hall residents were under twenty-one.

Books were put away. Differences between neighbors were set aside. DJ's, bartenders, and party planners filled each need as necessity arose. Students set up tables for drinking games like beer pong, flip cup, and games of bags (or corn hole or cornhusker, colloquially). Friends and classmates took to the evening like it was their first night alive, acting on any entertaining idea that came to mind. Beyond the parties and dancing, board game tournaments, DVD screenings, and hearty conversations soon delighted students on every floor of the building.

*   *   *

By 5:30 the gathering in August Hall had grown into the largest party the dorm had ever seen. By six, it was the biggest party the NEQ ever hosted. Shortly after six, drawn by the noise in the dorm, an actual crowd began to gather outside.

Inside, the party raged, music blared, and laughs carried far and wide. As the noise complaint total ratcheted up (also setting a new Wednesday record) University Police knew the PPC's supposed non-issue had become a serious predicament.

Chapter 17: Two Seats to the Right of Asbury

"WHAT IN the fuck is he doing?" Provost Asbury bellowed, brashly ushering the beginning of the PPC's first emergency board meeting in just over four years. Listening to the Athletic Director's plea was admittedly his own fault. That admission did not stifle his indignation once seated among his associates who actively did nothing as the situation first presented itself.

"It sounds like he's having a party," a timid person replied, unsure if their response would be met with acclaim or scorn.

The adult members of the board wordlessly prayed Asbury would not reprimand the entire audience for the comment. No one could confirm why or how the situation escalated but all were easily assured their latest problem would not fade easily. Even worse, in addition to the after-hours meeting, the PPC was also under the close watch of five new guest members from various departments, notably one director level employee from the office of the President. (No professors from the History, Political Science, Criminal Justice, or other academic departments were added to the mix.) Even Kathie, who had been focused on the celebration she would execute when Lockwood was carted out of Pemberton by the collar of his perfectly starched shirt, was focused on one newcomer in particular.

That visitor, whose bag and brightly colored yoga mat were waiting for her by the board room's entrance, was wearing somewhat damp yoga clothes and a muted irritated expression. Kathie noticed this girl's seat, which was two spots to the right Asbury, was distinctly closer to the committee's lead than Kathie had ever sat. (Kathie reminded herself that she deliberately chose her own seat that night next to the university's head of compliance, the rarely attentive individual who ensured the school's amenability with vendor contracts. The VP, who for the purposes of this story will be known by the alias of Fredrick, would soon become pivotal.)

Eva Yesterday, meanwhile, knew little about why Asbury's secretary ventured out to Eva's afternoon exercise class to personally invite her to the meeting. At the time she was still under the impression Lockwood had been shut down. Thanks to a few minutes of pre-meeting chatter, she gathered that the school had done nothing to release the students held in August Hall and the "protest" had devolved into a party thanks to an abundance of alcohol.[14] After harvesting what she could from whispers, she prepared questions for the Provost, not realizing her queries would not matter once Asbury gained speed.

Eva was so focused on her questions that she didn't notice Kathie's venomous looks, which she shared whenever another student visited a PPC meeting. Though only a onetime guest and not a provisional member of the board, seeing Eva scorched Kathie's latest plan: slowing Asbury down as much as possible. The example with the AD, who swiftly turned down Asbury's invitation to the emergency meeting, showed that lurking in PMU's practices there must have been a bounty of ways to hamstring the administrator. Kathie

---

[14] Incidentally, the previous year Eva's student action committee spoke out against several of the caterer's practices to no avail. None of the infractions of which she was previously aware were anywhere as "ghastly" (her word) as the practice of storing alcohol in a student dormitory.

spent her afternoon trying to uncover progress constrictors. Eva, who knew Lockwood really wasn't leading a protest, could step in as the voice of reason. Would she? That, Kathie decided, was entirely up to her.

Asbury continued with a public shaming. "For anyone who offered no counsel earlier: do you have anything to say yet? Has anything you've seen or heard prompted any emotional response?" The audience continued to sit in silence, unsure how to react to the question Asbury loaded so much that it became nearly impossible to answer. "This boy has locked up students. He is force-feeding them alcohol. He is mocking everything from our fire department to our truancy guidelines! Is that not enough for you?"

The dearth of replies disheartened both Asbury and Eva equally. Kathie glanced at the head of compliance, who was assuming his typical meeting stance of furtively scanning emails unrelated to PPC business.

"This isn't just about moral delinquency. " Asbury produced a piece of paper and angled his head so his bifocal lenses hit the sheet's text just right. "He's already cost us five hundred dollars for the fire alarm and at minimum two thousand dollars damage to the dorm's security. Who knows what other horrors this scene will produce? And what is this entry..." He squinted for a better look the last line item. "Forty five dollars for clothing reimbursement?"

A fairly embarrassed Bursar's Office representative responded. "After leaving the NEQ, the negotiator we sent discovered someone had painted the words 'ass fan' on the back of his shirt during the encounter. We have been asked to reimburse him."

Asbury turned his head enough to let out a forceful bone cracking that startled the room. "I want answers! There are teenagers running free in a building that somehow is full of alcohol! How are we getting them back in classes? How are we handling security? What are we doing?"

At this, many tried ducking into their notes or glaring angrily at their laptops, hoping to piggyback off Asbury's ire by appearing they, too, were searching for answers from others instead of giving the answers that were required of them.

Asbury tried to retract his intensity momentarily. "Someone please explain this silence."

While the board members shied away from posing truly dangerous answers, Kathie had drifted from angered to disappointed. She knew which way she wanted to steer the conversation but she needed something to pilot. Someone— anyone had to talk to move everything along.

"Perhaps you, Miss Yesterday, could explain what happened here," Asbury continued, shifting squarely to Eva. "Lockwood placed hundreds of our students in danger, not to mention thousands of dollars of private property and an entire dormitory building! Would you mind telling us where you were today when you were supposed to monitor this situation?"

Eva took offense but outwardly displayed only the tiniest amount. "In a roomful of people considered to be esteemed campus leaders, I'm the one who deserves the blame?"

(Kathie did her best to hide her smirk.)

"We sent you there to check on the safety of our students."

"No, you sent the man without a clean shirt to check on their safety. You sent me to check on their first amendment rights. I am not here to monitor for underage drinking. You asked if what I saw was a protest and I said that it was not."

"Whether we ask you to investigate drinking or students hurling themselves in front of tanks, you have your honorary position for the sole reason of protecting them," Asbury shouted.

Unperturbed by the antiquated show of chauvinistic educational leadership she felt was more suited for the 1950s, Eva provided the half innocent, half snarky reply of: "Is that not the exact reason everyone in this room has their paid position, as well?"

The reply steamed Asbury but he chose to move his meeting along, knowing in his heart that the blame should be shifted equally around the board room. "The remainder of the board will discuss that in private. For now, what I need is to know why you didn't report this potential danger earlier. The reply you shared with me over the phone was short and far from descriptive."

Eva cocked an eyebrow at the question. "My reply was short because I described a display so stupid that it should have been stopped immediately." This prompted Asbury to grow more exasperated upon seeing few colleagues were taking Eva's tirade personally. "What's almost worse is now I have to see how the school's leaders have no idea how to solve this."

"That is patently untrue, young lady!" bellowed Asbury.

"How so? You yourself mentioned hundreds of trapped students in the same breath as minimal costs you're losing thanks to property damage and burglarized beer."

Eureka! Kathie thought. "I'm sorry to cut you off," she said disingenuously. "I get that you're not familiar with decorum, but Provost Asbury did not suggest the school is more concerned with stolen property or broken contracts than it is with its students."

At this, the VP of Compliance stirred. "Excuse me? What broken contract?"

Asbury wasn't sure which attendee deserved more concern: Eva for her insubordination, Kathie for her eerily robotic support, or the high level administrator who was displaying less than sound judgment. "Have you been listening at all, Fredrick?"

"If I sound this shocked," he replied unapologetically and indignantly, "then yes, I missed something. Tell me what he stole."

Kathie emitted a lighthearted laugh, which she had been rehearsing since reading the school's food service contract earlier. "This confusion may have been my fault. Mr. Provost and I were trying to explain to Eva that the school's first order of business is getting those students away from Chip Lockwood and the alcohol he somehow procured from behind locked doors—"

"He got into [REDACTED]'s north campus cache?" Fredrick replied bewilderingly fast. "This is bad."

Asbury studied the incensed VP who had gone from uninterested to furiously typing in seconds. "Of course this is bad. That's what the adults in the room have been talking about."

"Be snippy later. When did the theft take place?"

Asbury looked to his left at the trusty Registrar's Office representative. The staffer looked through her notes and replied: "Less than three hours ago?"

Before letting anyone reply, Fredrick rattled off an unexpected explanation. "Our food service, like some of our other service-based contracts, states it is our duty to report grand scale destruction to or theft of third party property or products within a two hour window. This gives vendors who choose to work with us a very reasonable of amount of time to determine if they want to levy legal action against the university and/or those directly responsible for the theft."[15]

"Are you kidding?" Asbury shot back. The aged administrator recollected that the PPC had little room to move when it came to contract disputes, which were handled entirely by Compliance. He mulled over the aggravating possibility of being forced into immobility again.

"We needed them on the phone an hour ago. I'm emailing them now to catch them before they leave the office," the VP continued at a frantic pace. "How much was stolen?"

The Registrar's Office aide read off a tally of what the university believed had been in the caterer's freezer unit earlier in the week.

Eva watched the scene unfold with a dreadful look inscribed on her face. "You can't be serious. When you thought this was a protest the best you could do was send in an idiot to talk Lockwood down. When you knew it was dangerous you did nothing. *Now* you want to act?"

Although her message bounced off of the VP's ears, he stated decisively: "We need to get ahead of this."

---

[15] These perhaps absurd-sounding clauses existed to reduce PMU's liability and to encourage corporate partnerships. In the 1990s, Compliance gathered that schools that were tight-lipped about theft and vandalism often came across as unwelcoming partners who might be willing to betray a vendor if a student tore down a goal post or defaced a sponsor's logo on campus. As PMU was eager to invite mutually beneficial relationships, they readily agreed to such clauses.

"I agree," Asbury replied. "We need to end this swiftly. Then we can return the students to normalcy, return to [REDACTED] its property, and deal with Lockwood."

"Oh no, no!" Fredrick shook his head. "That would make it look like a cover up. If we don't talk with the catering company immediately, we could be considered just as liable as the student who did the ransacking. If the company finds us in breach of contract, it could cost us five times the value of everything taken, plus a sizeable upper six figure settlement."

"What?!" Asbury and Eva simultaneously exclaimed.

"I told you this is serious."

"Oh come now," Asbury bellowed. "We're dealing with a joke of a student. We need to go in there and wipe him out!"

"You mentioned a protest earlier, right?" he replied with more attention to the key pad than his superior. "A protest works. I'll say the company's property was misplaced in the midst of…political outcry. That will buy us time."

"I don't know what's more ridiculous: the idea that Chip Lockwood is staging our biggest protest in decades or that someone like him would stand up for the Native Americans." Asbury looked to his left. "Do we even have any native American students?"

The Registrar rep checked to make sure her reply was accurate. "Not many."

"How many is not many?"

The rep exhaled an attempt at a self-exonerating sigh. "At least fifty percent below the average for comparable schools."

Asbury tried the calculation but was too flustered. "Regardless, read my lips: we need to get him out of here now!"

Fredrick's computer emitted a "ding" to notify him of a new email. As he scanned it, he explained the board's next steps: "Debate later if it's a protest. The soonest they can talk with us is in ninety minutes. Until then, we cannot break those doors down."

A bewildered Asbury and a similarly flummoxed Eva stared down the speaker. His shock came from trying to discern how he was once again left without options to act. Her amazement was mixed with disgust at how it seemed decisions were made in her collegiate home. Kathie, meanwhile, who managed to incite the scene with only two comments, was content after buying her nemesis an hour and a half to further junk his reputation.

"So what do we do?" asked a representative.

The partially whiplashed Asbury looked around to ascertain who wanted an answer and who was only waiting to be released so they could go home. Most were in the latter category, but since he himself didn't like the only logical answer remaining, he didn't belittle their malaise.

Looking over Fredrick, Asbury asked: "We can't enter August Hall until this call?" A nod was offered. "But there's nothing stopping students from opening the doors themselves, right?"

Fredrick weighed the question. "I don't see how that could put us in breach."

Asbury turned to his right to face Eva. "You're certain this isn't a protest?"

Eva was disheartened by the meeting, though still empathetic for the portion of her mind that felt real change could be inspired by actions in the NEQ. "This is not a protest."

Asbury nodded. "In that case, we do whatever we can to prove to the students that Lockwood deserves to be ousted. Find another negotiator." As the bulk of the committee watched his movements for the signal showing they were allowed to leave, Asbury stood to gather his personal effects. "One of you better make sure Ass Fan's replacement goes in wearing an inexpensive shirt and does the research we're actually paying him for."

Chapter 18: Purgatory

AT EIGHT p.m., Lockwood stripped himself from the party to somberly examine the Quad from a dark corner room on the third floor. After so many novel failures, his latest plan was a success. Students were present, they were loud, and they seemed to be rallying behind a cause. The event may have looked more like an early tailgate for PMU's upcoming football game against the Southwest A&M State Cowboys, not a protest, but it was a victory nonetheless.

As he watched scores of students drink and talk merrily, a thought briefly entered his mind: this would be the last party he would ever host at PMU. He wouldn't let the thought distract him for long, but he indulged it for a moment. Soon everything he knew about PMU was going to become a memory. The smell in the air when the first signs of spring arrived, the camaraderie during all-night movie marathons when the cold of February forced everyone to remain indoors indefinitely, the feel of pulling his reliable PMU hoodie over his head as he forced himself out of bed for a 7 a.m. tailgate; all were about to shift to the past tense permanently. Knowing those recollections would only be felt in pain if he did not rise above his predicament, he returned to the tasks at hand.

In his hand he held a list of notes provided by Alf about what the small online PMU community felt about his actions. It was time to take that information, and with the help of his war council, convince the campus it was embroiled in a true protest. For that he needed Edie, who he knew was chatting up a lacrosse player in a nearby hallway, and William, whose whereabouts for some reason he could not recall...

*   *   *

Not terribly long after falling over in Lockwood's new favorite place in the world, William awoke in a terrified stupor.

The room around him did not fit with August Hall's decor, so initially his mind followed an illogical thought pattern that suggested he made it out of the building alive and away from Lockwood and Edie. Clutching to the idea for a sweet moment, a weak-bonded feeling of clouded joy overcame him.

He then took a closer look at the items around which he was engulfed, prompting him to consider the possibility that he did not survive "drain storming." Was he in Purgatory, in his own personal hell for underage drinking?

The troubled sophomore ran with this longer than he should have, wondering if it was his duty to finish the mountainous collection of kegs, or rather to avoid touching anything for an undetermined portion of eternity. (He was unaware that the guard outside had neglected his orders to move William out of the cold storage area long ago.)

He got to his feet with help from a stack of wine boxes. While his eyes searched for any way out, he found what appeared to be a door with no handle. This confused him until he realized he was locked inside of a room that likely didn't often have visitors. With a hefty push, the door opened and he found himself in a dimly lit area being guarded over by a tough looking student wearing a Pemberton athletic sweatshirt.

The student looked up from his magazine and laughed at the sight of William.

"Shit, look at you, kid!"

"Am I..." William began, stretching his jaw to let the frost escape, "Am I supposed to drink all of that?"

The jock chuckled. "Rookies."

The intoxicated William belatedly celebrated the victory. "So I'm still alive?"

The jock nodded vigorously. "Dude, if you think that room is crazy, you should see the freshman girls' hallway!"

This left William more confused as his memories since the numerous gulps of malt liquor were still missing. "You mean— you mean I'm still in August Hall?"

"Kid, you're pretty much on Poon Island! It's crazy! I even got a text from a chick upstairs who thinks she might be pregnant...so keep an eye out, but the rest are fair game, man!" The jock smiled and slapped William on the back.

The stubbornly shy sophomore steadily found his way into a part of the building he recognized, the Great Hall. He remembered seeing it the night before as a pleasantly boring unused space. Since then, it had become a dance hall complete with a flickering multi-colored light display and an ample supply of dancers.

As he continued the sights grew worse for William. Hallways were lively. Music and laughter seeped out from every direction. And one glimpse of the freshman girls' hallway sent the withdrawn boy practically running in the other direction.

The building's main entryway, previously the sight of Lockwood's failed daylight attempts at capturing students' hearts, was at night the scene of four dueling beer pong games. The study lounge, which had highlighted the students' disdain for joining the revolt had since changed into a lively bastion of students playing board games. Outside, the morning's lone protestor would no longer have a chance of being picked out of the excitable crowd in the Quad.

William's discovery that the students were finally keen on Lockwood's plan (or whatever it was) shattered his hopes that Lockwood would give up once no one responded to his antics.

With the desire to be alone, he turned to the only room in the building he felt he could go for solitude. The room belonged to a friend named Ralph, a sophomore living on Four East. He'd met William in History of the U.S. Treasury (HIST-292, offered WTR) and earlier agreed to let him use his room if he needed a place to stay.

Ralph's room was empty and thankfully not in the vicinity of any boisterous party. Once inside, William fetched from his backpack a long sleeved Pemberton shirt, which he'd packed to impress the spirited Carolina. He then scanned through Ralph's DVD collection for a movie to watch to calm down. With just enough time to grab his film of choice and hold it close to his chest, the door opened and Edie and Lockwood appeared.

"Hey buddy, welcome to the party!" Lockwood declared happily.

The sudden entrance startled William. "How did you find me?" he moaned.

"I'll be honest: this isn't the first room we burst into," Lockwood replied while sealing the three inside. "Also, Lats said you left and Ralph said your bag was here."

"You have people spying on me?" William asked angrily.

"Wow!" Lockwood replied with a relieved tone. "I thought you'd be more upset over us leaving you in the basement for two hours."

"Don't you mean leaving me in cold storage for two hours?"

The news shocked Lockwood but wouldn't show it in his face. Neither would Edie, namely because she didn't care. William complacently fell to the floor to sit. His head ached from the alcohol, stress, and hours on a freezing cement floor.

Edie, hoping to speed things up, recapped, "So you finally got attention. Now what you need is a cause, a declaration, and a better damn showing than you had at the last negotiation."

"Already got an idea on the cause," Lockwood said as he handed Alf's findings to Edie. "Let me know what you think."

Edie read the notes to herself and then aloud. "Alf wrote: Between the web search sweeps and the message boards on the *Nightly*, 120 people have posted about you. Ten think you're protesting for Native American rights, fifteen think you're protesting the Iraq War, seven think Afghanistan, five think you're actually protesting to stop AIDS, fourteen think you're trying to *spread* AIDS, and thirty five think you're trying in a mighty clever way to speak out about student rights. The rest had crazier ideas."

"I can dig it," Lockwood replied excitedly. "Student rights."

Edie's arched left eyebrow signaled her concern. "Why are switching back to an idea that you texted me about earlier and neither of us liked?"

"I've liked it all day but this isn't revolutionary France. I didn't think people rising up for attention would fly in 2005 but this says that it might." He paused to hand one opened beer to Edie and place a second one on the floor near the back of William's head. In response, William let out the sound an ailing dinosaur might make after being crushed by a larger beast. "If people are already imagining this is what I'm speaking out for, this might hit click with them…"

Edie interjected with a nod. "…and then we can ride it as long as possible."

Edie and Lockwood clinked their watery beers in a mock toast. Before the celebration could continue, William rolled over to rest the left side of his head on the ground. "One problem," he grunted. "Or two if you count how you're feeding thousands of gallons of stolen beer to underage students…"

"Hey, that was the catering company's fault." Lockwood nudged William's leg with his foot. "See? We're already exposing devious shit going on behind our backs."

This information would have normally impressed William, but he couldn't help but ignore it. "How do you abandon the Native Americans?"

"Didn't we already do that, like, as a country?"

William let out another howl. "What I mean is your audience might find it odd when Native Americans disappear from your speeches."

"You heard Alf. Most of the people know that it's not really about Indians."

As Edie sipped her beer, she reminisced to a time in high school where her parents sent her to live with family in the Midwest for two weeks as punishment for an indiscretion. During the visit she sat in on her cousin's student council meetings while her school debated switching their mascot from the "Bloody Mohawks" to something less insensitive. She recalled that most people at the meetings weren't really listening to statements about the broader, big picture, rather they were focused on what the change meant personally. "I remember when they tried to change the mascot in my cousin's high school. No one cared about the history of neglect. They were furious over '*my* mascot having to change' and 'being stripped of *my* culture' and shit like that."

Lockwood began to catch on. "So if I can find a way to connect Native Americans to something the students really can complain about...I'm good?"

"Absolutely. If anyone gave a shit about Indians, these problems would have been solved centuries ago," Edie replied. "Just figure out how to segue and never go back."

Lockwood sat on the bed and leaned back contentedly. There were missing pieces, yes, but he had something he could use. "That will work for anyone who's here in the Quad listening. We need to show everyone else how serious I am. And that's where William's declaration is going to come in handy."

Protesting scantily from beneath his veil of self-diagnosed alcohol poisoning, William replied, "No one knows who I am. Why would they care about a declaration I write?"

"Because you're going to put my name on it."

"No, no way. How many damn assignments am I going to have to write for you?"

Lockwood shrugged. "If we're lucky, or even if we're not, this will be the last."

Lockwood's browbeaten advisor, having been dragged into criminal actions, force fed alcohol, and hearing a plan most despicable, couldn't help but wonder when it would all end. "Why? Why are you doing this to me?"

"Doing what?" he replied, bereft of sarcasm. "This is the biggest party the campus has ever seen! I'm trying to make you a part of it. Isn't that what you wanted?"

"No!" William moaned as he turned over, DVD still firmly in his grasp. "I don't like parties, I don't like people! I just want to be—"

"Where do you want to be, Will?" Lockwood pried, leaning up in his seat. "Back home? You want to be a genius, amazing nineteen year old living at home, safe in a tiny comfort zone?" William shrunk back in his audacity. "Or did you want to do new fun shit and meet people like Alf and Carolina and whoever the hell is letting you fondle his movies?"

Instead of agreeing, William bullishly muttered, "I didn't want to make friends like this. You'd know that if you really knew me— or really listened to me."

"Really listened? Do you remember when we took you to all over town last spring?"

Had William possessed the ability to shudder, he would have. That was the only night he'd "let loose" in college, and worse, he did it in front of Lockwood and Edie.

William stole a look at a somber Edie. He then turned to Lockwood to hear more about the majority of the missing hours of his life.

"You got drunk on three beers and you told us you hated being this guy. You hated always having to choose between studying and being a smart, outgoing, kick ass guy." He watched as emotion crept into William's dejected face. "You wanted to be the guy who could help three people study for a test and then race them to a bar afterwards. You wanted to be able to talk to anyone. And this is your chance."[16]

Edie and Lockwood watched to see how William would react. (Not using the nickname they bestowed on him that fateful evening potentially improved their chances of success.) The pair knew there were few non-violent things more frightening at their age than hearing someone recite words they'd said while entirely blacked out under the influence of alcohol.

---

[16] As this discussion of which they spoke happened off campus, I cannot confirm or deny whether this really happened as Lockwood alleged.

William set down the movie. "Fine, I'll write the damn thing."

"That's my Creamer!" Lockwood joyously slapped his hands together.

With that, Lockwood finally had a cause, an audience, a statement of purpose, and more than ever, he had the momentum to use all three to his advantage.

Chapter 19: The Northeast Campus Lake Fill

SPEECH PATHOLOGY major Cammy Dalton was one of many students that evening who had heard about an alleged protest at August Hall. The idea was captivating but then disappointing as she didn't think the reality could defeat her mental image of a true demonstration.

At 8:30, after hearing rumors for two full hours, she could ignore the chatter no longer. Donning a light jacket, she left her sorority for the NEQ. On the way she coaxed herself into believing it was her duty as a student to go, either as one who was interested in important social causes or as one who needed to do homework uninterrupted by gossip.

Cammy served PMU well since meeting the university on a recruiting visit three years earlier. She was her sorority's treasurer, an avid PMU athletics fan, and an organizer of the annual Cancer Research Bike Marathon. As an all-around courteous student, she was exactly the type of young adult the PPC didn't want wandering near August that evening.

By the time she arrived, she was far from the only one whose curiosity had directed them.

The scene instantaneously intrigued Cammy. Some students were drinking joyfully while others had lively debates over what was happening inside the building. The scene looked similar to PMU's tailgates, so it wasn't wholly unfamiliar, but she felt there was something more to it.

After joining up with a few friends, she latched onto the name Lockwood. Having never met him, it did not take long to believe full-scale protest was his forte (as opposed to flooding sororities and slathering like-colored condiments on handrails).

The most overwhelming item of the NEQ by far was the sight of August Hall as lights flashed and noises, like raucous laughter, pulsated from it in waves. Each sound weaved in and out between the tracks of countless songs. The dormitory's energy was something neither Cammy nor any other student present had ever encountered. Between the wildly keen spectators and the relentless enthusiasm from inside, the moment seemed "Gatsby-an" in her mind.

Then, having been spared the fate of others who waited hours without seeing anything more exciting than kegs opening and colorful placards appearing, Cammy saw heads turn towards a nearby parking lot. Her eyes instinctively followed the movement.

She couldn't see who was approaching, but judging from the wave of cups being heaved onto assorted lawns, she knew it was someone important. A small force of police created a path for a team of five men. One shuffled papers as fiercely as one could with such a mundane task. Another gripped a megaphone so tightly his leather gloves looked ready to pop at the knuckles.

Cammy's eyes followed her curiosity up to the rows of lit windows along August Hall's façade. With so many students and administrators present, she couldn't help but think about Lockwood. *Does he know how many people gathered because of something he dreamed up?*

As minutes passed, Cammy fixated on what she wouldn't give to see Lockwood at the precise moment before he came out to greet the crowd that eagerly awaited his arrival.

*   *   *

Unbeknownst to Cammy, at that exact moment, our story's misguided protagonist was shoving a beer can with a gaping hole in its side against his mouth and chugging its contents.

Delicately holding the can in his left hand afterwards, Lockwood shook off the round of "shot gunning" by high fiving three other young men who participated.

He then backed into a hall with Edie following. The pair made their way past a group of students playing a card-based drinking game and Edie began prepping Lockwood. "Alf texted me and said they just pulled up. Are you set on the plan?"

"I talk from Alf's room and—"

Edie rushed in to guide him. "First: keep it vague. No tribe names, no nothing. Second: don't get stuck in anything stupid. Just latch onto something and make it about students." They arrived at Alf's room and Edie took a moment to examine the young man she once endearingly described as a "SoCal-bred cologne-smothered" frat boy. *Swagger, charisma, possibly one drink too many*, she thought. *This just might work.* "Tell me you understand, Chip."

He remarked "I'm feeling—" before unintentionally burping and effortlessly rebounding into one of his most charming expressions. "Don't worry, I got this."

*   *   *

With a crowd surrounding him on three sides and the team of high-ranking university officials behind him, the new negotiator pointed his megaphone towards August Hall and lifted it to his mouth. "Attention, residents of August Hall. My name is Mr. Walters and I am here to speak with whomever has locked the doors."

The square's guests quieted to watch the scene unfurl.

With a healthy but not widely seen nudge from one of his cohorts, Walters raised the megaphone for a repeat attempt. Only a speck of sound escaped before the lights in every window on Four West shut off. The crowd let out possibly sarcastic "oohs."

Moments later, the curtains in the center room swung open and the lights flashed on, revealing Lockwood with outstretched arms and a two-foot tall headdress atop his head. (The adornment was not Edie-approved.) Those watching did not seem to notice or care about the slight transmitted by his costume: the man they were there to see had arrived.

"I take it you are Chip Lockwood?" Walters asked.

Lockwood guffawed, attracting praise from anyone hoping to see insubordination.

Chatter and muffled laughter popped up as Cammy smiled at the tension-tightening reply.

Walters pressed on. "At least some measure of decorum is called for. I am here to get those students out of the building safely before you end up in a lot of trouble."

"I'm already in trouble, we all are!" an impassioned Lockwood replied, with spectators balanced between entertained and hesitantly intrigued. "Every student here should know their futures are being endangered by the people running this school!"

Edie and Alf, watching stealthily from a nearby dark room noticed some students respond with nods even though Lockwood had said very little. Edie appreciated their support but still disliked them, assuming they were the same people who grinned and wrote unimportant memos when professors brought up obscure facts in lectures.

Walters offered, "If you would open the doors, we can talk like civilized people—"

"Don't assume I'm uncivilized because of how I speak with my tribesmen. I am here to raise my voice above the tyranny that has silenced our tribe for years!"

"All of that will have its own time and forum, not now with everyone held hostage." Walters said sternly, pausing to allow his barb to strike listeners. "You do know you have students trapped at a great hazard to their health, correct?"

"These students are being treated well and they know their sacrifices won't be forgotten." Lockwood winced, hoping no one thought the statement sounded as villainous as he did. A quick sweep of the crowd confirmed he was not alone in his interpretation.

Walters continued the attack. "Do you wish to sacrifice their futures tonight? Countless students in there have GPAs to keep up, and without high grades, many may lose their financial aid eligibility. But...you don't have such financial aid obligations, do you, Charles?"

The junior sprung back quickly as his role from offense to defense. "No, I do not have all of the same obligations and that's exactly what lets me point out Pemberton's flaws. I can speak out for the erasure of the past that happens when we walk on this soil old men call theirs. Who said this land was yours? I didn't sign anything! The natives who occupied this land before Pemberton took it sure as hell didn't sign anything, either!"

Walters seized the first hint that Lockwood hadn't done his homework. "Are you protesting for Native Americans who were living on this land right here?"

"What land do you think I mean?" Lockwood cried back. "Of course this land!"

"Well the land we're standing on right now was reclaimed from the lake in 1954 by the Engineering Department."

The shocking response surprised even Lockwood, forcing him to mutter "Say what?" a little louder than he expected.

"The land we're on was shipped in via barge from sand dunes near Lake Erie in the fifties. This was done to expand the campus during a freeze on the sale of county land. This land could not possibly have been owned by any tribe before Pemberton poured cement over it." (This fact, as unlikely as it may sound, was true. The NEQ land reclamation endeavor was similar to a project later undertaken in Illinois in the 1960s. Oddly, William knew this but didn't have the chance to share it with Lockwood as he was still recovering from his time on ice.[17]) "If all you were fighting for proved to be incorrect— what does that mean for those you locked inside that building?"

The faux chief, experiencing another first, was caught without an answer in front of the class. Despite the urge felt by many to look

---

[17] Perhaps even more bizarrely, in 1952, when a move to use Canadian sand for the project was blocked by one of Edie's relatives who spoke strongly against "unpatriotic" filler, a state park in Ohio was chosen as the sand donor for the initiative. So Lockwood was, in fact, claiming land belonging to a state into which he was not allowed to step foot.

away as he showed he was dumbfounded, all continued watching.

Amid the break, which took no more than twenty seconds, Lockwood scanned the crowd for help, and somehow spotted the placard that would change his entire campaign.

At first glance, it looked unintentionally goofy. Other posters near it bemoaned global injustices or political issues that did nothing for Lockwood. But the sign that read "Colonial Hall 2003–2004 term Avg. GPA 3.7, Avg. Jan/Feb thermostat: 55F" had just the right amount of pertinence and selfishness to remind him of what he needed to say.

"If you think all I want is land," he stated with more daring than expected by listeners, "You're way off. I'm fighting for my people's proud heritage!"

The statement intrigued students but not enough to buy in just yet.

Walters proceeded with a placating tone. "And what fine heritage would that be?"

"Unbelievable," Lockwood jeered. "Before we came to Pemberton you would be embarrassed to ask so sarcastically about our past." In his pause, some faster students picked up on his meaning. "We're not here because we're bad at what we do. Show me hands: how many of you came here as valedictorian of your high school?"

Three-dozen hands went up.

"Keep your hands up. How many of you were class president?"

Another twenty hands were raised. Thirty more joined in after he queried who had started their own club in high school. Nearly ninety more upon asking how many were varsity athletes.

"When you carefully chose PMU, did you realize those honors would get stripped once you got here? Did you any of you know your hard work would only give you the chance to live in dorms so rowdy they have to lock garbage cans to the walls? Or eat unhealthy food provided by contracts that benefit VPs and Directors who never ever have to talk to you?" An energetic Lockwood could feel the growing vigor of his crowd. "Why do admins you'll never meet get to complain we're just partying? And why did we work so hard to get here if the school just wants us to forget we did anything good before we arrived?" To cap off his finale, he put his right arm out to the side and made a motion as if he were dropping a microphone.

A chorus of cheers erupted. His call to action may not have been perfect, but it was enough to stoke the controversy. Grins flared, drinks were raised, and Lockwood waved heroically before retreating to his lair. And inside the storied August Hall, the party raged on.

*   *   *

The scene, even its less impressive moments, moved Cammy deeply.

The talk affected her so much that it inspired her to place a phone call to her parents in Denver to ask about a subject she never thought to ask about directly: how her own parents were able to afford to send her to Pemberton. Having never really thought much about how college was paid for until she saw those impactful placards in the Quad, she was keen to learn more.

Over the phone her father explained that he and her mother were so committed to giving their daughters the best college education available that they had been saving dutifully for years. The goal was to allow Cammy and her sister to get through college without any student loans. The story took an unexpected turn when he explained that due to skyrocketing costs that her parents learned about almost accidentally, they had to severely adjust their savings plans while she was still in grade school. By the time she arrived at Pemberton, they had made two more adjustments, showing their original, very conservative seeming estimates had been far off. He finished with a heartfelt reminder that he was very proud of her achievements and he thanked her for being the daughter her parents had hoped to raise.

After the call, her appreciation for her father's sendoff and her overwhelming passion for the student voice led her to conclude that she had to help Charles Lockwood. She knew the rumors that brought her to the NEQ could soon reduce the truth down to a story of a wild party. It would be her duty, she affirmed, to tell students what was really happening in August Hall.

After toiling over words for thirty minutes and wrestling the thought of sending out her treatise with her name on it, at 10 p.m. her fiery declaration was ready:

Fellow Students,

Tonight junior Charles Lockwood addressed a crowd of students about problems we face every single day as on this campus but are blind to.

Tonight many of us saw a brave man dressed like America's early patriots who stood up against tyranny by dressing up as Indians to dump overtaxed tea.

We fought hard to get here. But now that we're here, look what we've let happen. We fight to learn interesting skills and facts while professors battle for their right to avoid talking to us. We strive to make this our home but we can't even meet the people making decisions for all of us.

Yearly tuition increases, crumbling services, and no chance to speak our minds was not why I applied here. Is that the Pemberton Way?

Lockwood, who is willing to shout for what we never thought we were allowed to ask for, is asking you to think about your rights, and what you really wanted from PMU. Shouldn't we all be willing and ready to help his cause?

—A Proud Pembertonian

*   *   *

Within thirty minutes, the email was read by scores and forwarded to hundreds more. After an hour, three fifths of all undergraduates had the email lodged in their inboxes.

Chapter 20: Glazier Hall's Lawn Decathlon Arena

ACCORDING TO the university's servers, Eva Yesterday received Cammy's email from friends at 10:07, 10:09, and 10:10. She deleted all three at 10:12 p.m. without opening them. When two more arrived a minute later, she opted to read one.

Fifteen minutes later I spotted her streaming east towards the NEQ. Six voicemails about August Hall served as the soundtrack that accompanied her quick-footed walk. Ten more remained unheard by the time she found her destination.

She arrived to a strikingly different scene than what she saw earlier. August Hall was lit up with an overpowering vivacity. Dorms around it looked just as rambunctious, as did as two fraternities, which joined in by setting up barbecue pits and draping cases of beer across their lawns. Stepping further into the Quad in search of any familiar face, she was more surprised by what was filling the spaces between the buildings. There were easily hundreds of students present— far more than she'd ever seen at a sanctioned student protest.

Many appeared to be jovial despite the unhidden police presence. In the midst of those with bright plastic cups, which were no doubt filled with alcohol, Eva found some students forming sit-ins (i.e. students who appeared to be protesting in a fashion she could appreciate).

Beyond her jealousy at the crowd's size and the joy she felt upon seeing students assembling, something felt awry. The scene was certainly impressive, but its pieces suggested something unnatural was positioned at its core.

It may have been sleep deprivation or the chance that the student body may have evolved beyond her comprehension in the few hours she spent at her apartment, but she sincerely couldn't tell if she was viewing a protest or a party.

That confusion was common not only in the NEQ, but also among the administrators who were still in their offices. Unsure of what to do after the failure of the second negotiation and the lack of response from the PPC, those left in charge classified the gathering as a less gloomy early pep rally for Saturday's upcoming football game. This move, which involved updating an official campus log maintained by University Police, let officials monitor the situation without technically failing to do their jobs.

The result, as Eva Yesterday saw, was a baffling mess. *How did hundreds of people make it to a protest in the middle of the night? And how did they manage to make it look like a rave that had sex with a pep rally?* Most seriously, she wondered what could have possibly happened in the short span of time between Ass Fan's departure and the birth of this gathering of Woodstock-like proportions.

As Eva looked around, the heap of questions continued to grow. *Was Lockwood really that good?* Or rather was he simply a strong enough tick that had burrowed under the skin of a behemoth too big to care?

Among the questions irking Eva was what Provost Asbury had to say about the scene. Ruefully for Asbury, he had spent most of the night wrestling with the Kathie-provided topic of how to handle the stolen goods at the epicenter of the party.

At the start of the conference call between PMU's Compliance team, Asbury's staff, and the catering company, the university provided an update on the situation (stopping short of sharing anything that suggested they had lost control of part of their campus). In response, the company's mouthpiece irately shot back a specific directive: it was the school's responsibility to promptly recover all stolen goods in proper working order or risk paying fines upwards of eight times the value of the property. To this, Asbury chastised the company for leaving so much alcohol in a very full dormitory. The vendor glibly replied that "according to the best of *our* records" all of the kegs in August Hall had been empty since the previous football game, as were the dozens of bottles of wine and liquor, which were all in storage waiting to be recycled.

Asbury, having heard what he considered to be a boldfaced lie designed to mitigate the company's risk and place blame on the students, was stunned into a venomous silence. With one more reminder about the university's obligations to the vendor's property, the meeting ended. The provost spent the remainder of the evening cursing those who'd tied his hands and debating with his staff what it would take to "minimize damage" in the NEQ. (While the debate seethed, Lockwood and Alf were competing against Edie and Dipshit in a long throw-style game in which they took turns seeing which pair could heave the building's sole empty keg farther down the hallway.)

Eva went in for a closer look at the sit-ins near August Hall. Half expecting to see posters with messages like "Support Boobs, Mandatory Bras for Fat Chicks" and so on, when within range she was pleasantly surprised. In one spot, students were civilly chatting under a large banner reading "Bring PMU into the 21st Century: Overhaul Minority Student Recruitment." Another team, some of whom Eva recognized, were clustered under poster boards taped to the exterior of the captive hall. Their placards read: "Stop Teaching Half the Story" and "Teach *all* Types of History, Please." Looking closer, Eva saw students sporting Pemberton colors happily conversing with these well-known advocates for change.

A third group, sitting under a banner that read "Financial Aid REDUX: A Basic Student Right" instantly attracted her feet. Looking more closely at the group, Eva spotted a friend (known here as Julia) who was actively talking to a handful of students near the main entrance of August Hall. Eva approached and tapped her shoulder.

Julia's face brightened at the sight of Eva. She hugged her firmly, knowing she did not often have the chance to brag with one of her idols. "Eva! How are you?"

"Fine," Eva replied while masking an ounce of betrayal she couldn't swat away. (Julia's phone number was not listed in Eva's phone under Missed Calls.) "But I'm a little confused."

"I knew I'd see you. No one else could organize like this."

Eva tried unsuccessfully to focus on the compliment and while blocking out its sting. "That's not quite right but I appreciate it. What's going on?"

Julia nodded, which puzzled Eva. "I...love it...whatever's happening. Sure, the music is loud and there's more nudity than I planned on seeing, but we're finally getting the word out!" Julia pulled from her bag a stack of leaflets. "I made these pamphlets six months ago and no more than two people picked them up at fairs. Tonight I've given out, like, forty!"

Eva wanted to believe Julia but something was holding her back: the boy in the Native American headdress. The Lockwood she saw was not bright enough to orchestrate this. "Are— are you sure this is all real?"

Julia smiled to assuage her friend's worries. "I'm not going to lie: some people are here for the party. But when they come over to ask what we stand for— oh I wish you could see their faces! It's..." as she located the words, her voice took on an undeniably appreciative tone. "It's what it feels like to not be ignored."

With Julia's heartfelt explanation, for one instant, every regret Eva had regarding the fiasco disappeared. Before she could ask her next question, Julia's eyes lit up.

"Oh my God you just reminded me I'm up next at that super cute guy's beer pong table at Glazier!" Julia turned to start to trot away. "Talk soon! Beer Decathlon is calling!"

"Uh...thanks?" Eva replied to the back of Julia's head.

Eva sought to head home to collate the data that was piling up, but her journey would not last long. After standing and changing course, she nearly walked into a boy who had been standing far closer than anyone would have considered polite.

"You want to know what's really happening here?" he asked indignantly. "Who the real evicted Indian is?"

Eva considered not answering, but thanks to how regrettably close the "off" looking boy placed himself, she could hardly ignore him. "You don't look Native American to me."

"That's not the point!" Squanto whined. He pointed towards the top floor of August Hall. "Those jackasses stole my ideas, kicked me out of my dorm, and now they won't listen to anything I have to say!"

For some reason, perhaps stress, or maybe a typically buried trait she shared with Kathie, Eva pondered the boy's words. Might he have scandalous tips to offer? Did she have an "in" with this scene? "So this protest was your idea?"

"Hell no! Indians got what they deserved. There's only two kinds of Indians: ones who want to steal your car, and ones who haven't seen your car yet." He laughed heartily, oblivious to the disgust blanketing Eva's face. "I'm saying they should have to let me back in!"

Eva proceeded with hope of learning if the callow stranger was in league with Lockwood or against him. "So you want to be in there to support Lockwood's protest?"

"Fuck no!" he furiously replied. "I want to be in there because chicks' faces are getting juiced!" He followed his statement with rowdy laughter, implying he felt there was nothing wrong with sharing such disturbing sexual goals with a complete stranger in a crowded square.

Eva's hands shot up to shield herself from any follow-up that remained. "Stop. Now."

"You think I'm sick? I'll tell you sick. You want to know about Lockwood really wa—"

"Not! Another! Word!" Eva declared.

Just then, from above, both heard a female with a Southern twang call out: "Squanto, why don't you leave that poor girl alone and let her have a good time like the rest of us?"

Eva and Squanto looked up to a second floor window which

Carolina was using to take in the NEQ. Squanto asked, "How could you be having a good time in there while I'm all the way out here?"

Carolina smiled. "It's the happiest and safest I've felt since moving in. Now scram!"

Squanto crudely displayed to Carolina his middle finger (while trying to steal a look at her breasts), shot in Eva's direction one last glare, and scampered off.

"Thanks," Eva said to Carolina.

"My pleasure! I'd rather see the protests over him, too!"

Eva's interest was piqued as the words came from one who didn't strike her as a person likely to care about protests. "Which protests do you mean? It's kind of hard to tell which parts are just parties from the look of it."

"I'm from the South. I know what a tailgate looks like. I also know what very angry protesting looks like and I prefer to see the kind that's happening around here!"

Interesting, Eva thought. *Was Lockwood's "protest" actually inspiring students...or am I just projecting?* "Why aren't you enjoying the party inside? Why stare out here?"

"Inside is great, but I want to see what it looks like when people start caring a little more."

Deciding to be more forthcoming with the girl who was so open with her, Eva replied: "That's what I really came here to see but I just haven't seen it yet. I mean, look around."

Eva turned her head towards the quad's frat houses and Carolina followed her gaze. The pair promptly got a clear look at a group cheering on two boys in swim trunks leaping into a broken hot tub full of icy water. Eva glanced back at August Hall where a student was vomiting out of a third floor window onto a 2004 tsunami memorial.

The two young ladies made eye contact again as Eva grimaced. Carolina offered a welcoming grin and nodded. She then pointed towards Glazier Hall. Eva turned, and after first only seeing Julia cavorting, on closer inspection she could tell the six students surrounding Julia were each intently looking at her pamphlets. All six seemed impressed and keen on listening.

*   *   *

As she made her way away from the NEQ, Eva was as torn between desires as she'd ever been. Something in Lockwood's plan was working, which was great. What was awful was how she hadn't been a part of the planning, execution, or promotion. In fact, her only links to it came when she distanced herself from Lockwood earlier that day.

Her moment had finally arrived, but due to the PPC, Lockwood, Kathie, or some other horrible factor, she found herself voiceless among those who possessed real power.

She laughed as she strolled with a stress-laden conscience through the quieter parts of campus and wondered again whether Lockwood was a nemesis, a pest, or an ally.

Knowing Lockwood would ultimately get credit for any breakthroughs, could Eva tolerate helping from the background after having led the battle since her first day at Pemberton? On the other hand, could she really prevent a brighter future for PMU's students just because she didn't like supporting a spoiled, drunk frat boy?

*   *   *

Around that hour, Kathie was drifting through Liberty Hall, enjoying her victory lap.

What started as a bland but annoying day had turned into a glorious one where she took her nemesis' failing sophomoric prank that would have fizzled in hours and turned into the gem that would lead to his expulsion. To prolong the crisis, she distracted Asbury and got Eva out of her way, too. Soon the administrators, who she felt lived without convictions beyond self-preservation, would act against her enemy, and she could experience the immeasurable joy knowing that she orchestrated Lockwood's utterly disgraceful exit from PMU.

While roving, she felt the urge to call someone to boast. This perhaps too typical feeling was followed by the equally common, repressed sorrow of realizing she had no one to call.

She looked at her phone anyway out of habit and she was happy to see an unanticipated image: a voicemail was waiting for her!

Her excitement dissolved speedily as an ill-mannered male delivered his message. "I hope you check your fucking phone more than your email! I've been writing for hours because I have info you need about Auggie Hall, beyotch! Check your fucking email and call me back!"

She ended the call without deleting the message. The unquiet fear about what awaited her pushed aside her annoyance at the boy's disrespectful language. She made quick work booting up her laptop before trying feverishly to connect with the building's new wireless Internet network. She could feel her pulse intensify as the seconds of unknowing ticked on.

Her pumping adrenaline nearly prevented her fingers from typing in her password. She went into her "junk mail" folder and scanned for messages that stood out.

Her mouse stabbed at an email labeled LOCKWOOD A FAKE-- URGENT and she froze as the document popped up. Her mouth and throat dried instantly. Her skin burned. Her fingers locked as her eyes jumped over blocks of text. Passages like "entirely faking the protest" and "trying to get kicked out, probably because his grades suck" attracted her eyes readily.

Tediously channeling the muscle capacity to lift her left arm without flailing it, Kathie slowly achieved her goal of closing her laptop without launching it. Then, in the middle of an empty hallway, she appeared to figuratively short circuit every synapse in her body at once.

Chapter 21: Alternative Study Breaks

WHILE THE bacchanal that Eva, Squanto, and others witnessed in the NEQ thundered, August Hall itself continued to teem with activity, as well. The alcohol provided by Lockwood's treasure hunt did start many residents off in a somewhat stereotypical direction, but not everyone chose unbridled partying as their entertainment of choice while "in captivity." In honesty, the breadth of the students' undertakings that night was impressive, and in certain cases, also profound.

Yes, the parties, game nights, and movie marathons did endure, and some extracurricular tasks did stray closer to illegal (e.g. the set of sophomores who erected a casino in a fourth floor study lounge after gathering supplies from six dorm rooms). But for the most part, the students who pulled away from the larger gatherings opted to focus on hobbies for which they normally did not have time. In one example, five students, three of whom were multi-instrument Music majors, decided to start a band, a dream that most of them had carried for years. In honor of the lock in, their repertoire would highlight British protest punk music from the 1980s.

Shortly after the band formed, a set of students from the Engineering and Architecture Departments excitedly ended their board game contest for a challenge of their own making. After an extended discussion about the destructive force of Hurricane Katrina, which made landfall weeks prior, the students organized a design contest seeking the perfect weatherproof dormitory.

In another case, a set of film students banded together with one Economics major and two Chemistry students, to plan out a short film they would write, tape, and edit during the siege. The non-film majors were all intrigued by movies but they did not have the time in their class schedules to dabble in such projects. (In fact, the Econ student did try to follow this hobby once at Pemberton but was spurned when the film criticism class gave his transcript what he considered a harsh C minus, which was his only non A in college. He noted in his review of the class that the professor only showed up twice all semester.) Incidentally, if the project was seen through to completion and if they could find a professor to back it, the students could have submitted the film as an independent study for class credit.[18]

The most interesting component circling all of these activities ranging from partying and gambling to studying and creating art, I should note, is that none of the indoor activities (save a pair of them) had anything to do with protest. Lockwood had certainly nabbed the attention of many students, but his creation was far from an expulsion-worthy protest.

Just shortly after Eva Yesterday departed the NEQ, only Edie, Alf, and William, who was punching away at Lockwood's declaration, were focused on the protest. That number, thanks to Carolina's efforts, was about to dwindle.

Fresh off of a revitalizing observation session near the Quad, she was ready to have fun and she knew exactly which acquaintance of hers needed the same thing.

*   *   *

---

[18] As for another example of students pursuing for credit work, about a dozen students in August Hall were still studying independently amid the madness. Many didn't realize the revelry around them, which was significantly louder than usual, was tied to something grander than an average weeknight party.

William was back in his associate Ralph's dorm room, alone, and using Ralph's laptop to piece together Lockwood's mission statement. At his feet was his open backpack, where his recently used toothbrush and a set of 3.5 inch floppy disks in a water proof container stared back at him. Resting next to the laptop were two sheets of handwritten notes and two of the case's disks, which were labeled Spring Semester 2005 A and B. Words flew out as uproarious sounds from the outside world occasionally crept into the room. Each set of noises started sounding more intriguing than the last, and soon William's mind wandered. *Wait*, he thought, *how did his speech about me breaking out of my shell just end up with me doing even more school work?*

The door creaked opened and William didn't stop when he saw a visitor out of his peripheral vision, having assumed it was Lockwood or perhaps Edie. When Carolina offered a chipper "hey there, William!" he turned and stopped his work immediately. He then thought: *getting interrupted by a beautiful woman while doing schoolwork is at least a step forward.*

Carolina advanced, prompting William to put his notes and disks away in a hurried fashion. "Whatchya working on?" she asked playfully.

William's attempt to be sly faltered almost instantly. "Uh you know, just some stuff. Stuff for Chip. I'm helping him...edit something."

Instead of pulling up Ralph's roommate's desk chair or sitting on Ralph's bed, Carolina lifted herself up onto Ralph's desk in the space previously occupied by William's papers. She then gave an exhausting sigh. "I hope this doesn't sound rude. But why aren't you having fun?"

"I will soon. For now I've got some very important work...you know, for the cause," William stated, assuming playing up his proximity to Lockwood could only help him. Suddenly, a terror-filled hiccup stopped him. *She totally knows Chip's full of shit and faking this thing, right?* As the mental debate played out, he hoped that his face didn't suggest to Carolina he was not interested in her. "This is how he's going to get the word out. Everything could depend it."

Carolina's beliefs in Lockwood aside, she was not letting

homework win William's attention over her. "That's nice, but I meant why don't you *ever* have fun? I never see you at bars or the union or football games. Now with all this is going on, you just happened to be in the building because you were finally visiting me...and now you're in here editing a paper?"

William began to worry Carolina's frankness would open up a wound that would force him to revert into his hole. "I'm working on that but it's not my time to have fun yet."

"Why not?" she pressed. "Everyone else is having fun, why can't we?"

Entirely missing the final word of the question, William stated: "They're having fun because they don't have to worry about getting expelled if this goes bad. Or arrested. Or worse!"

Carolina pondered how to help. "If you have that much more to worry about, then you should be extra entitled to a good time, right?"

William considered the question briefly before realizing she was right. *The week has to have more in store for me than thoughts of expulsion and hearing other people have sex to crappy R&B music.* "You're right," he solemnly stated. To prove to himself that he was ready to push out of the library's quiet zone, he followed up with: "You wanted to know why you never see me?" Carolina nodded. "I haven't told anyone this, not even my best friend back home. I've stayed in all but one Saturday night since I got to Pemberton. I spend Fridays and Saturdays in the library until four. Then I go to my dorm where I eat food I snuck up from the dining hall and I watch movies until I can fall asleep to the breaks in the hollering from out in the streets." Carolina's empathetic expression made William want to end on a brighter note. "But thanks to some big loud idiot with a giant, very offensive hat, all of that is coming to an end this week."

Carolina smiled and playfully smacked his leg. "That's what I want to hear! And yeah, it is offensive. Let's go hide that hat."

"Agreed," a grinning, refreshed William replied. "Just give me fifteen minutes to put the final touches on this and then I'm all yours."

*   *   *

Meanwhile, Alf and Edie were chatting over two bourbon-based concoctions from Alf's private collection. Their conversation switched between progress updates whenever new information came in (due to the late hour, bulletins were sparse) and reflections on the day's absurd events. Their latest topic focused on how the campus might remember Lockwood's stunt.

Alf offered: "My seventh grade history teacher told us that back in the Depression they named crappy stuff after Hoover because he messed up so bad, like Hoover flags for an empty pocket. Maybe Pemberton will one day have Lockwood flags or dollars or something."

"What would a Lockwood flag be?"

Alf shrugged. "An empty condom wrapper?"

Edie grinned and took a sip of the drink, which even after letting the ice in it melt for fifteen minutes, was still stronger than expected. Facetiously, she proceeded. "One day they'll call him the biggest hero the school ever had. He brought equality back by taking students of all races, genders, and sexual orientations and locking them up in the same building."

"He gave the students a voice *and* a beer and fearlessly challenged tyrannical administrators. Then one day they'll say he did it with one hand tied behind his back."

"And we'll both know that the hand probably belonged to a perky half naked brunette doing some kinky shit with him."

A portion of the crowd outside roared in reaction to an intense drinking game. The pair inside, knowing they helped arrange the mess, couldn't help but take some joy away.

Alf raised his drink. "The biggest Pemberton tailgate and protest to ever hit the NEQ."

"The first Pemberton tailgate to ever single out a full ethnic group."

Not wanting their naming session to cease, Alf offered an idea he'd been sitting on for a few hours: "To the Pemberton Tea and A party."

Edie nodded and happily accepted the challenge. "The...Trail of Truancy."

"I believe what you were looking for was the Trail of Beers."

"Well played," Edie replied before dreaming up what would become my personal favorite name for the day's events: "The Faux Zulu Uprising of the Northeast Quad."

Alf tapped his drink's vessel against Edie's just before watching her reaction change from jovial to concerned. "What's wrong?"

"How is he going to get booted for protest if this never looks like anything but a party?"

Alf nodded at the valid question. He then mentally sidelined his question about whether the team should have thought of the answer long before getting in as deep as they did. "Isn't Chip putting together that declaration?"

"Chip's not, William is. Do you think that'll help? What happens when it's out? How do we get the people who believe in it?"

"I don't know how to do that. Does anyone?"

Edie gave a somewhat defeatist chuckle in response. "The Pemberton Eight did."

With this, Edie found the lightning bolt for which she'd been craning. Setting down her drink and leaping up, she put her hands on the back of Alf's chair and rolled him to his desk.

"Look up our student group directory," she commanded. "The Pemberton Eight didn't win because they pissed off the school. William said they got spared because they were campus leaders who were connected to a ton of the student body. We need to find out who's in charge of the best and loudest student groups and make them fall in love with our little douche bag."

With the computer screen showing a long list of student groups, Alf opened up a search field, and turned to Edie. "Who should we look for first?"

"Activism groups. They'll wet their pants when they find out they can get in on this."

Alf typed in Edie's search terms and three groups came back, each of which listed Eva as their main contact.

This result displeased Edie. She knew little about Eva but she distrusted her anyway. "Nope. Try environmental groups."

After Alf executed the command, two results came up, one with a faculty advisor listed, and the other with Eva Yesterday shown as the group's lead.

"Damn it," Edie spat. "Does she go to class less often than Chip?"

"Since I have no clue who she is, do you mind if I ask what's wrong with her?"

Edie produced her phone to type a text to some friends inquiring if they knew anything useful about Eva. "There's something weird going on with her. Also I can't tell if she'll be able to sniff through Chip's bull shit."

As Edie sent out her exploratory text message, Alf signed into the university-run online student directory. "Since that doesn't sound super solid, let's not write her off yet. Let's see what she looks like. Maybe we've run into her and we don't know it." Alf typed in Eva's nickname and her self-tailored profile page materialized. The page displayed only one profile picture, which was of a bulky and sweating male aid worker cleaning oil off of a smug looking seal. Alf replied with: "Hot!"

A less than entertained Edie headed to the door. "Let's see what Chip thinks about her and just maybe we won't need that husky Inuit after all."

Chapter 22: A Baited Trap

AROUND 11:00 P.M., in the midst of a rare quiet moment, Chip spent fourteen minutes surveying the spectacles around the Quad, wholly impressed by his classmates' passion. Though the acts that pushed the event into motion were carried out with goals far from noble, to him, the resulting momentum spewing forth was a thing of wonder.

This brings me to one of my greatest challenges of writing this document. Despite having access to data gleaned from hundreds of sources and my own knowledge of campus and its inhabitants, the question of how to portray this young boy was long a confounding one. On one hand, his desires to protect the Lockwood line at all costs (despite the cost of actually studying) could paint him as a tragic hero. Alternatively, his years of mocking of the educational system, a practice which led to his ill-conceived move to hold hundreds of students against their will, make it very easy to describe him as a careless villain.

What complicated his character even more was this one moment, which he counted among his happiest at Pemberton. This assessment befuddled me for several reasons.

For one, he was nowhere near achieving his goals. He still needed to involve many more students and do so on a much more intense level. Many present were convinced they were at a party. Others had already left disappointed upon thinking they were beckoned to a tailgate for Saturday's football game versus Southwest A&M State, not the start of a revolution. Additionally, one of his strongest allies that day was his sworn enemy, who at that approximate time, was painfully evolving from ignorance to enlightenment, and brewing an assortment of evil for him.

His problems were not only external to August Hall. The residents were happy, but as Edie warned him twice before, if officials took away just precious one utility before Chip had enough of a foothold to assure expulsion, they would most definitely be in trouble. If they didn't forcibly cut off the water or electricity, the food in the stronghold still would run dry before long.

So from a strategic perspective, or really any viewpoint, this was not the best time in Chip's week. He saw things differently.

Initially I thought he was merely incompetent regarding the impossibility of his situation. Then I recognized that this was the first and perhaps only moment where he grasped that he could really help the student body.

Pemberton had never been a chore to Chip, but in reflecting on the evening, he surmised the school perhaps never carried the honor it should have while he lived there. That night showed him a different type of ardor for Pemberton. While engulfed by support and basking under calm October skies in one of the nation's greatest campuses, for that instant he almost didn't care if he reached his goals. The classmates with resolve in their eyes and desires to improve Pemberton were the ones whose success really mattered.

His journey was far from over, but with a lively hum of school spirit in his bones and a patriotic intensity emanating from over five hundred of his fellow classmates, he felt proud of what he'd built. Then, after another thirty seconds of thinking, he recalled that his *personal* success really did matter; the victory of many could not be counted as a win for Chip Lockwood. It was a time, he deemed, to continue doing whatever he could, regardless of the cost, to let the passionate students around the Quad push him towards an early winter break in Fort Lauderdale. (Even after his "studying" earlier or his moment of awakening, he's still not quite a folk hero just yet.) The Quad was packed with PMU-focused crusades awakened by his actions and with more people present there was no telling how much change for Pemberton he could help inspire, namely the change that would lead to the permanent alteration of his student status.

In spite of his burgeoning good will and fresh victory in front of his gregarious classmates, he remained a young man in need of brighter circumstances. While his brief flirtation with altruism would not entirely fade from memory, he was still far from realizing that he didn't simply want more student support, he needed it for survival. How would he get it though?

For that answer, he realized, it was time to consult his favorite residents in the building. Before he could call Edie or the others, he saw a text message from Alf already awaiting him. *Check your email*, it instructed.

In his inbox he found a list of articles and facts on someone named Eva Yesterday, who Alf thought might become useful. The points summarized her work focused on promoting human rights and improving on-campus conditions for students. He then reviewed some of her treatises and noted that she bewilderingly never used capital letters. It was the articles from the *Pembertonian* that led him to confirm Alf's believe that she would indeed come in handy at some point. One recent example stuck out as specifically intriguing.

Over the summer she managed to rally the tiniest amount of interest in the shuttering of the NEQ's KRC dormitory, which Residential Affairs closed for eighteen months of repair work. She posited that the school really moved to close the building to drive up demand and prices for on-campus housing. An apathetic populace and proof that the building was truly in disrepair helped cull the spat before it grew. Alf's research showed that another group quietly protesting the closing of half of the campus' eateries was making a similar claim, but as they appeared to have disparate goals at surface level, Eva was unaware that the connection existed.[19]

With more reading, Lockwood guessed she actually could have cobbled together a fairly potent campus protest herself if she had focused her efforts more. She had passion for her mini crusades, links with various campus groups, and access to information on virtually every alleged and real misdeed undertaken by the university.

But would she have the desire to join Chip before he'd made any really solid progress?

For that answer, another council meeting would be necessary.

*   *   *

After blowing out of his room with an enthusiastic glow to see the revelry abounding, he located Edie within two minutes. Chip was somewhat surprised to see Edie and Alf chatting amiably. He was more shocked to see William and Carolina playfully flirting. The two pairs converged and during a very short discussion, which Chip could not hear, a single piece of paper of William's was snatched up by Edie, then William, then Edie again, and finally Alf, who began to scan it. Carolina began to pull William away, and as he was happy to oblige, his conversation with Edie promptly became an argument. The two bickered and as Chip approached he couldn't help but think that thanks to his involvement, Edie was warming to William. He arrived to stand next to Edie as Carolina succeeded in pulling a beaming William away.

"Nice!" Chip exclaimed. "I might be rubbing off on that guy after all."

Edie, aghast, studied his face for sincerity. "You see nothing wrong with this?"

"Why would I? Is someone getting jealous?"

Edie's stern brow did not disappear. "Jealous? No, I'm shocked that you're letting him get carted away without letting him know

---

[19] By the time Chip read Eva's theory, the KRC renovation project was entering its fifth month and no work had been done besides encircling the dorm with a fence.

she's totally got VD."

Chip considered the statement for a moment, scratched his head, and offered his sparse reply: "Hmmm…How about that?"

Turning swiftly back to the task at hand, Edie led them into Alf's room while Alf suggested that they read William's declaration before sending it out with Chip's name on it. The two read through it at the same time.

The declaration was well written and craftily worded. The note (which, at the strictest request of the university, will not be recited in full) began with Chip outlining his request for greater student rights. It then covered three despicable and very well researched trends: alleged lies told in admissions statistics, PMU's failure to address a crumbling infrastructure, and injustices in the financial aid system. The miniature treatise declared the ideals on which the university was founded had "been shat on for too long." Due to this, Chip was making it his solemn duty to trim the garden of inequity and greed surrounding Pemberton.

"It works," Chip stated. "It has the right amount of passion to get people moving."

The slightly more skeptical Edie replied: "Is this really something that will get people to jump out of their beds to protest? Don't forget: our classmates are programmed to be quiet. It's going to take a major leap to get the numbers you need."

Alf offered: "I say we try to pull in Eva Yesterday. The Pemberton Eight got theirs because they involved the right campus leaders."

"I say we don't call her," Edie counteroffered. "If she was really that great, she would have done all this herself."

"We definitely need her…" Chip stated through a widening grin, "but I have a feeling if we straight up ask her for help, she's not going to want to. But if we get all those hyped up and boozed up people outside to send us their opinions and make it seem like their voices really matter, then maybe that could be the bait."

Edie began to nod. "Figure out which overachievers want a piece of that action without the work and make them come to you."

"Exactly! It's the bait-and-Chip."

"Oh how proud the Lockwoods should be of their little master baiter."

"One little problem, though," Chip admitted. "I have no clue how to get people to send in everything they think is wrong with this place."

"I think I have an idea," Alf offered, thankful that he could once again simultaneously help their collective cause and impress his own Professor Russell, as well. While internally determining the best way to document this work in his independent project, he explained his plan rapidly. "We need a spot where everyone can to submit suggestions, complaints, etc. and where everyone else can see the other ideas. Online is the easiest and strongest option, as long as it's not a page that the university can control. I'm whipping up an Internet forum now and it should be up pretty fast."

"Nice!" an impressed Chip stated.

"Next question: how do you get everyone to the forum?"

In an attempt to piggyback off of Alf's quick work, Chip shot out the first idea that came to mind. "Well, we gotta get the declaration out, too. What if we email the declaration to everyone on campus and throw in a link to the forum. Alf, do you have a way to get every student's email address?"

Alf did have a way and he knew it. The easiest solution was to use the information he had at his disposal thanks to his part time job with the university. He held his answer, though, while he tried to determine what his professor would think about him breaking his employer's trust to expose personal information. Feeling this would be detrimental to his grade, job, and relationship with the professor, Alf began calculating ways to pull in student email addresses using legal means. "I can handle that. But two problems. One is it's really risky relying on university email to get your message out."

"But I need the school to know it was me who sent the emails."

"Okay we can send it from your account but we'll CC a personal email account in case people want to reach you. Problem two: if the school shuts down email access, you're screwed."

"The school could do that?" Chip queried, almost in shock.

Alf nodded. "Damn right."

Edie, who'd been mentally running at full speed to try to get looped back into the conversation, jumped in with a sure-fire suggestion: "The *Nightly*."

"Yeah, if we could get them that would be great," Alf balked, "but they're probably not going to cover this until the morning."

"I don't mean the articles themselves," Edie replied, thinking back to when she was reading up on Eva and the newspaper's website gave her the chance to write a scathing and inappropriate comment about the article's subject. "Each of their stories has this stupid 'add your comments' section. If we put the link in every article's comments page, the school would have to do a lot to hide every copy and every link. Plus the school definitely won't have the balls to shut down university email *and* the student newspaper."

Chip, smiling at the idea, turned to Alf with an expression that asked "that's a home run, right?" Alf nodded at the wordless question and continued his work.

"That's what I'm talking about!" Chip shouted with his arms raised in the air. "I'd say it sounds like it's time for a nice box champagne break for all of us."

Having felt they'd accomplished their latest challenge, the three set aside their work for a walk to Chip's room. This led them to start a human anatomy themed trivia challenge in a study lounge (grand prize: a bottle's worth of high end vodka poured into a mint flavored condom.) This episode ultimately brought on the idea to lurk outside of Carolina's room to have an impromptu dance party to the soundtrack of Carolina's "sex mix" (Chip's words). That scene then led to Alf finally getting to work.

And so, with a still fuming Kathie pacing about Liberty Hall, Chip had the rebuttal he didn't know he so desperately needed. Whether it would counter Kieft's inevitable upcoming attack, however, was yet to be seen.

Chapter 23: Digital Arms

WITH HUNDREDS enjoying themselves and scores who were already put off by the lack of a "true protest" at August, it should not be assumed that the campus was full of students who were friendly with, apathetic about, or ignorant of Lockwood's quest. What's more, the man at the helm of the August Hall lockdown was also certainly gaining enemies. The enraged junior Business Institutions major known as "Soup" (originally "Super Nate") was one of those foes.

Throughout his upbringing near Minneapolis, the student, whose real name was Louis Cassidy, had always had a condescending streak and penchant for bragging. His nickname was bestowed on him during his freshman year of high school at a track and field meet where he'd spent fifteen minutes lecturing his coach about how a classmate's running style was costing them victories. As the student thought the common runner's affliction "supinating" was called "Super Nate-ing" after an Olympic runner his grammar school coach once told him about (the coach fabricated the tale as he wasn't very fond of Soup), he looked like a fool throughout the diatribe. As the scene led the high school coach to such bountiful bursts of laughter, a nickname was immediately bestowed and it stuck. In the runner's junior year the coach retired, and he successfully shortened his alias to "Soup" and generated a phony origin story for it.

As a teenager, Soup developed a caustic habit he would keep for life: he odiously hated the smell, sight, and act of underage drinking. Starting in high school and continuing in college, his number three focus after schoolwork and running track was battling the amber liquid-powered delinquency of his classmates. He patiently earned the right to drink legally and he was entitled to enjoy himself without the annoyance of loud, green, underage drinkers.

Expectedly, what he saw around the NEQ that night was relentlessly nefarious.

He was surrounded by hundreds of young students openly treating a Wednesday night on their college campus like a Friday evening in an old Western saloon. There were unhidden drinking games, freshmen tossing empty beer cans onto the lawn of the KRC, and athletes wiping suds from their faces with the sleeves of PMU athletic hooded sweatshirts.

He saw nothing that came close an expression of First Amendment rights or upstanding behavior and he shuddered thinking of the conditions in which the students held in AP Hall were toiling. (Those inside had actually been relishing their place as campus celebrities.)

After taking in the scene for five minutes, Soup aggressively broke free from the madness and found the quietest space he could: up against the chain link fence engulfing the KRC.

Gripping the latticed wire with both hands he let his fretful head hang down. Everything around him was an abomination. Lockwood's reign of terror and the university's complacency were perfect examples of Pemberton's infuriating tradition of honoring the modern aristocracy. Soup believed college should be about classrooms whose desks could feel the hardback binding of books, not parties and the veneration of legacy students.

Looking at the abandoned dorm, he thought back to his earliest memories of Pemberton, and realized that if not for the pervasive presence of alcohol, he actually might have joined the front lines of the protest, too.

Thanks to his speed on the track and high academic marks in high school, Soup assumed he would get a full ride at the college of his choice. He was happy with his PMU acceptance yet disheartened by seeing that he'd only received a vaguely worded eighty percent "educational" scholarship. After a high school counselor informed him that Pemberton occasionally provided local baseball players with full ride scholarships, he accepted the offer immediately. Soup despised baseball players, but he liked the sound of being pampered by a school like Pemberton.

Shortly after accepting the offer, he learned his scholarship only covered eighty percent of tuition and it did not touch any of the other costs he'd meant to ask about. This news took some of the pep from his stride, and the student loan application process stole more enthusiasm. His Pemberton prep packet outlined that as part of the underwriting of his track scholarship, he had to choose one of the university's two preferred lenders, both whose loans carried a slightly higher interest rate than he was hoping. He chose the larger bank and cast the process into the recesses of his mind as a single necessary evil in exchange for a lifetime of opportunity.

Before moving to campus, he grew to trust the university's priorities less upon hearing that the catcher on his high school baseball team received an actual full scholarship from Pemberton. Soup had long known that most scholarship dollars for males went to football, basketball, and baseball programs. He never appreciated that fact less than when wondering why PMU had less appreciation for his own talents and more for the catcher, who celebrated their high school graduation by goading police into pulling him over while driving recklessly with a significant amount of marijuana in his vehicle.

Scarred but committed to the choice he made to be true to Pemberton, Soup cast aside all thoughts of the catcher, or whether he should have read his offer more closely. After inquiring about which dormitory usually housed the freshman on the baseball team, he decided his residence would be as far away from the behemoth known as "August Hall" as possible, and he pushed to make the best of his college experience.[20]

---

[20] Thanks to Kathie's diligent research, the university found out

After setting aside his memories and the hurt feelings surrounding his scholarship offer, Soup pushed himself away from the
ghost dorm to glare at the heart of the hive: August Hall. This was not
the pursuit of liberty. It was a travesty. *We all have issues here*, he told
himself, *that doesn't give us the right to wreck the place.*

He then turned to the building that was selfishly commanding
the campus' attention and wondered where Chip Lockwood was at
that exact moment. Where was the man who for some reason thought
there was a connection between binge drinking and protest and who
thought it would be honorable to so brutishly exploit that link?

*   *   *

At that precise moment, Chip was sitting in as a volunteer DJ
for a hallway party helming an intense set of songs. With the online
forum set up and email to the student body ready to go thanks to Alf
and Edie, respectively, the three opted to have some fun before revealing the next, undoubtedly loudest step in their plan. Secretly,
Chip was hoping to use the interlude to calm his nerves before taking
the stage. To do so, Chip blasted at full volume a popular hip hop
song and those around him went wild. As the tune continued, each
guest took turns supplying the lyrics to a verse. As Alf (who was
astonishingly adept at reciting the lyrics) took everyone through the
song's bridge and back into the chorus, Chip strutted towards his
audience.

*   *   *

Soup's eyes followed the arched necks and mesmerized "oohs"
and "ahhs" up to the central window of August Hall's fourth floor,
where he saw the man he'd hurriedly learned to hate. His upper body
poked out of the window as he posed arrogantly with a grin plastered
onto his overly large head. His right hand held a plastic cup as his left
waved. The crowd cheered and quieted as a number of radio speakers
dimmed to make way for the reckless Chip Lockwood.

"Hello beautiful Pemberton students!" he bellowed with an out-

---

about the catcher's unreported incident and placed him on probation
for his first year at the university.

stretched arm and cup. Many replied with nearly unbridled screaming. "Thank you for caring so much about our quest!" He raised his
cup and styled his face into a gleeful look. "To liberty for all at Pemberton!"

Nearly every student in the Quad raised their cups in response
and toasted.

"We are here as the voice of not only the Native Americans who
were silenced, but also the students who have been locked for years
in this steel and concrete beast. This should be a home, a place to
thrive!" Amid another round of cheers, Chip did his best to look as if
he were addressing each student one by one. "It's time to see what
you want here, not what the school wants! Shout ideas to me! What
do you want to see change at this place?"

A student confidently yelled, "I want professors who care
enough to know who I am!"

Chip nodded. "That's reasonable! Does that sound like a basic
student right to you?"

"Yeah!" countless audience members shouted back in an off
kilter unison.

"What else do you guys want?" Chip asked.

Another student shouted, "Access to better on-campus medical
facilities!"

Heads bobbed up and down and Chip's followed. "Sounds like
something we should've had a long time ago! Anyone else? What do
you want to see at PMU?"

Having been too embarrassed to voice his sophomoric suggestion earlier, a cookie-cutter fraternity member shouted, "More hot
chicks!"

Chip replied by slamming his left hand on the window frame.
"Damn right! More Hispanic and Asian chicks! There's a group
around here rallying for minority admissions. Go talk to them and
show them some love." Some chuckled while others tried to decipher
if Chip misinterpreted the request. "We can get those things if— and
only if-— we start spreading this love across campus! While those
ancient, selfish suits who run this place are sleeping, we need to make

sure every student knows what they stand to gain or lose here!"

Soup lofted his voice to shout in return, "But how do we do that without getting in trouble? You're safe because of your family. But if we speak up, the school fucks us!"

"Believe me, I know it's hard," Chip replied with only the slightest amount of proof that he was ignoring the man who pitched the question. "If you're afraid, I have a way to make sure the university can't blame you!"

Soup grew furious for unwittingly setting up Chip's next great scheme.

With conviction, Chip continued: "Each of you now has an email from me in your inboxes. That email has an explanation of why I'm doing what I'm doing. You'll also find in that email a link to an online forum where I want each of you to write about the issues you have with this university." Chip let the nodding heads reassure him he was on the right track. "Maybe there's a promise this place failed to deliver on. Maybe there's something it should be doing that it's not. Maybe you want to tell the admins what you think of their rules. Whatever it is, you can share it with us. Be anonymous if you wish, but know that your voice will be heard tonight."

Chip wasn't entirely certain, but it appeared this latest speech might have been exactly on target. Before sending them off, the orator then remembered one of the most important pieces: ensuring they would come back afterwards. "So I ask you to stop what you're doing just for a few short minutes to go to a computer, read the email, and post what you like. Then, share it with your friends and come right back here to keep this going!"

A raucous roar of joy enveloped the Northeast Quad.

"Speak up and let tonight be the start of the best nights in PMU history!"

* * *

Soup was catastrophically sickened by being so close to anyone who would cheer such a madman. His fingers tensed up from adrenaline, his legs yearned for a release, and from the feel of the blood pulsing around his eyes, he assumed he would soon develop boils on forehead. To prevent further internal damage, he pivoted away from the Quad.

Thanks to "the cushion of incompetence cradling the treasonous" students around him (his words), he felt the world had been tilted askew. As he departed, he cursed aloud and vowed that he would teach Chip Lockwood how terribly fearsome of an enemy he'd made that night.

Fortuitously for Soup's damaged spirit, an austere looking brunette donning a red baseball cap approached before he could move too far. Not only had she heard the upstanding question he asked Lockwood, but she loved how fervidly he posed it. She told him she had a proposition for him. She, too, knew Lockwood was poisoning students, and if the runner was willing to help bring down the maniac, she had the perfect job for him.

He accepted immediately.

*   *   *

Within minutes of Chip's departure, students hurriedly exited the Quad, eager to declare their freedom by posting their grievances online. Shortly after the mass departure, an amazing number of students took to the forum quite rapidly. The reasons they were doing so, however, were not all exactly in line with Chip's desires.

It was clear a number of students visited the webpage took his request to heart. Comments about unfair distributions of funding for certain departments, issues with the nutrition of the food available at campus dining halls, and others steadily trickled in despite the late hour.

Other students, almost instantly used the forum as a way to post practically anonymous party invites for their classmates. Their goal, while not specifically to undermine Chip's efforts, was to get information out about their own August-inspired gatherings without the university having a clear way to determine who exactly sent each invite.

While valued visitors plugged away on the forum at a steady pace throughout the late evening hours, those from the second group increased in size and ferocity in the hour after Chip spoke. Some who visited the site to promote a party did also throw in a comment or two about the state of the university, but often only as an afterthought.

As the majority of the PPC slept quietly with their laptops and phones tucked away for the night, thousands of student computers accessed countless notices about off-campus bashes and on-campus "protests."

The time of night did not protect the university much as countless students in residential halls woke their neighbors out of fear they would miss out on the "sanctioned" unruliness as the phenomenon was dubbed by a late night internal PPC memo.

Students swarmed four of the seven local grocery stores and all three nearby liquor stores. According to a health department investigation conducted days later, night managers of the larger stores instructed staff to closely examine identification for every alcohol purchase. Each store reported that even when underage patrons couldn't prove their age, the items they tried to buy rarely went back to the shelves as others in line were willing to purchase them.

(I must pause to note the beauty of this reaction, as if Chip had been a listener instead of the speaker, he would have been among the first to sully the forum with a non-protest post.)

A cacophony of disorder descended onto PMU's placid campus, all thanks to Chip's quest for liberty for a group of Native Americans who never stepped foot on New York soil and a ploy that was successfully building up his legitimacy.

By 1:00 a.m. every residence hall, four out of five fraternity houses, and approximately seventy off-campus apartments melded into the largest party to which Pemberton ever played host. In the midst of correctly singing every third line of lyrics from various eighties songs, students in every pocket of Pemberton sung the praises of Chip Lockwood using either their own vocal chords or the online tool the young firebrand gave them.

Chapter 24: The Southwest Quad's Sticky Handrails

UNBEKNOWNST TO Chip, Edie had grown wary of her position by Thursday's early, pitch dark hours. Despite their invigorating evening, her inclination wore out quickly and forced her to question whether her dedication would yield dividends.

She knew Chip was not careless about her contributions, but she couldn't help having these thoughts. Chip always handled his schemes' big brush strokes, leaving Edie to fill in the tinier gaps and ensure success. That week she'd spent hours doing just that. She'd had athletes clean and fill up storage bins with water in case the school turned it into a scarce commodity and she then stored a cache of emergency food in the basement. As of Wednesday morning, three of her sorority sisters were on call at all times with cars ready in case any August student needed medication picked up and snuck into the building. This served as added proof that Chip selected his lieutenants wisely: he knew Edie would battle against inactivity at the first sign of tedium.

Edie was great at her job. The problem, though, was whenever it looked like there were no more blemishes to fix, thoughts of her usefulness followed while she staved off her desire to lose interest entirely. By two thirty a.m. she'd logged forty five minutes of time scanning Chip's forum and confirming that his cause was gaining megabytes of support. The following day would surely have its trials, but it was beginning to look to Edie like her services would soon be irrelevant.

Reminding herself that she would have plenty of time in the following weeks to decide if Chip really needed her while he had mere hours left at the school, she shed her pessimism by writing two of her own Pemberton protest proclamations.

She warmed up with an unsigned post about not having adequate access to professors. (This was sadly based in truth. During the previous school year, professors in three of her ten classes failed to show up even once. While these instructors tended to their research, teaching assistants led some classes while students were directed to read specific passages in their assigned texts during other sessions.)

Her second anonymous post touched on the hot topic of student loans, something she never personally needed but she found fascinating when it came up classes.

The brief epistle was expertly written and cutting. Between ferocious statements, her email asked: "Would we really all get the chance to experience the greatest years of our lives if each day we spent here didn't generate more interest money for banks?" Edie dubiously dreamt that her note would spur vitriolic debates amongst its readers. To help those arguments along, her note concluded: "For so long college was reserved to let the rich relax and expand their minds. It will become that again. It would have already happened if college wasn't such a great way to whittle money from the middle class." With one click, the note streamed out to the world.

Feeling satisfied for helping while lessening her characteristic urges, Edie departed the room to seek out a lively section of the building. Her mood improved, especially after finding a handsome gymnast who happened to have the same phone charger she was desperately missing back in her sorority house. Regardless of her improved spirits, she couldn't entirely dispel the feeling that there was a variable she was missing after alcohol and other substances led her mind to think too casually. There was something about the popular forum phrases "power grab" and "student leaders" that made her feel less at ease.

At that moment, as it was nearly three, with her phone charging, and having a welcoming, very athletic companion for the night, she decided her duties for the day were officially fulfilled.[21] Whatever component they may have forgotten, Edie thought to herself, it certainly wasn't going to manifest itself overnight.

*　　　　*　　　　*

Meanwhile, across campus, a security guard making his rounds at the darkened student union discovered someone that evening had methodically glued quarters to every single vending machine's change receptacle.

The guard's call to the central office to report the incident was interrupted by another call noting that students had covered every handrail on the western half of campus with viscous substances (white handrails had mayonnaise, black had a thick layer of honey, and red rails were dotted with ketchup).

At the same time in Monterey House, which was the home of one of the few sororities avoiding the campus-wide gala, for the second time in as many years, the basement dining area began steadily filling up with water, debris, and globs of breakfast cereal.

---

[21] With her eye for trends, Edie believed that being able to date extremely fit men would not be an option well into her thirties or even her twenties. So despite not seeming like jocks, while at PMU, her occasional amorous advances were focused on the campus' supply of athletes.

Chapter 25: One Lonely Red Placard

BEFORE APPROACHING the start of the daylong PPC session to watch his cohorts worriedly avert their eyes, Provost Asbury resolved to make the NEQ his first stop on Thursday.

His primary goal was to see how devastating the evening's activities had been. Moreover, although he felt the chance that this was a real, action-oriented assembly was low, he intended on scanning for evidence that a figurehead (an entirely revamped Lockwood or someone else) had made an appearance. With a large crowd and a passionate current, any student with a platform, a voice, and magnetism would be considered very dangerous by Asbury's office. Having been on campus during the Pemberton Eight's infamous stunt in his Associate Professor years, he could still recall what the university heads should have looked out for.

Upon his arrival at the NEQ, the cranky administrator was met with little fanfare other than a quick hiding of beers by a few of students who were still out. About fifty students remained through the evening. Some had set up booths for their causes the night before. In large part remained as they felt if they left their spots they would never again get the chance to speak with the student body again on such a large scale. Other stragglers spent the early morning hours drinking what remained of their beer while waiting for the sun to rise. One final set of students was still frolicking to music quietly pumping from a radio in the center of their dance circle.

All Asbury saw was destruction and delinquency. The students who were still present should have been asleep or readying for class. The beautiful Quad, for which his office helped secure resurfacing funding only two years earlier, was paying the price for being the welcome mat for what he considered the university's biggest mistake in decades. To further complicate matters, amid the beer cans and other trash, several placards taped to chairs, tables, and buildings gave the haunting impression that this truly was a justified assembly.

Asbury wondered if the students who made those signs did so jokingly. If they did not, did those who pedaled their views alongside the signs realize their audience was there solely to litter the campus with mayhem? The amalgam of impertinence, waste, and activism gave Asbury a dreadful impression that this was what this generation considered venerable behavior. The thought was so aggravating that he nearly forgot how he helped allow the charade to take place.

He did not forget this connection for long.

He began roaming for a closer look. One of the first things of note he found was a defaced four foot tall miniature billboard that lived in a garden near the NEQ's gym. On most days the friendly, school color clad sign read "Welcome to the [REDACTED] Northeast Quad!" That morning, thanks to graffiti, it read "[REDACTED] likes it in the butt Northeast Quad!"

Asbury recalled how the sponsor had been the focus of great concern for the AD, and allegedly, the president, too. As he realized neither had reached out about the sign's defacing, or for that matter, the disturbance, he chastised himself for taking their advice at all.

He then made his way to the building at the beast's core: August Hall. From afar, it didn't look like much was different. Upon closer inspection, Asbury could spy through the curtains of one study lounge what appeared to be a dimly lit casino. Another set of windows showed rooms displaying a light show one might expect to see in a discothèque. Also, he could clearly see the building's uncomfortable murals he'd heard about had not been exaggerations.

The AP Hall sight that stuck out the most was a fourth floor dorm window that had a large steel keg jammed into its frame. Miraculously, this reportedly long empty keg was steadily dripping drops of beer. He looked away from the keg in disgust, and interestingly, his eyes landed on a poster with a message about PMU's habit of making deals which net no positive affects for students. Instead of drawing any comparisons between the students who created that poster and himself, he moved on to view other placards.

In an attempt to avoid speaking with students while in such an odious mood, Asbury strayed from the areas where student protestors were still present. Perhaps it would have been a good idea to ask them why they felt this was the right place to be with their message instead of official school hearings. But either his stubbornness or his theory that his current state couldn't lead to genial conversations led him to focus on the placards whose owners had already departed.

Most of the dozen or so posters had no surprises and they packed little punch, in his opinion. As he approached Colonial Hall, a set stopped him instantly. These posters seemed different, as if they were written by a hand borrowed from a different era. The trio was written with a rhyming pattern Asbury heard regularly during Vietnam protests. The first read "Tuition skyrockets huge amount. Do $tudent$ still count?" The second said: "Welcome all, here's your dorm. Rats & bugs are the norm." It was the third, a red poster, which caused the already irritated man to take pause: "Hey, hey, Asbury, I'm a student — can you hear me?"

Asbury broke away from the sign speedily, fearful that students might notice that he took offense to it. He would give no one any easy victories that day, even partially deserved ones.

As he walked back to his car, the message stayed with him, forcing to the surface a question he would ask again a number of times that week: *how could I let this go so far?*

I'm happy to say that Asbury really did pose himself this question and reflect upon it. I'm less ecstatic to admit that he did so while ignoring a few factors, namely that he never thought the student body was capable of collaboration on such a grand scale. There was also Lockwood, but prior to that week it would have been extremely difficult to believe that such an infamously uncouth boy would have united thousands in protest.

What Asbury did not ignore was the fact that he could have acted but he did not. He knew as a leader it was his responsibility to "weed out the bull shit and tackle the real problems" (his words). It was true the officials who approached him had valid points that in at least some way could have had the students' best interests in mind. But he was not supposed to do their jobs for them. He was supposed to consider the students first.

It was time to take charge. Chip Lockwood's plans, the university's contracts, and the opinionated Kieft spawn would matter naught to Asbury from this point on. Between the noise and vandalism complaints the university had to have received the night before, Asbury felt he would soon have more than he needed to take executive action.

His first task was to have University Police confiscate all alcohol in the Quad and have a cleaning crew sweep up the trash and unattended placards. The next step would be to start the latest PPC meeting and explain why they were not to trifle with Asbury any longer.

Chapter 26: Adelaide Lockwood's Graffiti-Covered Statue

DESPITE HIS louder instincts, Chip arose early, shortly after the alarm on his phone chimed 7:03 a.m. Aided by the chipper sun, he gathered his phone and shoes and daintily moseyed out of the dorm room in which he'd spent three hours sleeping. With his head start on the day he hoped to see that his grandstanding made enough of an impact to make the remaining 29 hours he possessed before zero hour less stressful.

First he snuck into his room to check on the progress of the forum. After a few seconds of scrolling, he saw it was pulling in responses but not all of them focused on topics that pleased him. This prompted him to wonder what kind of gall it would take to unabashedly ignore instructions he doled out so selflessly. Before he could brainstorm any revenge for those who seemed to be out to ruin his plans, he recalled some of the dozens of times he'd likely done similar things to others' plans and the anger simmered down. With at least one lesson learnt on the day, he withdrew from his room bound for Alf's residence.

He was surprised to discover Edie there, already awake and researching his reach on campus. After asking about her progress, they opted to split the remaining tasks: Edie would continue looking through the *Nightly*, Chip would scan students' profile pages in the PMU student directory and his own email account, and Alf would finish his thorough sweep of the forum.

Accompanying their research were telltale signs of a gathering emanating from outside. The Quad was dotted with clumps of undergrads, some of whom had hand sheets and a cause, and others who circled around coolers and card tables adorned with snacks and drinks. A maintenance crew had removed all unattended placards and was slowly tending to some of the Quad's trash. Chip, who remained hidden from their view, welcomed the sight and sounds until he realized the rate of bottles opening was growing at a stronger pace than the protest cries.

The team shared their findings, first with Chip noting that he found very little on the school's social media site. A select number of pages mentioned him in some way, but none referenced his crusade or any of his exact words.

His personal email account fared much better. He had over fifty emails from students who believed in his cause. Eva herself, regrettably, was not among them, forcing Chip to ponder where this pivotal assistant was spending her time and energy if not with him.

(At that exact moment, Eva was battling Chip-inspired insomnia. As she explained to a friend later that day, she wanted to consider him as merely a loud voice broadcasting party directions to a populace willing to relinquish anything for fun. But if he didn't really need her concern, why was she fretting over what would happen to those hapless students if he was revealed as a fraud later? Also, if he wasn't a real force for good, why was Kathie texting her things like *"Admin says they'll shut down ALL protest groups if Chip isn't exposed as fraud"*? Finally: if Chip really wasn't worth her time, why couldn't she sleep through the night?)

Edie followed by confirming the party was astoundingly grand without a doubt but it was both his biggest victory and his most demanding obstacle to overcome.[22] This was exemplified on the website of the *Nightly Pembertonian*, which featured a post about the NEQ. The developing article had few details with the exception that someone spammed the newspaper's message boards the night before. Importantly, the article mentioned Chip, but its author, like most of its audience, wasn't sure if he should be taken seriously.

"I've got some good news," Alf began. "The reaction to the forum was huge. There's actually a lot to use here." Both Chip and Edie were intrigued. "I haven't read all of them yet but it looks like there's almost two thousand posts, including at least five hundred that may have legit points about the college experience."

"Two thousand!" Chip declared excitedly. "That's amazing, it's like fifteen, twenty percent of the school! Why didn't you say that earlier?"

"Calm down. It's great that we're getting this response...but..."

Edie volunteered to fill in the bad news, "It's impossible to verify which posts were written by different students— or by students at all."

To that, Chip suggested: "We could share *all* the emails with the school to show the spectrum of complaints that were voiced, even if they're not verifiable. Right?"

Edie scoffed. "If we do that we'd have to submit tons that just say you love to party."

"How bad are they?"

Alf scrolled through his notes. "Some blame you for the noise, some for enabling reckless underage drinking, and a few are pissed at you for flooding Monterey House."

"Monterey?" he replied caustically. "That was two years ago. Why bring that up again?"

"You did it two years ago," Alf noted. "Someone else did it last night...and a few people think it was you again or it was your idea."

---

[22] Reports later showed that all three grocery stores within walking distance of the campus sold out of beer, charcoal, plastic cups, ketchup, and for some reason, denture cream.

"That's ironic it would happen last night." He chuckled uncaringly. "What are the odds?"

Chip's question churned uneasily in Edie's mind. She looked up from her phone to see that Chip had not identified her concern yet. "Alf, do you have info on calls the U.P. responded to last night?"

Alf rocketed into a typing frenzy. "I can try. I know they feed stuff to the Criminal Psych department for a few law enforcement classes. And here it is." Chip and Edie hovered over his shoulders to look through the list on the Department of Criminal Psychology's website. Alf scrolled and asked, "Are we looking for places where Chip has gotten trashed or would it be easier to call out where he's been sober?"

By the time the question was posed, it was clear they were not wrong for examining the list. The feed revealed that four of Chip's "greatest hits" pranks recreated in just hours.

As the details seeped into Chip's alcohol-shrouded skull, the mystery outlined an obstacle he should have considered earlier: someone was determined to convince people that Chip was trying to distract the campus while he blanketed it with pranks. Following a protracted mental struggle around who could do such a thing, Chip berated himself for not storing a contingency plan for something he should have considered from his first steps. "Kathie fucking Kieft."

Chip remembered their first encounter freshman year differently than Kathie, although he, too, knew there was nothing great about what he put her through. What he was doing the day he spotted Kathie in the lecture hall was looking for someone random, not anyone in particular. The person he spotted just happened to look like the bratty girl who ruined his grandfather's PMU garden dedication in 1992 by drawing on the statue of Adelaide Lockwood using permanent marker. Chip did not believe the outwardly woeful girl's apology. He knew knock off sincerity well and he would forever remember her oversold tears and her eyes' sinister gloss.

What he didn't realize while choosing Lynette Darcy's victim was she didn't just *look like* his old enemy, she *was* his old enemy. Even when he learned her full identity after the Darcy Incident,

Kathie spent years hating him while he went on enjoying his life, much to Kathie's added dismay.

Chip should have known his path would be deterred by her wrath. Edie was just as enraged for not thinking of Kieft's meddlesome presence earlier.

Hangover, lack of sleep, and terrible planning aside, Chip knew he had to start steeling himself; this was no longer a battle against time or academia, but it was one that pitted the Lockwoods versus the detestable Kiefts, who were led by the worst of their kind.

Chip and Edie broke out what they'd cobbled together of the plan. At some point, Kathie figured out Chip's real motivation. She didn't want to simply tell the school his motives since his family could easily come to his rescue. Simply saying he was a selfish fraud wasn't enough. She had to persuade the university, the students, and his family that he was laughing at them.

To counteract Kathie, he needed concrete proof that he was using his position for good. It also wouldn't hurt to give solid alibis to his close friends to show that they weren't running around campus flooding buildings and taping freshmen to walls.

Marshaling more strength than he should have had at 7:45 a.m. after the night he'd endured, and utilizing an impressive tactical fervor, Chip set himself in motion.

First, at Chip's insistence, Alf blasted the university and the forum readers with an invite to an urgent 8:30 a.m. meeting that required their attendance. Chip then sent instructions to his fraternity house detailing their activities for the day and followed with direct calls to friends explaining that they had to set up daylong volunteering exercises for their houses. Chip assured his cohorts outside of August that each organization that helped out would receive a prize in the near future. Alf, Edie, and Chip then scoured the hallways for active student body leaders who could help gather volunteers, as well.

Shortly thereafter, the attendance in the NEQ ballooned, growing to around three hundred students. Newcomers were greeted with a bit of confusion from the die-hard attendees.

At 8:32, Chip appeared in his usual spot to address the groggy crowd. His pitch was simple: it was time to show the school that the students were capable of great things when given the chance. They were not just there to drink, he explained, or to sleep through uninspiring classes for which their parents were charged hundreds of dollars a session.

To show they could accomplish so much more than what the school prescribed, Chip urged the students to unite and give back to their community that Thursday. He challenged them to make a visible difference on their campus and in neighboring communities between nine and five. Their revelry the night before did not go unnoticed. Instead of being embarrassed by unforgiving stares, Chip urged the students to prove that they could be noticed for greater things.

His final call to action began with a flourish. "Your classes will be there tomorrow, the day after that, and all the way until this semester becomes a memory. There are people to be helped." He continued by guiding students towards an Alf-built website comprised of hyperlinks pointing to websites with local volunteer opportunities. "The people who say this is their land want you to sit in classes today to get one third of a percent closer to earning a document they claim makes you educated. You know what I say? Take today and show them you're already educated by caring about your community!"

With that, the students rose up.

Chapter 27: The Great Lockwood Debate

THURSDAY MORNING in the administrative offices began a few brief hours after the previous evening's parties ended. In an unusual twist, some administrators spent their mornings much like August Hall's residents.

Like their undergraduate counterparts, any PPC member who arrived at the early morning session with any knowledge of the prior evening's happenings direly hoped to avoid eye contact with anyone who knew more than they did. Next came their drink of choice. For August's residents it was a sports drink or more beer. For those who worked through most of the night and Kathie, whose night of boastful sleep was ruined by a two-hour search for her lost phone, coffee was the first order of business. PPC members also found their email accounts brimming with startling piles of messages forwarded from professors. Like many students in August Hall, the more they examined the available documents, the more they wondered how they could have let the events of the night get away from them.

As the board members pieced together their stance for the day, it seemed none of them (with the exception of Kathie) noticed the stoic and sharply dressed newcomer at the table. The tall, thin, and devastatingly staid new arrival was seated in front of a black leather folder. Kathie guessed correctly that the other adults didn't bother examining him closely out of an assumption that he represented a department with which they never did business. But she was intrigued.

What captivated the teenager in addition was the question of how the PPC would react to the busy hours since they last spoke. While pretending to focus on her laptop and bran muffin, Kathie was pleased that it didn't take long for the board to answer her unspoken question by launching into the most vitriolic discourse of her tenure. The group was so ready to fight that they did so before Asbury even arrived.

What started as rumblings evolved into an argument involving nearly everyone present. Professors, local business owners, and students assaulted their email accounts and phones all night, and the statistics available were nowhere near calming. ER visits quadrupled the night before (twelve total, all alcohol related), propaganda was racing through campus, and a new noise complaint record had been set. Between the countless spoken and written assaults, the normally uninterested group's boiling point had been reached, and they were ravenously divided.

Some, who considered this the dawn of a new age of assembly, called for a dialogue with student leaders. They hated seeing disobedience brewing in their own home, but after supporting such activities earlier in their lives, they could not opt for a big stick over an olive branch. Others were convinced that Chip should be stopped as soon as possible. The alcohol, truancy, and messy handrails all pointed to the student's utter lack of appreciation for Pemberton. This side felt Chip was gaily laughing in the faces of those who stood by him and the only way to support these misguided children was by authorizing a quick strike against their leader.

Thus the "Great Lockwood Debate" was born, which asked if Chip was on campus to promote academic and civic harmony or to simply drink and encourage others to break the law.

One side felt the school had a duty to negotiate to return balance to the campus. The opposition balked at this, noting that it gave credence where none was deserved. Additionally, the opponents noted that the longer they pretended Chip's crusade was bona fide, the longer they were inviting to campus real agitators hoping to capitalize on what Chip's masquerade started.

Those who believed Lockwood's primary goal was wreaking havoc pressed for his immediate shutdown. The more pacifistic side decried this, reminding the board that breaking up a protest of this size and nature, especially if done uncaringly, could have a devastating impact.

From the sidelines, Kathie reveled in the confirmation that her revised plan was working. Spectacularly, all it took was a late night strategy session and the ability to pick from a crowd the people who most despised Lockwood.[23] The board was torn and bewildered thanks either to their gullibility or Kathie's brilliance, and it would take days, if not weeks, to land at a reasonable solution. Meanwhile, Chip's time would tick away and his grades would become final, leaving him sorely out of luck.

To Kathie, it was truly inspired. That is, until she zeroed in on the only other quiet party present: the guest. Who was he? More importantly: how much would Asbury listen to him?

Her questions would be answered in brutally quick fashion.

Asbury pushed through the doors brimming with disapprobation and spite. He examined the room as Kathie watched his skyrocketing spirit sink the instant he saw the well-dressed newcomer. Kathie tried to hide her fervent interest as she followed Asbury's gaze to see the suited stranger was looking back at Asbury in (dare she think it?) a reprehending manner. It only took one look before Asbury no longer knew if he should feel agony or irascibility. The reaction, needless to say, startled Kathie, as did the man's presence.

Provost Asbury, in reality, was stunted as he knew what this man represented: another potentially insurmountable hurdle.

Although a number of the board members were covertly happy that Asbury overheard the morning's quarrel, which showed they

---

[23] She noted in the diary she kept lodged in her phone that it was likely "the greatest example of quick thinking in PMU's history."

were actually engrossed in the ongoing debacle, the talk simmered once he entered. Asbury languidly made his way to his seat and before the double doors could close behind him, a middle manager from the President's team rushed in. His face feigned regret for his tardiness, an expression meant specifically for the dapper gentleman who had a seat at the table thanks largely to intervention by the university president.

The middle manager gave a brief introduction of their newcomer. Once he mentioned the large bank that employed the guest, board members either glared irritably or watched cautiously while each trying to recall exactly what they shared heatedly in the man's presence. He was then introduced as Bromhead, a nickname he'd been given the previous year by a university official who had mistaken him for a dear friend's nephew, Jeremy Bromhead. No mention was offered explaining why he preferred to use an alias while working with the PPC, but no one objected.[24]

It was not discussed in the sanitized primer, but Bromhead's presence could undoubtedly be described as an unfortunate reflection of the times.

Bromhead then provided a little more background. Although he was a representative of a major bank, he explained, he was there to preserve the best interests of the student body. It was unknown whether his company's interest in the students was based on a commitment to their personal growth or the bank's own vaults. (Such an occurrence seemed less clandestine after news of the 2007 student loan scandal broke, but at the time, it was a closely guarded secret that a representative from a major bank was brought into these proceedings.)

Bromhead's presence on campus, like his employer's grasp on it, was no accident. Gradually over the latter part of the Twentieth Century the large banking facility for which Bromhead worked was able

---

[24] As for why he is known only by Bromhead in this text, per an agreement with his employer, to protect his ability to serve his clients properly, his real name will not be used.

to coerce a series of PMU officials to declare their bank as the university's preferred student loan lender.

Several miniscule changes followed and the partnership eventually allowed the bank to become the overseer of the vast majority of the university's student loans. Hardworking Pemberton students paid fair to slightly higher than fair interest rates after taking out these loans and an overwhelming number paid back their loans in full without delinquency. Without their knowledge, the dollars they repaid went to the coffers of a bank those students very likely would not have sought out or found on their own.

The initiative's success was so prodigious that by the late 1980s the bank decided that for privacy's sake, it was a necessity to cloak the company's link to the university. To cover the bank's tracks, in the early 1990s, PMU for the first time in years allowed students to elect to take out loans from one of six banks instead of just two. What students did not know was that four of the six options were subsidiaries of Bromhead's bank and the other two were too small to take on a large percentage of the school's loans.

By the time Chip acted up in 2005, over eighty eight percent of student loan dollars being pumped into Pemberton came straight from Bromhead's employer. A small team of students camped outside August Hall were actually aware of the cause for alarm, but the errant rumors they'd heard about the abstract banking entity only amounted to a fraction of the truth.

This is why the man who was perplexing Kathie could have silenced Asbury so quickly. The aged official knew that while he could have and should have turned down the previous two requests he'd received, whatever requests Bromhead was about to make were not optional. His presence showed that each of the highest levels of PMU leadership was fearful. Any major scandal could lead to catastrophic shifts in enrollment, university prominence, and the bank's bottom line. Those to whom Asbury reported had sent Bromhead to protect all three.

With indifferent eyes scanning either the representatives' faces or hairlines, Bromhead dryly stated, "Please allow me to skip formalities. My team and I have already begun enacting a three pronged push to reduce your risk associated with this...incident."

"How do you define risk?" one board member prodded. "As a financial measure or as something rooted in the wellbeing of our students?"

Without moving any muscle superfluous to his desired action, Bromhead shifted his eyes towards the questioner. "One of your dormitories is on lockdown with hundreds of students inside. Those students are missing classes while drinking alcohol you placed there. How do *you* define risk?" The administrator met the question with a slouched reversal in his seat. Bromhead continued. "The first step involves my team analyzing attendance records, undergraduate demographic information, application statistics, and other documents as needed. For this we will need the assistance of many departments, primarily the Registrar. Are you compliant?"

The Registrar's representative dutifully nodded. Kathie, meanwhile, tensed up at the presence of the action-oriented speaker. What could a person like this do to her aim of a drawn out, delayed deliberation about Chip?

"Second," the banker continued, "since the information shared with me to date didn't reference this, I assume you have not decided what to do with Lockwood after he has been apprehended." The room provided no responses. Asbury shook his head ruefully at this lack of foresight. "To be prepared, we must know every option of recourse at the school's disposal."

"My team will work on that," offered Asbury, whose acquiescence bewildered the sole student present. This prompted her to wonder: *what the hell can I do to get around this guy?*

Bromhead nodded at the senior member of the board. "Third: before you completely lose control of your students, we must immediately determine how much of this is a protest and how much is sophomoric duplicity." Bromhead produced a paper that recounted some of his team's research. "As I have read, he is capitalizing on easy targets, including various infrastructure issues, and encouraging others to amplify these weaknesses. A stronger grasp of his intentions is needed."

To this, a pugnacious board member asked: "Why should we heed anonymous sob stories that could have come from anywhere—even from authors with no link to Pemberton?"

Bromhead, opting for a reply meant more for the entire table, focused on his research notes. "I will read from you a forum entry which was written quite eloquently early this morning. It asks 'Would we really all get the chance to experience the greatest years of our lives if each day we spent here didn't generate more interest money for banks?'" He paused. "What matters is that your students are being encouraged to read statements like this. It no longer matters where they came from. It is time to find out how serious he is."

With this suggestion, much of the board felt relieved that they may finally have a sturdy plan. For similar reasons, Kathie was infuriated at the progress the team made in just minutes.

Bromhead continued: "How has the university gauged student reaction so far?"

At this, the aide from the President's office opened his arms in Kathie's direction, as if to say "please proceed!" Kathie reacted outwardly with an awkward smile (and internally with a note to make that administrator's life a living hell the next chance she had).

Hoping a kind tone might siphon more consideration from Bromhead, Kathie warmly replied, "It's been a very trying couple of days for the students. I've been receiving emails almost non-stop, so it's definitely made a mark on the week."

"Specifically, please, how are they reacting?"

"I'm sorry to say it, Sir, but they appear to be pretty split. Some seem very determined that Charles is trying to push for real change. Others are just as positive that he's pulling one of his famous practical jokes, especially after the sorority flooding incident."

"Do people really think he snuck out of a locked dormitory to flood a sorority...again?" one board member asked.

Kathie, hoping control the conversation, added, "I think that—" before getting cut off.

"Thank you for your data," Bromhead replied over her. "We can work on gleaning insights into student body opinions shortly. First, we still need proof of his intentions."

Glossing over the bitterness of the interruption, Kathie fought to brew up a way to sway the conversation back into her hands.

"I have an idea for that," chirped the representative from the undergraduate school of Mathematics and Science. He was more than eager to speak after his suggestions during the Lockwood Debate were called too theoretical by irate representatives from other academic disciplines. "We need a litmus test, a very public one. Simply: we put him in a position that forces him to show us exactly what he's up to, and once he does, we'll react accordingly."

The room gauged the idea before anyone dared to respond. Kathie at first hated the suggestion (namely because it didn't come from her) but she soon came to adore the idea. If the protracted deliberation she'd been hoping for was no longer a possibility thanks to Bromhead, a very public example highlighting Chip's idiotic behavior could work even better. The PPC could determine definitively that he only masterminded a gargantuan party, ending the standoff and allowing his grades to inelegantly escort him away from the campus.

"Furthermore," the Math and Sciences chair added, "if he is fooling people who want a protest, he'll let them down himself. We won't have to intervene and risk distraught onlookers disliking us as the messenger."

"That may work," the President's Aide stated. "But if he isn't the real protest leader, your plan does not solve our dissent problem. Very important omission."

"I disagree," Bromhead retorted. "If we prove he is not the leader, we can limit potential Lockwood family interference. We will also be closer to finding out who the real leader is if it truly is a third party who saw the potential to act."

For Kathie, the question of pinning the punishment onto another intrigued her, but it would have to wait. She was willing to abide by the latest proposal, but it was imperative that she choose how to enact the suggestion. A conclusive test of Lockwood's character would only be useful if it could guarantee his failure.

Bromhead, having heard the PPC's reputation for being nonresponsive, repeated the proposal: "We need confirmation that Lockwood is either orchestrating a practical joke or he is speaking out for causes he never once referenced as an interest prior to this week. Who has an idea to obtain this verification?"

After a tough but efficient search inward, Kathie realized she had the answer. Relishing the scenario she was picturing, she expertly continued acting her role as an unbiased observer and stated: "I have the perfect idea."

Chapter 28: Noonish Beer

EVEN BEFORE the PPC could approximate the impact of Chip's boisterous call to action, early estimates suggested it was enormous. By 10:00 a.m. it was clear that low attendance records would again be smashed as the campus took off in dozens of directions.

Many used Alf's online list of nonprofits to find their destinations for the day. As the ledgers of organizations he'd listed filled with volunteers, students started requiring a broader selection of worthy groups. William, fresh from his late awakening, funneled new organizations to Alf, who regularly edited his post to ensure it was as up to date as possible and to note which volunteer opportunities were full. Chip and Edie, meanwhile, continued promoting this possibly too brash addition, which he'd presented to a community that recently drank itself into a collective stupor until 4 a.m. Chip's fraternity and others that housed close friends leapt into action before nine. Various sports-related clubs followed, their appearances punctuated by bloodshot eyes, mussed hair, and room temperature energy drinks.

Edie took on the task of recruiting the female contingent of the Greek community. Although she was far from the most sociable girl at PMU, Edie brought six full houses and four tiny campus clubs out of their beds and into the world all before nine thirty. While I'm not permitted to share any of the language Edie employed in her communications that morning, I can assure you her tactics were as brazen as one would expect.

Impressively, their reach went far beyond the students they contacted directly. When statistics were gathered later that afternoon, more than 1,500 undergraduate students skipped at least one class that day to volunteer. In all, it would be found that the undergraduates logged between 5,000 and 6,000 volunteer hours in a single day. (It is important to note that only participating in the day's activities and loaning explicit support to Chip remained, for many, utterly separate.)

Before the day was done, seven neighboring towns' community centers were renovated, painted, and brought into the 21st Century. To-do lists were wiped clean at a dozen local houses of worship, and virtually every nonprofit in town went from being dangerously behind on its work to two to four months ahead of schedule. The impact stretched beyond the township's borders as villages as far as thirty miles away felt the benefits of the actions of students. Even tasks at PMU were getting tended to, mainly in departments that were aware of the university's conflagration with Chip but had plenty of envelopes to be stuffed.

*   *   *

By noon, the PPC still hadn't responded to Chip directly. It was early enough that the day's official statistics hadn't been calculated yet but late enough that the prevailing trend had undeniably presented itself. The Provost's Office did exercise some level of interaction throughout the morning, but none with Chip himself. Shortly before lunch Asbury threatened to dangle select houses' charters as bait to get students to return to campus, but he knew he'd never be able to make his punishment stick if the groups were merely doing what they did every semester while scrambling to make up for a dearth of volunteering hours.

Everyone on the board agreed that while the volunteerism had benefits, it was dangerous to get that assistance at such a cost and amid troubled times. Those who were frightened by Chip's power, however, were reminded by Asbury that it didn't take much to convince a 19 year old who wasn't paying for their own college education to skip a day of classes.[25]

Other PPC members, while enraged, were not convinced that this urge for activism was anything more than an extension of Chip's push to fool the university. Throughout two of the louder moments of doubt, Kathie patiently assured the room that her very public test, which would take place at 2:00 p.m., would definitely show what Chip really stood for. (She was able to preemptively brush away suggestions that she was biased by reminding the board that the reveal of Chip's intentions would help students far more than anyone else.) The questions died down before the lunch hour, but the concerned looks did not.

As the queries continued, Kathie actually for a brief instant admired Chip's intention to counter the effects of her previous night's actions, the first and last of his ideas to earn her esteem. That admiration smoothly morphed into self-satisfaction when she reminded herself that the students' selfless activism would dovetail nicely with the spectacle that would extinguish Chip's credibility.

With Kathie dreaming of the upcoming one-two punch, the PPC powered on around her.

*   *   *

Following his morning rallying as many people as possible, Chip spent hours dutifully reading forum replies. The self-assigned task would have been more effective had it not been paired with a beer around 11:30 or its cousin "noonish beer" which helped encourage their mutual friend "raging, skull screwing hangover" (Chip's

---

[25] Interestingly, Cammy Dalton attended every class that day despite being one of the most committed followers Chip found that week. Though sympathetic to the cause, after calculating how much money her parents paid for each hour of her in-class instruction that semester, she opted to attend each class (instead of wasting hundreds of dollars by ditching just a few sessions) and then between classes volunteer at a local home for adults with developmental disabilities.

slightly censored words) to depart.

The emails pleased Chip, as did the scattered reports noting the productive volunteering that was underway. Wanting to go a step further, he located Alf in his dorm room and provided him with a supplemental suggestion. Alf was to take the best forum entries and post them on any local, highly visible web site he could find. He then provided Alf with eight public posts he could use as a start and left. Alf posted seven, ignoring only one that went "Chip: tell chicks my frat will pledge eight hours a day to hospitals for a month if they show their titties in the NEQ tonight. Sincerely, Poon-a-saurus."

Upon departing Alf's side, Chip's innocent glance at the clock on his phone immobilized him. He had less than twenty four hours to become officially detached from the university. The reminder startled him, but his nerves cooled when he recalled his progress.

(While aware he'd forged through a lot and involved countless students in his quest, what Chip didn't realize was how many of his own associates were touched by topics being brought to light underneath the umbrella of his actions. For instance, Alf's older brother was toiling with his third year of unemployment while living with their parents despite having bachelors and graduate degrees from very reputable institutions. As such, Alf was happy to promote the cause of those students speaking out for better job placement assistance. William, meanwhile, who had always been bashful and quiet about his student loans, felt empowered by those who proudly wore the badge he'd hidden and were willing to speak loudly for their rights. One crusade even touched the Kieft clan. In 2003, the credit of one of her cousins was ruined just months after starting at a university in a state where it was legal to give away trinkets like t-shirts and free meals in exchange for signing up for credit cards. She'd amassed fourteen new cards in her first semester alone. A group camped near the NEQ's welcome sign was asking for passage of a national law protecting students against such aggressive practices.)

He then intelligently set out to brainstorm Kathie's upcoming moves. This would ensure that he would never again have to play catch up or defense that week. The idea, while a great one, took a backseat almost immediately when his mind prompted him to take a poorly timed but physically necessary nap before his brainstorming session could produce a single countermeasure.

*   *   *

At approximately the same time, one of Pemberton's most perplexed residents was sitting in her favorite study spot on the sixth floor of the library. The study nook hosted only five desks and was congested with bookshelves, dusty books on British literature, and little foot traffic. She was visiting to address in peace the cascading layers of emails and phone calls about Chip Lockwood's "wild success." Between bouts of mental reflux, she was taking the time to courteously reply in a humble manner to the emails that thanked the campus for the support.

After hours of analysis, thoughts of Chip's siege remained far more tightly packed in Eva's mind than she desired and new concerns mounted as her classmates repaired countless things that she warned had long needed fixing. Furthermore, although she'd dreamed of leading a similarly sized (or larger) movement for years, so many questions unfurled that morning that had never occurred to her in her years of dreaming. She wondered if this really was her destiny, if she could have missed so much of the dire minutia for so long.

Her anguish also came, at least in part, as a result of her research into Chip's declaration. During breaks from her emails, she'd followed up on each of his claims linked to the university abandoning a student. Despite being outwardly jockish, insensitive, and possessing so many other behaviors that defined youthful selfishness, the young man knew how to deliver a solid, factual message. Her digging found that his declaration contained only painstakingly accurate real life examples of students left behind without recourse against the institution. What was worse, Chip's stories were being told to droves of people who were willing to listen.

With Lockwood's mixed signals, Kathie's scornful texts, and the student body's newfound drive for community involvement, it became too hard to focus. At first Eva told herself to be thankful that beneficial work was happening. In the first batch of emails, excited students humbly boasted their classmates were finally working alongside of them. Then came emails from local community leaders who were ineradicably thankful for the student support.

One such email came from a local group called C.A.N.S., who had been trying to bring modern, compartmentalized recycling bins to the town for months but until that morning they lacked the manpower to construct or distribute them. The email noted that every bin would be ready by the end of the day and thirty percent would be delivered directly to homes, too. As Eva had been trying to help C.A.N.S. all semester, she felt divided over the outcome considering her own lack of personal success. Thoughts then followed that the students were helping construct the garbage receptacles just so they had more prime locations in which to vomit after a long night of drinking. These crude thoughts then led to moments of self-hate.

As she read on, she battled to determine if she was being harsh or simply realistic. It was fantastic that worthy projects were getting attention. However, the day's growth was not under any circumstances sustainable, even if Chip's crusade wasn't brought to a crudely foolish end.

An angelic, hopeful voice in her head told her the impetus for the community didn't matter, rather students supporting one another and using their time wisely did count.

But Eva could not listen to that voice.

As much as it hurt, she deeply despised how the volunteerism rose out of two days of a spoiled legacy's hard drinking and pontificating. It may have been a byproduct of her pride, but with each email describing a success, she grew to dislike even more the man who was fixing in hours what she could not repair in years of conscientious labor.

The aggravatingly complicated flow chart of issues in her head led Eva to believe it was time to lean on her favorite method of feeling better: a call to one of her parents. Such conversations always helped her productively shift perspectives.

Before withdrawing her phone, she imagined the pending conversation. As she pictured the words that would no doubt leave her mouth if her call went through as dialed, her excitement waned. Yes, she had real questions, like what would happen if students found out they'd volunteered to be the butt of a joke? Or: why, if he was a true leader, did it seem like Lockwood was shielding his true intentions? And: was there some way to talk to him to find out what he was really after?

Her parents could provide some answers, but her hesitation spread because she knew they would be able to see the real problem: Chip had written her out of a success story she'd been trying to compose for years. Whichever parent she spoke with would know of their daughter's ego, which she was often successful in hiding, but could not be suppressed in this case. The more Chip looked and acted like a leader, the more Eva would despise him. It was far easier for her to see him as a fool whom she could overlook while pushing ahead trying to solve the truly pressing student rights questions at hand.

Eva then asked herself something she'd been weighing for hours. Regardless of his intentions or goals, Chip would fall. What then? If she took his place, would she ruin her reputation as the stand in for a joker or would the action paint her as the shepherd of students in their time of need? Alternatively, could she do nothing and watch thousands get duped and convince themselves no cause was worth fighting for?

Chapter 29: Wisdom of the Elders

A NEARLY motionless Edie stared at the boarded up door of a sad closet-like room on Four South. It was a relic from another time whose status had grown obstinate due to disrepair. It was one of eight nearly identical rooms across the building which used to be phone booths.

For decades, students retreated to these windowed cubby holes for weekly calls to their parents, reminders for their out of state girlfriends or boyfriends that they weren't forgotten, or chats with distant friends. These private escapes made possible these rare windows between the student's world and what they'd left behind.

The booths meant nothing in 2005, nor had they for a long time, and they would regain usefulness only in some "we'll take care of this later" future. Edie's only notable memory that was associated with these alcoves was the night during her freshman year when she convinced the joyous jock Jake Longman to punch through one of the windows to see if he could. It worked, and thankfully, his RA was still awake to take him to the ER for two stitches and an exacting lecture. In the window's place went a characterless slab of plywood.

Some others still retained their windows, but that mattered little as they no longer hosted guests or a purpose. It appeared the booths, which could have been used for storage or a number of other things, were only there to be ignored, defaced, or used for uncomfortable sexual liaisons.

What Edie wanted more than anything was to make Kathie as unimportant as these phone booths. Kathie's latest selfish push to procure proof that she was a greater human than Chip made Edie long to make Kathie as useless and unwanted as possible. She felt it long before that week and it definitely did not wane when she saw Kathie's 2:00 p.m. surprise arrive in the Quad.

But Edie's revenge would have to wait. She and Chip had more pressing concerns as William led a dazed Chip towards the spot she requested.

"What's more urgent than my nap?" Chip asked through clouded eyes.

She ominously replied: "I take it you haven't looked outside."

The boys stood still, as if they thought whatever potential danger would disappear if they refused to move.

William was the first to speak. "What's out there?"

"A crowd half the size of last night, Asbury, and a few other admins standing around a skinny sun burnt guy in black leather pants and a funky turquoise vest."

Chip, who was still hoping the situation was not as desperate as Edie's conduct suggested, replied optimistically, "So...they're bringing us a dealer?"

*   *   *

By all known accounts, Warren Lightstorm was a fair and just man.

The proud member of the [REDACTED] Tribe had a degree in Central American History, another in Native American studies, a PhD in Public Policy, and over twenty-five years of experience as a community educator. His presence on Pemberton's grounds brought to the university a wealth of Native American history and tribal knowledge, among other topics that were central to the talks that he believed were happening on campus that day.

Despite being offered other jobs earlier in his career, Lightstorm resolved to focus on educating his community and others like it. He sought to teach students who would ultimately find few accessible four year college options, fewer scholarship opportunities, and likely an underwhelming number of job offers even if they completed a degree. And he strived to push them all to rise above those boundaries.

Among the other tasks assigned to him by his vocation was the job of educating outside collectives, as well. Often he had been called upon by educational institutions to have serious, structured debates about changing mascots or to give history lessons around Thanksgiving. While he knew these one-off talks could not possibly provide all the education students would need, he continued agreeing to visits because he knew students would benefit more from the few words they could hear from a real Native American, than they could from antiquated text books.

These talks kept Lightstorm's name high on the list of people to contact if ever a discussion about Native American rights arose in the state. His one hundred plus mile drive to Pemberton that morning was not the longest trek he'd ever undertaken, or the least useful, but early signs suggested it would be the strangest.[26]

He sensed right away something was awry.

From the little PMU explained to him, he knew he was not driving across the Empire State to explain why it was offensive to cheer on their culinary mascot. Beyond that, all he'd gathered from initial talks was he was expected to help with a mysterious issue.

The first notification Lightstorm received from PMU came around nine a.m. when a fairly callow young woman who rang him with a series of odd questions. Before answering any of them, he consulted the elders of his tribe. He was then met with a second call, this time from a kinder woman who said she worked with the provost. She warmly asked if he would come to the campus to consult with a

---

[26] Among his more unpleasant visits was a trip to a school that incorrectly wrote his name down wrong as "Lightstrom" and later refused to let him speak at their multicultural assembly as he had no knowledge of Nordic history, as his mistyped name suggested.

"disagreement we're having with one of our students." During the drive to Pemberton, he was in almost constant contact with members of his tribe who were compiling whatever research they could find about any sort of Native American activity happening within PMU's boundaries. They could not find much, but what they found was mystifying.

When he arrived, he parked a few blocks from campus and did not immediately notify the administrators he was there. During his scouting walk, he stopped students one by one to hear their perspectives on the protest about which he had only sparse details. He managed to gather some data, but within thirty minutes of his arrival, a staffer found him and his independent research ceased. Lightstorm knew a school with a more substantial Native American population would have taken longer to locate him, but he didn't let that distort his opinions just yet.

The staffer brought him to an office for a forty minute talk centered on what the university considered to be its problem. At no point did anyone ask what he thought, rather they kept mentioning he would have a chance to speak publically on the matter. Before he knew it, he was standing in the NEQ with a crowd behind him and a megaphone in his hand.

Had the administrators given him the ability to talk while spraying him with facts, it would have been easier to like them more than their evidently immature opponent. What Lightstorm truly required was a real understanding of Chip Lockwood. What were his goals? Was he worthy of praise? Most importantly, did he realize what impact his words would have on thousands of impressions of Native Americans? If Chip's classmates and guardians couldn't crack the enigma of this elusive student leader, Lightstorm knew would have to meet him directly for answers.

*   *   *

Chip, after a brief delay, embraced desperation. The visitor was the latest obstacle designed to show he had no intention of helping the student cause or really anyone. It had long been clear, at least in his own mind, that the Native American idea was merely a symbol for student liberation. Chip never intended on promoting the former without the latter. But still the two were inextricably linked. To make matters worse, his nap had left him fuddled and highlighted how his body and mind had been overworked that week.

"What the hell do I do?" he asked. "Who knows what the school told this guy about me?"

Edie pulled her gaze off the hockey stick she was gripping. "Would it be worse than anything you could have told him yourself?"

"Come on. I don't know shit about these Pakistani Indians."

William groaned. "They're Native Americans."

Chip pointed at William. "My point exactly. We can't let them know I don't know that. So what do we do?"

The sophomore trudged on. "If he knows anything about what's been going on here, he most likely isn't on your side, so I hate to say it, but...you definitely shouldn't talk to him."

Edie continued, "But you can't *not* talk to him." She then poked William's shoulder with the hockey stick. "We'll be close by and we'll help with your answers. But be serious because this guy being here is not good. It's probably why the school doesn't admit a lot of them."

William nodded in uncomfortable agreement. "As depressing as it is to say this, the only way you can win this is if you, the rich, privileged offspring of white American society totally ignore the Native American guy and his opinions."

Edie enthusiastically prodded William again. "Just look at him like a distraction. No one invited him because they care about Indians. He's here to make you look stupid."

Chip blearily picked up the torch. "So make sure he doesn't say shit or—" Chip paused to let out an enormous belch that took him by surprise. "Or turn his words around on him. Right?"

Edie, though concerned by the extra sound effect, supportively nodded as she knew Chip had to take the stage soon. "Right now your strength is coming from that website that students are still pumping crap into and I guarantee not one of them mentioned Indians."

Chip took a deep breath and pressed his fists together to crack his knuckles. "Okay. Should we find my Indian feathers for this? I think that'll help."

*   *   *

Some showed out of curiosity. Others arrived after reading posters throughout campus (the trusty Soup's handiwork again). The placards told students a real Native American was going to discuss Chip Lockwood's protest with him. This invite evidently intrigued many.

Lightstorm looked over the crowd, or what he could see of it through the administrators who continued to instruct him on a number of topics. As this went on, Asbury, the only adult there who was not lecturing Lightstorm, was surveying the Quad for the second time that day and admitted to himself he almost preferred the trash he'd encountered during the previous visit. The small set of campaigners displayed only a tiny drop of the vigor he'd seen during campus conflagrations earlier in his career, and as such, this was not at as horrible of an encounter as it could have been.

Standing far away from Asbury, meanwhile, was Eva, who was present out of concern. The posters her eyes scanned worried Eva as it did not look like they originated from within the cause. Similarly, the eager anticipation on her friends' faces suggested they, too, had no idea what to expect. Upon seeing the Provost lead the speaker through the crowd, she began to wonder if the anonymous postings were Kathie's handiwork. That least favorite undergraduate of hers did not appear to be in sight, she noted.

Hundreds of students, many back from hours of selfless volunteering, expectantly looked on. Regardless of his behavior the night before, Chip's appearance in front of Asbury, hundreds of classmates, and a man who no doubt knew more about the plight of Native Americans than anyone else present would be a major moment.

The onlookers hushed when the curtains of Chip's favorite spot opened to show a proud but haggard looking version of the week's leader.

Though trained from an early age to not make rash judgments about others, Lightstorm had already seen enough. It was obvious that the boy had been drinking for some time, confirming administrators' theories weren't rumors. He was not wearing the headdress as he had in photos from earlier that week (pictures which Kathie gladly provided), but the boy's carefree expression unlocked more about his opinions of the oppressed than any outdated adornment could have. He did help others achieve fine things that week, but strong initial indications showed Chip was not interested in helping any Native American tribes.

Chip attempted to launch into a speech before Lightstorm could speak. "Good morning all, and a better morning to you, good Sir, my—"

Lightstorm held up a hand and stated into the megaphone, "Please, if I may, I would like to say a few words to start."

All eyes watched Chip consider his move. "Absolutely," he replied.

Lightstorm gave an appreciative nod. He then took a look around to discover that with the exception of the administrators at his side, he had the most interested audience he'd ever seen on any campus. Outlines of students also began appearing in windows surrounding the Quad, including windows in August Hall itself. Edie and William were among the spectators, too, technically, as they were anxiously huddled near Chip's feet if they were needed.

"Thank you, Provost Asbury," Lightstorm began. "Thank you, residents of Pemberton, and others who have come here today. I also thank the elders in my community for allowing me to represent my tribe today. I am Warren Lightstorm of [REDACTED]."

The introduction commanded more respect than the students were expecting to give that morning. Lightstorm rightfully had the audience ready to listen.

"The community to which I belong and countless other tribes have not had pleasant histories. We have been massacred, prodded out of our land, and pushed to the bottom of society for the entirety of this country's bloody history. We have dealt with countless tribulations and that is why we are tending to today's situation with care. Our tribe met this morning, during my drive here, and this afternoon to discuss today's dilemma. Upon my arrival, I sought feedback from a number of students, gathered as many facts as I could find, and I examined this place's history, the present, and even what was said on this ground last night. After much discussion and consulting my tribe's elders, and we have come to a conclusion."

Spectators on in the square, those listening through their windows, and Chip himself leaned in a little closer to hear the result.

With his mouth still on the megaphone, Lightstorm turned towards away from Chip and towards the crowd to state: "My tribe and I have determined that Chip Lockwood is a complete and utter asshole."

Shocked gasps and stilted laughter escaped various listeners' mouths. No one dared to speak, fearing they would miss something even more shocking.

A positively stunned Chip watched from his perch.

From underneath the window frame, William leaned to Edie and said, "So are we getting arrested, expelled, or burned at the stake tonight?"

Edie, invigorated by the exchange, waved off the comment. "Shh, I want to hear how horrendous this gets."

Lightstorm continued. "Please forgive my bluntness, but to combat any possibility of misinterpretation, I feel stern language is necessary. Based on what I have seen, as far as I am concerned, every single Native tribe should decree that Chip Lockwood in no way speaks for us or any of our views."

"But my brethren!" Chip declared with a tone reeking of intoxicated shock.

"I am not your brother," Lightstorm snapped. "And I don't know what you think you are fighting for, but trapping people in their homes and forcing them to consume alcohol to no end is no way to stand up for Native American rights. I will say no more on this subject. Thank you Provost Asbury and students for your attention."

Lightstorm lowered the megaphone and stood patiently, waiting for guards to shuffle him to a dark room where administrators would declare that he would never again be allowed back.

Asbury and his team did no such thing. They were so pleased with Kathie's newest idea that some among them could hardly contain the urge to pat Lightstorm on the back.

The Quad buzzed with captivated whispers. Grins of faculty members squared off against awestruck students wondering what to think about their suddenly silent leader.

High above and huddled below the brick exterior of Chip's speaking dais, Edie, too, took a moment to wonder how Chip might bounce back from such a lashing. William punctuated the moment by mouthing "we are fucked." Edie responded by kicking Chip delicately in the shin.

Edie whispered, "Ignore him— everyone else does!"

Chip shot back to her, "I got nothing!"

"If people wanted to believe Indians over white men, then we'd be going to college in France and England right now and the U.S. would have a population of three million people!"

Before the distasteful remark could fling Chip into a heinous reply, a hissing noise from outside stole his attention. The sound was emanating from the still fenced up KRC. It was persistent enough to encourage dozens of listeners' heads to swivel in groups away from Chip.

After thirty seconds of mystery, a balloon shaped like a cowboy steadily inflated atop KRC. The figure, facsimiles of which might normally be seen outside of a used car dealership or at a high school sporting event, continued growing until it reached a height of about fifteen feet, where it continued to confound the spectators. (From inside August, Edie and William snuck peeks at the distraction, as well.) The balloon continued expanding, and as the pressure built up, the racket grew more menacing.

Then, an unidentifiable student in Native American regalia (a dear acquaintance of Soup's) appeared above a fraternity house and cried: "Pemberton Indians! Chip Lockwood wants to know: are you ready to rise up against the evil Southwest A&M State Cowboys on Saturday?"

The instant his war cry ended, the cowboy balloon vociferously burst open, spraying confetti everywhere. Moments later, previously unseen banners unfurled and covered the top level of KRC with messages like: "Kill those cowboys, Indians" and "Reclaim our heritage on the battlefield!"

Chip stood dazed, overlooking the possible disintegration of everything he'd worked for. The students then promptly reacted. Half cheered uproariously. The other half split into two uneven groups. The larger of the two angrily streamed out of the Quad, engaged in bitter quarrels. The second group looked on through eyes that were equally as confounded as Chip's. These students carried on many of the same conversations as their departing compatriots did, but they did so while remaining on their hard fought turf.

As the dumbfounded Chip was pulled back in through his window by the unseen Edie, it was clear he'd been dealt a devastating blow.

For two minutes the trio sat in silence. After having dealt with enough tension, William stood to leave for a happier setting. Chip fell into his couch and the fast talking girl who prided herself on being prepared for anything remained quiet.

Finally, Chip looked at her with a bewildered expression and said, "Well, I know who I'm not inviting to Thanksgiving dinner."

Chapter 30: Eva's Olive Branch

THIRTY MINUTES later, Provost Asbury was gliding through Liberty Hall wearing a smile behind his aged eyes. In his hands he had the Registrar's latest report on the matter in the NEQ, and in addition, notes detailing what he would order University Police to do as soon as the PPC voted to cease Lockwood's reign.

Despite not being able to vote on the matter immediately after the debacle, Asbury remained confident in this outcome. He was faced with delayed debate due to Bromhead, who set down a directive prior to the two p.m. summit stating that each PPC member had to spend one hour speaking with their departments gauging their opinions of Lockwood's actions. Asbury ignored the directive and went straight to the campus' Chief of Police to map out their attack. Waiting an extra hour was fine as long as he could act the nanosecond the PPC's decision was finalized. For Asbury, the worst possible outcome at that point was the one in which the young brash student had a chance to surrender.

While he desired nothing more than to see Chip hang, the victory would be less sweet if the wily boy handed himself in before the tactical team could squeeze the life out of his party.

If that were to happen, he knew the same imbeciles who called the parade a protest would positively implore Asbury to seek a less brutal punishment. He knew he could not expel the boy, but Chip's penance would still be unforgettable and ruthless, and Asbury would tolerate no news denoting that his ability to inflict punishment had been lessened.

Despite this slim possibility, with his notes firmly in hand and the Chief of the UP waiting by his office phone for further instructions, Asbury was happy with the course of events that lay ahead: vote to end the circus, cease the calamity, and eventually determine the identity of the actual mastermind who sought to rile the campus up into an anarchic fury.

While he certainly had thoughts on who that mystery candidate was, he set them aside for more pressing matters. Clasping the set of papers in his hands (and feeling a little surprise at how much joy this act brought him), he continued towards the PPC's conference room.

*   *   *

Kathie, similarly, could not be happier. Finally she was close to the end of her impossible, beautifully sweet mission.

Like Asbury, she was at least partially transfixed on what could possibly derail her quest. Since no one knew what she had been up to, her success seemed fairly guaranteed. While she did receive help along the way, she was careful to ensure the connections could not bring about any unwanted attention. The email and voicemails from her first assistant, the dimwitted dunce Squanto, had long been deleted. Also, as she never responded or acknowledged in any way that she received his messages, she felt this "loose end" was tied down particularly well. Soup, her much more prominent assistant, never received her full name and nor did he ever meet with her outside of dimly lit areas. What's more, he did not have her phone number, email address, or anything else he could use to definitely finger her as his puppeteer. With the two pawns out of her way, she could soon enjoy the bounty of her efforts while watching her nemesis crumble. Ruining Chip Lockwood was *indelibly* guaranteed.

As she continued to ponder the triumph, she concluded that not every aspect of the fiasco would be resolved once Lockwood was whisked away. If the week's proceedings showed her nothing else, it introduced to her a scenario in which the university was obligated to seek Eva's counsel in order to resolve a potentially calamitous event. The likelihood of this situation ever occurring again during Kathie's time at Pemberton was extremely low. Nevertheless, as there was a situation in which a student could assume significant power and Kathie was not that student, she found a new enemy even before her previous adversary's departure had arrived.

Kathie knew that Eva, with her outwardly altruistic nature and a desire to do well academically, was a significantly different opponent than Chip. This battle, should it ensue, would take an entirely novel set of tactics. Unless, she realized, she could tie Eva's and Chip's failures to one another before the week's end.

And so, before she had a chance to enjoy an instant of her celebration in the war against Chip Lockwood, Kathie began mobilizing for her battle against Eva Yesterday.

*   *   *

Incidentally, one of the things that Bromhead and his team were working on at that time had the same focus. For the most part, thanks to an agreement signed years ago, I am not at liberty to explain much about the tasks undertaken by the team Bromhead brought onto campus. I am permitted to note that one goal of their team's extremely detailed, *nearly* all-encompassing research was to determine who could have orchestrated the ostensibly legitimate protests.[27] Even though a sizeable number of events that week were centered on parties, anyone who focused on the grand scene could see that underneath the week's acts were the seeds of a populace taking tangible, if not infuriating concerns to heart. Someone had to have deliberately driven them in that direction and this group set out to learn who that someone could have been.

The issue was of great concern for Bromhead's team for nu-

---

[27] Pride might be getting in the way while discussing the consultants whom someone felt could do a better job than our internal staff, but I write "nearly" because in all of their research, Bromhead's team did not once mention the possibility that Chip was trying to get expelled.

merous reasons. For one, if the school was going to act against a member of one of its alumni community's most powerful families, PMU's leaders needed to know exactly what the boy was guilty of prior to exacting punishment. Additionally, on a broader scale, his team wanted to investigate the likelihood that Lockwood's removal would solely curb the kegger but not the protests.

The abridged version of their findings contained only a short list of candidates. Chip was listed prominently, although it was noted that his interest was likely a superficial one. Beyond Lockwood and a few potential external agitators from around the region, only one other student's name appeared on the list. Unsurprisingly, that name was Eva Yesterday.

Bromhead's team's data on Eva suggested it was very likely that she had at least some role in the orchestration of the unrest. What the report lacked was solid proof that any of her actions could be directly tied to specific cases of truancy or law-breaking.

Upon reading the report, Bromhead instructed the team to continue working on all other aspects of their Pemberton research and also double the amount of resources investigating Eva. He then departed for the meeting with notes on the young protest liaison in hand.

*   *   *

Eva at this point was walking towards Liberty Hall with a determined stride and a clear conscience. Sadly unaware of how many minds were pondering her involvement in the week's events, she was approaching the administrative offices with a heartfelt smile.

Thanks to a call to Asbury's office, she knew the PPC would soon be voting to determine what to do with Chip. Considering the amount of pomp and red tape that seemed to get attached to all of their other decisions, Eva assumed a hand-delivered message that Chip did not stand with the students would help the board greatly during this meeting.

Unlike her decision to volunteer this information to the PPC, initially arriving at the conclusion about Chip was no easy task for Eva.

After his latest spectacle, it had become evident that no positive change could come from his embarrassing mockery. The latest scene and Chip's lack of response poisoned any chance of amending to his name any successful campaign for change.

In Eva's opinion, it was best for the students, the school, and the causes to which she and her friends were devoted to start mending fences. Her life's large, gallant battle would no doubt happen at some point, she assured herself, but it would have to wait. Of this she was sure.

There were, indeed, factors suggesting that Chip wasn't really all bad, like his flabbergasted reaction when he saw the cowboy stunt. There was also the odd scene Eva witnessed when leaving the Quad where the loud boy from the stunt who dressed as a Native American gave a high five to a callous looking bully in a PMU track jacket, who then "gave the bird" to August Hall. But these isolated occurrences were not nearly as strong as everything else she'd seen.

As she approached Liberty Hall, she reminded herself it was a time for positivity, openness, and community.

Within seconds that changed drastically.

Her first indication that her positive mood would be short lived came when she saw Asbury, whose expression swiftly changed to disgust. After asking if she could attend the meeting and explaining why she wanted to join, his face took on a dubious expression. She chalked the progression up to stress. Countless more signs that her humor was destined to change followed once Asbury led her into the board room.

She immediately felt like she was the person in an old Western movie whose entrance into the saloon made everyone take pause, but she told herself she was imagining it all.

In typical PPC fashion, most in the room promptly returned to ignoring her after their initial look. Of those whose gazes remained, two frightened Eva the most: Kathie, who looked bitterly stunned and suspicious, and a sharply dressed stranger. The latter looked judgmental upon her entrance, prompting him to ask the person next to him who the girl was. When he heard the answer, his eyes dispersed a sliver of shock (Bromhead's most visible emotion of day).

Why do people who don't even know me hate that I'm here? She wondered, agitating her suspicions. *Would it be too awkward to just back leave now?*

As Eva struggled, Kathie remained fixed on her new enemy's presence for a fantastic reason: accusing Eva of heartlessly using Chip as a marionette depended largely on not letting Eva defend herself. Did someone know Kathie's plans? If so, did they reveal them to Eva? Even more intriguingly: was Eva here as a symbol of something shocking to come?

Similar questions that were equally as intriguing danced through Asbury's head, but they did not carry enough heft to slow down the inevitable vote he wished to cast. He stood, and using the telephone receiver near his seat as a gavel, he brought the meeting to order. He nodded to an assistant, who closed the double doors just as Lightstorm had finally located the conference room. Lightstorm was then shown to a seat in the hall as the wooden barrier expeditiously separated him from the proceedings.

Returning the phone to its receiver, Asbury proceeded. "You've all read the latest reports. As far as I'm concerned, this is no longer an issue that deserves debate. It's a simple matter." Asbury hesitated for a deliberate look at Bromhead, a minute action he hoped the board would fail to see. Bromhead locked eyes with Asbury, and the banker nodded firmly. With a statement that normally would have made the apprehensive Eva disappointed to witness, Asbury declared: "I suggest then, that we move forward without a vote and—"

Before he could finish, the doors swung open once again, revealing a representative from the Media Relations department. "You have to turn on the campus radio station," he instructed as he rushed towards the cabinet that housed the room's audio equipment.

Eva could feel her pulse quicken. She tried to calm herself by looking around to confirm that she was not the only nervous person in the room. Seeing that many were watching the staffer try to pull in the radio station frequency calmed her briefly. When she realized Kathie and the man in the suit were looking directly at her, a lump began to develop in her throat.

The radio station flickered to life from inside speakers embedded in the ceiling, allowing an amazingly demure Chip to startle the entire board room.

"If you think this is only a tailgate or only a protest— you are wrong. I am responsible for that confusion," Chip's tinny voice called out sturdily. "But if you think it is one hundred percent party, know that you can expect nothing to change here after this ends." Asbury's face turned as blood red as a healthy human face could as other board members donned queasy visages. "If you want to gain nothing, keep thinking this is a party. But if you've heard anything that got you mad this week and you know there's something you wish was better here, get your ass down here to let the campus know."

Asbury listened angrily, assistants began plugging away at their spreadsheets, and Bromhead took out a pen for a set of notes that his team would use throughout what could likely be another long night. Kathie tried to calm herself after locking onto thoughts that Eva had been in on this scheme the entire time and was there to mock her to her face.

At the same time, Eva wondered if she should say something to let them know she, too, was shocked. She stole a peek at Kathie. The girl's fiery stare, which Eva caught by accident, confirmed she should stay as quiet as possible until she could regroup privately.

"Now hold on, hold on," Asbury demanded weakly. "This doesn't mean any—"

Before he could finish his plea, a Registrar's Aide entered with an announcement. "New protestors are appearing in the Quad. Estimates suggest he'll have more in an hour than he did before that...that guy spoke." As the doors remained open behind him, this moment was sadly the only instant "that guy" aka Lightstorm seized a look into a PPC session, when he craned his neck from the hall to see a flurry of activity but not an invitation.

Inside the meeting, Asbury re-seated himself as a furious Kathie scowled over her laptop screen at Eva, watching carefully for even the tiniest glimmer of smugness. When the object of her hatred looked back, she saw in Eva's face only defiance (not the truth, which was that Eva was merely focused on hiding her own fear).

Nearly all others in the room couldn't help but focus on the most pressing of questions: how did Lockwood manage to smoothly return from the dead after such a gargantuan blow?

Chapter 31: "Porcelain Angel"

THE SIXTY-FIVE minutes between the confetti explosion and the PPC's decision to treat the situation as still hostile were far more stressful for Chip's cabinet.

After a minute of muted despair following the departure of his audience, Chip arose over the jeers and laughter, stumbled away from the window, and set his sights on the refrigerator. Upon reaching it, he first used it for balance before rummaging through it.

Edie had too many emotions pummeling her focus to be concerned by Chip's scavenger hunt at first. Over the course of their friendship, she had become proficient at guessing Chip's thoughts with merely a single expression. But following Kathie's spectacle, Edie was surprised to see a unique countenance: dumbfounded acceptance. The look aggravated her enough to leave the room for what she considered to be a vital sojourn into the nearest empty dorm room.

Upon her return, the peppier but still agitated young lady was disappointed to see Chip taking sturdy swigs from a bottle of inexpensive vodka. Acting immediately, she pulled the bottle away and threw it in the trash as he reeled back and forth.

Edie knew he needed to strike back swiftly, so she decided the bottle's recently dispelled contents would have to find another place to spend the afternoon.

Grabbing Chip by the shoulders, Edie briskly led him to the hall with the hope that only a limited number would see him in his state. Fifteen paces later she pushed through a door labeled WOMEN and maneuvered him to the first empty stall. Once there, she set Chip on his knees with his face towards the toilet and forced two fingers down his throat until his body responded.

The heaves continued in spurts with fantastic results until Chip sank back and leaned against the stall's side wall. He wiped his mouth off with the back of an exhausted arm as Edie used several ply of toilet paper to wipe off her right hand.

Chip squeezed his eyelids tightly as he fought against the wavy aftershocks. Edie managed to get most of the alcohol out of his body before it could be processed, but not all of it.

"Speaking of something totally different, like plans…" the still slightly intoxicated Chip muttered. "I hope you have one because my contributions might be *extremely* limited for a few."

Edie grabbed Chip by his armpits to hoist him up. "We're getting you on the radio. People need to hear this distraction won't keep you from continuing your work."

"We have a radio?" Chip asked as Edie led him to a sink.

Moving past the question, as well as the inquiry of whether Chip felt they'd reached an utterly helpless point, Edie pressed on. "William will write you your speech, which you will read verbatim," she stressed the last part sternly as Chip dunked his face into the sink's icy cold rushing water. "Alf will get someone on the phone from the student radio station and Carolina is going to nurse you the hell back to health."

Chip lifted his face from the water and through squinted eyes asked, "Nursed as in how much? Like, under the shirt?"

Using one of her recently washed hands, Edie turned Chip's face towards hers. "Rest that stupid voice and idiot mouth of yours. Starting now."

*　　　　*　　　　*

It took no time for Edie to locate Alf and get him up to speed.

During Edie's slightly more tiresome search for William and Carolina, she laid her eyes on the Quad multiple times to observe real protestors leaving. She would have to fix that, she resolved. Soon the entire team could work to pack the Quad with true believers. But in the interim, people who merely appeared bona fide would have to suffice.

She found William and Carolina enjoying the dance party going on in Three South's Disco Room and she rapidly gave Carolina her important task. Then, while pulling William away for his assignment, Edie made a mental list of friends of friends who could be counted on to paint vague protest placards and start filling up the emptying Quad. As William set off to write the most compelling speech he could, exonerating Chip of the cowboys and Indians prank without explicitly mentioning it, she dialed one number after another on her trusty phone.

Edie knew it would take more than a radio broadcast and straw men with generic poster boards (or "poseur boards" as she called them on the phone) to get Chip where he needed to be. First, though, they had to stop the bleeding.

*   *   *

Just short of seventy minutes after the multi-pronged disaster, Chip took to the microphone (actually a dorm phone in a random Two South room) to address the theoretical entirety of the campus. At least, that's what Edie wanted the PPC to think.

The broadcast was intended entirely for the university's disciplinary boards, not the student body. Edie assumed that Asbury's team was so out of touch that they would believe students were listening to the radio station in droves. The only students expected to hear the speech were the *Nightly Pembertonian* writers who would receive quality sound bites of Chip sounding like the charismatic leader he was pretending to be.

During the transmission (which I am obligated to not repeat out of fear it might incite unrest at other institutions), Edie thanked Carolina wholeheartedly for getting Chip back into shape. She didn't know what did it, or how much this distressed mission ate into their already low supply of sports and sports drinks, but the work she did was fantastic.

The minute the speech ended, Chip dropped the receiver, and sprinted to the closest bathroom. In his wake, Edie's associates trickled into the Quad with freshly decorated signs.

*   *   *

As Edie smoked a rare cigarette one stall away from Chip's second round of vomiting (which he said he needed to "get out of the woods"), she couldn't help but direct her energy back to her hatred of Kathie.

"If I wasn't so fucking pissed at her," Edie stated, "I'd almost admire what she did." She took Chip's lack of movement as a suggestion another onslaught was coming. "Are you alive?"

"Augh...porcelain angel..." came his muffled response.

"Get your head out of the toilet and back in the game. You've got less than 24 hours, your audience is bonging beers instead of burning bras, and she's got the school thinking you're the party animal you really are."

"You're looking at it all wrong," Chip replied as he pushed himself up to his feet. "Kathie just helped us."

Edie stubbed out her cigarette and stepped out of the stall to watch Chip wash his face. "Are you vomiting bullshit now that you're out of puke?"

As Chip explained, the afternoon's painful recuperation process left him with time to think. Big open-air talks with the school only worked under really specific conditions, and thanks to a lack of initiative, no one in the crowd could help push the protest any further than he already had. He had to start reaching out to the people who truly wanted the protest to thrive. "Kathie showed us that the group outside is on our side only as long as there isn't a cooler party somewhere else."

"Please tell me you're not going to just try to make this a cooler party."

Chip pulled open the bathroom door and the pair entered the hall to see three young ladies dressed in ghoulish Halloween costumes chase a male student piloting a unicycle while juggling three rubber sex toys and being taped by a student cameraman.

Chip continued with, "Cooler party? Ain't no such thing. No, we're going to appeal right to the real leaders on campus. They can carry this thing over the one yard line for us."

"So..." Edie began amid a shoulder check to see if others were in earshot. "We need people to do the work for you."

"Pretty much," Chip replied. The pair slid into Alf's room and shut the door for privacy. "You, me, Alf, and William will get a list of all of the people in charge of important student groups and beg them to help us teach everyone what's at stake here...starting with Eva."

Edie uttered a deliberately audible moan while Chip scrolled through his phone's recent text message list. As Edie had already grown tired of dealing with another bossy student who wielded more power than she deserved, she wasn't terribly fond of admitting Eva could have so much say over the outcome of Chip's week. "Why do we need her? She's just going to wait this out and jump on the winner's side claiming she's been there the whole time. I say we stick to the student directory and call up every other group we can find."

"We'll need to do that, too," a distracted Chip noted as he located Eva's phone number. "But I don't know if this part can work without her."

Edie leaned against the wall farthest from the dreaded phone call. "You sure you can handle this? I know you're not used to calling girls when you know their full name."

Chip laughed and put the phone up to his ear. "Hold on, it's ringing."

Edie watched Chip's patient but enthusiastic glow give way to a softly confused expression. "What is it?"

"She didn't answer."

"Leave a message! It's not rocket telephony."

"Okay, quiet." He cleared his throat to aide a change into a smooth, rehearsed, and usually very successful tone. "Hey, this is Chip Lockwood. I'm hoping we can talk. Give me a call. I'm at three-two-three, [REDACTED], two-two-five-seven. Again, three-two-three, [REDACTED], balls." A puzzled Chip disconnected the call. "That was weird."

"Don't pretend you've never had a girl send you straight to voicemail."

"I can't lie. I gotta say it's never happened."

"Well maybe it should have considering what's stumbled out of your apartment. It's like rejects from a DMV."

Chapter 32: "Ask Eva Yesterday."

THE INDIVIDUAL outreach ploy may have been Chip's best idea of the week, albeit one he should have conjured far sooner, considering he was low on time and resources. Not only could the act of promoting these student leaders' causes in a grand fashion generate healthy symbiosis, it was also the most unselfish of Chip's decisions that week.

Some students with whom he spoke initially sounded intrigued, even excited to receive a call from the man at the center of the spectacle. Almost without fail, though, each person's tone shifted, adopting the unadorned voice of someone following orders. No one could agree to any solid support on their own.

Each person directed Chip to Eva Yesterday, who remained essentially unreachable during Chip's marathon of calls. Between the dozens of suggestions that he speak with her and her refusal to reply to his earlier voicemail, Chip was struggling with questions around what she was thinking and feeling while ignoring him at such a crucial time. (I must admit, I too, was interested in a glimpse into her thought process. As she left campus for home following the PPC meeting, my view into her psyche went hazy and remained that way.)

Knowing he was faced with an ever-shrinking mound of sand in his hourglass, Chip determined the evening would not be an entire wash. Between half hour bouts on the phone, he played fifteen-minute sessions of beer pong and then spent the remainder of the hour addressing the NEQ. Regardless of what awaited him the following day, he had to make the most of what was very likely his last night as a Pemberton Blade.

In each of his hourly trips to address the NEQ (which each started with a scan of the audience for anyone with a megaphone or a visible faculty ID badge who might try to thwart his efforts) he quieted down the majority of the partiers, singled out at least one of the somehow still present legitimate protest groups, and had them share their goals with everyone within earshot.

The move turned out to be quite smart. He knew whatever was keeping people from buying his telephone-based pitches would not block groups who were starving for support from espousing their platforms to the hundreds of students who were happy to listen thanks to Chip.

At nearly 7:00 p.m., after three hours of futile phone calls, a 2-0-1 record in beer pong, and three admirably engaging talks, Chip moved to reassemble his cabinet for an update.

*   *   *

As the hours passed Edie grew more troubled, as well. The worry was not for Chip, rather, her own behavior as they waited.

The Pennsylvanian knew it would be a long time before she'd again be at the heart of something so exhilaratingly far from ordinary. Still she found herself drifting into boredom amid the bedlam. Within days Chip would be either in jail, on an extended vacation, or rushing to gather whatever cash he could before fleeing town. Regardless, she would remain at Pemberton and nothing would change. Her grades were impeccable, her family support was beyond solid, and no one outside of a small, trusted circle knew what she'd really been up to that week. Her place was secure, but that did not mean she was necessarily happy.

By no means did she dislike Pemberton. But the PMU in which she would live in a few short hours would undoubtedly be a blander one. She could look forward only to Business Department functions, typical sorority mixers, and conversations with coeds so boring they would make William sound wild.

After the few minutes of daydreaming, she let more pressing thoughts expunge the others. Regardless of what mysteries awaited her, at that moment she had a mission. Chip had to reconnect with the students with enough zest that Kathie's rebuttals would amount to naught.

At Chip's request, she gathered Alf, then William, and shifted to Chip's room for the 7:15 p.m. regroup.

*   *   *

Chip examined his advisors as they entered the room with less vibrancy than he would have hoped. Alf trotted in with his laptop looking discouraged and upsettingly, more than a little hungry. His spirits were nowhere near as lowly as William, who looked sorrowful even for him. Edie's eyes were jousting with disappointment, as well.

He could tell they didn't have anything grand for him, so he tailored his expectations by recalling the bit of progress he'd pushed through thanks to his fireside chats, as well as his near flawless second beer pong victory minutes earlier.

"But beyond that...short version of my calls: bad," Chip bluntly stated.

Edie nudged William. "Do you look nervous because you have bad news or because I know you were watching cartoons when I picked you up?"

"Both, but mostly the news," he remarked. "I made about forty calls and I only got three groups on board. But they're barely connected to social causes."

Chip exhaustedly chuckled. "Three? Hell that's almost more than I got."

"Me too," Alf added timidly.

Chip queried: "Which groups did you get, Will?"

"The Bike Marathon group, Pemberton's Historical Society, which only has eight members, and PMU Action Role-Play Club. Wait— did you only give me nerdy groups?"

"About eighty percent of the groups are nerdy ones," Edie explained. "And yes, you got the nerdiest."

"Regardless, the vast majority aren't talking to us."

"Your favorite pain in the ass Eva set us up to fail, Chip," Edie coldly cooed. "Most people besides William would have realized three accidental yes's and thirty-seven identical no's is not natural."

Alf added: "The key word is 'identical.' No matter what we say or who we talk to, if they're important enough to help out, they say 'ask Eva Yesterday.'"

Chip wistfully shook his head at the double meaning. "That's cute." He'd received a number of similar replies in his quest. After hearing the first few refusals, he decided to not waste precious time arguing with each person, and he instead listed out each one who employed the response, in case that information could come in handy later.

Alf went on. "Even groups who were helped a ton by the volunteer rush you kicked off won't talk to us. It sounds like Eva wants us to know that without her, we're on our own."

Chip took in the statement but couldn't help laugh at his latest realization: for the second time that week he'd been boxed out by a secret voice telling allies that they weren't allowed to come to his aid. Odd, he thought, that a student rebel would employ the same methods of control as the institution against whom she was constantly battling.

Edie suggested, "I say we ditch the bitch. We need to show the school you're serious, not stop to celebrate how Eva's waiting to figure out which jersey to put on when the game ends."

Chip waved off the idea with a look at the Quad. "I still feel like she's the key."

"You couldn't depend on her even if you did get her on the phone! If she cared this much about you or the student cause, why didn't she help you earlier in the week? Does she even have any real help to give or just empty threats?"

"That's why this is so great!" a rejuvenated Chip said with a smile. "No matter what she is, all I need to do is talk to her and we'll know what to do next."

"I don't follow you."

"If she's a fair weather fan, then it will be easy to convince her I'm the right choice. If she's some true believer then I'll ask what she really can contribute. If it's zilch, we leave her behind, go back to the people we just called, and convince *them* that I'm the one to bet on."

"But what if she does have serious pull?" William asked.

"Then she would have fucking used it months ago and I never would have had a chance to protest for student rights!"

Though impressed, William couldn't help but point out Chip's error with a mumbled response of, "Technically you protested for Native American rights…"

"Not a bad idea," Edie offered, "…if you knew how to get her on the phone."

This prompted Chip to ponder a blunt question: how did he ever get anyone to do what he wanted in desperate situations? While thinking, his eyes drifted from the Quad, to Alf pecking at his laptop, and then to William before concluding the "Creamer Method" was his answer. "We get her talking by convincing her she's already the person she never wanted to become."

Removing his phone from his pocket, Chip hit the redial button and braced himself for the single beep before being sent to voicemail (something he swore he would not remain accustomed to). "This is Chip again. My friends and I have been calling student groups for the last three hours and most were nice enough to pass along your message. Mission accomplished. You just had everyone shoot me down in the exact same way the school shot me down when I brought my concerns to them. So good job. You're telling students to use the same tactics that are used by the administrators you love speaking out against. Think that over. You know my number." Chip closed his phone to disconnect the call.

Edie's reply came first. "Think that will work?"

Chip shrugged. "It could definitely help."

"It better help, because this really only gets you part of what you need. You also need a way to shut Kathie up, and a way to end this."

Chip nodded intently, almost to the point where his audience wondered if he was really focused on the question or the drinks he'd consumed during his beer pong tournament.

William prodded, "So do you have one? A grand finale?"

Chip grabbed a softball and started tossing it to himself. "I'll have that all set soon," he stated, hoping he was not lying.

The short, pensive silence that followed cued Alf to bring up another pressing question. "Speaking of other things we'll figure out soon: where are we on supplies?"

Chip tossed the softball to his top lieutenant. "Can we make it until noon if we have to?"

"I don't know how long the booze can last," she replied. "I think we're down to maybe two or three kegs and random hard liquor. We can scrounge for food for the next few hours. The other big problem is water. If they shut that off we have hundreds of pissed off, thirsty, hungover people and the worst kind of cluster F."

"And we don't want that," Chip replied as Edie tossed the ball back. "Okay, for water let's knock the tops off empty kegs and—"

A rhythmic buzzing coming from Chip's pocket startled him. Dropping the softball, he reached for his phone in his pocket. "Someone's calling me."

"Someone's calling at this hour?" asked a startled William. (It had been a while since his phone rang and it wasn't a relative.)

"Dude, it's only like seven thirty," Chip replied, with an extra-long stare. "You really got this dorky in just one year?" He examined his phone and his face lit up "It's Eva!" he declared, excitedly shaking his phone. "I should send it to voicemail, right?"

Chapter 33: "That's the worst invitation I've ever heard."

CHIP EXPEDITIOUSLY donned his most charming persona before clicking a button on his phone and brightly saying, "This is Chip."

The voice on the other end, which Chip previously knew only from her voicemail prompt, was not as pleased. "You're one reckless ass, did you know that?"

A ready to sweet talk Chip continued, "I didn't think anyone who cares for the students would mind strong initiative."

"Bold action is one thing, what you did to confuse everyone is totally different."

"That's why we have to talk," he pleaded, hoping his tone hid his deceit. "I know you're the go to at PMU when it comes to student rights."

"You knew that and you still did all this without asking me if it would be harmful?"

Realizing penitence might be needed instead of ego stroking, Chip altered course. "I'm sorry and I was impatient. But I need your help. The whole school does and I know you wouldn't let a problem between you and me stand in the way of the all the students."

Chip pictured Eva grimacing. "You're not dumb," she stated

(not knowing much about his most recent set of midterm scores). "But you don't get it: I can't trust a single word you say."

"Why not?"

"I can't separate the person I've been hearing about all week from the one I saw on Tuesday who reinforced every frat-tastic rumor about you."

"I can guarantee the Chip you'll be dealing with is trustworthy and honest."

"I wish it was that simple, but I've put so much into this. So forgive me if I can't blindly trust the guy who once switched the photos in the Animal Protection Club's Cute Pets calendar with pictures of morbidly obese people on tractors."

Chip covered the cell phone's microphone as he restrained himself from laughing. "You got me, I've pulled some pranks here and there but please know: this is not one of them."

A lengthy coda followed. Chip glanced at Edie and William, whose faces were growing more anxious with each exchange.

"I want to talk to you about this," Eva offered.

"Thank God! Thank you. First up: what can you—"

"Stop. It's not that easy," Eva quickly retorted. "I've been in this fight for years. You've just pulled your head out from under Sorority Row to join in. If I'm supposed to risk everything for you, I need to be one hundred percent sure I can trust you."

"You can. You absolutely can," Chip said hurriedly. "Now let's get down to it."

"No, not on the phone. I'm going out on a limb so you have to, too. I'm willing to talk but only if you meet me at my apartment to do so."

The smile, energy, and shockingly even his characteristic tan vanished from his face. Who was she to demand something so reckless? "That's the worst invitation I've ever heard."

The gap in conversation that followed grew into an awkward one as he realized his response was likely a more insulting one than Eva was expecting. While he stood silent with a flat expression, Edie sought to kick him back into reality.

"What is it?" she asked after the foot tap.

Chip shook his head. "She wants to talk in person. At her place."

"That's fucking nuts!" William blurted before slapping both hands over his mouth.

Edie cocked an eyebrow at the absurd proposal. "Doesn't she know what's going on? We can't even do carry out. Delivery is out of the question."

"Tell me about it," Chip said. He removed his hand from the phone. "You can't be serious."

"I've thought hard about this and I can't come up with a better way for you to show your commitment."

"Better than getting hundreds of students to donate time and energy on the same day? Better than amplifying their voices when they want to speak up? Your idea isn't better, it's extreme." Chip declared. He didn't want to sound rude, but it sounded like all Eva was offering him was the chance to stick his target-covered head out in the open. Moreover, she sounded like she was all talk and no substance. "Even if I could leave, which I can't, why would I risk it just on faith that you'll help?"

"Good point," Eva replied plainly. "Do me a favor and look out of your window."

Chip stuck his head through a break in the curtains. "What am I looking for?"

"Concrete proof. What do you see?"

"A bunch of people here to see what happens to us in AP Hall," he replied with a shred of impatience.

Chip heard a beep as Eva sent a text message without disconnecting their call. "And now?"

With Edie and William peeking through slits in the curtains, the junior examined the crowd carefully. He was too far to see the half dozen people whose cell phones received Eva's message. He was able to spot the six make announcements prompting about one hundred fifty students to raise their left hand in unison. He nearly dropped the phone before the students lowered their arms. This was not an outcome that anyone in Alf's room had considered possible.

Eva directed: "I don't know how many other people you've got out cheering you on, but the ones you just saw will disappear the moment they find out you're mocking their beliefs." Eva paused to shift from the threatening tone, which she was not used to utilizing, to one of sincerity. "Don't forget: I'm risking everything trusting you. You have to respond in turn."

Despite the lack of foresight that could have predicted this turn of events, Chip was not willing to roll over, especially not after seeing the student support he so desperately wanted waiting just outside his grasp. He scrambled for any alternate idea he could conjure. "How about we find a dorm room in one of the dorms nearby where you can see into a room over here? You and I we'll be able to talk and see each other. Right?"

"Not happening."

"Come on!" he stated, hoping he didn't sound exasperated. "I get where you're coming from, but that's impossible. We can't open the doors before the school caves."

"I've been told if there's one person who can do absolutely anything on this campus, it's you. So if you want to talk, I suggest you find one more miracle tonight."

At this, Chip's mind leapt from the image of the raised hands to a sight of the statue of his Aunt Adelaide, then to the bust of his great grandfather in the campus' concert hall, and finally to the plaque of his aunt Laura Lockwood honoring her years of post-Pemberton service in the Peace Corp. Was he angry at Eva's reply? Aroused by her daring? Impressed at her secret weapon? Whatever he was thinking, the pitch and the adrenaline it gave him was impossible to ignore. "Give me fifteen minutes to figure this out. Be by your phone."

"Fine," Eva said.

Chip hung up and gently lobbed the phone across the room onto his bed.

"Well? What are we doing?" asked a curiously eager Edie.

"We're going to all get a drink."

*   *   *

While Alf and his laptop moved through the security checks

he'd been running every three hours, he, Chip, and the other advisors sipped at low quality beer and argued over Eva's motivations.

Neither the danger nor the irony was lost on anyone. If they proceeded with their courtship, Chip's only way to prove he could command such power from inside a locked off building was by surreptitiously exiting the building in front of the entire crowd he'd attracted.

Thanks to text messages from trusted colleagues, Edie was well aware of the rumors that Chip had been freely walking in and out of August Hall all week. She was indelibly suspicious of the idea that asked Chip to prove false rumors right for the purpose of proving his earnestness.

To Edie, Eva's pitch amounted to sabotage, and she was not shy in sharing that thought. Eva was nothing more than a selfish birthday girl who couldn't stand that someone who was barely trying was doing a better job than she at pinning the tail on the donkey at her own party. Chip countered by explaining how he felt her sincerity on the phone. If she were really trying to ruin him, it wouldn't be by setting an elegant trap that would undoubtedly hurt the student body. In no way could students gain anything that week if their only two leaders were found tearing each other limb from limb.

Despite what he believed of her credulity, Chip knew Eva's suggestion really was a rock solid way to force him to prove his worth. Successfully passing the challenge would certainly show he was part of the fight. It might even be enough, he thought, to convince her that he was the "real deal" even without pleading his case beyond merely showing up for her.

"I thought," William began, in an attempt to be the voice of reason, "that we were going to stop and re-think all of this through if we found out she actually did have some power."

"No, you just wanted to hear that," Chip replied. "The call did exactly what we wanted: it showed that she's got the students that we need to get my ass booted."

"But what do you know about those people besides that she made them put on a good show?" William pried. "If so many students had her back this whole time, why didn't she ever use them?"

Edie scoffed: "Because she's never had a sucker stupid enough to ask for her help. Now she's got Chip."

Perhaps due to his confidence, which society had helped stroke for years, Chip would not be deterred. "I need those people, and I know, I freaking know I can get her to give them to me."

"*We* know that," Edie noted. "How are you going to let Eva know that without leaving?"

"Not quite sure yet," Chip replied while circling the room and bumping his friends' beer tops with the bottom of his own. The cue to finish their beers wasn't very well received. "Ideas?"

William avowed: "The only idea we need is the one that convinces Eva this is out of the question."

Chip crushed the empty beer can in his hands. "She's dead set on this, so we either find a way to get around her or a way to get to her. Get me a beer, bro."

William opened the fridge and pulled out one of the remaining cans, noticing how shallow the vessel's bounty had become. "She's willing to meet but couldn't come up with anything remotely better than her shitty idea?"

"Two things," Edie said while discarding her beverage. "One, if she had better ideas, she would've had a crowd at her protests long before Chip's posse came along. Second, she has a valid point. Anyone who knows shit about Chip from before this week would know he's not taking this seriously."

"Of course you like the idea," William complained. "It's stupid and reckless."

"I didn't say I liked the idea, Prince Whiny," Edie replied. "I think it's as stupid as giving a frat guy a hand job on the bus ride to his winter formal."

"Stupidity aside, we need her!" Chip insisted. "She could be the fastest way to get the voices I need. We can't argue all night. Final votes, let's go."

Unsure of who should speak first, the conspirators looked around to gauge what other responses might get offered.

William posited: "I think it's too risky to do but I don't have any better alternatives."

Chip looked to a pensive Edie, who added, "I'm still not sure it's not a trap but I guess she can't afford to totally screw you over."

Alf, having only been half listening, nodded into his laptop and provided Chip with an outstretched thumb up.

Chip fist bumped Alf's hand and gave an excited grunt. "Nice. Time to get pumped." He then opened up the door and pulled William into the hallway. "Let's go. Everyone."

The revelry in the hallway calmed their nerves slightly as they recalled there were at least some supporters in their midst. (As they convened, at the end of the hall, the head of an overly intrigued student popped out of a study lounge. He remained unnoticed as he approached.)

"It's time to enjoy ourselves," Chip instructed, "while I figure out how to do this before we realize it's too f-ing complicated to bother."

As Chip spoke rosily of a path with fewer obstacles, the aforementioned young man strutted towards them unnoticed, with his weasel-like smirk ready to mark their grand reunion.

Chip continued, "If you get any ideas before I do, find me. We cool?"

The guest's lamentably familiar voice replied: "Oh we always cool, muthafuckaaah!"

Edie and Chip, whose backs were turned toward the peculiar voice, could only watch the bewildered William and terrified Alf for clues about the visitor's identity. Chip turned and forced himself to mask every emotion upon realizing he was standing face to face with Squanto.

Chapter 34: "Three birds with one...stone."

"YOU DICK mustards have no idea how long I've been trying to get back in here," Squanto said while being more than lightly nudged out of the hallway. He was so exuberant to be near Chip again that he didn't realize it wasn't a compliment when his "friend" pushed him into a dorm room to get him out of sight the instant after he saw him. While this went on, Edie whispered hushed instructions into Alf's ear and sent him on his way to find Carolina, who would likely be willing to help with their latest sticky situation.

"Get on with the story," urged Chip. "Just tell us how you got in."

"You thought you were smart, didn't you, you jack ass?" Squanto hissed. "First I was going to wait you out, thinking you'd let me in once you got bored."

"How'd that work out for you?" William asked drably.

"Ha, ha!" Squanto shot back. "Funny, dick face. Anyway, then figured I could climb in. I made it part of the way up a few times but some guys on Four noticed me and kept dropping water balloons on me until I backed down."

Chip squinted at the statement. "All it took was water balloons?"

"They moved to...warmer liquids after the first few."

William responded with a shudder as Chip and Edie chortled.

Squanto plowed on. "I switched to a different wall and I finally made it up to a level that had windows but I lost my arm strength when I looked into a room where some lucky bastard was creaming all over Carolina."

"That was you?" an angry William queried.

"That was you?" Squanto replied, just as enraged. "Shit, I knew this guy was fucking me over. First taking my friends, then my pussy." The observation was paired with a shove into William's chest.

"Hey screw you, man," William called back, ready to lunge at Squanto with the indignation of his former jock self, whom a happily entertained Edie and Chip had not yet seen. "I'm sure every girl in here is happy you got locked out— that's double for any girl who sleeps."

Chip put his hands up to separate the two. "How did you get back in, Squanto?"

"Oh, that. After crashing in the library I figured you missed something, since, you know, you took this whole idea from me. And boom— I found an old version of the floor plan that had these weird lines from Colonial Hall all the way here. So I busted into Colonial and tore up the basement until I found an old door that was wallpapered up. That led me to a dirty as shit underground tunnel that no one knows about!"

The explanation fascinated and frightened Chip. On the one hand, it did give him both a way to meet Eva and to oust Squanto once again. On the other hand, if word of this got out, the hearsay that he'd been masterminding the whole week between off-site visits would strengthen. "Just how secret is this secret passage?"

Squanto replied with a reptilian sneer of self-satisfaction. "Real secret. I had to go through six maps before I could find it and it wasn't on anything else I found in the reference library. I guess they forgot about it. But it's still there! It brings you right under the Quad and into a storage closet."

"Did anyone see you use it?"

"Hell no! You guys didn't share for days and now I ain't sharing with nobody!"

Edie was hesitant but was drawn towards asking: "Share what exactly?"

"Poon, bitches! I know people are getting ass here, especially if this scrawny shit is getting some. They're gonna love me now that I'm back."

Despite always wanting to limit their interactions, Edie couldn't help but initiate one more query. "So after not showering for days and getting covered in piss, you snuck in here expecting to get unlimited ass?"

The contemplative pause before his reply only made the answer worse. "You offering?"

All stared back with blatantly unimpressed looks.

An exhausted Chip stated, "Please tell me you at least took the map."

In one fluid motion, Squanto reached into one of his jeans pockets and produced a folded up blueprint. Chip snatched it up straight away.

*　　　*　　　*

Minutes later, Chip, Edie, and William were basement-bound, snaking through the interlocked gatherings of the third floor. Thanks to Edie's quick thinking, their guest remained behind, forcibly unable to make the voyage with them.

Upon the presentation of the map, Carolina and three of her closest friends entered the room right on cue. The four carried an absurd bounty of alcohol and flashed smiles entrancing enough to strip Squanto of his desire to leave, not to mention his suspicions that he was being held prisoner. Their instructions from Alf via Edie were to keep the outsider's face out of sight, his BAC elevated, and his cell phone battery drained.

The walk through the halls brought the three schemers better news. The energy in the dorm was inexplicably high, and despite a lack of luxuries, like the ability to go to off-campus bars or engage their brains with lecture attendance, August's residents were unflappable. Much to Chip's delight, he learned that the residents even managed to solve one of his biggest logistical dilemmas: the imposingly finite amount of food, water, and alcohol.

Around six p.m., an innovative Political Science major who lived on AP Hall's third floor called upon friends who lived in a nearby dorm to purchase cases of beer and toss the cans to his room. The idea, though it carried only a middling success rate, caught on, thanks in part to Dean Sheridan's plans for the building that kept the first set of dorm rooms far too high for anyone to climb in or out. Within an hour, countless sodas, sports drinks, and food items were soaring into August. Some students made a game of it by daring each other to see who could throw the most cans consecutively without a miss. This display prompted an unexpected partnership to bloom when the student booster club joined with a protest group to pledge to lob into the dorm two bottles of water for every beer they saw fly in.

This endearing show of support was much appreciated, but the event's organizers knew they had other more critical concerns, namely the ever-shrinking expulsion deadline and the lack of security, the latter being the reason the trio went to take a look at the passageway.

During their walk to the building's lowest floor, the three bickered as stealthily as possible about Squanto's foreboding presence.

Edie felt disquieted by the fact that they had no proof that he truly did keep the passage a secret or that he'd gone unnoticed in Colonial Hall. Chip urged her to think little of these factors during their quest to expunge Squanto from the building once more. Secretly he, too, felt the uneasy pings realizing his confidence about security had been misguided during the entire siege.

As they went on, Chip pointed out how beneficial it was that someone who thought he was helping the cause made the discovery instead of a university employee.

The three entered the basement's Great Hall to see a set of students setting up for a concert. No one present seemed to be looking for the same thing they were and none among them could see a conspicuous hole in any wall. This quelled some fears.

They moved along, hoping to draw as little attention as possible. Although the map said the corridor jutted out of the building's northwest corner, Chip led them to the southeast for the door that earlier brought them to the cold storage unit. This opening was one of four that led from the Great Hall to the perimeter of windowless dorm rooms turned storage closets.

Once out of the Great Hall, they first moved past the guarded entrance to the supply room with the dwindling keep, and then headed down to Basement South. To their left, the hall was lined with storage rooms whose doors had been left open after getting raided.

As they pivoted to approach the basement's western corridor, Chip's worries about the secrecy of the passage dwindled when he saw that none of the hallway's rooms or their locks appeared disturbed. They continued to the end of the hall where they stopped in stupor upon seeing no sign of forcible entry anywhere or anything that looked like Squanto's handiwork.

Using the light from Edie's phone screen, they examined the map and realized they had gotten lost on the way to finding the hall, bolstering their assurance in the passage's secrecy. After doubling back they found a door halfway down the hall that led to a westward bound hall. This corridor soon led to another, which presented Chip with a final set of four storage rooms, one whose door was wide open.

Hearing of the secret pathway was menacing to Chip's mental wellbeing. Seeing it personally then should have been devastating. Instead of a morose concession, upon examining the entranceway, Chip only reacted with a confounding and simple, "Well…that kind of sucks."

Despite its remote location, the room into which the pathway opened was being used for storage. The hall's existence was evidently a mystery to even the theater troupe whose props were piled up around it.

Chip's eyes were quickly drawn to the signs of Squanto's forceful push in, which was evidently the first use of the knob-less door in decades. His action stripped off a floor to ceiling streak of wallpaper thick enough to mask the creases between the door and the wall, and dusty signs of its lack of use covered pockets of props around the room.

Edie opened the door wider for a glimpse into the nondescript, dark, and grimy hallway. She and William simultaneously noted it would have been a good idea to bring a flashlight. At the same time, Chip pulled himself away from his mental debate over the Eva quandary as an interesting realization came to him: nothing he'd built that week was ever really impenetrable.

Instead of a gloomy response, again Chip marked the actualization with humor. "Thank God the school is listening to their bureaucrats instead of their engineers."

Chip returned his focus to what he could see of the pathway as questions tore through his mind. The most troubling among them was whether this was too good to be true.

He agreed that the hall did seem perhaps a little too lucky, but then again, so many things that came to him at critical moments were also borne almost entirely of pure luck. Furthermore, as there was no way Eva Yesterday knew who Squanto was, so there was little to no chance she could have known of his discovery, making Chip's arrival that much more stunning.

Soon the quandary reminded Chip of one more fact: he was Chip Lockwood and nothing so far that week had stopped him. Now that he had a way to reach Eva and astound the campus leader while convincing her to do the heavy lifting for him, Chip didn't see an all too convenient option or a compromise to his secure lair. He saw a practical way to complete a mission that would sound impossible to nearly any person but a Lockwood.

"This will work," he declared, instantly stopping his friends' dispute. "Give me ten minutes and I'll show you how we're making this happen."

*   *   *

Back in August Hall fifteen minutes later, Chip placed onto his bed a large map he'd drawn up. It depicted the buildings of the Quad, the passage to Colonial Hall, and also, for good measure, it contained a giant drawing of a set of male reproductive organs.

"Listen," Chip began, "we can knock out three birds with one penis shaped stone here: get Eva on our side, ditch Squanto, and seal up that exit before anyone else finds it." His plan followed, along with failed attempts at eye contact with Edie, Alf, and William. They would need more than a map to allow him to carry out such a plan and he knew this. "This might not be the choice we want but it will get us what we need. You with me, William?"

William nervously rubbed his nose. "Did I ever have a vote?"

"No, but if it makes you feel better, don't forget: I know if I go face to face with this girl, I can get her on our side."

In a moment fueled by her belief in Chip's titanium-laced charm, not to mention a desire to see which unimaginably exciting routes their night could take if they went through with such a plan, Edie winked, denoting she was onboard.

Chip hopped to his feet, grabbed his phone, and dialed Eva's phone number. After two rings, she answered. "I almost didn't think you'd call back."

"Are you kidding? We're definitely on. But we can't do it now."

"Um...how late do you plan on coming?"

Chip, who was trained on the countdown clock, skipped the dirty joke he would have made under normal circumstances and replied, "Not late, but not now. What's your address?"

"Seven fourteen Orrington, Unit E. Go up the back porch to the third floor."

The former French Studies minor smiled at the number before responding. "Fine. Don't expect us before ten thirty. Good?"

"Fine."

Chip disconnected the call and pointed one hand at Alf and another at Edie. "Alf, get as much booze into Squanto's room as you can. Edie, get your sorority on the phone and have them tell all the houses that tonight's protest is about to become a costume party."

Chapter 35: "Enjoy College Out Loud"

AT ASBURY'S insistence, the pair would meet in a private staff room in the recesses of the campus library. He had no desire to speak with Bromhead, but he knew he had to, thus the inconvenient location. He felt the banker deserved to have to ask permission to access at least one of the campus' buildings (he left the man no instructions on how to get past the turn styles). What's more, Asbury wanted Bromhead to see at least some real students that week, many of whom were still studying in droves despite the hubbub.

The two were meeting at the insistence of the university president. The reasoning, as it was told to Asbury was that the head of the school felt his key campus leader should have as open of access as possible to Bromhead's findings. The unspoken subversive suggestion Asbury heard, meanwhile, was that the school wanted him to have one advisor whose voice stood out. He'd been in "the game" a while, though, so a short meeting he could tolerate, especially if it were under his own terms.

Once the talk began with a series of questions from Bromhead instead of the guest listening quietly, Asbury knew it was more than just an informative meet up. This loud behavior suggested to Asbury that he wasn't in charge. He had been summoned.

Focusing on doing his duty and getting the consultant out of his way for the remainder of the night, Asbury answered Bromhead's lead query of whether anyone had bothered to contact Lockwood's parents that week. No one from his office contacted the boy's parents, he explained, and he assumed no one else at the school did. Asbury bemoaned the family would tie up as many phone lines later that week upon finding their cherub in jail.

Bromhead then requested a status on how the school felt the students seemed to be reacting. Asbury explained that his team found that online chatter was still abounding on campus (this was consistent with the media inquiries, which were starting to trickle in), and a healthy crowd was still present outside of August Hall. They knew students were listening, but they did not know what message they were ingesting. Finding the pulse of the student body was made more difficult due to the fact that late reports explained students were arriving at the NEQ in costumes. A number were wearing protest-themed outfits, like some theater students on scene who touted readymade outfits taken from their few costume vaults that weren't in August's basement.

At this point, Bromhead stepped in, ready to offer suggestions that would help Asbury determine Charles Lockwood's real agenda, which could help them stifle the unrest. The three most likely ways to strip positive public consensus away from Lockwood were:

1. Proving he did not write the declaration he distributed on Wednesday.

2. Showing that August residents truly could come and go s they pleased that week.

3. Revealing that Lockwood and Yesterday were partners.

The idea behind the first option was simple: if Chip were really the crusader he claimed to be, he would have written the tome by his own hand. If he was not serious, he would have had someone else fabricate it for him— or worse, he would have stolen it.

This thought was first presented in one of Kathie's rants, but the banker's interest was not piqued until after hearing from an assistant about an academic dishonesty deterrent PMU called the Duden

System. Every essay ever written by a PMU student was destined to make its way through the Duden System, where it would have its writing patterns analyzed for plagiarism. Every time an essay was submitted for a class, TA's would add them to the Duden System's server, which would categorize them by student, matriculation year, and course.

The tool, which cost PMU nearly one million dollars to research, build, and maintain over its first eight years had been used at most four times per semester. Still, in 2005, the Duden's archives held every essay and term paper from every student who was on campus at the time of Chip's attempted uprising.

After deciding the Registrar's Office would send the document through the wringing process, the team proceeded to the second point, that Chip secretly exited and reentered the locked down dorm all along. If the students heard their fearless leader didn't abide by the rules his prisoners followed, their enthusiasm would dampen.

By that point no energy was placed into these rumors, although the PPC did receive some notable emails on the subject. Eight people stated that they saw other students who were not Chip addressing large crowds from August Hall, including one who insisted a TA named Jia Xiong spoke to the students from the window everyone believed was being used strictly by Chip.

The importance of the third metric was slightly shrouded. If it turned out that Chip was really just Eva's puppet, the university could explain to its students that the person who was allegedly looking out for them felt she had to first dupe them into listening to a ventriloquist's dummy in order to help them. Students who had inherited their protest vigor that week would disperse immediately and return to classes angered yet determined to ignore Eva and Chip.

Bromhead admitted he and his team had been investigating Eva's history, political leanings, and other factors for hours at that point. Several signs already pointed to her being the singular mastermind behind the upheaval, and there were easy ways to pick apart Eva's character in front of the students, should they need to do so.

This last set of notes would have normally infuriated Asbury, but behind the focused look in his eyes, he was not listening with anywhere near all of his attention.

Nonetheless, Bromhead continued extolling the merits of his three metrics.

Prior to starting his last barely disguised demand, he stated for the record that neither he nor any employee of his company wanted the incident to go on longer than necessary. However, the data showed that there were ideal times to end the siege. At the end of the business day on Friday would be preferred, notably as it was near the end of the news cycle. Concurrently, midnight to three a.m. and ten p.m. to midnight were bad and worse, respectively. Due to the alcohol present, disrupting students after midnight had the highest likelihood of a violent outcome, and deposing Lockwood before midnight could lead to someone else replacing him, if the right figurehead stepped forward.

Bromhead then realized he'd spoken for a number of minutes without hearing any replies. After a logically short exchange of pleasantries, he excused himself and departed.

Asbury remained in the room for a few minutes before proceeding slowly through the library as he tried to determine which part of him felt empty due to the rendezvous. What started as a task he believed he was doing out of his duty to the school turned into something far worse.

He thought of his meeting with Bromhead and began mentally cycling through his preferred on-campus protest examples. In each of those cases, he mused, whoever turned the situation from simple to calamitous must have had started off with reasonable, coherent thoughts. What was the last completely rational thought they had before they started shifting their campus down a dark, destructive path? Along those lines: what was the first only somewhat irrational thought that regrettably comforted their grasp of right and wrong?

As he pivoted deliberately towards the history hallway, he asked himself when exactly his own thoughts started following the same pattern. What steered him from leading a standard PPC meeting to listening to a man like Bromhead try to educate him about the best way to run his campus?

Asbury's feet stopped him in front of the same Pemberton Eight photographs that Chip, Edie, and William examined days earlier. He found in them another message than Lockwood did. With his eyes affixed on an image of his dearly departed colleague, Asbury saw Dean Sheridan doing everything he could to quell the nightmarish, antagonizing situation.

This man acted differently, he thought. *This man acted nobly.*

Sheridan, Asbury argued to himself, fought to understand what was happening since no precedent had been set on campus. Asbury knew what had to be done, and instead of acting, he battled against action by letting nonessential quarrels get in his way. Sheridan didn't deal with sports drinks or banks or Internet usage settlements.[28]

Asbury took a step back to examine the picture with a broader view. He had done his chores by meeting with Bromhead. But now it was time to act. With one last unreserved sneer directed at one of the pictures early on in the Pemberton Eight set, he was on his way.

As he strolled out of the library, he browsed through the list of helpful catalyst suggestions that Bromhead offered and let his mind explore. As soon as he could find a course that would make action look student-driven, it would be time to finally force Chip's hand.

---

[28] For pacing's sake, earlier I skipped why disabling August's Internet access wasn't considered even though the PPC did discuss it. In 2002, the university was one of several institutions that were sued because students were using the university's high speed Internet to illegally download music. To avoid an ugly outcome, PMU's Residential Affairs Department conceded to promote legal purchases and agreed students would hit stressfully high download quotas each semester. Shutting off the Internet in any part of campus during a week where music usage seemed to be at its peak was simply not an option. (In a related twist, in 2003, Bromhead's bank started its "Enjoy College Out Loud" campaign, which gave each PMU student who carried a loan with them the perk of five song downloads at fifty percent off each semester they were undergraduates.)

Chapter 36: "The Strait of Squanto"

AROUND EIGHT p.m., a large number of people in the Quad, including many who were there with the intention of promoting student rights, started to wonder if they had missed an email encouraging the cool kids to show up to the year's biggest party wearing off-color costumes. After arguments at various sit-in sites and flip cup tournaments, dozens of students casually tiptoed away in shifts to find outfits of their own.

As the night progressed, bizarre attire continued to materialize. Students decked as promiscuous police officers and escaped convicts mingled with nuns, cellular phones, and a student dressed as a box of condoms. Another visitor later arrived as the state of Oklahoma in a costume that looked far too professional to have been spontaneous. Some who had evidently not been paying close attention to Chip's alleged goal even returned as scantily dressed caricatures of Native Americans and cow girls.

Cammy Dalton's sorority, not wanting to be outdone by other impeccably coordinated groups, mandated that every member had to attend the evening's "killer protest party" dressed as "cartoon princesses with tight dresses" (with loose morals, it seemed).

This pattern astounded outsiders who showed up without prior knowledge of the recent change in the dress code. One particularly confusing scene took place when some thought it would be funny to restrict the sorority of Native Americans from going more than ten feet away from the student dressed as Oklahoma.

Although it may have looked like a mess to a casual observer, it seemed brilliant to Chip.

*　　　*　　　*

The costume-littered Quad was just one factor of many that required perfect execution that evening. Another was Chip explaining the plan to his lieutenants.

It would begin with Chip addressing the crowd in the NEQ. Immediately following the speech, Squanto and Edie would lead a food run through the passageway with two anonymous, masked freshmen wearing costumes he'd located with help from one of Carolina's associates. Once through to Colonial Hall, Edie and Chip (the first costumed "underclassman") would claim to guard the door and William (the second) would lead Squanto to a group of Chip's fraternity brothers, who, instead of handing off boxes of food, would whisk Squanto away to an all-night party far from town. William would return to watch over the hall's entrance while Edie and Chip met up with Eva. Upon their reunion, they would sneak back into the dorm and Chip would give another speech (ideally to a larger audience) to cement his constant presence in August Hall.

Edie thought the scheme was perilous but terribly exciting, with the exception of having to be close to Squanto, whom they desperately needed back outside to re-solidify the mirage of the dorm's impermeable security. Alf dutifully did not voice any concerns he had over the other conspirators leaving him in the building practically alone shortly after Chip whipped the crowd into a frenzy. He knew the other tasks were more challenging than his. Chip chalked up William's lack of opposition to the fact that he finally had a reputation with a lady to uphold.

Chip and Edie moved onto the next obstacle: giving Squanto nothing short of an amazing reason to leave the building he clawed to reenter.

The pair returned to the room in which they left Squanto to

find him derisorily drunk and ignoring his phone. That solitary window to the world, should he get separated from his friends again, had been quietly broadcasting a local weather service's five day forecast repeatedly for over seventy minutes thanks to Carolina.

Chip in quick fashion explained to Squanto that he needed his help with a daring food run to save the dorm. Squanto was ecstatic to hear Chip needed his help, and astonishingly, he was too intoxicated to realize the price for his assistance was tremendously high. Squanto's only objection came when Edie handed him a bundle of cloth, which was so heavy he could barely carry. Edie admonished that the maneuver was so secret that everyone leaving the building had to don disguises.

He instantly agreed to help, and while keenly eyeing Edie, downed more beer.

Chip's next battle would be his grand speech.

Even though he was expressly focused, the trek towards his last public appearance before disappearing underground was nearly sidetracked first by one last beer pong game and second by a visit to a study lounge screening of a raunchy comedy film. He was able to bypass the first after realizing college drop outs, too, could still play beer pong. The second and more difficult obstacle was expunged from his mind thanks to Edie's question of "why did you think you needed one more drunk, confined, homoerotic experience this week?"

At a little after ten p.m., Chip appeared in front of a savagely cheering audience. The speech that followed was one of his more concise yet forceful addresses. He began by reciting verbatim the latest cease and desist order he received electronically from officials. He then somewhat brilliantly compared the note to prose on PMU's admissions Web site. He quoted, "'...We remain a world class institution thanks to a commitment to our students, who know the value of a university that never stops asking: what do our students want?'"

Straining his voice to overcome the notably loud movie screening, he asked spectators one by one about the last time Pemberton polled them about what they truly wanted. He argued, amid roars, that such acts were fictitious since PMU's leaders "no longer respect our contract."

And with that, he was off.

*　　　　　*　　　　　*

While running through Basement South, Chip smoothly donned his costume, which consisted of sandals, a giant robe with generic imitations of African-looking icons, and a mask from a multicultural musical revue that was staged in the early 1990s that would cover his whole face and head.

He arrived at his destination to find Edie dressed as a samurai with a helmet under her arm and William in a billowy Roman toga complete with a silver battle-ready chest piece, and confusingly, the happy, comedic half of a set of plaster theater masks. As the helmet that matched the costume would not cover a face, Chip's costume assistant improvised with the rose-cheeked, oddly bucktoothed mask.

William, though ready for the task ahead, felt the need to declare the obvious. "I take it everyone noticed how absolutely ridiculous these costumes look."

"These will be fine," Chip insisted, "deal with it."

With an extra look at their garb, Edie asked, "Anyone else wondering what the hell kind of racist theater department we have?"

Chip lowered the mask over his face until it fit snugly and tested his range of vision from behind the eyeholes. "Can you tell it's me?"

William shrugged. "You don't look like someone who would get in here, if that's what you're after."

"Nice. Get yours on. And don't forget: only Edie talks once Squanto shows."

*　　　　　*　　　　　*

Eight minutes later, the parka-blanketed mess flushed himself out of a stairwell and into a zig zag stumble across the Great Room floor and then the hallways he'd navigated with more finesse earlier in the evening.

When he arrived at the rendezvous point, Edie tried with unsurprising ease to look as annoyed at his tardiness. William and Chip stood soundlessly behind her.

Squanto crept to Edie. He stopped to stand with as much stability as a top nearing the end of a spin and hoisted the parka's hood over his head. "Okay— let's—" he sputtered into the heavy fabric before his voice took a darker tone. "Who the fuck are these guys?"

"They're with me," Edie demanded, pushing herself between William and Squanto, correctly guessing Squanto's imposing lean was agitating the soldier/performer.

"They can't answer for themselves?"

"Come on, we're late," Edie insisted. "Show me how to get out of here."

Squanto grunted to signal agreement and inadvertently regurgitated up two ounces of beer. "I still don't know why Chip didn't come. Don't get me wrong, I'd fuck the shit out of you. But this is a mission for dudes, you know, guys who know each other like only dudes can."

Edie pushed past the putrid comment, taking solace knowing it wouldn't take much for Squanto to fall asleep after his walk to Colonial Hall. "I need to tell you something."

Under the weighted garment, Squanto pushed his forehead down and fought to lift it back up to complete a nod.

"After we get back you're going to get one nut punch from the biggest athlete I can find for every time you break the silence. Understood?"

"Got it," a distracted Squanto mumbled, noting that the unforgiving hefty folds in the hood were making it more difficult to see.

Following Edie, and with the unnervingly silent pair behind him, Squanto launched into a stagger and said, "Feast your bitch ass eyes on the Strait of Squanto. It feels like it goes on forever and then it points slightly to the left. And if you like long stuff that points—"

"Shut. Up. Now."

Once inside the hall, Edie scanned it to see it was four feet wide, dusty, and mostly bare. Its cinderblock walls and lack of lighting suggested it had not been designed for frequent use. The poor visibility and potential for hidden obstacles prevented the four from walking faster than a crawl. Edie knew this would not do.

At about one third of the way through, Squanto piped up. "You in that Jap mask. Don't I know you from like classes?"

"Shut it," Edie shot back as she sped up. "Practice shitty pickup lines some other time."

"Jeez, bitch. I'm just trying to keep the conversation going, you know?"

"We don't need your conversation," Edie insisted, remaining affixed on moving forward.

Not ready to give up, Squanto sniffed at any clue he could find. Upon leaning closer to William to get a smell of either his costume or the person inside of it, William pushed him away.

"What the fuck are you doing?" Edie asked, directly in Squanto's face.

"I'm wondering why these guys are being so quiet. It's freaking me out!"

"They're quiet because they aren't trying their hardest to fuck this up like you are!"

"Why you being such a bitch?"

"Do you have any idea how dangerous this is? Pull your shit together, now!"

"No way, man," a jittery Squanto replied, leaping backwards a step towards August Hall. "Something's whack. All of a sudden you— you and Chip need my help? And it's the most dangerous thing you've done all week? Then these guys ain't talking..."

"I told you— none of us are supposed to be talking! Top— secret— asshole!"

"Well how top secret is..." Squanto blurted before springing at William and yanking his mask to the ground, shattering it. "I knew it!" he yelled in William's face. "This fuck again! Every time I'm about to get dicked in a bad way, I see this guy!"

"Quiet down *now*!" Edie ordered.

"Quiet? Hell naw!" an energized Squanto shouted at a volume designed to cause neighbors to notice. "I get it. You're trying to screw me again!" Determined to let as many nearby ears hear, he repeated it mid-hop. "You're screwing me and there's noth—"

Chip, having measured his options, decided it was time to end the uncontrollable Squanto's involvement with a strong punch to the face, knocking him out.

Chip looked at his friends. "I always expected Eskimos to be quieter."

A suddenly tense William asked. "But what do we do now? Drag him through Colonial?"

Not wanting to admit he hadn't thought that far, Chip ignored the questions. Instead, he imagined a map of the campus with a little dot for each person who knew his plan. As the dots kept spreading out more and more (Alf and Carolina, Squanto, and more concerning, the recently re-unnerved William, who could feel the desire to depart at any point), he decided to make some changes. "We leave him here. The priority is getting to Eva's as fast as we can. On the way back we'll hand him off to my buddies."

Then, before he could protest, William was grabbed by the robe and pulled along, his job as guardian of the hallway having been forcibly forfeited.

*   *   *

After finding the end of the hallway and blocking the door behind them, the trio stopped by Colonial Hall's basement laundry room to find William with a new mask. Edie located a thick athletic headband and a pair of sunglasses, and rearranged part of William's toga into a turban, covered most of his face with the sheet and put the sunglasses on to shield his eyes. To make him more nondescript, she pushed him to lose the breastplate, as well.

The three students responsible for much of the week's ado then experienced for the first time the sheer vivacity of the Northeast Quad from the ground floor.

Chip, Edie, and William all knew the aftershocks of Chip's actions had been immense, but they were awestruck as they stepped out into the torrent of fierce energy coated in rumors and smelling of ramen noodles and beer.

Despite the scores of partygoers mingling with the sit-ins, the commandos could tell all were there for the same mission. For once, their emotions were channeled into a single energetic cause that could benefit each and every person present. It was greater than a sporting event or an aced exam or an invitation to one's favorite club; it felt like nothing the students experienced before. Some present went as far as asking if this was the defining moment of their generation.

The full blooded W.A.S.P. sneaking through the Quad dressed as a cartoonish sendup of an African tribesman, though thoroughly impressed by the grand reactions set in place to secure his own expulsion, had other plans than creating their era's quintessential snapshot.

Trying to keep moving through the irrefutably entertaining scene, Chip nudged Edie on as they walked through the crowd. Thankful for the cover supplied by coolers of beer and disguises, Edie led the way breezily out of the NEQ.

Once the noise settled down to an intoxicated whisper, anxiety struck each of the three. It wasn't until walking through what Chip had created that they fully realized the risks involved with their late night run, and to a lesser extent, every one of his recent actions. He would not let fear paralyze him, so instead of dwelling on new perspective, he pressed on.

Ten minutes into the exit, William revived the talk.

"I gotta ask," he stated hesitantly with a look over his shoulder towards strangers who were not actually there. "What if Squanto wakes up?"

"Chill," Chip replied casually. "He'll be out for a while."

"How do you know that?"

"He's shit ass drunk, sleeping under 40 pounds of fur, and covered in piss. He's not waking up."

"Okay then," William pried, "Do you know what you're going to say at Eva's?"

The lengthy pause before Chip's answer gave Edie and William cause to doubt his sincerity. "I've got it figured out."

"Seriously?" William pressed, as a tall man dolefully searching for his car headed unseen towards them. "You still have no clue what you're going to say?"

Had William's question not been so pointed, Edie and Chip likely would not have taken their eyes off the sidewalk to scold him. Without this distraction, William likely would not have directly plowed directly into Warren Lightstorm.

For thirty seconds that felt to the students like thirty minutes, the three stared up at Lightstorm's scorching glare, obsessed with identical questions. *How much did he hear? Could he recognize Chip's voice?*

The three were not aware that decades of tireless days in schools with minimal lighting and summers informing visitors about his tribe in screaming heat had dulled some of Lightstorm's senses. Having long since lost the strength in his night vision and his ambient noise detection, he knew the youngsters in front of him only as a small part of what he called "the degenerate culture dutifully trained by Pemberton."

"What a foul mess this campus is," he stated derisively.

Chip didn't know what to say.

"You're all white as snow under there, aren't you?" Lightstorm asked.

Chip instantly relaxed, remembering he was wearing a mask that strategically covered his face (but showed vibrantly his cultural insensitivity). He nodded.

"I thought as much," a dejected Lightstorm stated. "In that case, can any of you tell me how this is the most diversity I've seen on this campus all day?"

The students were stumped. That is, until Chip had the idea to raise his right hand and chant "how" like a Native American cartoon he'd seen years earlier.

Lightstorm, disgusted, maneuvered around the students, and with them at his back, muttered, "School full of morons."

Chip and Edie watched Lightstorm walk away until deciding he did not show signs of wanting to turn around to follow them.

"Well that was freaky," Chip noted as they continued walking.

With barely enough time to shake off their potentially hazardous run-in, Chip took notice of their location near Eva's apartment with a triumphant smile. "Nice!"

With Chip in the lead, they sidled towards the five story building's exterior staircase and hiked up the exterior staircase. When at Eva's door, Chip rapped on it four times.

Seconds later, a young lady dressed plainly in muted colors opened the door. They watched her expression turn from one of anticipation to dismayed annoyance.

"You've got the wrong address," she stated.

"No, wait!" Chip urged eagerly. "It's me! Remember? I'm here for our talk!"

Eva squinted for a closer look at the guests in her doorway. "It's going to be a long night, isn't it?"

Chapter 37: "You are no Abe Rayburn."

THE DÉCOR of Eva apartment, as William later recalled, was stunning for someone who was outwardly a populist hippie. In addition to bookshelves crammed with textbooks and classic literature, the living room housed an impressively sized television, ornate sculptures, and a tanning bed in one corner. (After discarding the protest spirit of their youth, Eva's parents settled into lucrative careers in banking and advertising.)

Chip affixed his attention to their uneasy host as they sat opposite each other on plush couches. William assumed she was confused that they made it, but something beyond surprise lurked in her face. As valuable seconds passed without grandiose strategy suggestions or flowing praise from her lips, the silence became unsettling.

William sat to Chip's right with his back to the door while Edie hunkered down near what looked like a billiard room. Her mask stayed on, which caught William's curiosity only after he removed his own sunglasses and face covering.

Eva declared, "You all look ridiculous. You know that, right?"

"We've been over it," William replied. "Can we get on with this?"

Eva shifted and shook her head. "I honestly don't know where to start. I thought this meeting would mean something...then you show up like this?"

"We had to go through hell to get here," William stated, somehow comfortably easing into the "bad cop" role as Edie stayed back.

"What my friend means," Chip suavely interjected, "is given the circumstances these costumes were our only hope of making it here."

"I'm starting to think you shouldn't have come," Eva replied curtly.

"Cut the bullshit," Edie demanded with a tone vastly more effective than William's. "You could've given him the cold shoulder risk free over the phone. What's your damage?"

Eva sat defiantly quiet, confounding the guests who needed immediate support.

The samurai pushed off the wall and walked to the center of the room. "Fuck this. She can play with the stick up her ass all she wants when we're gone."

Before Edie could take two steps towards the door, Eva threw both arms out. "No! Wait—" she called before recomposing herself.

Chip sought to seize the moment. "You didn't think I would show. It's okay. I would've thought that, too."

With her eyes locked on whatever it was she found so encapsulating behind William, Eva clicked her tongue against her teeth. "No, I did not think you would," she announced contritely.

"But," Chip started, "I'm here. And it looks like you just straight up don't want to talk."

"Forgive me if I'm hesitant to trust people who can cause this much trouble while staying perfectly calm and suntanned in mid-October."

"Seriously?" William declared. "From someone who owns a tanning bed?"

"The tanning bed and pool table are my roommate's!" Eva instinctually replied.

William blurted out, "Who do you live with? A gay frat president?"

"What I'm saying," Eva replied through gritted teeth, "is a person who looks this relaxed after causing this much chaos could only be someone who doesn't really care."

Chip snatched the chance to prove his sincerity. "If I didn't care why would I be here?"

"If you *really* cared you would have come to me before starting this circus."

"I didn't want to get you in trouble!"

"That's what worried you? Did you worry at all about pulling two years of my progress down with you?" Eva let out a tension-soaked laugh. "I am not covering your ass on this."

"I'm not here because I want you to save me," Chip stated sincerely.

"What?" asked a startled Eva.

"I need you to let me take the fall!"

Eva appeared even more dumbfounded by the follow up. "I don't get it. You could have just stayed away if that was your plan."

"No, I couldn't," Chip said as he gazed into Eva's eyes and turned on his charm. "I can't leave this place a mess before knowing someone's going to look out for the cause when I'm gone. I needed you to know that before I ended this."

Eva, though seemingly content with the suggestion, was curious about the hidden fees underneath the luster. "I'm still not seeing where I fit in."

"If they bust me and no one steps in, all that follows is trash talk and people calling me a screw up. Nothing positive happens for the students. It all just gets shit out."

Instead of replying, Eva once again let the discussion falter. This behavior continued to confound William and he could see her very apparent reservations were grating on Chip as well.

Edie, meanwhile, thought nothing of Eva's behavior. Years later she explained to me that since the moment the opposing forces sat, she believed the perilous talk would lead nowhere. Instead of listening, from behind her mask, Edie was committed to plotting their return trip.

The mercurial hostess sat up straighter in her seat for her long awaited reply. "First, there's no 'we.' If you really were worried for the students, we would have met years ago while sober, not tonight sitting with a trio of racist caricatures. Second, I can't believe you think I'm going to gamble with the students' futures."

William balked at this. "If you can't make a deal with another student who shares your concerns, how the hell are you going to get anywhere dealing with administrators?"

"He's right," Chip said patiently. "Ever since the lock went on AP Hall's doors it's been a fact: someone is going to have to go down for this. That's why I'm here. I want to make sure whoever is here can carry this through."

Eva glanced once more behind William, and with placidly building enthusiasm, asked, "So what do you propose?"

"You get me the campus' support now and wait it out until they want real negotiations or until I'm busted. If I go down without backers, it just looks like a weeklong prank."

At this, William tried to decipher Eva's reservations, too. Chip proved he was reliable, gutsy, and willing to compromise. He even showed generosity by offering the clearly lost, if not egotistical, leader help she wouldn't find elsewhere. What was left to consider?

"If those are my only options," Eva stated, "I refuse. I'm not willing to place any one person's gain over the student body."

"Unbelievable!" William moaned. "What is wrong with you? Are you trying to fail?"

"Hold on, Will," Chip demanded. He inched towards the agitated girl and looked into her eyes in search of an answer. All she could offer was a hint of interest. "I'm here because I'm scared of the thought that this place could become a corporation. They already make so many decisions for us where someone else gets the benefit. Our food, our loans— someone's making money off of all of it and that someone doesn't give a shit about what we learn here."

Through what looked like appreciation for Chip's words, Eva still managed to respond bitterly. "If you came to our meetings you wouldn't have taken over a dorm to learn that. Also don't forget: your family's money bought that building. You're part of the corporation."

This was a powerful suggestion. William later recollected the words were chilling, and they also convinced him he would soon be studying for his finals from a New York State prison.

Similarly, had she been listening, Edie may have found the exchange inspiring. But she was still unashamedly ignoring it. All she had to do, she told herself, was give him another minute of arguing to drain any chance that he would want to stay. Then they could return to August and brainstorm the show stopping grand finale.

Instead of listening to Eva and Chip babble, she strolled down the hallway to take in the two bedroom unit. While wandering, she questioned whether she really did have a problem. There they were, besieged by the direst of consequences and still she couldn't shake the thoughts of how blasé the upcoming week would be.

After being unimpressed with the refrigerator's animal-free products, she closed its door. As she scanned the kitchen, her eyes fell upon one of her most favorite sights: an unattended cell phone.

Considering Edie was incurably annoyed with the protestor, it was as good of a time as any to enact her pet prank. She picked up the smart phone, scrolled until she found a directory entry labeled Arthur, typed in her favorite text about their "late friend," and sent it.

She then returned the phone and ambled toward the argument to initiate their exit.

Chip beseeched, "I'm trying to give them the leader they deserve!"

"You can't give them someone you are not and you are no Abe Rayburn. He was a real leader, not a careless drunk!"

Finally seeing fit to raise his voice, either due to fury or the desire to be heard over his buzzing phone, Chip belted out, "The leader I'm trying to give them is you!"

Amid the charged atmosphere, Chip located his phone in his robes, opened a newly arrived text message, and his wrath grew more distressed. "Can someone tell me why the hell Kathie Kieft is texting me she's pregnant?"

"Kathie Kieft?" Edie and Eva simultaneously exclaimed.

Chip looked at the deathly-frightened Eva before his eyes sliced across the room to the patches of fabric under which he assumed Edie's eyes were gaping back at him.

"Say something," a stunned Chip requested.

The startled Edie replied: "I think we just got slaughtered by a vegan."

Chapter 38: "It's what you'll be remembered for."

IT APPEARED the real reason Eva could not sell her soul to the smiling demon in front of her was she already made a pact with a shorter, far less amusing one.

The scenario was set into motion earlier off campus. Kathie's initial goal was to set her enemies against each other in a ferocious way. She would maneuver to make Eva so appalled at Chip's actions that she would cannibalize her entire mission to stop him. This would not only paint her in a negative light, it would also convince the school to declare Chip a clownish pawn, not the true ringleader, letting his grades become "deservedly, perfectly final."

Although she wasn't fond of creating any record of their interactions, she felt the best way to reach Eva was an email, which would soften up the principled girl before meeting.

The note stated that she would not be writing were it not for the grave circumstances. The PPC concluded that Chip was indeed the fraud Eva said he was, but since the student body was irreparably attached to his overly amplified messages, the irked PPC hoped to expose Chip in front of the largest audience possible.

When Kathie saw the school's leaders were happy to let real

protests bleed to death with Chip's sordid stunt, she knew she had to contact Eva to see if they could find a better outcome.

This email prompted a near immediate response. In sparse detail, Eva implied she was interested in a solution that might help the student cause *if* that was truly Kathie's goal.

Skipping over Eva's caveat, Kathie insisted they should meet. In fewer than ten minutes, Kathie was in Eva's living room, sitting in the exact spot in which Chip would later lounge.

"Thanks for letting me in," Kathie began. "It's way worse than I expected it would get."

"Things getting worse for Chip isn't really bad, is it?" Eva casually replied. "Everyone knows he's just an idiot who must think he's on some enormous hidden camera show."

Kathie looked morbidly shocked. "Didn't you read my email?"

"Come again?"

Kathie looked perplexed, as if she was surprised by how little Eva knew about the (entirely fictional) situation. "The school doesn't just want to burn Chip. They want to destroy all chances of a student uprising. That means they're going to try to remove you, too."

Even if she did not believe them, the words devastated Eva. For a split second, all thoughts of her comrades in arms disappeared from her mind. Not only would there be no revolution, she thought, there would be no Eva, through no fault of her own.

"You're kidding. You're just messing with me because you don't like me."

Kathie ruefully shook her head. "They said it earlier in the last emergency session. This…it's what you'll be remembered for. I had to come because that sucks."

Kathie continued with her overblown tale, providing made up quotes from PPC members that were too brash to bother repeating. Eva sat stupefied, unable to produce any response that would show she didn't feel utterly destroyed. Her guest slowed down, and in an effort to make the scene more casual, she removed her shoes and shifted to sit cross legged on the couch. For comfort, she placed on the table her dorm keys and her pink tinged smart phone.

Still stunned, all Eva could say was, "My roommate has that same phone."

Kathie earnestly proceeded: "I hate that they're trying to link the two of you. That's bad business, and unthinkable behavior for a school."

Without converging on the ever so slightly ridiculous idea that PMU intended to bulldoze her life's work (rather, her "two year's work"), Eva asked herself whether there a way to push forward by separating the good from the fratty spectacle? "What's the school scared of?"

"Right now? They're afraid of a riot."

"That's partially true," Eva stated as some of her virility returned. "They're afraid of that and they're that the students will stay united. How would a riot start?"

"Maybe...when everyone realizes Chip fooled them," Kathie replied, trying to keep up. "Or, if they don't find out how badly he's mocking them, it starts when he gets arrested."

"Then it's simple: we make sure no one sees him get arrested."

"How do we do that? There's hundreds of people in the Quad."

"We find a way to sneak him out of the Quad," Eva declared pragmatically.

Kathie's pause in response as she processed the pitch was perhaps a second too long. Upon her return to campus later that evening, I found out that she would have been satisfied if the meeting merely prompted Eva to retreat entirely out of fear of retaliation. Alternatively, it would have been nice if she charged ahead with a full verbal assault on Lockwood and the school. What she was not expecting was a gem such as this from the "moral compass of the student body" (a quote about Eva listed on one of her club's websites).

Eva stated that it was in the best interests of the students to get Chip far away from the crowd where the PPC wished to castrate him. This was impossible as he trapped himself in the heart of campus, a fact Eva had been grappling with all day, as she'd sought to learn about his true stance but couldn't due to the barriers between them.

The hostess then asked about a solution she had dreamt up earlier but didn't feel was fitting at the time: if she could lure Chip to a location of her choosing, what could Kathie do to ensure he would be apprehended privately and quietly?

Kathie suggested she could convince campus police to let her borrow a small team to help with a scuffle-free arrest far from the NEQ. What's more, she could also report to the PPC that Eva had been integral in capturing Lockwood. This would block the university from expelling her and it would let her continue her work in a productive (i.e. "un-Chip-like") way.

It was risky and dirty, Kathie admitted. But it would spare heartbreak and prevent students from learning that their dreams for a brighter Pemberton were only fodder for a drunken prankster's ego. (Truthfully she didn't think the meet up would ever happen, but she was willing to let Chip and Eva waste their time while trying.)

Sensing that she likely appeared overeager, Kathie opted to give Eva space by making herself a cup of coffee and letting the girl brainstorm (or sit with her dying morals in solitude).

As Kathie exited for the kitchen, Eva's eyes landed on the pinkish phone on her table. The first idea that came to her stuck, evidently. She hated the idea of taking a phone for collateral, but she also despised that she had to trust Kathie at all. In a compulsive act, she snuck into her roommate's room and swapped out Kathie's phone for the one sitting on his dresser.

Eva then summoned Kathie and told her she had her vote. Before leaving, Kathie instructed her to text the time and the place of the meet up once she knew it and departed.

The minutes that followed for Eva were filled with a wild thrashing of emotions.

She thought of her crusade and of the students who she last saw lighting the night sky with passion for progress. Her thoughts drifted back her initial letter to the PPC, and then to her current options, and of the only person who bothered to offer her better footing.

Later that night, as if Kathie knew Eva had been thinking about her, while the woeful activist sat at her computer, another email arrived. It read: "Cannot find cell phone. Send email with time and place if still willing to help students. Then delete both emails."

The reply unsettled her (not just because it was apparent that her roommate was short a cell phone). Feeling her fate had long been sealed, Eva typed her reply in her typical lower case-only style: "set to arrive sometime after ten p.m. i will be at home reading."

Eva sent the message, snatched up a book, and crept into the living room to read away what she hoped would be the only minutes she would have to wonder if her covert actions would save the students she loved or if they amounted to the worst choice of her life.

*   *   *

Chip appeared as if he could feel fate crushing life out of him one memory of benevolent fortune at a time. This was not the reaction Eva expected from people pulling an elaborate prank.

"Dozens of kegs," William muttered. "Crates of hard liquor…so much stolen cheese…"

"Dude, let me think," Chip began to repeat with a growing hint of desperation.

Edie pointed Kathie's cell phone at Eva. Neither was sure if she would launch it into Eva's face. "You're the biggest sack of shit at this school."

"What?" Eva replied, straining to sort out the reactions. "Chip forced me to do this! I'm trying to protect the students!"

"Don't give us that shit!" Edie spat, equally mad at Kathie, Eva, and herself.

"We just gotta let me think…" Chip sputtered.

"I had no choice! It would have been a disaster if everyone learned Chip was faking!"

"He is who he says he is! Why can't you believe that?" William stated. "He came here to find the students a real leader. Now see how he feels for trusting you."

"Just give me time to me think!" Chip said to the television screen.

Edie called back: "We don't even have time to pretend to think. You can't let Kathie find you here with your pants down."

With sudden determination neither William nor Edie expected,

Chip stated, "That won't happen. Eva, tell me every detail of what you two planned."

"You were supposed to come over and Kathie was going to have police officers catch you before you even stepped inside."

"What went wrong?"

"I don't know! I told Kathie I'd be here doing homework and it's like she just bailed!"

"Were those your exact words?" Chip demanded, emphasizing each syllable.

Eva reached up to brush her hair back and stopped halfway to scratch her scalp. "I— why? I told her I was here reading, that— that I would be at home reading all night."

"Perfect," he replied as he scrolled through his phone's directory. Holding his phone up to William, he said: "Call this number on your phone and ask if anyone's looking for me there."

William punched the numbers into the cell phone while Edie pulled back a corner of the curtains to see if anyone was outside. Nothing looked out of the ordinary.

The voice inside William's phone said, "Home Reading, this is Jim."

"Hi, there isn't, uh, a group of people waiting for Chip Lockwood there, is there?"

"Yeah," Jim replied with a laugh. "One chick and a crew of guys with flashlights and handcuffs hiding by the dumpsters. Is this for some theme party I should know about?"

"No, thanks, we're good," said William before hanging up. "She's there."

"Amazing!" Chip stated. "Thank God Eva doesn't know shit about capitalization."

Edie leapt across the room and employed gestures suggesting Chip should move. "Great. We have to get back before she wises up."

"No, not yet," Chip affirmed. "I came here for Eva's word and the student body's support and that's what I'm leaving with."

"You kidding me? She can't do shit for you even if she wanted."

"I heard her admit she got into a deal she doesn't know shit about." Chip reply was so grave it commanded Eva's utmost attention. "You don't know what Kathie is capable of."

"Why should I believe you?" Eva retorted.

"Because you have two enemies now: the school and Kathie. You may be able to handle one but you sure as hell can't tackle Kathie. Once I'm out, she'll throw you to the dogs."

Eva continued to put up a stoic front, likely as part of an attempt to scare off Chip so she could find a way out of the mess alone.

Chip added, "Don't believe me? Cool. Ask yourself: who do you think Asbury will choose to lead the movement if you and me are both gone?" Chip nodded as the wrath started to show in Eva's irises. As he stepped towards her, for a single instant her expression suggested everything else evaporated behind the ease of his smile. "Alone you're facing a lot. You let us get back to August, and we'll make sure no one fucks with you or the cause."

Between her piercing anger over bargaining with Kathie and her mixed feelings over the words of the potentially dishonest young man facing her, Eva looked as if she could take years to make a decision. (The scene prompted William to wonder who of the pair cared about the students more at that moment.)

With their timeline in mind, Edie stepped in and grabbed Chip by both shoulders. "This is where you draw the line. Tell the skank she can call you when you get back to the dorm."

Chip's eyes danced from Edie to Eva before pivoting towards the doorway.

"No wait, I—" Eva stammered with futility.

"That's the plan," Chip said. "And it's the only one that doesn't end with this story being told to students without your name in it."

Eva watched as Edie re-donned her mask, kicked open the screen door, and scanned for possible obstructions. William followed, with Chip in tow.

"Wait!" Eva cried, evidently inquisitive about her options that didn't involve solely trusting Kathie. "If I choose to help, the students will need a battle cry to rally behind. Any suggestions?"

Chip later admitted the question had confused him as a battle cry seemed needless, but he didn't want to unnerve Eva by ignoring the request. His eyes darted around until he could find anything to help him think. After landing on William as he nervously scurried away, Chip leaned into Eva and whispered something. Her face contorted as he shared his reply.

Eva shook her head, repulsed. "Are you serious? What does that even mean?"

"Don't worry, it's going to do the trick." Chip stepped back before stopping himself. With his last chance, he added, "Adults deal with backstabbing and shitty bargaining all the time. We shouldn't have to deal with that too in our last years of freedom." Then with a wink, he slid backwards into the darkness.

Chapter 39: "August Hall is no island of freedom..."

ALF WAS growing weary. With each thought about the evening's clandestine run, he couldn't help but wonder what the outside felt like. The opportunities he could explore, the new, yet familiar faces, and how even the simplest task like lounging could mean so much more to a person who wasn't holed up.

It was nearing eleven thirty and he knew the meaning of the hour well: only ten and a half more hours until his favorite Tex-Mex establishment opened. If he had the chance to walk out the door in ten hours and seven minutes he could get to the pristine haven in twenty three-minutes, right on time. If he were to get his usual order, he would require only seven dollars and sixty cents. That exact amount was already staring back at him from his desk.

Alas, he was in no position to change that currency into a meaty bundle of cheesy ecstasy. His situation required focus and lacked burritos.

He was committed to helping Chip, but his hunger to stray from the claustrophobic mission grew stronger. These thoughts did not emanate from selfish reasons, but thanks to his position as the lone sentry in August Hall. As so many terrible ideas marinated in his mind, it was only natural that a meal would take their place.

The unhappy thoughts were the outcome of Chip's latest plot. From the moment he heard Chip finish his latest speech, the evening changed. Sounds and scenes from the parties seemed subdued, as if they were being played through a wall of water hovering in front of him.

Earlier, at around eleven, he received a text from Edie nothing that they arrived safely. With the news, he knew he could set aside at least some of the scenarios playing in his head.

The serenity did not last long.

At first he thought it was a joke when he saw four people arrive in the Quad in the same dark costume. He guessed they were from a fraternity or dressing like characters from a film. When he noticed six more identical outfits, he wondered if the team was donning costumes from any recent movie or television series that featured police officers. He began listing the potential shows in his head, but when a dozen more uniformed officers followed, he realized none were dressed as fictional characters.

He watched uneasily as the increasing number of officers mixed in with the students. Some undergraduates hid their beers while others gauged if they should take the new arrivals as a threat. The officers did not seem hostile, but Alf knew there was something unquestionably odd in their movement patterns.

Then he realized what was happening: starting with Colonial Hall, guards were lining the entrances to every building in the NEQ. Every building, that is, except August Hall.

By the time the guards took their places, clumps of students began decrying their presence to no avail.

Convinced he was overreacting, he tried to imagine that Chip, Edie, and William were somewhere safe. Then he told himself it wouldn't be long until he received notice that they were all securely back inside the dorm.

*   *   *

William, once again pinned underneath Chip, who tackled the sprinter moments earlier, asked: "Have you seen what we look like?

How will us tiptoeing look any less suspicious than sprinting?"

The three had managed to get halfway back to campus before William provided the suggestion to run back to save time. Like earlier in the week, Chip replied by chasing him down and jumping on him.

Chip casually replied, "This is college; shit like this happens all the time."

"He's right," Edie added, taking a seat on William's calves. "You'd know that if this wasn't just your second night in college of having balls."

"Excuse me for being a little nervous!" William replied in a harsh whisper.

William wasn't the only one on edge. Eva's betrayal hit Edie the hardest, mainly because she knew she should have looked harder for it. The trip, although potentially costly, did place into Edie's hands a fantastic weapon. As she and Chip remained perched on their colleague, she tapped Kathie's phone into her right palm and blessed its utility.

Chip was energized and optimistic about Eva, perhaps more than he should have been on both counts. At a moment when too many obstacles to count could have been speeding through his mind, he took solace in knowing that he, Charles "Chip" Lockwood, had gotten this far and certainly was not going to be stopped anytime soon. "Things are going to be okay, William."

As Edie stood and Chip pulled William to his feet, the youngest asked: "But how can you be sure Eva isn't going to screw us again?"

Starting on their way, Chip dismissively replied, "You ever met Kathie?"

"Just once. She was kind of a piece of shit."

"Exactly. Now that Eva's met me, she'll know the safer bet is not that bitchy priss." With a pat on William's back, he added, "So all we have to is find a way around Squanto, which shouldn't be hard, then call my frat buddies to sneak into Colonial—"

Chip stopped upon feeling his cell phone buzzing. He reached for it and activated the call. "Talk to me, Alf...Uh huh...uh huh...no, that was not in the plan…" (At this point, Edie assumed Chip's expression was weakening under the bulky mask.) "So that means…shit…no, that's not what— fuck, man!…No, I'm going to fix this. Keep your phone on."

Chip disconnected the call and adopted a much brisker pace.

After a half dozen steps, Edie pressed, "You going to tell us what that was?"

"Alf says University Police are in riot gear and lining the entrances to every dorm."

"Oh we are fucked!" William muttered, throwing his hands up.

"Quiet down," Edie insisted.

William persisted. "What a surprise that some part of this turned out shitty."

Edie replied with a healthy physical slap to his face and a second one for his ego. "You want to know what else turned out shitty? Carolina has chlamydia. Now shut it."

Deep inside the turban, William took on a visage of deeply rooted disappointment. "Wait, but…Oh God damn it, this place fucking sucks!"

"Let's all calm down," Chip suggested. "Alf was probably just stressed. I guarantee we'll be fine…I mean, we'll be fine getting back in. The chlamydia sounds like something you should get checked out."

*   *   *

Five minutes later, while taking in the NEQ from behind a row of bushes, Chip's assessment of the situation speedily changed.

"Shit. We're totally fucked!"

Edie nodded. "It does look that way."

The trio was aghast as they took in the wholly different scene from the one they saw an hour earlier. Officers were lining all but one of the dorms and students were angrily realizing their consequence-free good time was ending.

Healthy packs of undergraduates both costumed and not, who only minutes earlier had been gregariously socializing, grew affixed to smaller teams who were decrying the presence of the guards. The atmosphere of freedom and community had been replaced by ire towards the uniformed officers and the administration that sent them. The guards, in actuality, were there to achieve this exact result. Asbury had no intention of waiting until Bromhead's acceptable timeframe so he sent in the guards to throw the evening off kilter. He was more than content to proceed with this action, especially after the Duden System confirmed Chip was indeed the author of the declaration of war against the administration.[29]

Chip found himself once again facing ostensibly insurmountable opposition. While he and his co-pilots fiercely endeavored to dream up a break-in route, shouting matches, angry students, and rows of police blended into a giant mess. The crowd's size and fury would be a perfect combination for his success if he could only get back into August Hall.

"Do you think Squanto talked?" William asked.

"No way. He wanted to party, he wouldn't have sent in the troops." Chip's halfhearted answer suffered as he was fixated on Colonial Hall and the beefed up security blocking him from claiming re-entry. "How the hell are we going to get in there?"

"Let me try something," Edie said, producing her cell phone and wildly typing.

The pressure was seeping into Chip's mind through every crevice it could find, and with the enormous protest and one hundred and thirty-two year tradition hovering above his head (which was still

---

[29] Chip Lockwood managed in his first four and a half semesters to take mostly math and French classes, along with non-essential electives. This posed a problem for the Duden System as the vast majority of his grades were based on multiple-choice exams or responses written in French. Staffers eventually managed to find one class in which Chip handed in an eight-page essay. That class was AMER 212-2, and the term paper, like the declaration, was, in fact, written by William Allton. As William utilized "bad punctuation and a reliance on a few specific words" when writing as Chip, the Duden System matched the papers immediately.

covered in a mockery of a tribal mask), negative thoughts had more than enough openings.

Edie noticed a friend dressed as a "sexy nurse" strutting up the stairs of Colonial Hall. "Look!" she instructed. "I asked her to see how serious security is."

The three watched as the girl's progress was met by officers shuffling to block any way through to the dorm.

"Shit," Edie muttered. "Okay, that's a no go. Got anything yet or don't ask?"

"Still working on it," an agitated Chip replied.

"Work faster," William noted with a nudge towards a bustling area where a stately elderly man huffed through the crowd with associates in tow. "Asbury just showed up."

"Fuck!" Chip declared. He sank back behind the bushes and tried to force his brain to do whatever it had done so well every other crucial moment in his life. Were all those years of coasting just preparation for fate to taunt him here? He was about to face the most public failure that could be endured and his time as a student *and* a Lockwood had evolved to a pathetic end. What was worse was that he failed surrounded by close allies and countless others trying to assist him. To his dismay, among those present were abhorrent theater students.

Chip stayed focused on the overly emotive teens as they leapt about and advertised their upcoming plays to the audience he fought, bled, and binge drank to furnish.

He watched in agony as the students brought out more props, like a scarecrow and a harmless guillotine, the latter of which was built for a 1989 musical review and later reused for a poorly received S and M themed version of a set of Greek tragedies. In that moment of hatred, all thoughts of the end evaporated, leaving behind a superbly illuminated path "I got it!"

The provocative proclamation urged Edie and William to slide in closer as Chip used his phone to dial Alf. "Everyone needs to be in one hundred percent. Like balls to the wall, full fury, check for rash in the morning *all in*."

William ashamedly slouched. "I got the last one covered, I guess."

"Great," Chip replied. Into his phone he rattled off instructions: "It's me…Yeah, it's pretty fucked. Do two things for me. One: in five minutes shut down the overrides you have on the security system and unlock the front doors. Two: find or call Carolina. Tell her to find the girl I spent last night with. Yeah, her neighbor. Have Carolina get that chick to meet me on Four West in five. Thanks, dude!" Chip closed his phone and jumped back up to a squat for a better view of the Quad.

"So…" Edie began anxiously. "What's the plan?"

"We…" Chip stated with determination, "are going to Bastille this shit."

Although happy with Chip's vibrancy, Edie was confused. "We're going to go power mad and start killing our own? If so, I want to start with Eva."

Chip scanned the crowd to see whom they could recruit for his bizarre idea.

"With all these cops, August Hall is no island of freedom; it's a prison. We need to find students willing to believe they're liberating the place and we'll be golden. Everyone's already riled up and there's no way Eva's not helping out. We all bust in, ditch the costumes, make it look like I never left, and let the school in so they can catch me. Cool?"

Edie spotted in the distance another newcomer arrive with a team of officers. Within seconds she knew how to handle this addition. "We better move fast. The Wicked Witch of the Bitch is here."

"Kathie? Perfect." Chip scoured the scene to ensure he'd chosen the best groups he could. "I'm going to take those guys behind that ROTC group. William, grab those people hovering around that cutie in bike shorts. Edie, find any sorority but yours or Carolina's."

"Got it," Edie replied.

Before anyone could move, William blurted, "I don't think I can do this!"

"Yes you can! Now that you finally know you don't need it, rip that stick out of your ass and start beatin' the man with it."

"That's right," Edie agreed. "Teach them a lesson with your jagged little Will."

Chip and Edie couldn't see William's face under the turban that was matted to his skin, but they could tell he was ready to make his stand.

Chip held up a hand and William high fived it. "You get five minutes, then look for the signal," he said before darting away.

Seconds later, Edie and William each left the bush sanctuary to approach their respective groups amid hundreds of increasingly agitated students.

Chapter 40: "*We* say it doesn't end here."

BEFORE CHIP could make it to his intended audience, he heard a gruff sounding man in a PMU track hoodie tell his associates he would do anything for ten minutes alone with "that sick sumbitch Lockwood." Suddenly the idea of exerting effort to convince a different, possibly less enthusiastic group of students to break into the building with him seemed silly.

Chip stopped among the group and they eyed the costumed stranger apprehensively.

"Who the hell are you?" Soup demanded.

"You guys want to show that sucker who's boss?" he asked. "Because I got just the idea to get us in there."

It only took a few seconds of consideration from the slightly intoxicated Soup before he nodded to his men and looked into Chip's mask. "We're in."

*　　　*　　　*

William could see Chip making progress with a group who would have torn his limbs out if they knew who he really was. Similarly, Edie found success with two costume-clad sororities after spinning a yarn about a Chip-themed scavenger hunt among the top houses.

As he drew closer to a group of students anchored by Cammy

Dalton, William reached into whatever remained in his soul after his year of emotional slaughtering and called out. "Did you all show up to stop the school from silencing freedom?"

"What?" Cammy asked. "They're just trying to scare us."

"Scare you from what? From realizing they've taken back August Hall and trapped those students?" Some began slowly accepting his words. "Everyone in there was free yesterday. But now look! There are armed police surrounding the peaceful gathering students created. The school trapped them again and now they're laughing at us!"

"Oh crap," Cammy murmured. "He's right."

"Our classmates stood up for all of us and the school turned them into prisoners! Is that why you came to school here?"

"No!" one student replied emotionally. "Of course not!"

"We're not here to let them trap our classmates!" William bellowed, feeling his passion infect the students. In this brief instant he forgot about not only the danger he was in, but also that he, a white male from suburban Cleveland, was lecturing a crowd while dressed in faux-Middle Eastern garb. "They've sliced up student liberty for decades and now they're going to try to shut down the only real freedom we've ever seen. *We* say it doesn't end here. Not them!"

The team around him cheered in reply.

"But what can we do?" one shouted over the hooting.

"Chip Lockwood liberated every student in there when he claimed the land for all of us. Now we're going to re-claim it for them by freeing the dorm ourselves!"

*   *   *

Meanwhile, oblivious to the three movements developing, a costumed Eva appeared in the Quad. Dressed as a giant bear (the only costume she could find that included a full mask), she crept through the crowd noting the mood and the security personnel. Their presence disappointed her, and she couldn't help but wonder if they were there because of her own dealings with Kathie. Bargaining with both Kathie and Chip left her angry and confused, and as such, she arrived still unsure who to trust.

Taking advantage of her anonymity, she decided the best place for decision-making would be right next to the reliable old curmudgeon Asbury, who was visibly distressed.

Asbury's dejected expression resonated with the innocuous bear, and in an unexpected moment of empathy, Eva found herself supportive of him and his nearly eternally hidden appreciation for the students. Not knowing he was the one who created the confrontational atmosphere, she continued feeling sorry for him, especially since she knew he wanted nothing more than to chop into the locked doors himself. The endearing moment would have lasted longer if not for the curt entry of Kathie.

Asbury moaned as Kathie shuffled over and insisted, "Sir, this must end, now!"

Eva fought the urge to back up out of fear Kathie would spot her. Asbury continued to ignore Kathie's presence.

"Sir, listen to me. I didn't find him at that bar like I promised but I know how to get the students to realize they weren't following the right person. Just give me a chance!"

"Kieft, I have had almost enough of you!" Asbury declared.

"If we show the students they're following a puppet," Kathie firmly posited, "they'll re-think everything, and we can restore order!"

This latest plea made Asbury's slightly more malleable, but to the nearby eavesdropper, the words felt like knives into every inch of fabric in the bear costume.

"If UP goes in there now," Kathie noted, adding a sinister smile eerily similar to the one she gave Eva when reassuring earlier, "you can clear that liar's name, and I'll get you someone who's waiting to walk right into that bear trap to take the blame."

Inside the steaming costume, Eva froze. She then he pulled off one glove, located her phone inside the costume, and dialed a number.

On the other end was a student poised by a computer displaying a text messaging website that allowed users to send mass text messages to several phone numbers at once. Behind the web browser pane were two similar web pages designed for subscribers of other popular mobile service providers. The student picked up their phone, heard a muffled "go ahead" and clicked a link that sent texts to forty-seven cell phones in the Northeast Quad.

While Asbury and Kathie were still conversing, the message arrived.

At first the chant began softly through self-conscious voices whose owners were afraid they had misread the text message. After three or four repetitions they learned they were not alone and the chant grew more assured.

Dispersed students continued the chant, and more joined, uniting the text's original recipients with others hoping to have their opinions heard in any way. The Quad was soon brought to life by hundreds proudly chanting: "Save Creamer! Save Creamer! Save Creamer!"

Eva examined the disgusted faces of Asbury's companions and couldn't help but emit a self-satisfied grin...until she realized what Chip's phrase really sounded like with a crowd of hundreds behind it. It was powerful and gratifying to hear such unity, but the words themselves left a discomforting aftertaste as they echoed through the Quad.

Kathie was appalled by the explicit uproar. She grew more concerned upon seeing the Provost's face. With the haggard expression of a man faced with his darkest ghost, a stunned Asbury muttered, "Jesus, Mary and Joseph..."

The repetitions continued while Eva and Kathie wondered was what wrong with Asbury. The man who had been an educator during the Sexual Revolution, the cocaine-coated 80s, and the birth of Internet pornography, and who was never visibly offended by anything on campus immediately insisted on leaving the Quad.

* * *

Chip pivoted towards Edie and William, raised his arms with palms out, and shook in a manner reminiscent of a layperson's interpretation of a Native American rain dance. Assuming amid the maddening shouts that this was Chip's sign, the others readied their crews to break back into the heavily entrenched August Hall. Inside, Alf turned off his security program that helped separate them from the outside world that week. His command went through just as the blaringly loud protest rock concert began in the Great Hall.

With one movement, Chip set it all in motion.

Leaping into action with Soup, Chip ran towards August Hall's front doors with his team behind. Seconds later the other groups followed.

During the sprint, Chip became excited beyond belief at the sight of a garbage can that wasn't chained to a wall. Instinctively, he ripped can from the ground. Before any guards stationed around the Quad could react, Chip and the track star scaled the front stairs and hurled the vessel through one of the full-length windows that straddled the dorm's front doors.

Safety glass spewed from the damaged window as the metal netting in the glass pushed the can back into Chip's hands. Gripping the garbage can, Chip hit the window's wiring with two more blows before they gave way, allowing him to lead his team in. The men then tore at the second set of doors, tugging on one so hard they pulled it off its hinges. They then quickly dispatched the desks set as obstacles days earlier.

August Hall had been breached.

Chip hastily went for the nearest stairwell. Flinging open the door, he rushed in, and stated, "He lives on two! Open every door until you find the bastard!"

Chip led the team up the two flights and allowed the pack to pass, enabling his departure. He could hear garbled startled reactions as the herd blew into Two West, but he cared little for the noise as he tugged off his cloak and continued up the stairs.

* * *

Not far behind, William led Cammy and company past the jumbled desks and bolted for the basement.

Unfortunately for the boy, August Hall's first uninvited guest, who recently vanished from William's mental list of problems, awoke minutes earlier thanks to the chant above his hidden bed and the concert. He pieced together recent memories, recalling "the shit bastard William" whom he believed was sneaking out to destroy Chip's party. Leaving his parka behind, he let the concert lead him back to the Great Room to warn Chip. He arrived just in time to see a masked Middle Easterner startle some of the sixty students enjoying the band.

Reacting to his hardboiled racism, Squanto ran for the turbaned stranger. As he approached he remembered a key fact: that was no regular Arab, it was William the Douche.

William, who had merely been looking for a place to ditch his outfit, was immobilized by the sight of a nearly naked Squanto barreling towards him. Reacting on what little he had left, he rushed back up a stairwell still wearing the damning costume that could link him— and Chip— to the liberation of the hall.

*   *   *

Effortlessly moving through the debris left in Chip's wake, Edie and her team entered August Hall unharmed and brimming with uncut energy. Trotting to a stairwell, Edie insisted, "I think he's on Three somewhere! Don't forget: his room's name tag is worth fifteen points and a piece of his clothing is twenty!"

Edie escorted the girls up four flights of stairs and unleashed them on the populace. Much to the pleasant surprise of the male residents, the costumed ladies rampaged through Three with hardiness. They opened doors, shoved their heads into study halls and alcoves, and left no corner unexposed in their search for Chip.

Their leader, meanwhile, split off, tossed her costume into a garbage can, and stole away to a room on Two overlooking the Quad to await the dormitory's next esteemed visitor.

*   *   *

At that very moment, the student on Edie's mind watched August Hall in horror. As the strident chant continued, Kathie's rage built as the dorm sank deeper into anarchy, potentially paralyzing her plans.

After two minutes of watching through every open window what looked like a steroid-infused chase scene from a campy old movie, Kathie knew it was time to act.

Maddeningly, she was informed by the UP sergeant present that only Asbury could give them orders to attack, based on the provost's explicit instructions. Until he gave the go-ahead, none of the officers standing guard could enter the building.

Kathie, enraged that someone would dare use the same red tape with her that she'd been using all week, shouted: "But he's not here, you idiot!"

"Call names all you like. Until he returns or answers our calls, you'll have to rely on the county sheriff's officers to go in but they're still on their way."

"That's the dumbest thing I've ever heard!" Kathie grasped for any alternate ideas she could grab. "My men were on a special assignment," she callously informed the sergeant. "Their orders don't prevent *them* from doing your job. We're going in."

*　　　*　　　*

Back inside, Chip located a room on the third floor to remove and hide his tribal costume. However, just as he stepped into the hallway, six young ladies spotted him exiting a room wearing nothing but boxer shorts.

"There he is!" one shouted. "Get him!"

Despite his moral compass, Chip ran *away* from the flock of spirited women. The drastic measure did not sit well, but he had only minutes at his disposal, maybe only seconds.

William, though, still needed a safe place to lose his inflammatory robes.

He managed to outrun his foe in the basement but with the new wave of outsiders rushing in there was no place on One to covertly change. Opting to head to Two for the first room he could find, he dashed into a stairwell and took the steps three at a time.

Swinging open the doorway to a frantic scene on Two West, William found himself at odds with Soup and five of his men. At first William had difficulty deciphering why they were glaring at him with such derision. Then he remembered his wardrobe.

"I fuckin' knew it!" one clamored. "Towel head bastards again!"

"Oh shit," William moaned, turning to flee as fast as he could.

"Let's get him!" another shouted. With that, they started chasing the turbaned William through the obstacle-laden August Hall.

*   *   *

Upon crossing the threshold of broken glass and later the cups dripping flat beer, Kathie knew she was nearing glory. Navigating the mess of a lobby, she guessed at Chip's whereabouts, reminding herself that if she could find any proof that he'd snuck outside, she could consider herself victorious. Kathie ordered the men up to the second floor to start the sweep.

Kathie's team burst onto Two and she followed. She barely had a moment to gape at the state of the hallway before getting yanked backwards and thrown into a converted payphone closet. As the door swung shut, she was unceremoniously locked in.

The startled Kathie watched as the black haired, green eyed demon culprit rushed up to the squad and declared, "Officers, there's a urine soaked naked guy running around trying to show girls his penis! Please stop him!"

The officers ran off, leaving Edie alone with her target.

"Let me the fuck out!" Kathie insisted at a smiling Edie. "I'll have you exp—"

"Can it, Queeft," Edie replied. As much as it hurt to not to relish Kathie's imprisonment in a sex closet, Edie knew she had a strict time limit.

"Go grind on a chainsaw," Kathie defiantly spat. "I can tell the board whatever I want about this!"

"I'm counting on that, sweetie." Edie said, lifting her secret weapon into view. "Thanks to your stunningly clear notes in here, I know you'll have lots to say to them."

Kathie slammed herself against the glass. "You bitch!" she shouted, seething at Edie's rich delight. "If you touch a single button with your powder-dusted fingers, I will—"

"I've already forwarded some gems for safe keeping, you miserable cold sore."

"But I— I..." The stutterer stopped upon realizing she had no choice but to listen.

"The phone goes back on two conditions: one, you don't get in Chip's way again, and two, you don't go after Eva when this is done. *Oui, oui, chienne?*"

"You can't be serious."

"Serious as a guillotine."

Just then, screeching female voices and frantic waving arms distracted Kathie. Edie turned, too, to see an entirely naked Chip streak through the hall with six giddy girls following, including one victoriously waving his torn boxer shorts in the air. Chip leapt out of view and Edie looked back upon the trapped Kathie.

"Deal," Kathie begrudgingly muttered. "Now let me out and go fuck yourself raw!"

Instead of replying with one of the countless clever quips she wanted to use, Edie simply pocketed Kathie's phone, playfully tapped the glass, and skipped off.

*   *   *

Somehow William found a room to disrobe. Only then did he realize he wasn't wearing much underneath. Having no other choice but to use an item from the room in which he changed, he stepped into the hall wearing boxer shorts and a tiny pink t-shirt made for a sorority formal. His goal of distancing himself from the garb before getting arrested seemed possible until he was dragged into a gaggle of females looking for the naked grand prize they'd just lost.

The pack picked up speed with a determination that frightened William. Upon turning a corner he tried to split off into a stairwell. However, just as he opened the door, Squanto leapt out with the intention of landing on or near him.

With nanoseconds to spare, William slid to his left and let Squanto slam into a wall. William's escape was blocked again, this time by officers in pursuit of Squanto. Not knowing what else to do, William rejoined the scavenger hunt contestants.

The team sprinted through a full hallway until nearing Soup's squad. William slowed them, hoping to prevent the teams from merging. "Wait! You've been down that hall already!"

"I think he lives on the fourth floor, let's try up there!" one girl shouted.

The note landed squarely in Soup's eager ears. "He's on Four, let's move!"

As Soup's men joined in with the hunters, William tried to split away, but the force of the stampeding pack prevented his egress. Once the boys joined the group in the stairwell, the men took a harsh view of the half-dressed William.

"You some kind of pervert?" one accused, pushing the barefoot William.

Needing an answer fast, William went with his first thought. "Some Arab stole my clothes!" (He instantly blamed the reply on spending too much time in August Hall.)

"We'll protect you!" one male posited as he pushed William elbows first into a door.

The two packs streamed onto Four. One girl ungracefully pushed aside a drunk freshman and offered to William, "I can't believe he took your clothes!"

Another girl, who noticed his shirt, added, "I went to that party, too! Wasn't that the baddest DJ ever?"

"Um…" William fumbled without knowing why he was replying. "What?"

Soup slowed the group to a trot and put an arm around William. "Let's find this guy a safe place, he's been through enough." Soup halted at a door and the group stopped with him. As he reached for the doorknob, a squirmy William wondered why the door looked familiar.

Realizing where they were, William pleaded: "No, wait!"

It was too late.

Soup threw open Alf's room's door and the scene inside promptly slapped a look of electrified disbelief onto every face in the doorway.

In the room, a nude Chip was engaged in sexual intercourse with an equally naked female student, who, unbeknownst to the guests, Chip had only just met.

The shock lasted only seconds before the pursuers recalled their tasks. Soup ordered "Get him!" as one female charged her friends to "get your camera phones out!"

Twelve of the thirteen students rushed in, pulling the reluctant thirteenth along. Limbs, sneakers, and all connected parts careened as the pack ran like they were chasing a loose football after a fumble. The flurry capped off with a mass dive, creating a giant pile with the amorous pair, and somehow William, wedged at the bottom.

Squanto then hurled himself into the doorway. When he spotted William trying to crawl away from the stunning scene, he knew there was only one thing to do.

Just barely dodging the hand of an officer reaching to nab him, Squanto took three steps, leapt through the air, and landed directly atop the quantity of bodies. As he slid down the pile, for good measure, he punched William in the face.

Shortly thereafter, Kathie's officers found Chip at the bottom of the pile, naked, and chatting with a lovely female student from Scottsdale, Arizona. This evidence promptly squashed the rumor that Chip had recently been out of the building as Kathie had postulated.

Officers cleared the room of its occupants, sending some (including, per their report, "a whiny nineteen year old male with a broken arm and a black eye") to the local hospital. After allowing him to find clothing, they handcuffed Chip, and lead him out of the dorm.

August's residents were escorted to a triage center in a gymnasium for medical screenings, interviews, and an explanation of what they were not allowed to pass along to friends, family, or the press.

Chip had been carted off, but the protest raged on. Voices of fighters became ragged above the rustle of investigators' boots and screams of counter-protestors. After nearly thirty minutes of post-liberation bedlam, the crowd's behavior suggested the scene would turn unruly and a mob would emerge— something no one on either side wanted. Before such a moment could materialize, from out of the night came a plainly dressed and enormously rejuvenated Eva. Using every skill she'd amassed through the years of waiting, she took charge of the mass of students with a well-written, perfectly rehearsed speech powered by her favorite megaphone. The mood still remained tense, but the threat of violence dissipated quickly as she espoused her beliefs and honed the students' energy into constructive outlets. From this pulpit she would stand for hours, ecstatic to finally get the dream for which she yearned for so many years.

As the exhibition raged on, for the first time in days, nearby August Hall lay dormant.

Chapter 41: Academic Investment

I HOPE you didn't forget that capture was only part of Chip's plan.

With help from many others, namely Eva, who confidently carried the torch well into Friday, Lockwood certainly seized the student body's backing and garnered substantial attention from their administrators. But as he sat in a jail cell in the basement of the PMU Police Department that morning, it was still possible that his cherished namesake would be ruined for the remainder of his days.

Thanks to a series of early morning phone calls prior to their 8:00 a.m. meeting, all present at the PPC's most important session in years knew the stakes quite well. After several hours of widespread demonstrations beginning on Thursday night, segments of the story began to leak out in many directions.

Every trustee phoned the Provost's office, as did very stern representatives from three state government offices. The callers wanted answers and a swift resolution, as did interested parties who surrounded the meeting hall itself. Droves of students, forceful reporters, and angered activists swarmed outside Liberty Hall while the PPC gathered. Those on the front lines, concerned that one of their brave leaders was behind bars, wanted a hasty end to Chip's suffering in prison. But would releasing him help the university restore order or propel more unrest? It was the PPC's job to determine that answer.

Since Chip's arrest, Eva helped strengthen the fires of indignation that grew thanks to years of unattended conflict. The number of protesters gathering overnight was so staggeringly large that it made Wednesday's rally look like the tailgate it actually was.

When the news media arrived, the condition of the campus became their star attraction and the PPC's central sore point. Regardless of the average BAC level of the crowds the previous night, each media outlet received what it came for: pictures of tremendous protests from the steps of PMU's storied academic halls to the back porch of the student union. The campus was in far worse shape than expected and the cameras present were not departing any time soon.

What worried the PPC more than the professional photos were pictures which students had taken stealthily.

Early Friday an Assistant Provost discovered one student snapped a cluttered but rousing photo of August Hall's entrance as the crowd rushed through the broken doors. The picture was uploaded to the Internet and was forwarded to an estimated two thousand email addresses by morning.

Additionally, seven students nabbed pictures of police escorting Chip out of August Hall in handcuffs, one of which became an instantly historic PMU image. Much to the PPC's chagrin, in one of the first identifiable acts of student solidarity that week, by Friday at 9 a.m., one third of Pemberton's undergraduates had swapped in Chip's iconic arrest image as their PMU online student directory profile photograph.

This novel electronic unity showed the PPC that the students' concerns would not be silenced easily. The campus knew his name, actions, and of his imprisonment. There was a chance the nation, too, would grow familiar with the struggle that emanated from Chip meeting a far from observant freshman with misguided intentions.

The mood in the deliberation room was wretched. Too many questions berated the representatives. Was Chip acting for the students and school alike or was he manipulating PMU's masses? Did his actions warrant expulsion? Just how did his family's name fit in?

For the President's team, the verdict was a question of upholding university standards while minding their relationship with one of PMU's favorite donor families. For Media Relations, it was a question of promoting the best image. For Asbury's office, the goal was ensuring PMU didn't become an academic joke by ignoring right and wrong. At least, that was the department's hard line as of Thursday evening. (No one had seen that team's leader publically since his disappearance from the NEQ.)

Board members desperate for a peek into the student body's psyche looked to the only student with whom they had contact. Her face was chillingly free of the verve it usually carried; it was clear Kathie would offer no easy answers, no matter how badly others required them.

Regardless of how the PPC took her passionless glare, the truth was Kathie was still horrified that the repulsive Edie forced her to sit as a mute observer while Chip's fate was decided. Though nervous that he could have charmed his way out of yet another punishment, she squeezed some succor out of seeing her fellow board members sit so squeamishly.

One thing they all knew would not be decided during the meeting was the question of criminal charges. A full inquiry would be soon leveraged but the PPC was aware that it would be hampered by a few key facts. Shockingly, interviews with August Hall's residents showed they were consistently well fed and their "captivity" was the most exciting and thought-provoking two days of their time at the university. What's more, two images provided by Arthur Lockwood's law firm slowed the push for criminal legal action. Early Friday his offices sent to the President's office a photo of the two common bicycle locks separating the students from the thousands of gallons of alcohol housed under their beds. Next to that image was a picture of a typical garbage can in August Hall, secured with one half of the security the school gave to the easily accessible trove of adult beverages. This suggested serious criminal action should be handled by a team that was used to more delicate matters than the PPC.

The expulsion hearing itself would be based on procedures in the university's charter. There would be no open forum but rather only presentations by three people. The Dean of Students, Provost, and President would each get a chance to speak or nominate a proxy. Asbury, unsurprisingly, was the only one volunteering to speak for himself. (By this point of the meeting, Asbury had finally shown up looking a bit gaunt and aberrantly unshaven.) The mostly absent dean selected someone from the media relations team as his stand-in, and none were shocked to learn the president elected Bromhead to speak for him.

As the team waited for the presentations, they dutifully studied the latest status reports on tumultuous campus hot spots. Unlike most other documents shared with the PPC, these reports' margins carried zero doodles even after a half hour on the table.

The media relations rep began her plea by reminding the board that public opinion would be shaped largely by the methods used by the PPC to exact judgment. If a softer approach could be taken towards Chip's punishment, her department could craft whatever message the board wanted society to hear. The media industry grew bored quickly, she noted, but the campus would be less likely to tire. Students were finding solidarity and feeling like they were contributing more to their education thanks to Chip. Many might vow to continue the fight until they received some sort of payout, which the board could help engineer painlessly.

"If we resolve this early enough," she noted, "as soon as this afternoon we can we can regroup with student leaders to give the impression we're working to solve their perceived issues. If we appear to concede to some of their demands, they will grow enthralled with their progress and begin to forget. But that's only an option if we provide a soft approach for Chip."

Heads nodded as if their paltry motions proposed that anyone not joining in was far less integral to arriving at this hard fought resolution.

Kathie, a devout non-nodder, gradually started to feel slightly more relaxed.

"Thank you for your attention," the speech giver stated as she diverted her eyes to her notes to recall the banker's pseudonym.

"Now, please turn your attention to Mr. Brom—"

To this, one board member yelped, "We're really going to let an investment analyst tell us how to handle our own students?"

Bromhead stood while sharing an unenthused scowl at the indignant committee member, whose face was studying Asbury. Their leader's downtrodden expression suggested he, too, knew Bromhead's words would emerge regardless.

The banker pressed his fingers on a stack of pages on the board table. "We are limited on time, so please forgive me for not focusing on the emotional aspects of your decision. I will remind you that you cannot afford to vote without understanding every crucial fact."

Dismissing the eye rolls, he continued. "Regardless of his actions, expelling Charles Lockwood would be seen by many as an act of aggression towards academic freedom. According to my data, the enrollment fallout that would inevitably follow his expulsion will be enormous. The issues he helped surface are so deeply rooted in traditions this university cannot give up that at its worst, this crisis could cost Pemberton upward of three thousand of its undergraduate students over the next two semesters. As your media team will confirm, a well-publicized restriction of basic student rights would turn the campus radioactive for years. The media may grow bored of your town, but potential new business and prospective students will not soon forget any of this.

"In addition, application numbers will fare worse than your retention rate. As the admissions cycle has only been open for three of its twenty-four week window, the number who accept a Pemberton offer will be unprecedentedly small next semester and for several following it.

"Based on the typical educational loan debt per student and average number of semesters students will no longer require Pemberton's or my bank's services upon leaving, the loss of interest payments alone from transfers will amount to fifteen to twenty two million dollars over the next ten years. That number does not include late fees associated with delinquent payments, which would be substantial. Looking further into the forecast, the loss of potential revenue from students avoiding the university until memory of the incident fades an estimated eight years from now would cost my firm many, many millions more."

By this point, the educators, staff, and administrators of one of the most expensive schools in the nation understood why Bromhead was allowed to speak.

"I understand this is not strictly an issue of banking, but my bank cannot advise a move that will suffocate your ability to attract students for thirty two financial quarters. You will be a university simultaneously encountering a sudden drop in applicants, a constriction of alumni donations, and disappearing sponsors taking a wealth of funds with them when they depart."

Bromhead looked around the room to check that the board was fully intercepting his message. "His actions were not justifiable, but it is my suggestion that Charles Lockwood not be expelled from this university."

With that, minds were made before the third speech even started. Above the pens clicking and middlemen and women re-forming the weekend plans they thought were lost forever, one privately joyous attendee realized the gravity of the pending vote.

Somewhere, in a hallway of the administration building in her mind, Kathie indulged in the most satisfied smirk of her life.

Chapter 42: Toxic Terms

IN THE wake of Bromhead's presentation, for the first time in days, a contented wind drifted around the boardroom. Shortly after, the table was engulfed by a typhoon of golf-related messages emanating from electronic devices encircling the table.

Through suppressed joy, Kathie piped up to state, "Now a final vote before shifting to mending hearts and minds."

"I—" grumbled a torn Asbury, "I can't allow this."

Overwhelmingly disgruntled PPC members looked at the figure as he shook his head.

"It's no secret I want him out, but …you overlooked too much."

Like many others, Kathie recognized the humbled discourse Asbury adopted only when he gravely wanted to convey his point of view. She cursed Edie and prayed another would voice a counterargument to Asbury's brewing address as she returned to her compulsory silence.

Asbury continued, "Lockwood's ability to mold opinion is dangerous. Expulsion may diminish future class sizes, but what happens when his demands become unruly and we haven't acted? Concerns over the class of 2011 will be moot if we lose control in 2005."

"But do we really know he's that powerful?" one representative asked.

"Of course!" Asbury shot back. "He was drunk off his gourd and preaching for Native American rights and students responded in packs! Doesn't that scare any of you?" He examined the faces that hadn't made the proper connections yet. There were many. "Most of you wouldn't know this, but we once had a student activist here whose impact was so intense, so scarring to our image that for decades there was an effort to erase from campus all traces of his name and his work. Despite these laborious efforts, last night I heard hundreds of students who I thought never knew of his existence chant the name of Abe Rayburn for every ear to hear."

The audience replied with only stares, prompting a blip of fury to escape the unnaturally tepid Asbury. "We were so close! Only a few pictures remained of him alongside the fairy tale ending about the Pemberton Eight! Lockwood knew he was sending a crystal clear message."

A sheepish Bursar's Office representative asked, "Are we sure they were saying Rayburn?"

"What the hell else could they have been saying?"

"I just wonder if we're giving him too much credit."

Kathie mentally praised the staffer for the reminder that few would be willing to sway from the easy choice that Bromhead presented.

Asbury stepped away from the table to circle his audience at a monotonous pace. "I thought that too before. But I knew I was wrong when UP handed me the list of hostages from August Hall. One in particular risked everything by sneaking into the dorm beforehand and aiding Lockwood the entire week."

Kathie's pulse quickened when she realized she had not seen the data upon which Asbury was basing his thesis.

"Four non-resident students were in the building during the ordeal. One was Chip's best friend, two were students visiting friends in the hall when the lockdown began, and a fourth was a boy who signed in as a guest of another student but was seen with Lockwood nearly every step of the way. That student's name is William Allton."

The unanimous slate of unimpressed looks confirmed none

present knew the wholly anonymous sophomore.

Asbury arrived back at his seat, and while standing over it, picked up a sheet of paper. "This boy's file is almost bare short of a bad case of mistaken identity and one single document that links him to Lockwood. It was an assessment he wrote of his time as Chip's student tutor last year. I quote: 'Lockwood is the most selfish and depraved human being I've ever met. I would not suggest any other tutor be placed with him under any circumstances.'" Asbury lowered the paper and celebrated the befuddled expressions. "This was only five months ago. So before you vote to keep Lockwood, ask yourself this: if he can turn someone who despises him into an ally so easily, what could he do with a campus of students who *don't* dislike him?"

Stillness filled the room again, and once again, the PPC representatives were left yearning for anyone to offer a definite solution. Kathie, taking the last remark to heart more than she wanted, even let out a miniscule whelp. With a peek at the spot where her phone would be had it not been a prisoner of war, she dejectedly sunk back into her seat.

Asbury stoically presented his final thoughts. "I agree with Bromhead. We can't expel Lockwood, but if we hope to maintain order over this campus, we surely cannot allow him to stay."

With that the room fell anemic as the PPC reunited with their spot firmly lodged between the hardest stone and the rockiest place in the university's recent history. Not even Asbury could escape the uneasy feeling of being posed a question he did not have the ability to answer.

It was a tense moment, indeed, one with which I perhaps would have helped if I desired. (While I may interact with anyone on campus as I please, out of respect for administrators and the privacy of the students, I never do.) Thankfully, with the fate of PMU's future hanging in limbo, one person present was able to analyze the situation with a levelheaded perspective.

"Actually, we might have another option," the dutiful Registrar's Office representative began. "It came to mind when you mentioned the Pemberton Eight, who actually were awarded a partial degree, nicknamed a UPAC. That move helped keep the campus calm after the arrests. Maybe we could give him the same thing?"

Board members stared on, stuck between interested and bored by the suggestion. At the same time, Bromhead looked agitated that no one had informed him of this alternate option earlier. In the committee's defense, PPC members weren't expected to be well-versed in obscure bits of school history like the UPAC or the existence of the Strait of Squanto.

Seeing Asbury's unease, the speaker went on. "This UPAC was concocted to get PMU through an overwrought time. If I'm reading this summary right, due largely to Dean Sheridan, the degree was engineered to make it look like the school was granting the students a second chance elsewhere while privately dulling their chances of getting into a better institution." The mere mention of Sheridan convinced Asbury that this was the right move.

As the elucidation went on, it became clear that the UPAC could solve an enormous amount. Chip's days at Pemberton would end honorably, quelling his family's bile, and his on-campus influence would be curbed. Moreover, it could show students that their administrators were willing to handle their concerns diplomatically as long as treacherous figureheads never appeared again.

After ten minutes of arguing, rather grandstanding, over the notion of simultaneously venerating and dismissing Chip, committee members were satisfied enough to bring the matter to a vote. The decision to expel Chip Lockwood and confer upon him the ninth UPAC ever issued was prodigiously prompt, and nearly unanimous.

The proclamation sent dozens of hands into exultant applause. Asbury retired to his office to await the inevitable onslaught of phone calls, and Kathie counted down the seconds she would have to remain present to give the appearance she was not eviscerated by the pronouncement.

Chapter 43: Deferred Interest

WITH FEWER than eighty minutes before his deadline, Chip's student status was revoked indefinitely, the Registrar endorsed his UPAC, and he was released from his cell.

Somehow, after three days of attempting to rile up the administration, several weeks of ignoring his academic duties, and two and a half years of often nearly inexcusable behavior at Pemberton, Chip Lockwood got everything he wanted from his college experience.

At that point, the one thing that could have gone awry was sharing the news with his family. With the scores of Lockwoods who proudly graduated from Pemberton with full regalia, learning one of their own would not do the same would be piercingly difficult to acknowledge. At first, his parents were justifiably furious. This was not the first time he'd infuriated them, and his latest foray into confusing the people who gave him life was one of his most intricate. Were they really to believe their son led an uncharacteristic and self-sacrificing revolt?

Their first discussion ended the moment that Chip's mother smashing their lounge's phone to pieces. It was followed by thirty minutes during which neither parent spoke a word.

Over the course of the day, their minds gradually changed, thanks to numerous phone calls from prominent members of the

PMU community. By the second time Chip spoke with his parents, their fury wasn't wholly undeterred, but they were no longer opposed to their son taking time to bronze his ego and skin in Florida.

It was mostly thanks to Arthur that Chip was driving south instead of facing jail time. Arthur's firm had been preparing their arguments ever since Chip's post-arrest phone call, and by mid-afternoon they had deftly convinced PMU that a lengthy, negligence-exposing trial was not what the university wanted. Chip would not return to a cell, but, as the newly minted bargain outlined, he could not return to Pemberton or the state of New York for ten full years.

Conditions on campus were nowhere as tidy.

In the wake of the decision, the atmosphere was chaotic beyond repair. As the PPC feared, the remaining riot-style partying did not dissolve into a hangover-induced blanket of indifference by midday.

Instead, by the lunch hour, joining the thousands of PMU students protesting were at least six hundred students from nearby universities. Droves of outsiders arrived as well, alternatively hoping to witness young adults take hold of their education or to spew diatribes at them.

Oddly, one area where protests weren't persisting was the NEQ.

Despite the chaos, once they were allowed back inside, the vast majority of the students in August Hall were left exactly how Chip first found them: split between highlighting passages in textbooks and searching for an opportunity to impeccably use a semicolon in an essay. As they hadn't been as extensively exposed to the tone and type of the gatherings outside their walls, few among them felt the need to join in the fray after the long week they'd had.

Elsewhere, protests continued to rip through the campus. To combat the unrest, at two p.m. the President's Office announced they were establishing a committee of educators, students, and policy makers to work through valid student concerns in a public forum.

Prior to the announcement, the advisor who cooked up this scheme privately explained to select administrators that these meetings would focus only on a severely edited list of topics. What would emerge would be a story telling of courageous, intelligent students squaring off with an upstanding institution that had no choice but to forge conciliation. In short: the meetings would bleed the fighters of their time and energy, and in the end, not much would change.

Around the same time, virtually all who were directly involved with Chip's plot were asked to answer for their actions. Upon confirming (using the Duden System) that Cammy Dalton was the author of the initial email that drummed up support for Chip, Asbury confronted her with the choice of permanent academic probation or the chance to follow Chip out of town. The usually cheerful student opted for the former.

Eva emerged as the new/old leader of the student movement. Since Chip's arrest, she had led a flurry of endeavors, from shifting students to the most visible areas of campus, to ordering other students to write and distribute quarter sheets outlining each of the protest's central issues.

When it was proclaimed a team would be formed to repair the relationship between the students and the university, Eva was immediately chosen to lead it. She accepted, and then promptly whisked herself away to the *Nightly Pembertonian* office to be interviewed.

As for the young woman whose conniving helped embolden this saga, practically nothing of note happened to Kathie Kieft in the aftermath of this book's events. She retained her spot on the PPC, her midterm report showed a sterling 3.95 GPA, and although she left the proceedings with damaged pride, she went to classes Friday with the heartening knowledge that she would never again have to see Chip on her campus.

Though he avoided immediate punishment, the week would have longer term effects on Kathie's henchman Soup. On Friday afternoon the PPC realized it would need to pull money from somewhere to handle the mounting costs of the crisis. Since Asbury still intended to make the Athletic Director suffer for helping prolong the disaster, the PPC insisted that the Athletic Department provide the emergency funds. To pay the hefty bill, the enterprising division head decided he would funnel scholarship dollars away from upperclassmen in lesser known sports, starting with the Track and Field team.

Meanwhile, to lengthen the streak of luck that pasted itself to William since his first day at PMU, his Friday did not go terribly well. It began in a hospital where he received twelve stitches, an arm cast, and X-rays highlighting two bruised ribs. Once Asbury located him, he was threatened with expulsion unless he shared everything he knew about Chip's plans.

After asking what happened to Lockwood and checking his hospital room's clock to confirm it was well after twelve, William cracked, explaining his role and some secrets the university didn't already know (while deftly sparing details of Chip's core goal) in exchange for clemency.

I should note that if you're looking for a hero here, please look further than the boy whose original goals of college revolved around "living large" at the center of a frat party. Without the sway held by his better-connected colleagues, William sat largely without rights during the grilling and in this story, in which I was legally allowed to use his full name. The one term he strictly set down was that PMU could not publicly use any of his statements for twenty years. A ten year compromise was later negotiated.

It is important to note that this story owes some thanks to William, as several details that happened during Chip's nighttime run to Eva's off-campus apartment, which I could not supply myself, came from transcripts of his interrogation.

Carolina, concurrently, brilliantly denied she had any knowledge of Chip's actions and was sent on her way after only minutes of questioning. When William was released from the hospital several hours after she was set free from the campus police station, he found her waiting for him with a brand new PMU hoodie to keep him warm during their walk home.

Alf, after three days of relentless verbal pressing, agreed to talk with the university under the condition his real identity never be used when reciting this story. The offer was accepted once he demonstrated how he circumvented August Hall's security system.

Edie in the aftermath initially told the university she was merely a drinking buddy of Chip's. Once cracks started appearing in that reply, she referred all questions to her family's legal team, who gave investigators nothing. Oddly, when I contacted Edie years later while doing research, she had no complaints with her role being explained in detail, and neither did her family's legal team. I have surmised they were cooperative because they knew she would land on her feet regardless of how she came across in these pages.

(As a side note, I am convinced that Kathie failed to read the contract we sent that outlined our desires to reference her actions extensively herein. Perhaps she thought I had no choice but to portray her as selfless and she signed and returned the document promptly. Alternatively, perhaps she, too, had grown to dislike her younger self in the years since her college days.)

Edie did read the contract and by the time the research phase began she was extremely forthcoming, mainly to assure I would not mistakenly give any of her best quips to others. The strictest stipulation came from her family's legal team, who stated that their surname was not to be mentioned more than five times in the entire text.

The Lockwoods had no issue with the mentioning of their name in the retelling of one of their most recent triumphs at Pemberton. Still, they added conditions before signing off on this book. Also, after a short phone interview in 2012, Chip submitted to my office a list of his own demands, which did not appear to have been reviewed by any Lockwood. Paramount among the more bizarre requests were: 1) Chip was to be allowed to translate the epilogue for the Portuguese and German editions (two languages in which he has no known fluency) and 2) the last word of the book was to be "balls." Some of his provisos had to be ignored. However, as we had to allow some of them through, I will place my conclusions here instead of the epilogue so Chip may destroy his own words instead of mine.

*   *   *

As educators, students, and citizens of the world, we should aspire to achieve more than the "accomplishments" detailed in these pages. I hope I have made this clear. However, this note alone could not suffice as the story's moral or the core of its meaning.

In attempting to reach deeper in my analysis, I was actually able to find an admonitory aspect. This lesson, which is perhaps what the committee of university presidents had been looking at the entire time, was the plight of William Allton.

When tabulating William's wounds suffered as a casualty of his association with Chip, no one could state that this was the finest chapter of William's life. As such, some who asked me to write this story unabashedly want me to say that the message is this: if something wild or dangerous is about to happen at your college, unless your name is on one of the buildings, don't get involved. Why? Someone has to be found at fault, and it surely won't be any of the Chip Lockwoods of the world.

Personally, I would like to remain a bit optimistic, even as colleges evolve to act more like businesses and the price tag of education increasingly reflects a future of indentured servitude to loan providers instead of a path that vividly highlights opportunity.

I will continue to believe that colleges like Pemberton persist because of their ability to provide the stimulation and challenging situations that young minds need to grow and achieve the type of success that they crave. In the case of this tale's central characters, Pemberton did afford a way for Chip to escape responsibility, a way for Eva to stand tall, and a way for Kathie to feel better about herself while belittling others. What would be preferable, of course, would be filling universities with students who truly crave knowledge, and giving them the chance to learn without being hampered by unnecessary bureaucracy or institutionalized partying.

As I was saying, though, in the end, Chip got what he wanted, as did Eva, and oddly, so did Kathie. With that, I suppose we've come to the culmination.

But please remember as you carry on, although this is one of Pemberton's more lurid legends, there is so much more in this beautiful, historic institution than a story of self-indulgence, riotous carousing, and a stern distrust of Native Americans.

Epilogue

AT ROUGHLY five p.m. on Friday afternoon, while deciding between attending a post-liberation mixer or driving around the quieter countryside, Edie's phone spouted a personalized ring tone set up for one caller.

She engaged the call and with mock indignation stated, "A hasty call instead of an in person good bye. You're not calling to tell me I have VD, are you?"

"Ha!" Chip replied. "Sorry. They only gave me four hours to leave the state so I threw what I could into my car and hauled ass."

Edie enjoyed picturing Chip driving a weighed down luxury sedan across six states to get to his next adventure. She promptly discarded the idea to follow the escapade. "So that's two states you can't go back into now? Impressive."

"Ohio's still permanent, but I can go back to New York after ten years, they said. Either way, it's nothing two months of self-punishment in Florida can't solve."

"So your parents didn't issue a recall on everything you own?"

"Not yet," Chip replied through what Edie could tell was an apprehensive grin. "They were pissed until three of the Pemberton Eight called to thank them for what their son bravely did for the students. Then they got pissed again and ripped Uncle Arthur apart…until two trustees called to praise their caring, righteous boy."

"So…they're learning to live with a lie."

"Yeah. That'll have to do until cuzzy wuzzy Craig's transfer application clears. Plus once they start talking to me they'll be happy to hear I'm going to start my own round of apps soon."

Edie chuckled at the thought of Chip being let back onto another campus. "You want to go back to a real school after all of this?"

"I'll have to do something productive after a few weeks of what we both know is going to be pretty freaking messed up."

"Wow, so you did learn something in all of this."

"Shit, yeah, I guess," Chip said enthusiastically. "One huge lesson to tuck away in my massive brain from when I riled up an entire college campus to get myself expelled."

Edie rolled her eyes. "Ooh, sounds dramatic. Tell me about it sometime. I have to get going."

"Yeah, and I should focus on the road. I'm not sure any of the sleep I got this week counted as real sleep. Hug and kiss Squanto for me…if my buddies are done with him already." Chip paused, and in a relatively appreciative way, added, "If I didn't say it before, thanks."

Smiling, Edie replied, "Any time," and hung up without waiting for a valediction.

With that, as thousands of midterm grade reports were printed up to be mailed out across the nation, many of this story's players found themselves still very busy. Chip and Edie temporarily parted ways. Alf, Kathie, and Eva sat in meetings, each plowing ahead with what could become their legacies at PMU. William and Carolina ambled very slowly along the lakefront sipping fruit smoothies. And as dark storm clouds approached campus, Squanto was left trying to determine how to escape the precarious position that had him duct taped to the outside of a fraternity house thirty feet in the air, without any clothing on, and with only his hands to cover his balls.

ACKNOWLEDGEMENTS

The journey towards getting the chance to write an acknowledgements page was a long one, so I have plenty of people I'd like to thank regardless of whether they enjoy the story or not.

First there's the book's editor Daniel Solera, who deserves all the thanks I could give for the care and attention with which he treated my pages. If you'd like to see some of Daniel's own writing, please check out his blog Dan's Marathon (http://dans-marathon.com).

My family has been extremely helpful throughout this process, as well. My mother, Sheri Doniger, DDS, gets extra points for being a reader and helping review later drafts and changes. Similarly, my father Bob Pollyea helped years before the story even popped into my head. The anecdotes he shared with me about college helped create my mental image of what Pemberton looked like long before I dreamed up Chip and the rest of the characters. My sister, Erin Pollyea-Lane, deserves recognition for being the loudest and biggest fan of mostly everything I've ever put my heart into.

I'd also like to thank my wonderful girlfriend, Erin Elizabeth Doyle, for her support, her ever-attentive ear, and her energy for this book's sometimes beleaguering author.

This book wouldn't have been possible without some phenomenal teachers and mentors throughout the years. In particular I'd like to thank instructors Chris Schwarz and Dan Rusk, and my former bosses Lora Dennis and Don Lemon. Mr. Schwarz's always thoughtful advice, his exceedingly detailed European History lectures, and his tireless efforts to keep unruly groups of student government activists (like a younger, noisier me) in line made him a role model I was extremely lucky to know. Mr. Rusk's unbending enthusiasm for both class material and his students make him stand out as one of the best teachers a student could want to meet.

Don Lemon, meanwhile, trusted me enough to hire me as his newsroom intern at a point when there was little reason to believe I would do great work. His relentless habit of believing in me and his resolute training strengthened my work ethic, my writing style, and pushed me to always try to do more. Thanks to Lora Dennis, who patiently mentored me during my first "real world" job, I was given the chance to make writing a part of my job, and I've been able to keep it that way through every career change. What's more, her slightly crazy decision to have faith in the writing talents of the 22 year old news desk assistant version of me was an exceptional act of compassion that I will spend the rest of my career trying to repay.

Last but not least, for their help with various aspects of the book I would like to thank Alexis Crawford Douglas, Jennifer Gadus, Joseph Vanerio III, Jonathan Kreyer, Sohil Shah, Mischaela Advani, Jason Velkavrh, and Kyle Smith.

ABOUT THE AUTHOR

Ryan is a graduate of Northwestern University and Scotland's University of Glasgow. His other works include a web series that was awarded a Chicago/Midwest Regional Emmy® in 2008, and the screenplay for the documentary *Burning Greed*. When he isn't working or attending to various writing projects, he spends his spare time swimming, reading, and exploring Chicago. His next book will be about farts.